D0401936

A DANCE OF SHADOWS

SHADOWDANCE: BOOK 4

DAVID DALGLISH

orbit

www.orbitbooks.net

Copyright © 2014 by David Dalglish
Excerpt from *A Dance of Chaos* copyright © 2014 by David Dalglish
Excerpt from *Promise of Blood* copyright © 2013 by Brian McClellan

All rights reserved. In accordance with the U.S. Copyright Act of 1976, the scanning, uploading, and electronic sharing of any part of this book without the permission of the publisher constitutes unlawful piracy and theft of the author's intellectual property. If you would like to use material from the book (other than for review purposes), prior written permission must be obtained by contacting the publisher at permissions@hbgusa.com. Thank you for your support of the author's rights.

Orbit
Hachette Book Group
1290 Avenue of the Americas, New York, NY 10104
HachetteBookGroup.com

First Edition: May 2014

Orbit is an imprint of Hachette Book Group, Inc. The Orbit name and logo are trademarks of Little, Brown Book Group Limited.

The Hachette Speakers Bureau provides a wide range of authors for speaking events. To find out more, go to www.hachettespeakersbureau.com or call (866) 376-6591.

The publisher is not responsible for websites (or their content) that are not owned by the publisher.

The characters and events in this book are fictitious. Any similarity to real persons, living or dead, is coincidental and not intended by the author.

Library of Congress Cataloging-in-Publication Data
Dalglish, David.
   A dance of shadows / David Dalglish. — First Edition.
      pages cm. — (Shadowdance ; Book 4)
   Summary: " 'Prove that you can stand against the darkness and live.' Haern is the King's Watcher, born an assassin only to become the city of Veldaren's protector against the thief guilds. When Lord Victor Kane attacks the city, determined to stamp out all corruption, foreign gangs pour in amidst the chaos in an attempt to overthrow the current lords of the underworld. And when a mysterious killer known as the Widow begins mutilating thieves, paranoia engulfs the city. Haern knows someone is behind the turmoil, pulling strings. If he doesn't find out who—and soon—his beloved city will burn. Light or darkness: where will the line be drawn? Fantasy author David Dalglish spins a tale of retribution and darkness, and an underworld reaching for ultimate power in this fourth novel of the Shadowdance series, previously released as Watcher's Blade"—Provided by publisher.
   ISBN 978-0-316-24244-8 (pbk.) — ISBN 978-0-316-24242-4 (ebook) — ISBN 978-1-4789-5340-1 (audio download)   1. Imaginary wars and battles—Fiction.   I. Title.
   PS3604.A376D368 2014
   813'.6—dc23
                                                                    2013034369

10 9 8 7 6 5 4
RRD-C

Printed in the United States of America

To Devi, for making this whole transition a dream...
as well as pointing out everywhere I screw up royally

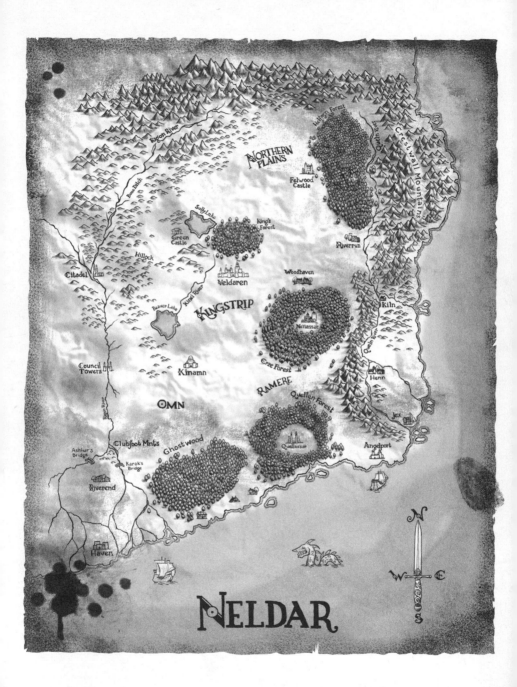

NELDAR

PROLOGUE

The city of Veldaren was his to protect, but Haern felt himself losing control more than ever as he watched the body bleed at his feet. It had rained just before dark, muddying the streets and back alleys. Blood mixed with the wet ground. The dead man's face was half-buried, mouth open in death, throat opened by blade, and both were filling with mud. In the moonlight, the green of the dead man's cloak took on a sickly hue. Haern doubted anyone would shed tears for the loss, but that was beside the point. He was the King's Watcher, enforcer of Veldaren, and such violence could not be tolerated.

Yet, despite the work of his sabers, the violence was steadily rising.

"I hope you find a better life beyond this one," Haern said, shutting the dead thief's eye so it no longer stared up at him. "No one should die in the mud."

He stood, pulling the hood over his face. In its shadow he peered about the alley. Come morning he'd alert a guard to the location of the body, but before then he needed to investigate. If the murder was what he thought it was, there'd be a sign somewhere, a message for the Serpent Guild where the guards might overlook it. On either side of him was a stone building, its walls slick from the rain. Haern slowly checked one, then the other, until he found it. Cut into the stone was a crude squiggle representing a snake. A jagged line crossed over its head. Below it was a fresh circle with eight tiny lines.

"Spider Guild is spreading," Haern whispered to himself as he rubbed his chin. "Or was this revenge?"

He knew of no particular bad blood between the Serpents and Spiders, but that didn't mean much. The thief guilds were all battling for territory, a direct result of the peace Haern had bought with blood. The three wealthiest families of Neldar, known as the Trifect, paid handsomely for protection of the entire city. Yet over the past two years, that amount had carefully shrunk, as had the size of most thief guilds. Every bit of land meant a higher payout. With the increase in killings and infighting, the number of guildless criminals had risen. They knew the risk the Watcher posed. They knew what he was capable of. But it was starting to no longer matter.

The thieves were getting desperate. They weren't afraid of him anymore.

Haern leaped to the rooftops, determined to rekindle that fear. Every night he scoured the city, often changing his route. He watched and listened, always wrapped in his gray cloaks, their shades mismatched so that no guild could be sure of any affiliations. For years he'd foiled wars among the guilds, disrupting their plans. But there were no more plans. The thieves were wounded animals, biting at everything they saw. Every night he found a new body, a new symbol, or a new message. He wasn't certain where the various guilds' territories ended anymore, and he doubted the guilds themselves knew for sure.

He ran east. Footsteps in the mud led that way from the corpse. Perhaps it was time he gave the guilds a message of his own. The steps grew fainter. Out in the wild, there were many who were better trackers, but within the confines of a city, Haern was the master. He ran along, still following the telltale signs. A knocked-over barrel here. A bit of mud brushed against a wall there. After a time he felt he was inside the murderer's mind, heading toward safer territory. Except that was wrong. Nowhere was safe, not from him.

Haern found the Spider talking with a guildmate, the two standing before a tavern that had long since closed. One held a knife, and he gestured wildly with it while telling a story. The blood on the blade was not yet dry. Haern worked his way closer, silently crawling across the roof until he was just above them, his ear leaning toward the edge of the tavern.

"...a little bitch," said the guildmate.

"Course he was. What you expect from a bunch of scum loyal to that Ket bastard?" said the man with the knife.

"Still, you'd expect him to die like a man. Put a knife at *my* throat, you wouldn't hear me blubbering like a child."

Haern drew one of his sabers, a dark grin spreading across his face. Was that so? Perhaps he should test that theory. Like a ghost he fell upon them, not a sound to give them warning. His knees crashed into the shoulders of the man wielding the knife. He heard a crack of bone, and the man dropped. The other stood stock-still, his eyes wide. Haern kicked, his heel crushing windpipe. As the man fell, Haern turned his attention on the boaster, who lay dazed in the mud from his head hitting the ground.

"So is this how a man dies?" Haern asked as he put the tip of his saber against the thief's throat. He shouldn't be wasting time, he knew. He was deep in Spider territory, and they would fight him if enough gathered together. Not that he feared them. Only their guildleader gave him pause. Thren Felhorn. His father.

The thief swallowed, the movement rubbing the tip up and down against his throat.

"I didn't do nothing," he said. "I've been here all night."

"Do you think I care?"

Haern knelt closer, his free hand grabbing the back of the man's head and holding it still. He stared into his eyes, then flinched as if he were about to thrust. The thief let out a cry. The smell of urine reached Haern's nose. He leaned closer, his lips hovering before the man's ear.

"I see tears in your eyes," he whispered.

The hilt of his saber cracked down hard atop the thief's head, knocking him out cold. Slowly rising, he drew his other saber and turned to his initial prey, the murderer. The man sat on his rear, both hands clutching his throat. He was gasping for air, the sound akin to that of wind blowing over the top of a chimney. Blood dripped down his wrist, to his elbow, and then to the ground.

"You slit a Serpent's throat," Haern said, towering over him. "Care to tell me why?"

The man coughed, crimson blobs flecking his pants. He gasped a few times, as if to hold his breath underwater, then forced out a word.

"Trespassing."

Haern shook his head. "Not good enough," he said. "Not even close."

He shoved his sabers into the man's chest, through his heart. Pulling them free, he kicked the body to the ground, then slashed open his neck. His throat dry, Haern turned back to the thief he'd left unconscious. He almost killed him. Almost.

But enough blood had been spilled that night, and it wouldn't be the last. Once Thren found out, he'd retaliate against the Serpent Guild. Back and forth, always back and forth without end…

Perhaps he wasn't doing enough, thought Haern. Perhaps it was time for him to come down even harder on the guilds and their infighting. No matter what, he couldn't go on finding the bodies of the dead filling the alleys every single damn night, regardless of their affiliations or crimes.

He sheathed his blades and turned to go, and that was when he heard the scream. It came from a distant alley, the deep, throaty scream of a man in horrible pain. Haern followed it, guessing which alley to turn down. The night was quiet, with no one foolish enough to be out and about so deep in Spider territory. At first he thought he'd guessed wrong, but then he found the victim. He lay on his back at the farthest stretch of a dead-end alley, arms splayed outward. His gray cloak signified he was a member of the Spider Guild. No wounds were upon him but for the tiny arrow embedded in his throat. Haern walked over to it, his stomach turning. Another? But by whom, and why?

Standing over it, Haern immediately felt something was wrong. The thief had been a smaller man, wiry, probably picked for his deft hands instead of brute strength. Hardly a whisker grew on his face. His face…

His eyes were closed, as was his mouth. That was it. A lethal hit with an arrow should have left him gasping in pain, his face reflecting that upon death, but it had not. The killer had shut his eyes and mouth to create the appearance of sleep, but why? Knowing he had little choice, Haern reached down, pushed two fingers between the dead man's teeth, and pried his jaw open. Starlight reflected off metal, and something about the sight sent a chill down Haern's spine. Lying on his tongue were two gold coins stacked atop one another. Haern took them, trying to decide the significance. A personal vendetta? A paid hit by another guild?

Laughter startled him, and he reached for his blade. He let it go when he realized it was just a drunken man curled against the wall, nearly invisible in the darkness.

"Sorry 'bout the scream," he said, drinking from the half-empty bottle he held. "Didn't mean to scare anybody."

"Did you see who did this?"

The drunk shook his head. "Like this when I got here. Nearly tripped over the damn thing."

Haern frowned. So the scream had been from the drunk, not the man dying. It didn't surprise him, given how dry the blood was across the man's throat. He yanked out the arrow, held it up to the moonlight. He caught sight of tiny white flecks of dried poison on the metal intermixed with the blood. A professional hit, but again, by whom, and why? He glanced about, looking for a message, and quickly found it. That he hadn't spotted it immediately upon entering the alley unnerved him. It was large, and written in blood upon the wall.

tongue of gold, eyes of silver
run, run little spider
from the widow's quiver

"The Widow?" Haern wondered aloud. The drunk's laughter stole away his concentration.

"You got competition," he said, then laughed again before staggering away. Haern looked to the gold coins in his hand and didn't see the humor. As he read over the simple rhyme, a thought hit him, tightening his stomach into a knot. Bending down beside the body, he carefully opened the dead man's eyelids.

"Damn it," he whispered. "Damn it all to the Abyss."

The man's eyes were gone, replaced by two silver coins staring up at the moonlight.

Haern left them for the guards to take.

CHAPTER 1

Haern returned home to the Eschaton Tower exhausted. He'd scoured the area surrounding the murder victim as best he could and tracked down several runners of the Spider Guild. The few he found had heard nothing, seen nothing, and even when threatened showed no sign of lying. Leaving Veldaren for the tower beyond the city walls, he'd felt nothing but frustration and bafflement. He kept repeating the phrase in his head.

Tongue of gold, eyes of silver...

As he opened the door, the smell of cooked eggs welcomed him home. Delysia was the only one awake, and she sat beside the fireplace with a plate on her lap. The orange light shone across her red hair, making it seem all the more vibrant. Seeing him, she smiled. The smile faded from her youthful face when she noticed his sour mood.

"Something wrong?" she asked.

"I'll talk about it later," he promised, heading for the stairs.

"Don't you want something to eat?"

He shook his head. He just wanted sleep. Hopefully when he woke up, he'd have new ideas as to why someone had killed a member of the Spider Guild in such a ritualistic—not to mention expensive—manner. Besides, the thought of eating twisted his stomach. He'd seen a lot of horrible things, but for some reason he couldn't get the image out of his head of the corpse's vacant eye sockets filled with coins.

Eyes of silver...

Haern climbed the stairs until he reached the fifth floor and his room. Hurrying inside, he sat down on his bed, removed his sword belt, and drew out his sabers. Carefully he cleaned them with a cloth, refusing to go to bed with dirty swords no matter how tired he was. That was lazy and sloppy, and laziness and sloppiness had a way of sneaking out of one habit and into another. His many tutors had hammered that into his head while he was growing up, all so he could be a worthy heir to his father's empire of thieves and murderers. He chuckled, then put away his swords. *Not quite according to plan*, he thought, imagining Thren scowling. *Not quite at all.*

Run, run little spider...

His bed felt like the most wonderful thing in the world, and with a heavy cloth draped over his window, he closed his eyes amid blessed darkness. Sleep came quickly, despite his troubled mind. It did not, however, last very long.

"Hey, Haern."

He opened an eye and saw his mercenary leader sitting beside him on the bed. His red beard and hair were unkempt from a night's sleep. He wore his wizard's robes, strangely dyed a yellow color for reasons Haern was sure he'd never hear. Trying not to smack the man, Haern rolled over.

"Go away, Tarlak."

"Good morning to you too, Haern."

Haern sighed. The wizard had something to say, and he wasn't going to leave until he said it. Rolling back, Haern shot him a tired glare.

"What?"

"Some fancy new noble is returning to the city today," Tarlak said, rubbing his fingernails against his robe and staring at them as if he were only mildly interested. "Lord Victor Kane. Perhaps you've heard of him?"

The name was only vaguely familiar, which meant the man had been gone from Veldaren for a very long time. If Haern remembered correctly, he was just another one of those lords who lived outside the city and liked to occasionally make a scene proclaiming how horrible Veldaren was, and how much better it'd be if their ideas were listened to. All hot air, no substance.

"Why should I care?" Haern asked, leaning against his pillow and closing his eyes.

"Because he'll be meeting the king soon, perhaps within the hour. Normally this wouldn't be a big deal, but it sounds like he's bringing a veritable army with him."

"As if King Edwin would let them pass through the gates."

"That's the thing," Tarlak said. "It sounds like he will. He sent a message to the king. I won't bore you with all the details. Much of it was the standard pompous nonsense these lords are fond of. But one comment in particular was interesting enough my informant thought it worth waking me up early."

Haern put his forearm across his eyes.

"And what was that?"

"I believe it was something to the extent of: 'Right now thieves police thieves, yet when I am done, there will be no thieves at all.'" Tarlak stood from the bed, then walked over to the door. "Sounds like someone plans on taking your job."

He left. The room once more returned to quiet darkness. Haern sat up, tossing the blankets aside.

"Damn it all..."

King Edwin Vaelor fidgeted on his throne, eager for the meeting to begin. Beside him stood his aging adviser, Gerand Crold, looking tired and bored. They'd emptied out the grand throne room of petitioners and guests, per Gerand's request. The adviser rubbed at the lengthy scar along his face, as if it bothered him. A sign of nervousness, belying the calm façade he showed. For some reason this made Edwin all the more impatient. Over the years he'd listened to what felt like a hundred lords talk about how they could do a better job policing Veldaren. A few had even tried, such as Alyssa Gemcroft, who had unleashed an army of mercenaries upon the streets for two deadly nights. Half the city had damn near burned to the ground because of it, too. If not for the Watcher's agreement's actually bringing about peace, as well as Alyssa's paying for the damages done by her mercenary bands, Edwin might have tossed her into prison for a few hundred years.

Yet at least Alyssa he could understand, given her belief at the time that her son was dead. Women did strange things when facing loss. This Lord Victor, though...

"You sure he has no family?" he asked Gerand.

"Quite sure, unless he has kept them in secret."

The king scratched at his neck. He wore his finest robes, lined with velvet and furs that were dyed dark reds and purples. It'd been too long since he had worn it, and it itched. Still, he wanted to show this upstart noble his wealth, to remind him of his regality and his divine right to rule over all of Neldar.

"What about a son? Or a daughter?"

"Forgive me, milord, but I do consider that family, and as I said, he has none."

Edwin shot Gerand a glare, and he bowed low in apology.

"Forgive me," he said. "I did not mean to speak with a harsh tongue."

"Try not to do so again."

He might have made a stronger threat to someone else, but Gerand had served him loyally for years. Any threat would have been false, and both knew it. He was too important to lose. But again, it showed Gerand's true nervousness. Why? What was it about Lord Victor that worried him so?

"You've met him before, haven't you?" he asked.

Gerand nodded, adjusted the collar of his shirt.

"My wife's family lives on his lands," he said. "I've spoken to him only once, but that was enough. He is not a man to forget, my liege, nor take lightly. If he says he will accomplish something, then he will accomplish it, regardless the cost."

"Then why worry? He's pledged to clean out the streets. Let him try, and fail."

Gerand cleared his throat.

"That is the thing. He won't fail. What he promises is war, the like of which we have not had in four years."

The king grunted. "You mean when that Gemcroft bitch went mad?"

"Yes, like that," Gerand said dryly.

Edwin leaned back in his chair and drank a tart wine from his goblet. Smacking his lips, he set it down and shook his head.

"If that's all he plans, then I'll laugh in his face and send him back to whatever runty castle he came from. The thieves are like rats, and they've grown exceptionally skilled at hiding in the walls lately."

On the opposite side of the room, at the end of the crimson

carpet leading to the dais, there came a knock on the heavy doors. The guards stationed there waited for an order. Edwin sighed, rubbed his eyes. Too early. He hadn't had much to eat, and coupled with the wine, it left him with a sharp headache. Stupid lords. Stupid, naïve lords thinking they had every answer.

"Send him in," he said, his voice echoing down the hall. "But only him."

Two guards bowed, and then they cracked open one of the doors and stepped out. A moment later it swung wide, and in stepped Lord Victor, flanked by the guards. The king studied him as he approached. He was a tall man, lean with muscle. His blond hair was cut short about his neck, his face cleanly shaven. Instead of the expected attire of nobles, he wore tall boots, a red tunic showing the symbol of his house, and a suit of chain mail. A sword was strapped to his thigh, and Edwin felt his ire rise, this time at his guards for being so dense as to let him keep it.

"Greetings, my king," Victor said, smiling wide. Gods he was handsome, his voice strong, confident. It made Edwin sick, and filled him with an irrational desire to slap him across the face.

"Welcome to my home," Edwin said, not rising. He gestured to the man's tunic. "I must confess, I have not seen that symbol in many a long year. I cannot remember its meaning."

Victor glanced down at his chest. Failing to recognize a family crest would normally be considered an insult, but he didn't seem the slightest bit bothered.

"It is a pair of wings stretched wide before the sun," he said. "Their gold melds together, as is appropriate. Our wealth comes from the birds of the forest, the fields that grow beneath the sun, and the strength of our kin rising every day, without fail, to do what must be done."

"You Kanes must be a proud lot," Edwin said.

For the first time that smug grin faltered, just a little.

"My father was a proud man," he said. "Proud as my mother was beautiful. A shame you will never meet them."

"Dead, then?" Edwin asked. He sensed disapproval, and that made him continue. He liked making Victor uncomfortable, reminding him that Edwin was in charge of everything, even their conversation. "Accept my condolences. If you are the last of their line, I hope you are busy finding yourself a wife."

"In time," Victor said. A hard edge had entered his voice. "Though matters here must be settled first before I take a lovely bride's hand in marriage. As a child, Veldaren was my home. Now I return, and I wish it to be my home again. But one does not move into a house full of rats and turn a blind eye to their droppings."

"Be careful who you call rat shit in this town," Edwin said, laughing. "It might get you in trouble."

His laughter died off uneasily as Victor stared at him with those clear blue eyes of his. It wasn't just strength he saw in them. No, what he saw was madness, and it was starting to unnerve him.

"Fine," he said, suddenly no longer having fun. He sat up, took another sip from his cup. "You've made plain your desire to clean up this city, though I have yet to hear how you will do it. So tell me, Victor. Let me hear your amazing plan."

"There is nothing amazing about it," Victor said. He crossed his arms over his chest, tilted his head back. "I have over three hundred mercenaries at my disposal, committed to my cause. They will aid me in this endeavor."

"Your lands cannot be large. How can you afford them all?"

"There is always coin available for what a man cares about most."

Edwin rolled his eyes and gestured for the man to continue.

"I know what it is you're thinking," Victor said, starting to pace. "You think I will unleash them like wild dogs, just as Lady Gemcroft did years ago. I tell you now that that is wrong. I do not do this for destruction, nor a desire for killing. I will not slaughter life at random, nor pronounce a colored cloak reason enough for death. I will abide by *the law*, my king. That is all I desire from you. Give me your blessing to enforce your laws. These guilds may no longer rob from your stores, but their hands are far from clean."

"And what do you expect from all this? A reward?"

"A home where I can live without fear will be my reward," Victor said, smiling. "That, and for you to cover the cost of the mercenaries, should I succeed."

"You ask for much while claiming to ask for little," Gerand said, and Edwin had to agree.

"What makes you so confident you can accomplish this task?" the king asked.

"The blood of the underworld will spill across your executioners' blades," Victor said. "Brought before your judges, lawfully condemned in your trials, and their bodies dumped into pits beyond your walls. Fear is how they have endured for so long, but I am not afraid of them. I fear nothing."

Laughter interrupted their conversation. Edwin felt his throat tighten, and he looked to his left. There, in a tall window at least twenty feet above the ground, crouched a figure cloaked in gray.

How in Karak's name did he get up there? he wondered.

"Come to join us, Watcher?" Edwin asked.

"I'm quite content to stay here," the Watcher said, turning his attention to Victor. "You truly think fear is how the thief guilds have endured? Fear is just the whetstone that sharpens their blades. Razor wire and poisoned cups are how they've endured. They fill their ranks with those desperate enough to kill just to have food in their bellies. You want to defeat the thief guilds? Flood the streets with bread, not soldiers."

"For a man of such reputation, you are incredibly naïve," said Victor. He didn't seem upset with the Watcher, only vaguely amused. "You think a little bit of milk and bread will sate their appetites? The guilds are full of men who will always want more than what they have. You used your blades to cull them, and took the gold of others to make them content. Your way is failing. You do not spoil a rotten child. You beat his ass with a rod."

Victor turned to the king, who chewed on his lip. This lord was fiery, devoted, and quick-witted. He truly seemed unafraid of making enemies, for few would have dared speak to the Watcher in such a manner. Even the Watcher looked surprised.

"Do not be afraid," Victor said, putting his back to the Watcher. "I have come as Veldaren's savior, and am prepared for the burden. Let it all be cast on me. Let it be my name the thieves hear. Let them know I am the one enforcing your laws. There is nothing for you to lose. Noble, beggar, merchant, thief…all will come to justice. The coin I ask for in return is a pittance compared to what you gain. Give me your blessing."

Edwin could tell Gerand wanted nothing to do with the offer, but for once Edwin saw a ray of light in his miserable city. For years he'd lived in fear of meeting the same fate as his parents, killed off because one of the guilds decided he was too meddlesome. Could this Lord Victor do it? Could he do what even the Watcher could not?

"If you truly desire to uphold the law, then so be it," he said. "You and your men may act in the name of Victor Kane, ask questions in your name, and deliver justice in a manner befitting the law. But the moment I hear of your own men breaking my laws, starting fires, and acting like the lowborn scum they no doubt are, I will banish you from my city, never to return. As for your reward..."

He stared into Victor's eyes, and Victor stared back.

"Every guild broken. Every guildmaster dead or gone. When I can walk down my streets without fear of an arrow, and eat my food without checking for sprinkles of glass, you will have your coin, as well as any portion of land within this city you desire for your home."

Victor's smile grew.

"Thank you," he said, bowing. "You'll never regret it. I swear this upon the honor of my house."

With a wave of his hand, Edwin dismissed the lord, who left in a hurry. A bounce was in his step. Unbelievable. Would he still be so cheerful when the collected might of every thief guild bore down upon him? How long until there were none left alive to taste his drink and sample his food? And when the chaos grew, and the real bloodshed began, was there anyone with enough skill to protect him?

He looked to the window, but the Watcher was already gone.

CHAPTER 2

Her servant women fussed over her, fitting clothes, applying rouge, and brushing her hair, until Alyssa Gemcroft finally sent them away, unable to take any more. They filed out, leaving her alone in her extravagant bedroom. Well, not quite alone . . .

"Come down, Zusa," she said. "Tell me what is wrong."

From a far corner of the room, hidden in a dark space unlit by the windows, a woman fell to the ground. Despite the many years since she had left Karak's cult of faceless women, Zusa still wore the tight wrappings across her body, strips of cloth colored various shades of black and purple. Her head, at least, she exposed: dark skin, dark hair cut short at the neck, and beautiful green eyes. A long gray cloak hung from her shoulders, the thin material curling about her body with the slightest tugs of Zusa's fingers.

"There is nothing wrong," Zusa said, crossing her arms over her chest and leaning against the wall.

"I'm used to you keeping an eye on me, but you only hide on the ceiling when you're nervous." Alyssa smiled at her friend. "You know I trust your instincts, so tell me."

Zusa gestured to the dress.

"You doll yourself up worse than a whore. Powder everywhere, rouge, perfume on your neck…and I must say, I pity your breasts."

Alyssa looked down at herself. She'd let her servants prepare her for her meeting, but had they gotten carried away? Her dress was a sultry red, tightly fitted, with a ring of rubies sewn along the neck. A gold chain held a large emerald tucked into the curve of her breasts, which, true to Zusa's words, her corset had rammed almost unnaturally high.

"This is what is expected of me," Alyssa said, sighing. She wanted to sit down but feared wrinkling her dress or, even worse, straining the ties of the corset. The realization made her blush, and she could tell Zusa knew her defense was a flimsy one.

"Since when did Lady Gemcroft do the expected?" Zusa asked, the last of her nerves fading away with a smile. "But you are beautiful, even if overdone. I only wonder why. Lord Stephen is but a child, young even compared to you. Your smile alone should impress him."

Alyssa paced, keeping her movements slow and controlled lest she muss her appearance.

"It's been a year since his appointment, and I have yet to meet him. I fear he'll think I have snubbed him, or deemed him unworthy of his position. I wish only to make a good impression."

Zusa sat down on the bed, shifting the daggers tied to her waist so they did not poke into the soft mattress.

"He will think it anyway," she said. "Though I fear his impression will be that you are making advances on him."

Alyssa opened her mouth, closed it, and then looked to her dress. She sighed.

"Help me, will you?" she asked.

Ten minutes later she was in a far more comfortable dress, and they'd wiped clean her face. Alyssa left her hair the same, having always enjoyed the sight of thin braids woven throughout her long red locks. Able to breathe and move far more freely, she hugged Zusa, then attached a simple lace of silver about her own neck.

"We have kept Stephen waiting long enough," she said. "Let's go."

A litter waited outside her mansion, and she and Zusa climbed inside. As they traveled through the streets of Veldaren, Alyssa felt butterflies in her stomach and did her best to belittle them. It was stupid to be nervous. Of the three family rulers of the Trifect, she'd been in power the longest and had clearly solidified her control of the Gemcroft fortune. Stephen Connington was but a bastard son of his father, Leon. Still, he was the only one with a clear biological relation. It'd been a couple of years before he'd been granted control of the estate from the caretakers. In the end they'd had no choice. Leon had killed most of his family members and steadfastly refused to name heirs, lest they drown him in his bath.

She winced at the memory of Leon. He'd been unpleasant at times, if not repulsive. The fat had rolled off him, yet his tiny eyes had always been those of a young, starving man eager to take, and take, regardless of the vice. She'd heard stories of what his gentle touchers—his private group of elite torturers—could do to a man to make him break. A shudder ran through her. She prayed that Stephen had inherited very little of his father beyond his name.

As for the last family of the Trifect, the Keenans, they'd yet to recover from the fiasco in Angelport two years before, when both Madelyn and Laurie had been murdered along with their temporary successor, Torgar. Their grandchild, Tori, was the biological heir, but it would be many years before she could take over rule. That had left Stern Blackwater in charge of the Keenan fortune down in Angelport. There was a benefit to this: the cessation of significant conflict with the Merchant Lords of the south who had done their best to destroy the Trifect families. Still, even Stern's rule was conflicted, and he rarely made any appearances beyond the walls of Angelport. If he thought the Trifect was no longer in his granddaughter's interest, he'd cast it off in a heartbeat.

That meant Alyssa was the pillar of strength of the Trifect, the one holding it all together. She had to be strong and confident whenever in public.

"I should have brought Nathaniel with me," Alyssa said as the litter bounced across the rough street.

"Your son is better served with an honorable man like Lord Gandrem than dealing with worms like the Conningtons," Zusa said.

Alyssa frowned and glanced out the curtained window to the passing homes.

"Perhaps," she said. "But it won't be long before he must put away foolish fantasies of knights and armies. I won't have all I've built squandered and broken like it did for the Keenans. In time he must learn to deal with the worms as well as the dragons."

Not long after, they arrived at the closely guarded Connington mansion and exited the litter. Thick, high walls protected the mansion from intruders, and armed soldiers with sashes about their waists to show their loyalty to the family patrolled the area. At the gate, two men bowed and opened it wide so they could enter. One of them sneered at Zusa's appearance, but the woman twirled, blew him a kiss, and then followed after Alyssa.

"Must I tell you to behave?" Alyssa whispered as they crossed the stone path toward the mansion entrance.

"I could have struck his head, if you would prefer."

Alyssa glanced back, saw the same guard watching them with a sneer on his face.

"Perhaps on the way out," she said, and they both quietly laughed.

Another guard stopped them at the door, and he glared at the daggers Zusa carried.

"No weapons," he told them.

"Zusa is my bodyguard, and will use them only to protect me," Alyssa said.

"There is no need. You are safe within these walls."

"Is that so?" Alyssa asked. "How long have you served the Conningtons, good sir?"

"Nine years," said the guard.

"That means you were here. Excellent. Please, tell me, where were you when your former master died?"

The guard swallowed hard. Leon had died in the mansion barracks, believed by most to have been killed by the Watcher.

"Very well," said the guard. "But do not draw them unless forced."

The doors opened, and they stepped inside. Alyssa had been there before, after its reconstruction following the fire during the Bloody Kensgold. The floors were still soft, deep-red rugs that she knew had to be a nightmare to keep clean. The ceiling was high above her, the wood columns decorated with various animals. But where there should have been vases, the tables were only bare surfaces. Where there should have been paintings and murals, there were bare walls.

"Much missing extravagance," Zusa said, keeping her voice soft.

"Perhaps their coffers are worse than we thought," Alyssa said.

Zusa didn't look convinced. She gestured to where many portraits of Leon were clearly missing.

"Or the son looked upon the father, and did not like what he saw."

At the end of the hall they waited until a servant stepped in, announced their presence, and then flung open the door. A practiced smile on her face, Alyssa went in to greet the new heir to the Connington fortune.

She knew he'd be young, only eighteen if their information was true, but she was still surprised by his small size, soft face, and even softer hands, as he bent on one knee, bowed low, and kissed her offered fingers. He had his father's brown hair, though it was kept shorter, and far cleaner. Alyssa felt her smile grow more natural. He may not have spent his early life in affluence, but he'd learned quickly over the past year.

"I'm thrilled to at last make your acquaintance," Stephen said, his voice tinged with a charming honesty. "I must admit, ever since my appointment, you were the one I was most nervous to meet."

"May I ask why?"

"Your beauty, of course," he said, and Alyssa caught his nervous glances about the room, his struggle to meet her eye. "That, and your unpredictability. Would you care for something to drink?"

They were in a cozy study, one wall covered with books, another with maps of Dezrel. Between the chairs was a small table, currently empty. When Alyssa agreed, Stephen noticeably calmed, calling out orders for servants and offering seats to his guests. Alyssa sat opposite him at the table, while Zusa refused, instead lurking behind Alyssa's chair, always keeping an eye on the doors and those coming and going.

As various cakes and fruits were placed before them, Stephen sat down and cleared his throat.

"I must confess, milady, that I asked you here with reason, one that you will...well, one that you'll find surprising."

"I've had advisers attempt to take my life, lovers turn to madmen, and my son brought to me from the dead." Alyssa smiled at him. "I daresay you have a difficult task if you think you can surprise me."

Stephen cleared his throat, but she saw a gleam in his eye piercing through his nervousness. He looked...pleased. She tried not to show it as she nibbled on a sweet cake, but a bit of worry crept up her belly. What if he did have something worthy of surprise?

"Alyssa...milady...what do you remember of your mother?"

The cake caught in her throat, and it took all of her control to keep her from launching into an unseemly coughing fit. Her mother? Why did he ask of her mother?

"She died when I was young," she said once she had swallowed. "The servants would not tell me the reason, and my father would only say that she left. I presume you think you know the truth of the matter?"

Stephen stood, as if unable to sit any longer.

"That I do, if you'd..."

She waved a hand dismissively, interrupting him.

"I am no fool, Stephen, and rumors are no stranger to me. I know what happened, if that is all you'd tell me. My mother was unfaithful to my father, and he..." She shook her head. "I love my father, but he was right to hide it from me. I'm not sure I'd have forgiven him, certainly not back then. She was given to Leon's...your father's gentle touchers. I can only pray they were merciful, if such a word even has meaning for their kind."

She felt Zusa's palm cup against her face, and she closed her eyes and leaned against it, accepting the comfort. When Alyssa looked again, Stephen was approaching the other door to the room.

"Well then," he said, unable to hold back a grin. "Everything you have said is indeed true. But you are still wrong."

He opened the door, then stepped back.

"Alyssa," he said, "may I present to you Melody Gemcroft."

Alyssa's heart stopped. Standing in the hall, as if afraid to enter through the doorway, was a woman from a dream. Her eyes had sunken farther, and many new wrinkles stretched across her lips and face, but the hair was the same, the ears, the nose, all the same as those of the woman who had sat on Alyssa's bed, candle in hand, and read story after story until sleep had taken Alyssa away. A thousand memories assaulted her, many long forgotten. Of brushing each other's hair. Of strict discipline and teaching of etiquette. The way she'd flicked Alyssa's nose with a finger whenever she grabbed the wrong utensil at dinner. The smell of crushed flowers every time they'd embraced.

"Mother," Alyssa whispered.

Tears swelled in Melody's eyes, but they did not fall. She took a few tentative steps inside, and then Alyssa was on her feet. Their hug was careful, slow, as if each was afraid of the other. When they separated, Alyssa looked deeply into that tired, pale face and was convinced beyond a doubt. She didn't know what to feel. Didn't know what it meant.

"How?" she asked.

"Not now," Melody said. "But...it is good to see you, Alyssa. You've grown to be so beautiful, just like I knew you would."

"She still needs her rest," Stephen said, gently taking Melody's hand. "I'll explain what I can. Servant?"

He snapped his fingers, and when the elderly servant arrived, he directed the man to take Melody back to her room. Feeling as if the world were spinning, Alyssa watched her long-dead mother be led away. Her stomach cramping, she went back to her chair, where Zusa remained leaning against the top, a guarded expression on her face.

"Is it true?" Zusa whispered as she sat.

"I think so." Alyssa felt as if she walked in a dream, one where the dead had come back to life. Would Maynard be revealed next, having lived in hiding after taking an arrow to the chest? She looked to Stephen, who appeared ready to burst with pride.

"How?" she asked again.

"Your father did give Melody over to my father's gentle touchers," Stephen said, sipping from his drink. "He even paid for it. But they didn't kill her. I believe my father fancied her beauty, from what I have learned. I will spare you all I know, but her detention was... unkind, as you can imagine. When Leon was killed, everything here was in chaos. It was several years before the caretakers would even acknowledge my presence, let alone my true birthright. None of us knew who Melody was, for we had no record of her existence. Even the gentle touchers didn't know for certain."

He took another drink. Alyssa felt chills, imagining what it'd have been like to be trapped in Leon's dungeon while the years crawled by. What "unkind" tortures might she have been subjected to? And for how long? Struggling to remember, she thought back to when she'd first heard of her mother's disappearance, a year before the Bloody Kensgold. That put it at near ten years. Ten years in darkness. No wonder her eyes had sunken in, and her thin frame had been unable to fill the simple violet dress she wore.

"I'm not surprised Leon kept it a secret," Alyssa said, trying to hold down her anger. "My father would have murdered him if he'd found out."

Stephen's cheek twitched, but his smile remained. "Maybe so," he said. "But when I finally accepted power, I cleared out all the prisoners, either through release or execution, depending on the measure of their crimes and the length of their stay. But what crime had this mysterious woman committed? She told the truth, of course, and as you can imagine, we did not believe her. Melody Gemcroft was dead. We all knew that. We all knew, but she persisted…"

He suddenly lurched to his feet, and before Alyssa knew what was going on, the young man had knelt before her and taken her hand in his.

"Please forgive me, Alyssa," he said, staring at the floor. "For a year she stayed, and I disbelieved. But she did not relent, and told us stories, memories, all to prove she was who she claimed to be. I should have known sooner; I should have believed her. Will you forgive me for adding torment to an already tormented woman?"

"I…yes," Alyssa said, carefully freeing her hand. Something about his touch made her squeamish. "How could you have known? I barely believe it myself."

This seemed to be enough, and with a jarring mood swing, Stephen was once more the charming boy.

"The finest physicians and priests in all of Dezrel have attended her," he said, grabbing a cake smothered with blueberries and wolfing it down. "Better food and bed have helped nurse her to health, and I am glad she took meeting you so well. Even walking at times puts her out of breath."

"I must thank you," Alyssa said, standing. "For everything."

"It is all I can do to make up for the sins of my father," Stephen said. "That, and to earn your forgiveness. I want us to be friends, Alyssa. May your next visit be far sooner than the last. As for Melody, we'll have her few things packed up and ready in just a few moments."

It was only then it hit Alyssa that it wasn't all a dream. Her mother was alive, and of course it was expected that she would go with her, to her proper home. Alyssa swallowed, and she felt her world crumbling. She hated it, how she hated it, but her immediate thought was nothing but an angry denial.

I am still ruler of the Gemcroft family!

She dug her fingernails into her arm as punishment. Such a selfish, childish thought was unbecoming of her. She was better than that, more mature.

"All the best," she said to Stephen, forcing a pleasant mask across her face. "It will be such a pleasure to bring my mother home."

To meet her grandchild. To see how the rooms had changed. To hear of Maynard's death, and the thief war that had nearly decimated the family.

To reenter a family of which she was the eldest, and the lawful ruler.

"All the best." Stephen smiled.

Alyssa grabbed Zusa's hand, squeezed it tight.

CHAPTER

3

Thren Felhorn crouched in the alley, watching the people pass. He wore the gray cloak of the Spider Guild, of which he was the undisputed ruler. Merchants, thieves, and lords quivered just hearing his name. At least they once had. But now someone had dared disrespect him, and even flaunted that he'd done so.

"Damn Serpents," Thren said. "Do they think I will let them go unpunished?"

Beside him, his second-in-command—a rugged thief named Martin—put a pinch of crimleaf between his teeth and bit down.

"They've only claimed the first kill, and marked it as such," Martin said, turning to spit. "That second one don't seem like them. Tongue of gold? What the fuck does that mean? Bert was hardly known for his pretty words."

Thren felt his insides harden. They'd found Bert the previous night, an arrow embedded in his throat. His mouth had been open, but no golden tongue there. The eyes of silver, though, those they had seen, and the memory still filled him with rage. They'd taken the coins and fled just before the city guard arrived. Some had thought it a hit by the Watcher, but Thren dismissed that immediately. It wasn't the Watcher's style. His two men accosted outside one of their taverns—now *that* was the Watcher's style. No, the coins and odd rhyme left in mockery had to be the Serpent Guild. Their new leader, Wilson Ket, was known for his pathetic attempts at resembling nobility instead of the street rat he was.

"Now," Thren said, and the two rushed out.

They'd been watching another tavern, a place where Thren had been told Wilson liked to drink in the early mornings. The crowds had thinned, and no Serpents were in sight. At his command he and Martin crossed the street, their hands on their hilts. But when he reached the door, he stopped and swore.

"Did someone warn him?" Martin asked.

Thren shrugged. He didn't know. Enough already didn't make sense, but adding this?

The door was broken inward. They stepped inside, their blades drawn. Not sure what to expect, Thren still did not find it within that tavern. Instead several Serpents lay on the floor, their arms bound behind their backs. Over a dozen armed soldiers were about, some tying ropes, others questioning the Serpents, while a few just stood around looking bored. That boredom vanished the moment they laid eyes on the two of them, barging in with naked blades.

"Oh, shit," Martin muttered.

An appropriate understatement.

"Halt!" several cried, but Thren was already on his way out. In the street he turned north and ran, jamming his swords into their sheaths. Martin followed, still clutching his dagger.

"They're chasing!" Martin yelled, and Thren glanced back to confirm. Only four, but they wore fine sets of chain mail that would turn weapons with ease. He almost engaged them, figuring to end the fight quickly, but then he saw another squad of soldiers turn the corner just ahead. They wore the same insignia as the others: yellow wings over a gold sun.

"Follow me," he told Martin, cutting hard to his right. They ducked into an alley, then dove through a window upon reaching a dead end. Thren landed hard atop a table, then rolled to avoid Martin's fall. Banging one of his knees on the way to the floor, Thren clenched his teeth and muttered a litany of curses at whoever had placed the table there. A woman stood screaming, and he slashed out her throat, not giving a thought to her corpse as they ran up the stairs. On the rooftops they were truly at home, and they leaped across with practiced ease. Once the guards were far behind, Thren stopped.

"Damn it," he muttered as Martin slowed up ahead, realizing his guildmaster was not keeping pace. A cramp stung Thren's side, and he tried to push it into a corner of his mind so it wouldn't bother him. It would have been easier if he weren't so desperate for air. *Old*, he thought. Was this what it meant to get old? Despite his training, despite his legendary skill, he'd still just be a weary man gasping for air while the young ran on?

"You feeling fine, Thren?" Martin asked.

"Don't ask stupid questions," Thren snapped. "What just happened there?"

Martin shrugged. "Looks like mercenaries going out hunting for thieves. We've seen it before."

Thren shook his head. "Yes, but not since the Watcher's agreement. Have they learned nothing? We nearly burned this city down before. Do they think we cannot do it again?"

Martin walked over to the edge of the roof, knelt on one knee, and peered down.

"Thren," he said. "You might want to look at this."

Thren joined him at the side, and if his insides were already hard, they now turned to iron. Hundreds of soldiers wearing the sun-and-wings insignia patrolled the streets. His mind flashed back to the bloody conflict four years prior, but it didn't match up. Back then Alyssa had unleashed a horde of mercenaries upon the city, smashing in homes, cutting down anyone suspected of guilt, and filling the city with fear. This, though...

"They're orderly," he said, with a hint of wonder. "Calm."

"Not just that," Martin said, pointing. "They're only talking to most. What do you think they're doing?"

Thren could spot a thief without even trying, and he saw at least seven weaving through the heavy crowd of the main street. None dared act. When one neared the soldiers, Thren thought they might spot the cloak and attack, but they did not.

"They're arresting thieves, but not at random," Thren said. "Who ordered this? Whose soldiers are these?"

Martin paced the roof until he was beside an alley jutting off from the main route. Waving Thren over, he pointed to a trio of soldiers marching below them.

"Think they'll know?" he asked, grinning.

Thren drew his short swords.

"Answers," he said. "One way or another."

When the soldiers were directly beneath, the two leaped to the ground, like hawks descending upon their prey. The soldiers' chain mail was finely woven, but Thren managed to jam a blade between his victim's coif and collar, piercing flesh. The thrust wasn't deep as planned, for the man immediately spun to one side and fell to a knee. Thren twisted the blade free, then made to cut across the throat with his other sword, but was not fast enough. A second soldier blocked the attack, standing protectively before his fallen comrade.

Thren gave him no reprieve, weaving a quick series of strikes to test his foe's skill. Much to his surprise, and annoyance, the soldier blocked them all. Curses filled Thren's mind. From the corner of his eye, he saw Martin battling the third soldier. Unlike Thren, he'd not managed a solid blow during his fall, his dagger failing to penetrate the chain mail. The two fought close, Martin trying to negate the soldier's advantage of longer reach.

"Who pays you?" Thren asked, feinting with one hand and then thrusting with the other. He expected no answer, only hoped to distract his foe. It didn't work. The thrust was parried harmlessly away, and then the soldier stepped in, expertly weaving his weapon in a beautiful counter. Thren flung himself to the side, bit his tongue as he felt steel slash across his arm. Blood stained his gray shirt and cloak. His fury growing, the rush of battle flooding through him, he lunged at his opponent with both blades. When the soldier blocked, Thren pressed on, hacking and slashing with such ferocity his opponent fell back in retreat. The wounded soldier no longer protected, Thren stopped for just a moment to stab him in the neck, then kick his corpse aside.

"What fool brought you to your deaths?" Thren asked as he swallowed, his mouth feeling dry. He was losing blood fast, he knew. Had to get it attended to. The soldier started to respond, but Thren spun, his attention no longer on him. Martin had fought the other soldier to a standstill, the two so focused that neither sensed his sudden appearance. Thren's short sword pierced the small of the soldier's back. A twist, a yank, and the man dropped. Martin nodded in thanks, and then the two turned on the last. Thren thought he'd run, but he did not, only stood his ground.

"Left," Thren said softly. When they both attacked, Martin did as told, veering to the left and cutting in with his dagger. The soldier shifted to the side, easily parrying it away, but the motion kept him from falling into a retreat. That was all Thren needed. A trio of slashes batted the sword out of position, and then his own blades sliced in, jamming through the soldier's throat. The man gurgled, his eyes widened, and then he dropped. Thren pulled his sword free, shook blood off it.

"Fuck!" Thren yelled, kicking the corpse. His arm stung, and when his battle lust faded, he knew it would hurt even more. Worse, they'd failed in their goal.

"Hard to interrogate a man who has no throat," Martin said, jamming his dagger into his belt.

Thren sheathed his swords, then checked the wound on his arm. Not too deep. It would leave a scar, just one more among hundreds. Glancing out the alley, he saw people passing, and several spotted the carnage. They wisely kept their mouths shut, but it would be only moments before someone wasn't so smart.

"Back home," Thren said. "We know too little. It isn't safe."

They took to the roofs once more and ran, Thren gritting his teeth against the pain. The chaos of the main streets vanished behind them until they reached the Thirsty Mule. Martin went first to ensure none of the mysterious soldiers were about. The way clear, he beckoned Thren in, and together they entered the cellar of their headquarters, disguised as a simple inn.

The place was abuzz with rumors and questions. Amid the pain, Thren estimated at least twenty of his guild milling about, swapping stories and making guesses. They'd fled home when the soldiers flooded the streets, but how many had not made it? At Thren's entrance the conversation quieted, and several tilted their heads with respect. No doubt they wished to ask him questions, but seeing his wound, they wisely let him be.

"Where's Murphy?" Thren asked as he took a seat at the bar, banging his fist on the wood in demand of a drink. One of the smaller thieves, Peb, rushed over, grabbing glasses.

"I'll get him," Martin said.

"What'll it be?" asked Peb. He was quick, and had big ears. They'd called him Mouse for a while, then switched to Pebble after Thren put a stop to it. No thief of his was a mouse. They were Spiders, lurkers, killers—even their smallest carrying dangerous venom.

"Hardest we have," Thren said. By the time Peb gave him his glass, Murphy had arrived, a small box in hand.

"How bad is it?" Murphy asked.

"Bad enough."

He downed the glass, then carefully removed his shirt so the stocky man could see. Of them all, Murphy was the only one with a modicum of training in the skills of the apothecary. A gap-toothed man with graying hair, Murphy loved to say he'd first learned to sew up cows, not people, but that the two were often the same. Deep down Thren believed Murphy had learned how to stitch and amputate because he loved causing pain while still getting praised for it. Had he been born of higher blood, he'd have been one of Connington's gentle touchers for sure.

"What's going on?" Thren asked as he motioned for Peb to refill the glass.

"Well, you're bleeding, but it didn't quite make it to bone."

"I meant with the city."

Murphy took out a long needle and some thread from the box. Thren grabbed his glass before Peb was even done pouring.

"I've been here all the while," Murphy said, threading the needle. He nodded to the rest. "Ask them."

"I have," Martin said, taking a seat on the other side of Thren. "All we've got is a name. Lord Victor Kane. He's been here hardly twenty-four hours, yet he's already stirring up trouble."

"What does he want?" Thren asked as the needle pierced his flesh. He didn't let the pain show. Not in front of so many. Pain was only a tool, and right now he had no desire for it. As Peb poured his third glass, an ache swelled in Thren's chest. There was a time when someone might have chopped off his right hand and he'd not have made a sound. Was he growing so weak that he needed the aid of alcohol for just a little cut?

Angry with himself, he pushed the glass away. Martin snapped it up for himself, drank it down, then let out a burp.

"That's the thing," Martin said. "We don't know what he wants. Early this morning, while we were stalking Serpents, Victor's men were rounding up merchants, lords, landowners... and then out they came again for us. From what I can tell, it's all been orderly, controlled. No one's been killed except those who resist. The rest are getting sent to the castle—whether for execution or interrogation, your guess is as good as mine."

Thren felt the skin of his arm tightening as the needle did its work. He used it to focus, to force things into perspective.

"Edwin's too much of a coward for this," he said. "That, and the status quo has served him fine for years. Someone else hatched this plan, and right now, the obvious one is Lord Victor."

"What about one of the Trifect?" Murphy asked, thread between his teeth.

"Victor might be in their pay," Martin agreed. "An expensive gambit, but by bringing in this outsider, they pull attention away from themselves and onto him."

Thren shook his head, then investigated the stitches on his arm. Clean work as always, but not quite done yet.

"Do it," he told Murphy. The old man grinned, then grabbed the bottle away from Peb. The liquid poured down Thren's arm. It burned like fire, but he gave no reaction beyond a tightening of his teeth. That done, he pulled his shirt back over his body. Despite his age, it was still pure muscle.

"We can do what we did before," Martin suggested. "Declare war against them, and rally the rest of the guilds to counter this new threat."

Thren met his eyes, saw the hopeful lie for what it was.

"We're too few now," he said. "Every night we've preyed on each other, and our numbers haven't recovered from the chaos four years ago. Besides... these mercenaries aren't normal scum with a sword. They're too good, too well armed."

Martin sighed, for he knew the same. Thren and Martin were easily the most skilled of all the Spider Guild, yet even they had suffered wounds in taking a squad down. The rest of the guild—clumsy men accustomed to threatening fat merchants for bribes—would stand no chance.

"We can't let this go unpunished," Martin said, dropping his voice lower. "The gold the Trifect pays us dwindles every year. It's not enough to keep everyone together, and I doubt we are alone in this. If every guild breaks, it'll be anarchy..."

"We will not break!" Thren said. All around him, men quieted, hearing the ice in his voice, the strength of his conviction. He stood from his chair, slammed a fist against the bar. "This is our city—*ours*. No outsider shall come in, bare swords against us, and expect to live. All of you, cowering here... get out. Now. I want your ears at every wall. I want your eyes on every street. Whatever information you can find, I want to hear it. Where this Victor lives, where he eats, where he sleeps, where he shits—I want to know it all. And if you fear being caught, or arrested, then don't come back. You aren't Spiders. You're worms."

They filed out, grabbing swords and cloaks on their way. Even Murphy left, though Thren knew he would only go upstairs to wait. Should anyone return wounded, the surgeon must be ready. When Thren sat down, he noticed a single man remained in the far corner, leaning against the wall with his arms crossed over his beefy chest and his strange hat in his hands. Thren turned on him, thinking a savage killing might do wonders for his mood. Then he better saw the man's face, and grinned.

"Grayson, you ox," Thren said. "I'll never understand how you can hide in a crowd."

Grayson grinned back. He was an enormous man, dark-skinned, and stood at nearly seven feet tall. The thin clothing he wore did little to conceal the muscles beneath. A four-pointed star made of gold thread was sewn into his shirt. His head was shaved, and he wore nine rings in his left ear, running up and down the cartilage. Where he came from, each ring traditionally represented a kill, yet Thren knew Grayson had been forced to adopt a new standard, with each ring counting for ten, lest his ear fall off.

Grayson joined him at the bar, slapping him once on the back.

"You banished our barkeep," said the man, his voice deep and rumbling.

"Would you make an injured man pour drinks?"

Grayson laughed. "I've never seen you injured, Thren," he said. "Just sometimes you're bleeding more than usual."

Grayson leaned forward, his long arms grabbing bottles and glasses from the wall. Mixing two liquors together, Grayson tasted his drink and then let out a sigh of contentment.

"From all I've heard, I thought you'd have little better than donkey piss and water," he said. "Looks like Veldaren might not be as bad as rumored. Either that, or you're the richest thief left."

Thren bit down a retort. Grayson was from the distant city of Mordeina, and was a legendary thief in his own right. In what felt like ages past, the two had worked together, building the Spider Guild into something fearsome. But then, one terrible night, it had all come crashing down...

"The gold still flows here," Thren said, careful to control his tone. "The protection money from the Trifect alone keeps the liquor flowing."

"That the lie you tell yourselves so you can sleep at night?"

Grayson took a shot, poured himself another. Thren's eyes narrowed.

"Things are not the same," he said. "Between the Bloody Kensgold, Alyssa's mercenaries, and now the Watcher, I dare say no thief elsewhere has faced such hardships as we have here in Veldaren."

"Ah yes, the Watcher. I've been thinking of hunting him down and seeing how good he really is. You know that word of him has reached all the way to Mordeina?"

"Is that so?" Thren asked, doing his best to sound bored.

"Yes. And you know what's worse, Thren? That's not the only thing reaching our ears. The nobles are hearing of your little setup, this game you play. It's giving them ideas, ideas I don't fucking like. Already they whisper of similar arrangements, of turning our guilds against each other in the name of protection money. Mordeina won't turn into Veldaren. The priests alone give us enough trouble. I'm a thief, and a killer. I won't let myself become some noble's bootlicking bodyguard."

Thren felt his blood turn to ice.

"Is that what you think I am?" he asked. "Some low-rent bodyguard for the Trifect?"

Grayson grunted. "That's what I'm here to find out. A lot has changed over the past ten years, and I want to know just how much." He stood, put a wide-brimmed hat made of leather on his bald head. "I have my own place to stay, so don't worry about offering me a bed. Not sure how long I'll be here, but I thought I'd drop in and give you my greetings."

"What are you really here for?" Thren asked as the big man was about to exit. "If all you wanted was information, you'd have sent an underling, not traveled across Dezrel yourself. You're here for more than that. What is it?"

Grayson stopped, looked back at him with a dangerous grin on his face.

"What if I don't feel like answering? Will you make me, Thren?"

Thren swallowed, and his hand drifted down to the hilt of a short sword. Grayson saw this, smirked.

"Careful," he said. "I have no desire to cross swords with you. Besides, it wouldn't be fair. After all . . . you're injured."

When he was gone, Thren took his glass and smashed it across the counter. The glass cut his hand, and he stared at the mixing blood and alcohol. His fury grew. Grayson had sensed weakness, and Thren could not refute it. Despite all his best efforts, his guild was weaker than it had ever been. All the guilds were. And if the Suns, or the Stars, or any other guild from Mordeina decided to move in . . .

Thren shook his head. No, there was no *if*, only *when*. Grayson would not have traveled such a distance without good cause. The only question was how the foreign guilds planned to make their attack, and how great their cooperation would be. Their first move, though, Grayson had stated clear as day.

The truce between the Trifect and the guilds would have to be broken, and the easiest step to that was obvious: ending the life of the Watcher.

"Good luck, Watcher," Thren said softly, doing everything to subdue his anger, to think clearly and carefully as he knew he must. Despite his frustration, he felt pride. All the way to Mordeina, Grayson had said. The Watcher's reputation had spread throughout the four nations, coast to coast.

"Good luck"—he wiped his hand with a cloth—"my son."

CHAPTER 4

The parade of men in chains seemed endless as Victor stood before the king's dungeon, a large, ungainly block attached to the side of the castle. They'd even started tying people with rope, having run out of manacles. *An excellent day*, Victor thought. He doubted it could have started any better.

"Milord," said Sef, leader of Victor's guard. He was heavy-set, bearded, and had been a battle-worn servant of the Kane household for almost two decades. "Sir Antonil Copernus wishes to speak with you."

"Send him over," Victor said.

Sef bowed, hurried away. Moments later Antonil arrived, wearing the regal armor of his position as captain of the guard and protector of His Majesty's city. His long blond hair peeked out from the lower limits of his helmet. Scars of battle marked his face. A shield hung from his back, and his long sword swung at his hip. The guard captain bowed low, and addressed him with sincere respect.

"Milord Victor, I come at behest of my king," he said, standing straight. "He thought it best I help oversee your endeavor, as well as ensure my own guards assist you in any way they can."

Victor grinned at the knight.

"Are you sure about that? I thought our gracious king might fear giving too much assistance, lest he earn the ire of both the guilds and the Trifect."

Antonil's smile hardened, and his voice lowered. "Perhaps. In all things, I protect the people of this city. You'd best remember that. Your men may carry weapons, and the king's blessing, but upon my word they lose both, and join the men they've arrested in a cell."

"All I do, I do for the people of this city, Antonil."

Antonil nodded, but did not respond. Victor felt his respect growing. The man looked tired, frustrated, but hid it well. An air of authority hovered over him, and whenever he cast his eyes about, even Victor's own men stood at attention.

"There are so many," Antonil said, turning to the lines before the dungeon entrance. "We cannot fit them all."

"We don't need to," Victor said. "Follow me, and I will explain."

Victor led the way. There were five lines, all steadily shuffling forward as Victor's soldiers brought in their latest catch. Though some wore the cloaks of the guilds, most did not. They were merchants, peasants, prostitutes, even the homeless and the beggars. Antonil took in the sight, and his frown deepened.

"They are not under arrest," Victor explained. "At least, not most. We are here for answers, Antonil, and to get them we must ask questions. Information is our greatest weapon against the shadows these scum cloak themselves in. It should please you greatly to know we fully abide by the law."

They stopped at the head of one of the five lines. An older man sat at a desk, a lengthy parchment before him, along with a large inkwell and quill. Before him was a fat merchant on his knees, two soldiers holding him still. His clothes were smeared with mud, and across his right cheek was an angry cut that oozed blood. At their arrival, the merchant glanced their way, and paused.

"Continue," said the old scribe before him. "Their names, if you know them."

"I...I don't."

"Then their descriptions. And remember, we will talk to them as well."

The merchant glanced their way. Victor put a hand on his shoulder.

"The law will protect you," he said. "Speak the truth, and hold faith. It will only be a matter of time. They cannot hide forever."

Their eyes met, just for a moment, and then the merchant turned to the scribe.

"The bastards' names are Jok and Kevis, both in the Wolf Guild."

His voice trailed off as Victor led Antonil away.

"I don't understand," Antonil said beside him. "We cannot just arrest anyone in the guilds. Our arrangement forbids it, for it is they who police the streets..."

"It should be you who polices the streets, not them," Victor said. "And you are no fool, so think. It doesn't matter if the guilds hold to the agreement, and do not steal. They still extort. They still kill. They demand bribes of merchants, smuggle goods to avoid tariffs, and flood your streets with powders and leaves that addle the minds of your people."

He gestured to the lines.

"Right now we gather evidence against them. We get names. We list crimes. When we capture them, we steadily move upward. We take everyone we can, then repeat the process. All of it, written and stored forever, unable to be killed or silenced. Time will not save them from their crimes. I will find them. All of them."

"But why here? Why in the open streets?"

Victor grinned, and gestured to the dungeon behind them.

"If they refuse, or lie, that is where they go. When their eyes wander, they see the fate awaiting them for such transgressions. Besides, let the whole city watch what we do. Let them know I am here, and will not stop. I will never stop, not until this city is a place of lambs instead of leeches."

Antonil swallowed hard, looked back to the line.

"You release them after you're done, correct?" he asked.

"The innocent ones, yes."

"And then they go home, having been seen by all, known by all to have talked. You know what will happen to them, Victor. You're sentencing them to death!"

Victor whirled on Antonil, leaned in close.

"If they die, it isn't by my hand, but the hands of murderers and thieves who should have never been allowed to live as long as they have. I do what must be done to save Veldaren from itself. I am no fool. This is a new kind of war, but blood will still be shed. If your guards do their jobs, those men and women will live. Stop cowering in fear of the dark corners."

Antonil met his gaze a while longer, refusing to back down. Victor's respect for him continued to grow. As the silence stretched, a man in a green cloak was led toward the dungeon door, then around to the side. Antonil noticed this, and gestured in that direction.

"Where does he go?" he asked.

"I shall show you."

Victor led Antonil around the back, to where two elderly men stood before a tall table. To the side was a hastily constructed platform, and in its center was a thick wood block. Seeing it, Antonil clenched his jaw, and his eyes widened.

"Calm yourself," Victor said. "They are your judges, those appointed by Edwin, not myself. They hear our evidence, read what we have collected, and then offer sentencing."

While the man with the green cloak was dragged before one of the judges, another climbed the two steps of the platform. His face was ashen, and his eyes remained locked on the floor. By Victor's guess he was fifteen, sixteen at most. Two of Victor's soldiers led him to the block, where a heavyset man waited, ax in hand.

"How many?" Antonil asked quietly as the thief was flung atop the block, his arms tied by ropes looped through holes in the platform.

"Seventeen today," Victor said. "By tomorrow it should be twice that. The list of crimes grows by the hour."

"Seventeen," Antonil whispered. "How many executed, and how many sent to the dungeon?"

Victor shook his head. "You still don't understand, do you? Your judges do. Mercy has been extended long enough here. All seventeen have met your executioner's blade. The dungeon is only for those who refuse to cooperate, who would rather bite their tongues than reveal the guilty. This is war, Antonil. War against the very culture that has twisted and perverted everything great about Veldaren and turned it into something wicked. We have no time for prisoners."

The executioner lifted his ax. Neither Victor nor Antonil looked away as it descended. There were no onlookers, no gathered crowds, so they easily heard the plop of the head hitting the wood, the sound of the blood dripping across the platform, and the untying of the ropes as men cleared away the body.

"I want every name," Antonil said. "Every crime, every shred of proof leveraged against the men who died here today."

"Of course," Victor said. "I understand your fear that we will execute an innocent. It won't happen, Antonil. I won't let it. The only sins I'll bear shall come from waiting as long as I did. Come with me. I'll tell Sef to prepare everything you need."

As they walked back toward the initial five lines, Antonil stepped in his way, grabbed him by the front of his collar, and pulled him close. Victor tensed, but he sensed no anger, no threat. Antonil's eyes met his, and they were full of fear...and hope.

"They'll kill you," Antonil whispered. "Something like this, so grand, so terrifying...they won't let it stand. I don't care how many guards you have, how careful you are, they'll still slit your throat, cut your body into pieces, and then scatter the remains about the city. You are a dead man, Victor."

Victor took a step closer, put a hand on Antonil's shoulder.

"Let them try."

He pulled away from the guard captain, then motioned Sef over.

"Everything he requests, fulfill to the best of your abilities," he said. "I must return to my room, and ensure no specters lurk in its corners. Oh, and Antonil..."

Victor sighed, tried to see things from the other's perspective. His grin faded, and he let some of his honest worry shine through.

"I know I might die doing this," he said. "But when? How

long? Because each day we do this, the sun shines that much brighter upon Veldaren. Succeed or fail…I'll have done something."

"What drives you, Victor?" Antonil asked as Victor put his back to him and walked down the street. "What madness would have you risk so much for so little?"

Victor waved good-bye, and did not answer. Unguarded, he walked down the street, but he never felt alone. His men were everywhere, always watching, always searching. They saluted as they passed him by, and each time, he smiled back. Just a small smile and a meeting of the eyes. He wanted each man to think he'd put special interest in him, watching closely for signs of greatness. For the most part, it was true. And when he received that night's report, listing the dead under his command, he'd recognize every name, remember every face. Steeling himself against the pain did little to help.

King Edwin had not offered them a place to stay, just as Victor had expected. The man was a coward, and Victor was lucky enough to have had the king go along with his plan, however distantly. But the castle was not a safe place anyway. It was too big, too grandiose, with all its windows, high ceilings, and lengthy halls filled with a million shadows. Most of Victor's men would be staying in inns scattered about the town. Victor had carefully chosen his home, though, and secured it before ever going to Edwin. Eyes watched him from rooftops, but it didn't matter if they saw where he slept. The constant surveillance only showed how frightened they were of him.

"Evening," Victor said to the two men stationed before the entrance of what would be his home for the foreseeable future. It had once been a tavern, shuttered for months until Victor bought it. Every single window was boarded up. All doors but one had been nailed shut, and then bricked. There was but one entrance, and it was to be guarded at all times. Upon his arrival he'd filled its stores with food and drink, carefully packed away. He would search no food for glass, require no taster for poison. Everything watched, everything controlled, just as he liked.

The outside soldiers banged on the door a few times, then called out Victor's name. Moments later, it was unbarred and opened by the interior guards. Victor nodded, pleased with their attention to detail, and then stepped inside. The interior was dimly lit, and while it had a vacant feel, it was still being meticulously cleaned. Servants moved about, and upon seeing him they quickly bowed and asked if he had any needs.

"Wine, if possible," he said, unbuckling his sword. "And something light to eat. Bring it to my room when ready."

The servants bowed again. Victor climbed the stairs as they hurried into the kitchen. Another of his precautions: the servants were all male, and had been in his service before coming to Veldaren. They stayed within the tavern, leaving only when they must. He'd even implemented rules with the guards that all servants were to strip naked, hand over their clothes, and then dress again on the other side of the door. A severe measure, but he could not be too careful. The fate of the entire city rested on his survival. He couldn't risk a servant's accepting a hefty bribe.

His room was sparse, his only luxury a bookcase full of carefully bound writings. The mixture was eclectic, from philosophers to kings to old wives who wrote children's fables. He was drifting his fingers over the spines, pondering what to read that night, when he heard the door close behind him.

"Well, aren't you a careful bastard?"

Victor's heart caught in his throat. He'd tossed his sword onto the bed upon entering, and he thought to leap for it. Instead he turned and stood proud and tall while confronting his no-doubt murderer.

"Not careful enough," he said, meeting his intruder's eyes. He was a dark-skinned man, with darker hair that grew down to his shoulders. His gray clothes were clearly that of a guild, but more noticeable were his eyes. One was a deep brown, the other a bloody red. "Have you come to kill me, thief?" he asked.

The intruder chuckled. "I could, but that wouldn't be interesting, would it? Allow me to introduce myself. I am Deathmask, leader of the Ash Guild, and I've come with a proposal."

Victor felt his muscles relax, but only a little. The intruder didn't seem particularly dangerous, and he carried no visible weapons. He leaned with his back against the door, his arms crossed over his chest.

"A proposal?" Victor asked, thinking to stall. He took a single step toward the man, shifting himself closer to his weapon.

"Two proposals, actually," Deathmask said. "First proposal is that you don't do anything stupid like calling for guards, or grabbing that sword of yours. Once I hear an answer to that one, we can move on to proposal number two."

Victor felt his heart skip a beat, and he stepped away from the bed, toward his bookcase.

"So be it," he said, clenching his fists at his sides. "I am listening."

"Excellent. Now, to make sure we both understand each other...you do know who I am, right?"

Victor nodded. He'd done extensive research on the various guilds before coming to Veldaren, learning what he could about their leaders, their habits, vices, and weaknesses. As for the Ash Guild...

"You're the one guild that made the least sense," Victor said. "Run by a man called eccentric at best, insane at worst. Four years ago you usurped control from Garrick Lowe, killing or disbanding nearly the entire guild. Estimates vary, but all claim you now have fewer than ten members. One man suggested there were only four of you, but that is ridiculous."

"Is it?" Deathmask asked, grinning. "No, that's true. There are just the four of us. Smaller than the rest of the guilds, sure, but I've found having a few dangerous, intelligent people is far better than having a guild full of mouth breathers."

Victor's mind clicked, and he shook his head in disbelief.

"And easier to split the rather handsome sum the Trifect pays for protection, correct?"

Deathmask shrugged. "That too."

Victor shifted closer to his weapon, then relaxed. If Deathmask hadn't killed him yet, he wasn't going to...at least not until he had an answer to his proposition.

"Why are you here?" Victor asked.

"I could ask the same of you," Deathmask said, tapping his fingers together. "A long-vanished lord returns with a miniature army, with the sole aim to clear out the guilds? Preposterous. But I do not care, because that is not how I operate, Victor. Why you do what you do is irrelevant to me. All that matters is that things go as I desire, and right now... I'd like to help you."

"Help me?" Victor lifted an eyebrow. "How?"

"I can give you names, locations, shipping dates...or I could bring you bodies. Either is fine with me."

Victor shook his head. "This won't protect you, Deathmask. I offer no clemency, not to anyone. I will not accept the help of the very criminals I have come to eradicate."

"You mistake me," Deathmask said, stepping closer. A fire burned bright in his mismatched eyes. "I seek no pardon, no clemency, for I won't need it. Tell me, of all the men who wilted before your inquisition, how many have spoken my name? How many pointed their finger at the Ash Guild?"

Victor had not studied the entirety of the lists, but he'd gone over them as the day wore on, and listened in on several confessions. Try as he might, he could think of nothing, and told Deathmask so.

"Exactly," said the thief. "And you will find nothing. We are not like the others. My guild is not careless, not foolish. No one will turn on me. No one will provide a single bit of evidence for you to use against me in any court, no matter how much of a sham it might be. Your...crusade...is no threat to me, only a nuisance at worst, entertainment at best. So then, now that we might understand each other, recognize that I could be your ally in this instead of your enemy. Let me help you. The destruction of the other guilds is something that would greatly amuse me."

His words were honey, but his eyes were death. Victor shook his head. "You may pretend, you may feign innocence, but I am no fool. You are murderers, thieves, butchers. I will not taint all that I do with your presence. Not if I am to succeed."

"I'm a dangerous man to have as an enemy, Victor."

Victor stood tall and spread his shoulders wide, as if daring the man to strike. "Kill me, then," he said. "I'll die eventually, but it won't be as a hypocrite."

They stared, matching wills, but then Deathmask broke into a smile. "You fascinate me," he said. "You won't die tonight, not by me, anyway." He turned to the corner of the room, put his hand against it. Shadows swelled, thickening as if into a liquid. The guildmaster looked back. His smile had hardened. "Those who loudest profess the law tend to have the greatest crimes to hide. I wonder just what secrets you have buried deep in the dark soil."

The darkness swelled, began to swirl. With a mocking bow, Deathmask vanished through it. Just like that the portal was gone, and Victor was alone in his room. He took a step toward the wall and ran his fingers across it. It was cool to the touch, as if a frost had settled over it. He struck it twice, unable to help himself.

"Magic," he whispered. All his planning, all his care, meant nothing to a man who could walk through walls. And if Deathmask could do so, then others could as well. How long until the Spiders or Serpents obtained a scroll to appear directly below his bed while he slept? He needed defenses, those of the arcane kind. Sleep could wait until it was safe. Grabbing his sword off his bed, he reached for the door, only to have someone knock from the other side. He jumped, then felt his neck blush. Deathmask's visit had unnerved him more than he'd thought.

"Yes?" he asked, flinging it open. The waiting soldier took a step back, surprised by how quickly Victor had come.

"Milord," said the soldier. "There's something we feel you should see."

Victor thought to ask, then just shook his head. It didn't matter what it was; he'd need to handle it in person. These first few days were the most fragile. Nothing could be left to chance.

"Lead on," he said.

CHAPTER

5

Haern rushed across the rooftops, and he was not alone. In the moonlight he saw many others in the distance, scrambling to and fro to avoid the roads. Most fled before his arrival, for they recognized his presence above all others'. He was their watcher, their punisher, their executioner. Victor might be a new enemy, but they still understood who was the deadlier threat.

Reaching the temple to Ashhur, Haern stopped, and atop a two-story building he knelt. The building was rented to large families forced to share such meager rooms. From within he heard a child crying, not loudly, just a constant whimper that put a damper on Haern's mood. As the moonlight dimmed, thick clouds slowly spreading across the sky let loose a heavy rumble. Rain. Pulling his hood tighter over his head, Haern chuckled. Of course it was raining. The perfect capstone to a long, terrible day. Pausing for a rest, he watched the streets. His brow furrowed when he saw a group of Victor's men rushing north. They appeared frightened.

His knees cracked as he stood, and he let out a groan. Night after night of stalking the rooftops was taking its toll. He feared one day he wouldn't be able to walk without a heavy stoop. Haern thought to follow the men, then changed his mind. The alley they'd appeared from led into Spider territory, and by the flickering light, he saw more torches within. The patrols had found something, but what? And more important, how willing would they be to share the discovery with him?

He dropped to the ground, drew his sabers, and then ran. He felt better with the hilts in his hands, cold and hard. In a fair fight, he knew of few who might challenge him, and even if overwhelmed, it was Haern who tended to come out unscathed. At the alley entrance he peered inside, saw three more soldiers standing around, torches in hand. Haern decided not to risk a scene just yet. Retreating back a space, he climbed the wall of the nearby home.

From the rooftop he heard them talking.

"What in blazes you think it means?"

"Means nothing, that's what I've been saying. Just nonsense."

"Can't be nonsense. You don't go to this much trouble for nonsense. It's a message."

Haern's stomach hardened. He desperately hoped he was wrong, but when he peered over the edge of the building, he saw he was not. A man lay dead on his back between the three. Judging by his cloak and dress, he was a member of the Spider Guild. When Haern looked to the wall, he saw the message written in blood, this time smaller, more hurried.

tongue of gold, eyes of silver
run, run little spider
from the widow's quiver

The three soldiers were still discussing the rhyme when Haern crouched closer to the edge.

"Widow, eh?" the tallest of the three asked. "Who's that?"

"Black widow, that's what I say," said another, a red-haired man with a heavily scarred face. When the other two scoffed, he pressed on. "This guy's a Spider, right? Think about it. They go out to some whore, only it ain't a regular whore. It's a black widow. And after she's done pleasing him, well…"

He curled two of his fingers and pretended to stab them into his neck. The three all laughed. It was nervous, forced. They were trying to make light of the corpse before them, to dismiss the mystery.

"And this?" asked the tall man, jamming a thumb toward the wall.

The redhead shrugged. "Whore fancies herself a poet?"

They laughed again, this time far too loudly. Haern was tempted to startle them, show them how unsafe they were, but he had no need. A loud voice called them to attention, and they jumped. Haern's eyes narrowed as he saw Lord Victor enter the alley with an escort of soldiers.

"What is the meaning of this?" Victor asked, approaching the corpse. The men shrugged.

"Just a dead thief," said the third. "But this one's a bit odd. Thought you should see. Liam, open his mouth and show him."

The redhead knelt, grabbed the dead thief's mouth, and pulled it open. The gold on his tongue sparkled in the torchlight. Victor muttered a curse.

"Not just this," said the tall man. "The wall, too. Looks like the killer left her name."

"Her?" asked Victor.

"Or him," the man corrected. "Guess we can't judge the tastes of a dead man, can we?"

Victor looked to the wall. Haern watched as the man's grip on his hilt tightened with each line he read.

"Is this a hit between thieves?" Victor asked.

"That'd be my guess," said one of the soldiers.

"And a foul guess it is," Haern said, his voice startling many into reaching for their weapons. He ignored them as they spun about, cursing or preparing for a fight. "Check his eyes."

As a couple swore, Victor leaned down, and his hand brushed over the face. Seeing the silver for eyes, Victor shook his head and frowned.

"Leave us," he said. At first Haern made to go, then realized Victor spoke to his own soldiers.

"Milord," said Liam, "are you sure..."

"That's an order."

The protest died. The men funneled out to the main street, leaving Victor alone in the alley. Haern put a hand on the rooftop's edge and swung himself to the ground. He landed silently, not even his cloak making a rustle. Victor stood over the body, and he let out a sigh.

"What is this?" he asked. "You know this city. Tell me."

"I'm not sure I should help you," Haern said.

"Forget your stubborn pride," Victor said, glaring at him. "A man died. I want to know how, and why."

Haern looked to the dead thief, saw the silver glinting in his eyes.

"I don't know," he said. "Twice now I have seen this... arrangement, along with the rhyme on the wall." He knelt beside the corpse and lifted it up. Finding what he wanted, he gestured so Victor might see as well: a tiny bolt embedded in the back of the man's neck.

"Poison?" Victor asked. Haern nodded, glad the man could make the connection.

"Quick, silent, hard to stop," Haern said. "I'm not sure it's what kills them, though. Look."

He pulled away the silver and gestured into the hollow eye cavities. One was filled with more blood than the other, and contained a puncture wound leading into the brain.

"So whoever it is paralyzes them, tortures them, and then kills them?" Victor asked.

"Appears so," Haern said. "Easy enough to understand, but then you have this…"

He gestured to the coins, the writing.

"You said a rival guild is a foul guess," Victor said. "Why is that?"

"Because a guild would either claim it, or destroy any evidence to avoid retribution. This is neither. This is mockery, or a riddle, or vengeance for a blood feud. Whatever it is, it isn't normal, and it isn't a guild. One, maybe two men working together."

"Or women," Victor said, glancing at the rhyme.

Haern stood, and he backed away from the lord. The shadows of his hood protected his face, so that only his eyes shone out. Most wilted under his stare, but this Victor was unafraid, and met them without flinching.

"Watcher," Victor said. "I've wanted to meet you since I stepped foot in Veldaren. Forgive my boast before the king earlier. I know what you've done, and it is truly impressive. But your way is doomed to fail, and that is why I have come. You can't control them any longer."

"They fear me," Haern said, shaking his head at the foolish noble. "That is why I can control them. What can you do? What terror can you inspire with a few scrolls, judges, and soldiers?"

Victor pulled the gold coins from the corpse's mouth, then stared into the vacant eyes.

"They fear you, for they know you are with them in the shadows." He looked up. "But they will come to fear me more, Watcher, for I will leave them with no shadows at all. That is my terror. That is the difference between us. You skulk and hide in their midst, and with every murder you become more like them. You are something they can understand. You are greater than them, you are frightening, but you are still just one man, and the moment you die, everything you've built will come crashing down. Let me help you. Let me save your legacy."

Haern heard no lie, no doubt. Victor meant every word. As much as Haern wanted to dismiss him, he heard the promise of another life, of a chance to pull the weight of Veldaren off his shoulders.

"You really think you can cleanse this city?" he asked.

"I can. I will."

Haern leaped, kicked off the wall, and then grabbed a windowsill. With it, he pulled himself to the rooftop, then spun, hulking like a gargoyle from a castle edge.

"Why?" he asked. "What gain? What reason?"

"You are the nameless man patrolling the rooftops at night," Victor said, a smile tugging at the corner of his mouth. "Yet you wonder about *my* intentions?"

Despite the seriousness, despite the body, Haern let out a laugh.

"Very well," he said. "Happy hunting."

Zusa had sent a runner back to the Gemcroft mansion to warn of their arrival, no doubt scrambling the servants about in preparation. Normally Alyssa would have thought to do so herself, but her mind was clearly elsewhere. After all, it wasn't often a parent returned from the dead. Alyssa and Melody sat together in the litter, with Zusa following alongside, ignoring the stares she received for her attire. There might not be room for her within, but she wouldn't leave Alyssa unguarded. The sun had begun to set, and so the guards escorting them carried torches. Given everyone's somber mood, it almost felt like a funeral.

Upon reaching their mansion, Zusa offered her hand to Alyssa, who took it as she stepped out. Together they looked upon their home, both quiet, both sullen.

"It will be difficult, but Nathaniel must be told," Zusa said.

"I know."

Melody emerged from the other side. Her clothes still hung from her thin body, but a bit of energy showed in her step as she looked upon her old home.

"Just as I remembered," she said.

Alyssa went to her mother's side and offered her arm for support. Melody took it, smiling, and then together they walked the path toward the door. Zusa followed after, feeling like an outcast. They were family, however distant. What was Zusa, though? Friend? Bodyguard? Not blood, certainly not that. Whatever family she might have had, it had been lost to her upon her entering Karak's temple, nothing but a sacrifice made to serve.

Melody stopped in the doorway of the mansion, her whole body trembling. She looked about, saw the paintings, the lush carpet, and the wood carefully stained and cleaned by an army of servants.

"Home," she whispered. For a moment she stood perfectly still, and then closed her eyes and breathed in deeply, as if she could pull the very essence of the mansion into her lungs. Tears fell down her face, and sobs tore from her throat. Alyssa held her as that tiny body shuddered with each breath. Whatever doubt Zusa felt vanished at the sight. The torment was real. The sorrow, the joy, all mixed, all confused. No pretender could pull off such a powerful display. Her insides twisting, Zusa hurried away, more than ever feeling like a trespasser.

Her room was out behind the mansion, in converted servants' quarters made flat and empty so that she might train. As Zusa hurried through the halls toward the back, she was stopped by a boy calling her name.

"Zusa?"

She turned, then smiled despite her worry. Nathaniel Gemcroft stood in the doorway of his room, dressed in his finest tunic. Already it looked tight on him, and she laughed at his obvious discomfort.

"You grow like a weed," she said.

He glanced downward, obviously embarrassed. He had his mother's features, delicate, soft, and with a mop of red hair atop his head. Though he was barely nine, he was fiercely intelligent, and Zusa had grown attached to him over the years, as had much of the mansion's staff.

"The servants say...well, you know. Is it true?"

Nathaniel looked up at her, and she saw the turmoil in his green eyes.

"It seems so," she said. "Why the worry? She is your grandmother, and will be pleased to see such a fine grandson."

Nathaniel shifted his feet and tugged at the hem of his tunic with his one arm.

"Because Mother will worry, won't she? Mother's enemies might want Grandmother to take her place."

Such intelligence for one so young. Zusa sensed John Gandrem's influence here. The lord of Felwood had found and protected Nathaniel after his near death at the hands of a vicious lover of Alyssa's. Ever since, the old man had played the father figure, and nearly every summer, Nathaniel went to his castle to learn to ride, wield a sword, and command himself before the people. Evidently he'd also learned of the many ploys men might use to gain favor and power. John was currently staying as a guest in their mansion, and Zusa tried not to think of how he might react to Melody's return.

Zusa knelt before Nathaniel, put her hands on his shoulders.

"All that matters is that you show her respect," she said. "Do not fear for your mother, and give no thought to her enemies. I'll be watching over her always, and no one is more dangerous than me."

"What about the Watcher?" Nathaniel asked, and he cracked a smile.

Zusa kissed his forehead. "Not even him. Now go, introduce yourself, and make sure John does as well."

He bowed, then hurried away. She watched him, biting her lip as he vanished around a corner. If Melody and Nathaniel got along, perhaps it would ease Alyssa's discomfort. Not that it would help Zusa any. She'd felt no discomfort when Alyssa took lovers and potential suitors. Why did this bother her so? She didn't know. She didn't care. Back in her room, she stripped naked, then tightened the wrappings about herself. Her mind drifted, as it often did during the lengthy, tedious task.

Alyssa had once asked why she didn't wear regular clothes since leaving the order of the faceless women. "Regular clothes get in the way," she'd told her, and there was some truth to that. She could not leap and climb in a dress. But mostly it was that in applying the wrappings, loop over loop about her slender arms, legs, and waist, she felt herself sliding away. They were poor armor, but they protected her from the minds of men. Anyone seeing her knew she was different, and had to treat her as such. In combat she was not a woman but a specter, a mystery. At times she even thought to hide her face as she once had, but could not do it. That was her rebellion, however shallow it might be. Those who died by her daggers would die seeing her face, and in her eyes they'd see no mercy, no grace, just a killer better than they.

Pulling her cloak back over her shoulders, she slipped out into the night. Alleys and rooftops passed by her, and she was dimly aware of them. At one time she'd been an assassin for her priests, and greatly feared by those aware of her existence. With enough coin given as donation, the temple of Karak could eliminate even the most powerful of lords. Rumors even told of kings and queens who had died by the faceless for daring to publicly condemn faith in Karak. But now she was just one of many dangerous killers crawling the night, with little purpose, little meaning. Alyssa was her ward. The doings of thieves and murderers meant nothing to her.

Well, almost nothing. There was the Watcher...

"What brings you out this night?" asked Haern, as if her thoughts had summoned him into existence. Zusa turned. She crouched atop a spire of a mansion belonging to some minor lord who'd long since moved out of Veldaren to safer lands. Haern stood behind her, leaning against the chimney with a subdued smile on his face. He'd pulled back his hood, revealing his handsome face.

"Sometimes even mansions aren't big enough," she said.

Haern chuckled. "I stayed in one for a few years, and was never allowed to leave except when at my father's side. I explored every inch of it a hundred times, and I daresay they can seem quite small when they're your whole world."

He joined her side, and together they overlooked the city. The night was deep, and in the starlight the city seemed calm, empty, but that was not what Zusa sensed. There was a tightness in the air, and glancing at Haern, she saw she was not alone in feeling it. Perhaps it wasn't just Melody that bothered her...

"Something the matter?" she asked him.

"Just Victor," he said, not looking at her. "Still torn on what to think, and how much to trust him."

"Victor?" she asked. He glanced her way, an eyebrow raised in disbelief.

"Where have you been today?" he asked.

"Busy."

He shrugged. "Look into it, then. I wouldn't be surprised if he pays your mansion a visit tomorrow. A change is under way, and from the way he talks, I don't think it is just the lowborn thieves he aims to scatter. Alyssa would do well to make friends with him."

"I'll remember."

They fell silent again. As he stared, she looked him over. Ever since their time together in Angelport, he'd been a far more subdued person. Even now, as they relaxed underneath the moonlight, it looked as if he carried a terrible weight on his shoulders. His encounter with the man known as the Wraith had shaken him to his core, sent him prowling the nights with increased zeal. Zusa shook her head. She wondered how long until he cracked, and could take no more.

Then again, she'd seen his strength. For good or ill, giving up didn't ever seem to be an option with him. Slowly, carefully, as if reaching toward a frightened animal, she put her hand on his shoulder and squeezed. She wanted to be reassuring, but such talk was awkward for her, almost foreign to her tongue. It didn't help that she was unaware of his deeper troubles.

"You are strong," she said. "None can defeat you, so do not be afraid."

"It doesn't matter," Haern said, but despite the frustration in his voice, he did not pull away from her touch. "I may kill thousands, but I will still die. What happens then, Zusa? What will I have accomplished? There will be no peace when I am buried, only a celebration of fire, theft, and murder."

Zusa swallowed. "Tears will be shed."

"Not for me."

"You are wrong."

He stood, but his head remained low, his back hunched. His cloaks curled over him like gray wings. Her admission seemed to slide off him like water.

"Fine then," Zusa said, feeling her temper flaring. "What if you're right, and it is pointless? Why continue?"

Haern chuckled. "Because I'm not dead yet. Have a safe night, Zusa."

"You too, Watcher."

Pulling his hood over his head hid his face in shadow, but she could still see his mouth, and the way it curled into a half-smile at the mention of the Watcher.

"Haern," he said. "To you, let me always be Haern. The Watcher should have no friends."

At this she laughed, then blew him a kiss as he vanished into the night. Staring where he'd been, she thought on his words.

"Victor," she whispered. "Who is Victor?"

Haern had told her to look into it, so she would, but not yet. With his absence, her mind drifted once more to the mansion, and Melody waiting there. Must she burden Alyssa with even more worries? Whoever this Victor was, Zusa hoped that he would indeed be friend instead of foe. Their life had been turned upside down enough as it was.

She once more took to running across the rooftops, the exertion welcome to her muscles. She was getting older, felt it in her bones. It had been nine years since she'd stumbled upon a frightened, endangered Alyssa. Zusa had been young then, but not anymore. It seemed everyone she knew was getting older. How long until even the Watcher was nothing but bent back and wrinkled hands? At the image she laughed. As if Haern would ever age. He probably wouldn't let it happen, too stubborn for even time to defeat him.

Old instincts guided her along, up walls, through windows, and across dark alleys many feared to tread when the sun went down. She was unaware of where she went, her thoughts elsewhere, but when she crept to the top of a roof and stared out across the street before her, she shivered. Sinking into old patterns, she'd come to the temple of Karak, hidden deep in Veldaren's wealthy district. A thousand memories assaulted her, most of them painful. The beatings. The trials. The methodical breaking of everything that made her a woman, coupled with the hiding of her body and face with cloth and wrappings. The priests had branded her a faceless, an outcast meant only to serve in penance.

But not all the memories were terrible. She fondly recalled her sisters Eliora and Nava, and their camaraderie in the face of such persecution. And of course Daverik's touch, the taste of his lips, the feel of his hands upon her, before they'd been discovered, been punished…

A chill spread through her chest, and she shoved such memories away. Looking to the temple, she muttered a curse, a hope that the earth would swallow up the obsidian pillars and lion statues, leaving nothing but a scar where the temple had been. And it was then that she saw the movement, just a shadow among shadows. The sight of it nearly stopped her heart.

"No," she whispered.

Drawing her daggers, she leaped from the roof and gave chase.

It had been heading north, a black shape with a cloak. But it was no thief she'd seen. Oh no, something far worse than that. Her legs pumped, and she was but a blur on the streets. When she lost sight of her prey, she leaped atop a nearby home and catapulted herself into the air. Calling upon the innate powers she'd developed over her years of training, she sailed forward, her arms outward, her daggers pointed down like the talons of a hawk. As she slowly fell, she once more spotted her prey. Twisting her arms together, Zusa spun, and she plummeted at a vicious speed.

When she landed, it was upon a large two-story set of homes, the roof long and flat. Before her, at the edge of the roof, was her nightmare. She wore black and dark-purple wrappings, tightly woven around her body. A white cloth covered her face, masking her features. A gray cloak trailed behind her.

Another faceless.

"Who are you?" Zusa asked as the other woman turned around, her own daggers drawn.

"You?" the faceless woman asked, her voice revealing her surprise. "Zusa, yes? The betrayer, the murderer of the faithful. They've told us of you, warned us of your blasphemy."

"They?" asked Zusa, her whole body tensing. "I was the last of the faceless. What cruel joke are you?"

"My name is Ezra," the woman said, adopting a crouch similar to Zusa's. Her body was thinner, and shorter. Judging by the voice and the hint of features she could see through the cloth mask, Zusa guessed her to be very young. "And I am the first of the new. The order has been remade, and it is my honor to deliver you to Karak so we might wash away your sins with blood."

"My sins?" Zusa asked, grinning. "Which ones?"

"You show your face," said Ezra. "You are a disgrace. A weakling. My faith will bring you low!"

Ezra's lithe body uncoiled, leaping out like a viper, her daggers twin fangs. Zusa fell back, surprised by the speed. Twisting to one side, she avoided a stab, then batted away the other. Planting her feet, she ducked low and cut. Ezra blocked with both her daggers, then tried to kick. A foolish move. Zusa spun again, her feet dancing. When she leaped forward, Ezra was out of position, the snap-kick having put her balance at risk. Her daggers flashed in, finding flesh. Ezra screamed, but instead of countering, she tried to retreat.

Zusa gave her no chance. Her grim smile remained. Ezra was younger, faster, but she was clearly new to the order, and could not hope to match the sheer skill Zusa had developed over many long years. She'd fought the Watcher to a standstill. This little whelp of a woman was nothing compared to that. A feint pulled Ezra's weapons out of position, and then Zusa stepped close, leg sweeping. Ezra hit the ground with a cry of pain. Blood spilled across the rooftop. Zusa fell atop her, knees pressing against her shoulders, locking them in place. With one hand Zusa clutched Ezra's wrists together, the other pressing a dagger against the woman's throat.

"You think your faith means anything?" Zusa asked, breathing the question into her ear. "You think it gives you the strength to challenge me? You are a fool, Ezra, as is whoever brought back our order."

"Kill me," Ezra said. "I am not afraid."

Zusa's eyes narrowed. She shifted her weight, tightening with her thighs so that she squeezed against the two stab wounds she'd given Ezra in her stomach. They weren't deep enough to be fatal, but they'd certainly hurt like the Abyss. Ezra clenched her teeth, but Zusa squeezed tighter until she finally let out a scream.

"You *should* be afraid of me," Zusa said, pressing the dagger hard enough to draw a drop of blood. It ran down the edge of her dagger, then dripped from the hilt to the dark wrappings. "I can do more than hurt you."

She picked up Ezra's wrists, then slammed them down to make her drop her weapons. With her unarmed, Zusa then took the dagger from her throat and began to cut, quick, calculated strikes. She knew where. She'd wrapped herself in a similar manner for over a decade. The wrappings about Ezra's face fell to the roof, exposing her small nose, cream-colored skin, and short brown hair. Her hazel eyes stared up at Zusa with a mixture of horror and fury.

"How dare you?" Ezra asked through clenched teeth.

"They hide your beauty to mask their own shame," said Zusa, "not so you might earn penance in Karak's eyes."

"I will not listen to your blasphemy."

"You don't need to." Zusa put the tip of her dagger against Ezra's left eye. "Tell me the name of the man who brought back our order, or I will scar your face so terribly at least you will have a reason to keep it hidden."

Ezra swallowed and looked away. Zusa could see her trying to be brave, to hold fast to her loyalty to Karak. She shook her head, annoyed. Leaning even closer, she let her cheek brush against Ezra's, let her lips touch her ear.

"Just a name," she breathed. "All I ask is a name. Who created you, gave you your lessons, your rules, your training? Do not make me mar your beauty. You suffer enough. Trust me, I know it well, know your loathing, your anger, your frustration that the man you fucked suffered only whipping and a banishment to a new temple while you must spend every waking moment as an outcast, humbled and cowering in hopes of forgiveness by our dear, beloved Karak..."

Ezra closed her eyes, struggled to maintain calm.

"You would have me condemn my soul to fire."

"I would have you speak a name, you stupid girl. Now tell me, or bid good-bye to your eye."

Ezra breathed in deep, let it out. Zusa sensed the defeat in it, and sighed in relief herself. She had no real intention of scarring the poor woman forced into such a terrible punishment. That relief fled the moment she heard the name.

"Daverik," the woman said. "Come from Mordeina with the highest blessings of the priesthood."

Daverik...

"You lie," Zusa said. "You must lie!"

Ezra tilted her head back as the knife pressed against her eye, and she let out a cry as the tip dipped in and out of the white of her eyeball. Blood pooled, and a red tear slid down her face.

"Do not insult me," she said. "Now do what you must."

Zusa thought to jam her dagger through the woman's throat, but could not. Ezra was only confused, her mind twisted, her faith a noose about her slender neck. She stood and took a step back as her insides churned.

"I want you to give Daverik a message," she said.

"Why would he care what you have to say?" Ezra asked, kneeling. She ran a wrapped hand through her brown hair, then touched where she'd been cut across the stomach.

"He will care," Zusa said. "Tell him...tell him Katherine must speak to him, and to find her along the eastern wall tomorrow night."

Zusa turned to leave, glanced back.

"And tell him to come alone."

"We'll find you," Ezra said, struggling to a stand as the wounds in her stomach bled anew from the movement. "My sisters and I will kill you for this."

"For what, looking upon your eyes and hair?" Zusa smirked. "We faceless saw far more of each other than that."

With a running leap, she soared into the air, leaving Ezra far behind. If only she could leave her troubles behind as easily. Daverik's face flashed before her eyes, so young, so handsome. Back before her name had been stripped away, and rebranded as Zusa. Before they'd been caught together. Before her love of him had doomed her to a life as one of the faceless.

She'd thought him dead. Thought him gone. Thought him forever out of her life.

She'd thought wrong.

"Damn you, Daverik," she whispered as she ran back to the Gemcroft mansion. "What cruel fate is this?"

CHAPTER 6

Alyssa slept terribly, and gladly welcomed the daylight when it shone through the violet curtains that covered her window. At least it meant she could get up instead of trying to fall back asleep. She bathed, and servants brushed her hair and helped her into a modest green dress. Through it all she keenly felt Zusa's absence. Normally she lingered like a protective angel, but this morning, when Alyssa needed her comfort most, she was gone.

"Keep the meal small," she told her servants. "And ensure John Gandrem is invited to our table."

"Yes, milady," one said, hurrying off to give the order.

Finally ready to face the day, she dismissed the servants and stared at herself in the looking glass. They'd done what they could, but the dark circles remained visible beneath her eyes, her face puffy. She'd spent much of the night in tears, all in confusion. She felt joy at having her mother back from the dead, and at times it nearly overwhelmed her. Other times she felt terror at the notion of losing control of everything she'd built, and if she closed her eyes tight, she could almost hear invisible gears turning, the machinations of a hundred different lords and ladies seeking to use this newfound change against her. Sometimes she wished Melody had remained dead, and then immediately followed this up with shame and regret for such horrible, selfish desires.

Yes, she was very glad the night was done. The last thing she wanted to be was alone with her thoughts. She was sick of them. Exiting her room, she crossed the hall to where her mother stayed. A servant was just leaving, her head ducked low and her eyes to the floor.

"Is Melody dressed?" she asked.

"Yes," said the servant, a pretty little thing with dark hair. "But I think perhaps she needs a moment alone..."

Alyssa dismissed her, and despite her advice, knocked on the door. No answer. She turned the knob and gently pushed it in. Stepping inside, she found her mother sitting on the edge of the bed. The image shocked her breath away. Melody wore an emerald dress that had long remained in storage, Alyssa being too short to wear most of her mother's clothing. Her long hair was tied back into a painfully familiar braid, one Alyssa used to tug when in a rambunctious mood. She looked like a ghost escaped from the past, and Alyssa could almost imagine her childhood self sitting beside her, book in hand. Except tears were in her mother's eyes instead of the smile she'd known in the past.

"Are you all right?" Alyssa asked, strangely timid in her own house. She remained in the doorway, her cheek pressing against its darkly polished wood.

"I will be fine," Melody said, dabbing at her eyes with a cloth. "I just... it's a bit overwhelming to be here once more."

"I can only imagine," Alyssa said.

Melody smiled softly.

"I have so many memories," she said. "Despite what May-nard...did, there were good times, many good times. But let us not dwell on that. Mindy said you have prepared us break-fast, and I don't want to keep John waiting."

Alyssa's cheek twitched at that. John Gandrem was staying in their mansion as an honored guest, and was very much a father to her son. When Melody had introduced herself, John had seemed quite taken, and they'd been deep in conversation when Alyssa left them to retire for the night. Idly she wondered what a union between Felwood Castle and the Gemcroft estate might mean for her son. So much added wealth and land...

She shook her head, dashing the ridiculous fantasies away.

"Indeed," she said. "I would hate to be rude."

In their grand dining hall, John and Nathaniel sat beside each other in the center of the long oak table, looking humor-ously insignificant compared to the food stretched out before them. They had not begun eating yet, and Alyssa was not sur-prised. John was most particular in his manners, and that was partly why Alyssa had first sent her son to be fostered in his hall. John stood at their arrival, and Nathaniel quickly fol-lowed. She smiled at her son, looking so small and youthful beside the older lord, who was dressed in fine green robes and a thin silver crown across his forehead.

"I fear your servants misunderstood," John said, tilting his head in respect. "We are only four, yet they cook for forty."

"The rest will eat after we are done," Alyssa said, taking a seat opposite her son. She glanced to an upper corner of the room. "And it is five, not four. Come down, Zusa."

Just a shadowy spider, Zusa climbed down from the tall rafter, hidden in shadows that clung to her most unnaturally.

Raking a hand through her hair, she joined them without a word or smile. She looked exhausted, and Alyssa knew without asking that she'd been out all night. Looking to her plate, already simmering with meats, eggs, and a choice of sweet rolls, Alyssa felt her stomach twist.

"Do you feel well, dear?" Melody asked.

"I'm fine," Alyssa said, forcing herself to nibble on some bacon so they would leave her be. From the corner of her eye, she caught Zusa's troubled expression.

"What is it?" she asked softly as John and Nathaniel started up a conversation about some jousting tournament to start soon on the outskirts of the city.

"We must speak soon, in private," her friend said. "One is of a personal matter, the other of Lord Victor and his foolish crusade."

"Crusade? What are you talking about?"

"Not now. And we must speak with Terrance. If he has made even the slightest error, your life might be in danger."

Terrance? Alyssa was baffled. Terrance was a distant cousin of hers, a young man she'd appointed four years ago to be her master of coin and trade after the previous adviser had secretly worked against her, eventually making an attempt upon her life. So far as she knew, Terrance was a good man, careful. How could an error by him put her life at risk?

"Zusa, I don't like how vague this . . ."

"Milady," interrupted a servant at the door. She was young, and looked flustered. "A man seeks an audience with you, and says it is quite urgent."

"It can wait," Alyssa said, more harshly than she meant. John glanced her way upon hearing the tone of her voice, but wisely kept his mouth shut.

"Yes, of course, milady," said the servant. "It's . . . well, he has many soldiers with him, and is very insistent that he speak with you."

"Soldiers?" asked Melody, her eyes widening.

"It's nothing," Alyssa said, pushing away her barely touched plate. "I will meet with him, though he'd better pray to the gods his matter truly is urgent. What is this whelp's name?"

"Lord Victor Kane," the servant girl said, bowing quickly before hurrying away. Alyssa paused a moment upon hearing the name, and she looked to Zusa, whose eyes met hers. A warning went unspoken between them.

"At my side," Alyssa said softly as both stood.

"Do you wish me to accompany you?" Melody asked as the two strode for the door.

Alyssa shook her head. "Stay, eat. I'm sure it is nothing."

Alyssa felt their eyes upon her as she exited. Zusa matched her pace, and together they walked through the halls, paintings of dead ancestors on either side of them.

"You had something to say about this Victor, correct?" Alyssa asked. "Now sounds like a good time to say it, and fast."

"He's been given free rein by the king to pursue his agenda," Zusa said as they turned a corner. "Rounding up every thief, merchant, and noble he can find who has broken the law. They are taken to the castle, judged, and more often than not executed on the spot. From what I've heard, he's been very thorough."

Alyssa stopped, her mouth dropping open. "How long has this been going on?"

"Only a day."

Alyssa ran a hand through her hair, trying to piece the puzzle together. The Kane family sounded vaguely familiar, but how or why wasn't coming to her. "Who is this Victor?" she asked. "What do we know about him?"

Zusa frowned. "A small lord, from an even smaller family. Inconsequential, really, until now. They own a meager castle, and control a modest but fertile stretch of land for growing wheat."

Wheat, that was it. Alyssa finally placed the Kane name. They'd had a few dealings before, nothing significant. A portion of the wheat market was controlled by their family. They weren't the dominant player in the market, nor the most aggressive.

"So now he enters Veldaren as if he's some righteous savior, come to arrest the guilty?" Alyssa asked.

"In short, yes."

Alyssa chewed her lip, then resumed her walk. Upon nearing the door, she found Lord Victor already waiting in the foyer. He towered above her, such a tall man. His pleasant appearance, carefully trimmed blond hair and a smoothly shaven face, matched what she'd expected. The chain mail he wore, and the sword he kept at his side, did not. Frustration bubbled over into anger in her chest. Letting the man in without first consulting her was stupid enough, but letting him keep his weapon? Inexcusable. At least he was alone, without guards. She felt no fear, for Zusa was with her. There was no chance he could lay a finger on her with the skilled woman at her side.

"Greetings, Lady Gemcroft," Victor said, seeing their arrival. His voice was strong, charming. If he was nervous at meeting her, he did not show it.

"Welcome to my home, Lord Victor," she responded, curtsying slightly. As she did, she took stock of the man. He was handsome, and his smile came easily to his face. Their eyes met, and that was when she saw the hardness hiding within coupled with a grim determination. She felt as if she stood before a charging bull, but she was no delicate flower, nor made of fragile glass.

"It is a fine place," Victor said, glancing about. "I would love to see the rest someday, but sadly do not have the time. I've come with both request and wisdom, if you would be so kind as to hear either."

Alyssa might have offered him a seat, or taken him deeper into the mansion, but something about his presence unnerved her, so she gestured for him to continue. He smiled at her, showing no hurry despite his claims. His chain mail rattled when he crossed his arms and tilted his head.

"I do not know what you have heard, so let me first make clear why I'm here. I have come to save Veldaren from itself. Those responsible for destroying it are legion, but for now I focus on the guiltiest. My men scour the streets, always listening, always watching. Know that I do not do this at random, nor recklessly. I follow the law, and will uphold it beyond all else. I have declared war, but it will not be chaos and fires in the night."

Alyssa felt the unspoken jab and did not let it pass unchallenged.

"You speak of the thief war," she said.

"I speak of the night you nearly burned Veldaren to the ground, all to mourn a son who was not actually dead."

A hard edge entered his voice, and she found herself taking a step back. Zusa was there immediately, sliding beside her with her hands on the hilts of her daggers. Alyssa started to defend herself, then caught the words in her throat. She would not defend that disastrous effort, for she herself was ashamed of it. It had been a foolish thing, her emotions overriding her judgment. Only Zusa had had the courage to say it to her face.

"And what makes you think your efforts will be so different?" she asked. Her blood felt like ice in her veins. "What delusion blinds your eyes to the strength of those who oppose you?"

Victor's smile returned. "No delusion, just stubbornness. Yesterday was the first, and the next week or so will probably be the most productive, but I have months if I must. All seventeen men we found guilty yesterday died by the ax. Those we capture today will give every name, list every crime they've ever seen, to spare themselves that same fate."

"They'll fight back," Zusa said. "They won't let you round up their fellow thieves without bloodshed."

"We do not march needlessly through dark corners hoping for a glimpse of a colored cloak. We learn names. We learn homes. My men move together, close, careful, and always with purpose. You do not remove weeds from a garden in a hurry, turning and grabbing every which way. You must move slowly, methodically, so you miss not a one."

Alyssa shook her head. "These are dangerous men, not weeds."

"Forgive me if I find them with more similarities than not."

He smiled at her, trying to win her over. Despite his handsomeness, she refused to let it sway her. She'd let one lover blind her to his underhanded dealings before; she wouldn't dare let it happen again.

"You said you had a request, and some wisdom," Alyssa said. "Have you given me either yet?"

Victor laughed. "Yes, yes, of course. For the request, it is simple. Your hatred of the thieves is almost legendary, and I would ask that you be my ally in this. Whatever you know of the thieves, turn it over to me. Any names, any crimes, whatever it is, we can use it. And if you have any house guards that you trust, that might help me secure the streets..."

"I will think on it," she said. "Your wisdom?"

Another smile. "That you say yes to my request."

Despite herself she snickered. "Perhaps. But we have entered into an agreement with the guilds, and now pay for their protection. What you ask jeopardizes everything. For once we have a semblance of peace. I do not want to ruin that now on some foolhardy outsider who has come to Veldaren with more stones than sense."

"Your peace is a mirage," Victor said, turning to the door. "It will fade no matter what you do. It is a house built on sand, a painting drawn in the dust. Oh, and remember this, Alyssa, for it is very, very important. All that I do, I do with the king's full authority."

He opened the door before she could respond. Waiting there was an old man, a heavy tome in hand. His hair was white, his face scrunched inward from age. Her eyes narrowed.

"What is this?" she asked.

"My most humble apologies," the old man said, bowing low. "My name is Henris Weeks, and I will do my best to work quickly and without trouble to your businesses."

Alyssa glanced to Zusa, confused. The smoldering anger she saw in her friend's eyes only confirmed her fear. Victor was playing a game with them, but what?

"Explain yourself," she told him.

"It is not only the thieves I hunt," said Victor. "Henris here must be shown all your records and all your dealings undertaken over the past few years. Not that I expect to find anything, not with such a lawful woman as yourself ruling the Gemcroft fortune. Still, I must be fair, for Henris will be scouring Lord Stephen's records as well. Though Stern Blackwater is safe down in Angelport, he still has property and caretakers here in Veldaren, and they will also turn over extensive documentation. I'd hate for him to be playing underhanded games with young Tori Keenan's wealth, after all."

Henris stood there, looking very nervous and uncomfortable. Alyssa felt furious, but she held back the rage. She could not err, not now. Zusa's warning suddenly made perfect sense. If Terrance had made a single mistake, if he'd avoided tariffs, smuggled in goods, or dealt in the more exotic spices and leaves illegal in Veldaren...

"Zusa, fetch a servant," she said. "Prepare a room for Henris. I fear this will take many days, and would hate to make an old man uncomfortable."

"Thank you," Henris said, looking relieved to hear of her cooperation. As Zusa left, the old man followed. Victor smiled at her, and gave a quick salute.

"Thank you for your time," he said. "I pray Stephen is just as accommodating as you are. Now if you'll forgive me, I must be off. I have a wizard to hire."

Alyssa thought of the young leader of the Connington household and could only imagine how the boy would react. Most likely better than she had.

"You're making many enemies," she told him as he exited her mansion. "I will not help you, not in this."

He turned back to her, hand on the hilt of his sword. No smiles this time, no amusement. He looked tired, weary in anticipation of the long day ahead.

"I am taking up the war the Trifect lost. I am fighting the enemies you could not defeat. Why do you respond with anger, and resist me? Just because I would hold you to the same standard as they? Or is it because your hands are just as dirty?"

She shut the door, pressed her forehead against it. In her anger she tried to deny him, to dismiss the easy accusations. It was far harder than it should have been.

A hand touched her shoulder, and she turned, thinking it

was Zusa. Instead her mother stood there, clearly worried. Alyssa closed her eyes and accepted the embrace.

"You poor dear," Melody whispered. "I remember well the difficulties of being one of the Trifect. Please, let me help in any way I can. Your father had me to share his burdens with, but you are so alone…"

"I've always been alone," Alyssa said, gently pushing her away. "I have been ever since I took up Father's mantle, and I fear I will be until the day they cast the first handful of dirt upon my grave."

"If you are alone, then it is by choice. That is the way it always is with our family."

"Is that what you told yourself when Father turned you over to Leon and his gentle touchers? He was just choosing to be alone?"

It was a cruel barb, and she didn't know why she said it. Her mother took a step back and touched her cheek as if she'd been struck across the face.

"Maynard was a cold, cruel man," she said. "Even on the day of our wedding, he had no warmth in him, not for me. Yes, he chose to be alone. He chose to keep his heart closed, and to love nothing but his trade, his power, and his coin. Is this why you've been so unwelcoming to me? Do you think those years of torture were warranted, were my *fault*?"

Stay silent, Alyssa told herself, but the words escaped her lips anyway.

"You insulted his name, slept with another, and because of that I lost a mother!"

"Then blame the man who cast me aside, and took me from you!"

There were tears in both their eyes. Alyssa felt exhausted,

frightened. Too much was changing without warning, without any time to adjust. She crossed her arms, tried to think. Meanwhile Melody leaned back against a wall. Alyssa realized how thin she looked, barely more than bones. At times it seemed like a miracle that she could stand.

"Do you know how I endured?" Melody asked. Her words were the whispers of a ghost. "How I managed to sleep at night in that...darkness? I thought of you. I prayed for you, for safety, for protection. Now I am free, and I can touch your face, see you grown...don't hate me. Don't do this to me. I can't stand it. I won't live through that terrible a cruelty. I'd rather return to the cage."

Alyssa cast her eyes to the ground. She could only begin to imagine everything her mother had been through, yet she'd had the audacity to blame her, to feel anger and betrayal for such a distant shame.

"I'm sorry," she said. She reached for her mother, and it pained her heart to see the way she hesitated, the wariness in her eyes. But even still, Alyssa was her daughter, and Melody came forward, wrapping her arms around her. Alyssa sighed, and let tears silently run down her face. Let her whole household be damned. She would not let her fears keep her from regaining what had been lost.

"I'm so glad you're back," Alyssa whispered. "Please, it's just so much, and I'm always fearful for Nathaniel."

"You have nothing to explain," Melody said. "Nothing to apologize for. I'm here. I'll always be here."

The door burst open, startling them both. A guard stepped in, then immediately bowed in apology.

"Forgive me, milady," he said to Alyssa. "I did not know you were...sorry, I was ordered to ensure you were safe."

"Safe?" Alyssa asked, wiping her face. "What is the matter?"

"Nothing you should concern yourself with. A servant was killed on the premises, and we fear the killer still might be lurking outside."

Pushing her emotions aside, she shook her head and straightened her back.

"I will not fear to walk in my own gardens," she said. "Let me see the body."

The guard looked between them, then submitted to his mistress.

"If you insist," he said, leading the way.

"I'll tell John," Melody said, declining to follow. "And make sure Nathaniel is safe."

Alyssa nodded, hurrying after the soldier, who looked as if he'd decided that if he couldn't prevent her from seeing the body, he could at least make the process as quick as possible. They curled around the front of the mansion, off a walkway, and into the smooth grass decorated with trees. All of it was surrounded by an enormous stone fence, the top spiked, but the Trifect had learned over the past decade how little use such fences were. More house guards lingered about, some searching for evidence of intruders, others scouring the fence for signs of rope or hook.

"Make way," the guard said as they came upon a cluster of four men halfway to the east wall. The men stepped aside, giving Alyssa access to the body. Seeing it, she held in a gasp. It was just a young servant boy, no older than ten. An arrow was stuck in his neck, having pierced his windpipe. Blood stained the grass red beneath him. At his feet was a pile of soiled clothes, the cleaning of his task for the early morning.

"Who would do such a thing?" Alyssa wondered aloud. "What harm could this poor boy have done to anyone?"

"There's a message," one of the guards said, sounding

uncomfortable. He pointed, and sure enough, letters were cut into the grass by means of something sharp. It was hurried, disjointed, but she could read it well enough for it to put a shiver down her spine.

tongue of gold, eyes of silver
run, run little alyssa
from the widow's quiver

"When did this happen?" she asked, glancing about. They were far from any door, and the body was partially hidden behind the trunk of a tree.

"He'd have been up before daylight to do morning chores," said the man who'd brought her. "Blood's pretty dry."

Her conversation with her mother, along with Victor, had already left her unnerved, but this awoke a brand-new fury. There was no doubt the servant child looked similar to Nathaniel. The strange killer mocked her, but why? Who would dare sneak onto her land to murder an innocent child?

"Bury him, and ensure his family is paid well," she said.

"Right." A guard knelt down, scooping the body into his arms. As he lifted, the boy's neck snapped back, and his eyes opened. Alyssa let out a soft gasp. Two silver coins stared at her. All around, guards muttered and cursed at such strange mutilation. Swallowing down her revulsion, Alyssa put her back to the body and found Zusa standing there, observing everything closely.

"Whoever it is wants Nathaniel next," Zusa said. "And they do it to torture you."

Alyssa glanced back, saw the guards pry open the boy's mouth and pull out two bloody coins of gold.

"Find Haern," she said, quietly enough that no one else

would hear. "He has to know who this Widow is, or what it means. And enlist that wizard of his as well. I will have this murderer found, no matter the cost."

"Will you be safe without me?"

Alyssa sighed. "No, but I trust no one else. Go, now."

Zusa headed for the front gates, then stopped. Hurrying back, she kissed Alyssa's hand and pulled her close.

"Something is wrong in this city," the faceless woman whispered. "Too many pieces are moving at once for it to be coincidence. We are lost in someone's deception. Be wary, and be safe."

With that she left, vaulting over the spiked walls with ease. Alyssa watched her go while absently rubbing her hand. She did not know all Zusa meant, but she understood the feeling well. Her mother, Victor's arrival, the Widow, plus Zusa had mentioned a personal matter...

"Stay safe," she murmured, staring at the wall Zusa had vanished beyond. Wrapping her arms around her chest as if cold, she returned to her mansion.

CHAPTER

7

Haern awoke a little after midday to the sound of the tower doors slamming shut. Instinct told him that something was wrong, a bad feeling in the air. Grabbing his sabers and cloaks, he slipped out of his room and down to the bottom floor. There, before the fireplace, he found Delysia sitting on a couch, her brother pacing furiously.

"The audacity!" the wizard muttered.

"Care to fill me in, Tar?" Haern asked, still on the steps. Tarlak heard him and stopped. His look was none too friendly.

"Honestly? No. I'm too pissed."

"Behave," Delysia said, and despite her brother's mood, she laughed. "You're overreacting and you know it. And good morning, Haern."

Haern joined Delysia on the couch, and together they watched Tarlak fume. Delysia leaned over, her head resting against his chest. After a sniff, she sat back up.

"Your cloaks smell like death."

Haern shrugged. "That tends to happen."

The priestess sighed and reached out her hand. When he removed his cloaks, she took them to the door and set them down to be washed later that day. As she did, Tarlak stopped pacing, and instead crossed his arms and frowned at the assassin.

"Lord Victor was just here," said the wizard.

"That so?" Haern lifted an eyebrow. "What did he want?"

"Wanted me to ward the home he's currently staying in, cover it with various protection spells so no clever thief can teleport under his bed and stab him while he sleeps."

"Doesn't sound like a bad idea," Haern said as Delysia returned, leaning against his arm and resting her head on his shoulder. "Why the fuss?"

"He wanted... bah!" Tarlak threw up his hands. "He wanted to pay us *after* his quest or mission or whatever this nonsense he's doing is over. Said he couldn't spare the coin just yet, something about mouths to feed. Worse, he actually hinted he'd appreciate me doing it for free. You hear that? Free!"

"Truly he is an evil man," Haern said.

Tarlak stopped and gave him a death glare.

"Care to share your opinion, Mister Cloak and Saber?"

"It's pretty simple, though you won't want to hear it. I think you should help him."

Tarlak blinked. "You do?"

Haern shrugged. He still hadn't fully made up his mind about the man, but he had little doubt Victor meant to see through to the end his attempt to clean the streets of Veldaren. If he could be trusted to at least do that...

"I think he truly believes he's helping. More importantly, I think he might pull it off. The thief guilds haven't faced a man quite like him before. Look at you. The only reason you're so bothered is because you're thinking of helping him for free, despite all desire otherwise."

Tarlak shook his head. "He's an egotistical ass."

"Hardly the only one around here."

The wizard glared as his sister covered her mouth with a hand to hide her laughter. "Careful," he said to Haern. "Otherwise I might turn you into an actual ass for a day and rent you out to a farmer."

Haern only grinned at him. With a sigh Tarlak relented, and took a seat in a wooden rocking chair beside the fire. Removing his yellow hat, he scratched the top of his head with his fingers, then ran them through his red hair to straighten it.

"If we help him, then he'll live long enough to actually accomplish something," Tarlak said, all his bluster and anger fading away. "That means the current peace with the thief guilds won't last. They'll react soon, and violently. But how? If they focus on just Victor, we might counter, but if they target the rest of the Trifect, Veldaren will fall to chaos within days. It'll be Thren's thief war all over again."

"We can't let there be another," Delysia said. She said it softly, but it weighed heavily on her heart. "The last one went on for more than ten years. So many died, so many..."

Haern shifted, feeling uncomfortable, especially with her so close to him. Her father had been just one of the many casualties of that conflict, killed by Thren while Haern watched. It had been his first true mission, to kill Delysia when she fled. But hearing her heartfelt sobbing for her father, and her prayers for safety, he had not been able to bring himself to go through with it. He'd later told her, and she'd forgiven him. He didn't know how, but she had.

"I won't let it happen," Haern insisted.

Tarlak shook his head.

"Then perhaps instead of helping Lord Victor, we should get him out of Veldaren as fast as possible?" said the wizard.

"Even if he has a chance to succeed?"

Tarlak threw up his hands in surrender. "If that's your idea of intelligence, then so be it. No matter what we do, we risk this blowing up in our faces, so might as well go for broke."

A knocking turned their attention to the door.

"Who is it now?" Haern asked.

Tarlak shook his head, for scrying spells embedded in the tower let him see the visitor. "Day just keeps getting better," he said. With a snap of his fingers, the door opened on its own, and in stepped Zusa, clad in her dark wrappings, her gray cloak fluttering behind her.

"Magic is a poor host to greet at a door," she said, sheathing her daggers.

"Yes, but it keeps my lazy rear in a chair," Tarlak said. "Come in, and share whatever terrible news you've brought with you. Gods know you're never here to tell us something good."

Delysia scolded her brother for his poor hospitality, and hurried up to greet Zusa. The faceless woman accepted her embrace, then set aside her daggers. A wave of Tarlak's hand, and a glass of wine appeared on the nearby table. Haern watched Zusa settle in, taking a seat opposite Tarlak. Ever since their trip together south to Angelport, the faceless woman had come to Haern and the rest of the Eschaton anytime Alyssa needed things handled in a way that could not be traced back to the Gemcroft family. Her visits were rare, and always odd. Though she tried to appear gracious, Haern could tell she was in a hurry, and that whatever brought her to their tower was urgent.

"Thank you," Zusa said, sipping the wine before putting it

aside. She looked awkward in the old wooden chair dressed in those strange wrappings of hers, but it seemed to bother her not at all. "But my time is short. One of our servant boys was attacked this morning, just before dawn. His eyes were cut out and replaced with silver coins, and two pieces of gold were put on his tongue."

The news struck Haern like a brick to the head. "A rhyme," he said. "Was there also a rhyme?"

To his dread, Zusa nodded. " 'Tongue of gold,' " she recited, " 'eyes of silver. Run, run little Alyssa, from the Widow's quiver.' "

With each word, Haern felt his fingers tighten against the fabric of the couch. After the first two murders, he'd thought it was just someone with an agenda against the Spider Guild, but to also strike the Gemcroft family, especially in such a petty, cruel way?

"Do you know of this…Widow?" Zusa asked.

Haern sighed, and he caught Tarlak staring at him, clearly also eager to hear. Nodding, Haern shared what he'd discovered, about the two bodies, and about Victor's also requesting help in discovering who it was. When he was finished, Tarlak leaned back in his chair, stroking his red goatee.

"He's taking their eyes?" he wondered aloud. "That's a little…odd."

"Odd?" said Zusa. "You insult a dead child saying such a thing. It is the cold, cruel act of a sick mind. Whoever this Widow is, let him kill Spiders night and day, but to threaten Alyssa's son…no. We must stop him. Despite your reputation otherwise, your Eschaton Mercenaries are the best. My mistress wants this killer found, and will pay you whatever it takes to enlist your services."

Tarlak's eyes widened. "Now that's what I like to hear," he said, grinning.

"He's striking at night," Haern said, glaring at Tarlak. "And he bears a grudge against both the Spider Guild and the Gem-croft family. Any ideas?"

"Perhaps a rival guild?" Tarlak asked.

Haern shrugged. "Maybe a rogue thief wanting the truce ended?"

Neither idea sounded right, didn't have that correct feel in the gut. And then Delysia spoke.

"What about Victor?" she asked.

Haern and Tarlak exchanged a glance.

"He's made his hatred of the thief guilds clear," Delysia insisted.

"He has no love of the Trifect, either," Zusa said, and she told them of Victor's visit to Alyssa's mansion just that morning.

"No," Haern said. It made sense, but still he shook his head. "I don't believe it. He's doing this with a sense of purpose, a sense of honor. Brutal murders, mocking rhymes...how does that help him? What agenda does that serve?"

Tarlak frowned, and he bit his lower lip as he thought.

"Zusa," he said, glancing at the woman. "Tell Alyssa we accept her request, and I'll have a contract brought to you before tonight. We'll start patrolling the Spider Guild territory come nightfall, see if we can spot him attempting kill number four. All of us except Haern, that is."

"You want me to watch Victor," Haern said. "Don't you?"

"Consider it protecting him," Tarlak said, standing. "That is, if he's innocent. And if he's not, well..." The wizard shrugged. "You'll be right there to stop him, won't you?"

Haern thought of the way Victor had responded to seeing the body in the alley. His anger, his revulsion...that couldn't have been an act. Could it? The timing would have been dif-ficult, but he didn't have to be the one committing the killings himself.

"It's not him," Haern said, reaching for his sabers.

"I hope it isn't," Zusa said as she went to the door. "Because his scribe sits in our mansion, recording our every deed. Find him quickly, Eschaton. Our city is dangerous enough without a madman."

Silence greeted them as the door closed behind her. Haern stood there, feeling unsure, then buckled his sabers to his belt.

"Where are you going?" Delysia asked.

"To speak with a contact," Haern said. "If the Spider Guild is being targeted, someone in their organization might have an idea why."

"Be careful," she told him.

He leaned in close to gently kiss her cheek.

"I will," he said. "I promise."

"You sure it's safe to be out here?" Peb asked as they neared the castle. His wide eyes darted every which way, as if guards were trying to sneak from all directions. With his big ears, the act reminded Alan why Peb had once been called Mouse.

"I'm not sure it's safe to be anywhere in Veldaren right now," Alan said, twirling a copper coin between his thumb and forefinger, something he did when nervous. "So why should the castle be any worse?"

Peb nodded toward the rows of men and women waiting to be interrogated by Lord Victor's men.

"Maybe because one of them people might be blubbering our names any second?"

Alan ran a hand through his long dark hair.

"Thren wants answers, wants something new, so either we get him something new, or we get a tongue-lashing...if we're lucky. Given the mood he was in, I'm not willing to gamble on that. I'd rather tempt the city guards than the boss."

Peb didn't look convinced, but Alan didn't care. The guy was a coward, and more important, he hated to be alone. He'd follow Alan so long as things still looked safe. Alan patted his own leg, glad for the dagger hidden there. Taking a deep breath, he summoned his courage and then walked out from the alley and into the main street, where the interrogations continued. Peb quickly followed. The two were in ratty clothing, their faces dirty, their hands callused. Anyone who bothered to notice them would think them nothing but poor, hungry peasants. At least that was the hope.

Alan led the way, faking a limp toward the lines. At the front he saw scribes jotting down the guts that their current pigeons spilled. Not that Alan blamed them. When your life was on the line, or the coin was right, honor was nothing but a hindrance. Making as little noise as possible, he listened as they got closer, hoping to catch an errant phrase, but a soldier noticed them before he could.

"Stay back, you two," said the armored man, his hand already on his sword. He stood between them and the tables of scribes. On his chest was a tabard bearing a crest Alan did not recognize, some strange circle with wings drawn in gold. "Any closer, and I'll think you a threat."

"Forgive me," Alan said, bowing low and turning away. Peb followed, saying nothing.

"That was pointless," Peb mumbled.

"Did you see Lord Victor?"

Peb shook his head. "No. You?"

Alan glanced back, scouring the guards, the lines, the scribes.

"Not here," he said. "But only twelve or so are set to talk. Yesterday had far more."

"He's slowing down?" Peb asked.

Alan shrugged. "Either that, or he's being more careful. Never know if…"

He had about two seconds to react before it hit. Alan grabbed Peb by the arm and pulled him hard into the side of a building. His shoulder throbbed upon slamming the wood, and Peb let out a cry when he struck his forehead, having been unable to twist in time. Still, it was better than being impaled by the barrage of arrows that sailed toward Victor's proceedings. Over twenty men stood far down the road, bows and crossbows in hand, their brown cloaks revealing their allegiance to the Hawks.

"Impatient bastards," Alan said before swearing up a storm. "Get down!"

The two dropped as another barrage flew. Screams filled the air. The first barrage had landed among the guards and scribes, but the second was aimed solely at the men and women brought for interrogation. People fled in every direction, while the guards swarmed in a panic, some flinging the older scribes to the ground for protection, others rushing to meet the new threat.

"We need to get out of here!" Peb said, scrambling out from beneath Alan.

"Thren will want to know what happened here!"

Peb spun about, shaking his head. "Then let him come count the bodies."

Alan looked back, saw the soldiers rushing with swords drawn. Arrows and bolts shot toward them, no longer in an organized barrage. Some men dropped, but most endured, even those who were hit. Their armor was thick, and the thieves used small bows and crossbows designed to take out fellow thieves, to pierce cloth, not metal. Alan thought to draw his dagger, then realized that might label him as being on the side of the Hawks. So instead he hunkered down and pretended to cower as the battle unfolded.

Seven soldiers, all bearing the same gold crest, crashed into the group of Hawks. At first Alan thought numbers would lead the thieves to victory, but the initial exchange proved otherwise. Victor's men had long blades granting them better reach, their armor protecting them from the quick, weak thrusts of daggers. Hawks dropped in a bloody clash, the thieves' attempt to swarm and surround failing miserably. Half were dead before they had the presence of mind to flee.

"Damn," Alan whispered, watching the display. Victor's men were well trained; he'd give them that. Glancing the other way, he saw the remnants of the interrogations. Most interrogators had fled into the castle, carrying parchments with them. Nine bodies lay amid the overturned desks, their blood mixing with ink. Alan chuckled. Would anyone be surprised? Victor had come in and openly mocked the guilds. Surely he didn't expect to go unscathed...

When he turned back to the battle, he expected to see a rout, Victor's men chasing in vain after a scattered collection of Hawks. Instead he watched the trap fully unfold. As the remaining men on the ground fled, twenty more emerged from the rooftops, all armed with crossbows. Bolts flew down like lethal rain. Despite their armor, the soldiers could do nothing, not against that many attackers. They ran toward the safety of the castle—the few who lived beyond the first volley—blood dripping from bolts embedded in their arms, legs, and chests. With even fewer targets to pick from, the second volley was worse. Alan winced as the last died, some with over five bolts thudding into their backs.

A trumpet sounded, bringing Alan's attention to the castle. He caught a glimpse of castle guards rushing out with swords drawn, but then something grabbed his cloak and pulled, hard. He was thrown into the same alley Peb had fled into, though Peb appeared long gone. Rolling to his knees, Alan looked up to see the Watcher standing at the entrance to the alley, a black shadow in the daylight.

"Stay here," he said, drawing his sabers.

That was it, that one command, and then he rushed off, moving fast enough to be a blur. Alan rubbed his neck, muttered, and rose to his feet. Despite the Watcher's fearsome reputation, he had no intention of missing this. Returning to the alley entrance, he peered out to watch the carnage.

Fifteen castle guards ran out to engage the Hawks. Unlike Victor's men, they wielded shields, and kept them raised to protect themselves from the arrows. For a brief moment, it looked as if the Hawks were going to make a stand against them as well. A few climbed down, forming a line of fifteen while the rest fired into the group of soldiers.

And then the Watcher arrived, tearing through their ranks upon the rooftop. He struck from behind, killing several before they knew they were under attack. The distance was too great for Alan to see clearly, but the gray of the Watcher's interlocking cloaks looked like a phantom, darting and weaving throughout their numbers, never still, never hesitating. One after another dropped dead. When the arrows from up top stopped, the soldiers below lowered their shields and charged. The Hawks, without armor or significant weaponry, did the intelligent thing and fled. They could easily outrun and outmaneuver the city guard. The Watcher, on the other hand...

Alan sank deeper into the alley, glancing about to see if any eyes watched. The last thing he wanted was to be spotted. He liked living, and wanted to keep doing it for many, many years. Minutes passed, and with ebbing interest Alan listened to the various trumpets and calls by the guards. At last he heard a soft rustle of cloak. Turning, he held down a startled cry upon finding the Watcher mere feet away.

"Did you know this was to happen?" the Watcher asked.

Alan reached out a hand. The Watcher glared, then tossed a small bag of coins at him. Alan caught it, and within seconds the bag had vanished into one of his many pockets. He didn't have to check it. The Watcher paid in silver, and always in significant amounts. Buying information from the Spider Guild was not cheap, and selling it wasn't safe, given how vicious Thren could be. But Alan wasn't one to let fear or honor get in the way of making a healthy sum of coin.

"We hadn't heard a word," Alan said, crossing his arms and leaning against a wall. "But then again, Kadish Fel's always been a bit of a hothead since taking over for his older cousin Vel. He's getting ballsy if he thinks his guild can take Lord Victor all on his own."

"What do you know about Lord Victor?"

Alan shrugged. "Just what everyone knows. Can't help you there."

The Watcher frowned, clearly displeased. "I'm starting to doubt giving you your coin."

Alan chuckled. "I never promise what I tell will be useful, or new to you. But I dare you to find anyone else insane enough to sell out Thren Felhorn."

"Enough. Tell me this, then ... what do you know about the murders, the ones being claimed by the Widow?"

Alan grunted, caught off guard by the question. Reaching into his tattered vest, he pulled out one of the silver coins the Watcher had paid him with and began twirling it in his fingers.

"Honestly, we don't know shit. I might have believed it was you, if I thought you had the ability to rhyme. The two dead, Bert and Troy, neither of them was special, or even important. No one's seen nothing, and no one's heard nothing."

"What were the two doing when they were killed?"

"Keep asking questions, I might think I don't have enough silver in my pocket."

The Watcher's glare made him chuckle, but his nerves were starting to rise. All it would take was one person telling Thren he'd been seen speaking with the Watcher, just a whisper of betrayal, and he'd be gutted from the Spider Guild's rooftop... if he was lucky.

"Fine," he said. "I don't know what Troy was doing, but Bert was out looking for whores. That help you any?"

"Perhaps." The Watcher pulled his dark hood lower across his face, then leaped from one side of the alley to the other, vaulting himself up to the rooftops. Once there, he spun on his haunches and spoke down to Alan.

"I'll find you three days from now, on your patrol by the south wall. If you can tell me anything about this Widow, I'll pay you in gold."

"Should be paying me in gold anyway," Alan said, but the Watcher was already gone. Turning to leave, he found a man leaning against one of the walls, his large frame blocking half the alley. His muscular arms were crossed over his chest, and he almost looked as if he were sleeping, with his wide-brimmed hat pulled low over his eyes. Alan felt a chill, but the stranger bore no cloak, nor any other sign of allegiance to one of Veldaren's various guilds. Hoping the man was there just to hide from the carnage, Alan walked past him toward the main street.

As he did, the man let out a soft whistle, that of a songbird. Alan didn't dare look back, nor acknowledge the blatant accusation. His hand dropped to his dagger. He slowed his walk, started to shift. But it was too late. Somehow the man was already halfway down the alley, his movement having gone completely unnoticed by Alan. The man turned, smiled at Alan, and then let out another bird whistle.

"The songbirds are singing," the stranger said, then laughed as he touched one of the nine rings in his left ear.

Alan fled. He knew he should return to his guild, to tell Thren everything he'd seen. But he couldn't. Not yet. Halfway across Veldaren he stepped into his favorite tavern, a silver coin in hand. He'd still tell Thren, but he needed a lot more alcohol in him to keep from shaking, keep his perceptive guildmaster from seeing the terror in his eyes. With every sip he took, he heard the whistle, the accusation.

It didn't matter which guild you were in, or even which city. Songbirds died.

"Keep it coming," he told the tavern wench, pushing away the change she'd brought for the silver. "Go until there ain't a damn thing left of it."

CHAPTER

8

Are you sure you would not prefer an escort?" John asked her as Melody put a simple sun hat atop her head and straightened it.

"I'm quite fine without soldiers following me everywhere I go," she said, smoothing out her dress. "But I've been shuttered in far too long, and I'd like to visit the market without it causing a stir."

John hardly looked pleased, but that didn't bother Melody much. She smiled at him, even when he crossed his arms and looked from side to side, as if trying to find the proper words.

"But you're Alyssa's mother, and she has many enemies. I would hate if they were to . . . harass you while unprotected."

"Her enemies are not mine," Melody said as she exited the door to the mansion. "For no one knows I exist anymore."

"They will soon," John said as the door shut behind her. Head high, she crossed the walkway, nodding at the guards stationed at the outer gate. She wore a simple dress, her hair tied back into a low ponytail. Nothing about her showed her station, showed her to be anything beyond a simple servant going out to the market on an errand. And it was true, really, except that the errand at the market was not that of making a purchase.

No, she had a meeting, one not for strangers' eyes.

A bounce came to her step as the mansion faded away behind her, soon lost as she took a turn southeast. It'd been so long since she'd gone to the market, she felt her heart begin to race as the painfully familiar noises slowly neared. The smells, the bustle, the constant murmur of discussion that washed over it all like a river. Everything invoked a life she had so long lost to darkness and the needles of the gentle touchers. Not that they'd come much for her, not even in those first few months after Maynard had given her over to Leon.

No, her torture had been far worse. Her torture had been the fat man's lips on her neck, his chubby fingers on her breasts.

But Leon was dead, she was alive, and the marketplace thrived with food and clothes and fruited drinks and alcohols of every possible strength and age. Stepping into the heart of the market, she felt lost and overwhelmed, and she loved every minute of it. She did not hurry, for she wanted to enjoy it, let it seep into her. People. Life. Everything around her was precious, was something that needed to be saved. And save it she would.

Everything she did, she would do, would be to save it from the coming nightmare.

"Interest a very lovely lady in perfume?" asked a boy far too young to be alone without his father, but young enough to use his cute face to his advantage.

"No thank you," she told him as she flicked him a copper piece. "But thank you for the flattery."

He smiled at her, most likely because of the coin, and not the actual act of kindness. He'd probably have smiled just as wide if she'd dropped the copper while walking past. But it felt good to give, and it was good to hear a man call her beautiful, even if he looked hardly older than ten. Any man, any boy, the very act helped wash away Leon's words echoing in her mind, always there when she lay down to sleep. It'd been two years since he'd touched her, but it didn't matter. It never mattered.

You're so beautiful, Melody. So beautiful, so charming. You're a light in my life, a light here in my dungeon...

Melody passed by dozens of stalls, only half-seeing them. Only at the end did she focus once more, looking for their designated meeting place. It was just one of many alleyways that cut in and out of the market, but the one she wanted was by a mustached man selling fake jewelry. She gave him a curt nod, polite but letting him know she was just passing into the nearby alley and that no business would be had from her.

The shade was welcome, and she took off her hat, fanned herself with it. Just looking as if she needed a breather, that was all.

And then the thin woman with long brown hair slipped into the alley with her, leaning against the wall opposite her with her hands at her sides. Her face she kept downcast, as if embarrassed.

"I'm glad you made it," she said.

"So am I—"

"Widow," the woman interrupted, glancing up just a moment. "When in public, I am the Widow. Do not use my other name."

Melody nodded, smiled as if they were just two friends meeting up while hiding from the sun.

"You've upset me... Widow. You know that, right?"

The woman's face flushed red. "I'm only doing what I was told."

"Were you told to kill that boy working at Alyssa's home? The very home I'm now staying in?"

"But you know Alyssa must be taken care of!" the Widow insisted. "Laerek said…"

"I don't care what Laerek said," Melody snapped. "You must give me more time. I've not had a chance to speak with my daughter about the simplest of things, let alone her faith. Must you be so impatient? Control yourself. Please, can you do that for me?"

The Widow looked up at her with her brown eyes, looked back down.

"If you say."

Melody crossed the alley, took the woman's hands in hers.

"Why does Alyssa bother you so?" she asked. "Don't lie to me. I can tell."

The strange woman swallowed, then shrugged her shoulders.

"I don't know. She just does. She doesn't deserve to be your daughter."

Melody sighed. That again. Still, there wasn't much she could do about it, not yet. The most important thing was buying herself more time, time to do what must be done.

"Is that why you killed her servant?" she asked. "Is that why a poor innocent boy had to suffer? Because you're *jealous*?"

The Widow said nothing, only stared at the ground and refused to meet her eye.

"You poor thing," Melody said, squeezing the woman's hands tight. "Do not fret, nor worry about my love for you. But please, understand, Alyssa will see reason. You just have to give me that chance."

The Widow bobbed her head up and down.

"I will," she promised.

Melody could still sense the edge on her, a bite to her words, a jitteriness to her movements that indicated her growing frustration. It was a habit, a sickness, a disease overwhelming the poor woman, and Melody knew exactly what would heal it.

"Go find another Spider," she said, letting go of her hands. "It will help you feel better."

"They're getting more careful," the Widow said. "I don't know if I'll find one."

"You will," Melody said, and she hugged her. Beneath her dress, the woman felt all bone and skin, and the sad state of her made Melody squeeze even harder. "You know you will. You're clever, you're fast. Go send another of those sinful wretches to the Abyss so they might be made clean."

"Thank you," the Widow said, and a tear ran down her face despite her smile. "And I will. They won't stop me. No one can stop me. Soon even Thren will suffer my sting. I can't wait, can't wait..."

Melody separated herself from the woman, kissed her forehead, then turned for the mouth of the alley. Just before exiting, she heard the Widow call out to her.

"Remember," she said. "If Alyssa doesn't turn to Karak, then I get to have her. Laerek promised me that."

Melody turned back, let her glare send the Widow retreating farther into the alley.

"I am well aware," she said.

She hurried back into the market, but this time the bustle about her was too noisy and bothersome, the smells too strong, the merchants too obtrusive with their shouts to buy, buy, buy.

"That'll do it," Tarlak said as he straightened up, wincing as his upper back popped twice.

"Are you sure it will hold, no matter how powerful the spell?" asked Victor, surveying the runes carved into the outside of his temporary home. Ten in all covered the large building, burned in as if by fire.

Tarlak raised an eyebrow. He'd spent the past six hours placing markings with chalk, rearranging runes, and casting a variety of spells that protected the building from magical attacks—from the subtle, like teleportation, to the less subtle, like giant exploding fireballs. Last but not least had been the requested surprise escape in case of an attack. His back hurt like crazy, his fingers were sore from all the measuring and writing, and he doubted he could summon anything stronger than a magical fart given how badly his head ached. And yet Victor wanted to question his abilities?

"If you didn't think I could do the job," Tarlak asked, "why request me in the first place?"

Victor sighed. "You're right. Forgive me. Today has not gone well."

"So I heard."

Word of the attack had spread throughout Veldaren like wildfire. Tarlak had gotten a firsthand account from Haern, at least of how the attack had ended. As for casualties, that was a little sketchier. Tarlak had hoped to glean more information from the lord, but so far had struggled to get the man to talk. Now that they were surveying his handiwork, at last he had a chance.

"Most of these runes I've burned in," Tarlak said, trying to keep Victor engaged, his mind on their conversation instead of elsewhere. "It'd take a lot to smudge or break them, but it is possible. Make sure your guards are always aware."

"What should they watch for?"

"Well, I'd say a man with a big mallet smashing the wood in.

That'd probably break them. Think your guards would notice that?"

Victor paused a moment, and then, miracle of miracles, laughed. Tarlak snapped his fingers. Finally he was getting somewhere.

"No one will lay a finger on the building," Victor said. "And I think even the least-trained man in my employ would be wise enough to stop someone from hacking at the wall."

"Praise the gods for intelligent help."

"Amen."

The two walked toward the entrance of the building. Guards trailed behind them. They'd watched Tarlak carefully the entire time, supposedly because they didn't want him harmed while casting the protection spells. Tarlak found the lie insulting.

As if he needed protection.

His balance teetered a bit as he walked with Victor, and he decided that maybe that wasn't so insulting after all. Victor caught him, inquired if he was all right.

"Just a little woozy," he said, rolling his head from side to side. "Ever had a headache so bad that it split your insides in half, making every light look ten times too bright?"

"I can't say I have."

"Then you're damn lucky. Consider me adding the cost of a drink to your expenses, because I need one right now, otherwise I won't make it home."

"Then consider it paid."

Victor led Tarlak to the door. The wizard made sure not to crack a smile. His head hurt, but not that terribly. Still, Victor looked as if he wanted those he hired to trust him, even respect him. A good sign. Anyone willing to buy beer for his underlings was a man with great potential. The guards let Victor pass, then stepped in front of Tarlak.

"All off," said one.

"All...off?"

Tarlak realized the guards meant his clothes, but Victor interrupted before he could protest.

"Let him through," said the lord. "I'm trusting my life to his wards, not much sense to fear him slipping a knife in me."

"Smart man," Tarlak said as he stepped inside and took a seat at a table. A servant hurried over, pitcher in hand. Accepting it graciously, he sniffed the contents. Strong scent of honey. Excellent.

"Only common sense," Victor said, dismissing the offered cup as he sat opposite the wizard. "If you wanted me dead, those wards would set my home on fire in the middle of the night instead of keeping out the more determined scum of the underworld."

"Speaking of scum, did you catch those responsible for the attack on your scribes?"

Victor crossed his arms and leaned back in his seat. His clear blue eyes bore into Tarlak, and Tarlak could sense the inner debate.

"Not as many as I would like," Victor said, sighing. "The Hawk Guild was responsible, that I know for sure. Guesses run from about thirty to forty that set up the ambush. We killed at least twenty...well, twenty died, I should say. My men can only account for seven. The Watcher took out the rest."

"He does tend to do that," Tarlak said, chuckling.

"If I'm not mistaken, he is a member of your mercenaries, is he not?"

Tarlak lifted an eyebrow.

"Aye, he is. Considering hiring him? Doesn't come cheap, but of course we're relying on future payments already. What's a little more debt between friends?"

"I just hope to know if I can consider him a friend in the first place," Victor insisted.

"Money tends to make such matters irrelevant."

At Victor's glare, Tarlak raised his hands and quickly apologized. "Forgive me, I tend to joke when I should grovel. If you're wondering what the Watcher thinks of you, I'd say right now he doesn't know. Just between you and me, I think you're a respectable-enough guy, but the Watcher tends to be a bit more distrusting."

Victor nodded, waved at the servants. Accepting a drink, he downed half. Tarlak shifted in his seat, wondered what troubled the lord so much he'd decided he needed alcohol after all.

"One of my scribes died in the attack," Victor said, his voice softer. He wiped a few drops from his chin with his fingers. "Good man, a friend. Several other innocent men and women died, having committed the crime of being in the wrong place at the wrong time. I've relocated all our interrogations to inside the castle, with King Edwin's permission. But things are souring already. My men must travel in larger and larger packs, lest they fall into similar ambushes. Only ten men went to the judges today, and they even freed one of the ten. Whatever tight mouths I thought people had, they've grown only tighter."

"You walked into a nest of hornets and started swatting," Tarlak said. "Surely you can't be surprised that they've begun stinging back."

Victor let out a halfhearted chuckle.

"I'm not surprised. No, what troubles me is that my men are afraid. The people we drag in here are afraid. The king is afraid. Everyone is afraid, so I can't be, yet I'm as terrified as any. How did it get so terrible here? How could an entire city live its life full of fear?"

Tarlak tapped his empty mug.

"This here's a start. But when your eyes are shut tight enough, you can convince yourself you're safe from anything. It's only when bold, brash outsiders come in braying and waving swords around that everyone remembers just how terrible the guilds can be, and how cruel a bedmate we've made."

"Indeed," said Victor, motioning for another drink. "Cruel, cold, and ruthless. But you know what frightens everyone most? The Spider Guild has yet to act. All the others—the Hawks, the Serpents, even the Ash—they're nothing compared to Thren Felhorn. The rumors I hear treat him like the reaper man, a monster from a child's fable."

"He started a war that lasted ten years," Tarlak said, feeling his mood grow somber. "And the only reason it ended was because he allowed it. Thren is the one you need to watch for most. He's getting old, but that won't matter. Long as he's alive, he'll be a danger. And if you're hoping someone will turn on him, mention where he lives or some illegal Violet he's smuggled in..." He laughed. "It won't happen. Unless you want to abandon this charade of law and order and declare full war on the guilds, you won't find him, won't send him to the executioner's ax. Not unless you kill him trying to kill you."

Victor frowned. His face hardened, as if the blood beneath his skin were turning to stone. Tarlak shifted, wondering what it was he'd said that angered him so.

"It is no charade," Victor said. "With every breath of mine, I'll tear them down, cast them from the shadows and into the light. But I won't let them drag me down with them. I won't become like them. That is why I must adhere to the law. I must be stronger, smarter, better prepared. The first day was too easy, and I grew soft."

He looked to Tarlak, and the earnest desperation was clear in his eyes.

"That is why I need you," he said. "Why I need the Watcher. I need you to trust me, to help me. I've looked into your dealings, Tarlak, and those of your mercenaries. You've helped others even when they couldn't pay. You've refused any assassinations, even when the Watcher could do them with ease. You have a sense of right and wrong, just like I do. You know they must be stopped. Please, help me."

Tarlak stood, smoothed out his robes.

"I must be going," he said. "Thank you for the drink, and the company. I'll consider your request, but I wouldn't hold your breath. You want my trust; so far you have it. What you don't have is my approval. I'm not convinced you'll make Veldaren a better place. The guilds were growing lazy, their numbers starting to dwindle. Already they were turning on each other, killing more and more."

"All it'd take is the Watcher's death," Victor said, shaking his head. "The Trifect fears the guilds, and the guilds fear the Watcher's wrath. Remove that fear, and their greed resurfaces, voracious and starving. Whatever growing pains I create are a thousand times better than the chaos that was certain to happen otherwise."

"Perhaps so." Tarlak bowed low. "I'll escort myself home, if you don't mind."

Victor gave him a sly smile.

"Headache gone?"

"Never felt better. Must be some amazing ale you have."

"Must be."

Victor stood, offered his hand. Tarlak looked at it as if it were a trap, then accepted it.

"Just give me a chance," Victor said. "I'll prove myself to you, to everyone in Veldaren."

"I'd be careful of that," Tarlak said, putting his pointy yellow hat back on. "The more the underworld sees who you are, and believes you're here to do what you say, the more frightened they'll be."

"Good," Victor said. "Let them be afraid."

"They fear the Watcher, they fear Deathmask, and they fear Thren Felhorn. Should your name one day be among theirs, I'll treat you to drinks at my tower."

Tarlak left, ignoring the cold glares from the guards at the door. While heading down the street, he stopped and turned back to observe his handiwork on the walls and think on the man hiding within.

"Crazy bastard," Tarlak muttered, shaking his head. "What in the world are you thinking?"

He headed back, feeling terribly annoyed. Worse, he wasn't sure if it was at Lord Victor's insanity, or his own for helping the man in his impossible quest.

Time was not on his side, but Peb felt confident he could finish quickly. Not that he'd brag about that to anyone else, or even admit it. But with such a daring mission approaching, Peb needed some release, otherwise he'd be a nervous wreck throughout. After Alan had told Thren everything that had happened at the castle attack, their guildmaster had fallen deathly quiet, talking to no one for a full hour. When he exited his study, his plan was simple, and his mind set.

Victor Kane died tonight.

"Like it'll be that easy," Peb muttered to himself as he headed toward the darkest alleys of Veldaren. He was in too much of a hurry to watch his surroundings, but he feared no attack, not so deep in the heart of their own territory. A few coins rattled in his pocket, just enough to pay for what he needed. He usually had his pick of the women, given how weak he looked, how unthreatening. The whores talked, Peb knew that. They knew he needed just a touch, just a kiss, and that he'd never hurt them, not like some of the others who needed to punch or beat someone weaker to get themselves off.

Turning right, he passed a dimly lit tavern, then veered into an alley beside it. He knew many men preferred brothels, wanting a bed where they could lie back and do nothing, or to have clean sheets they could ruffle and cast about. Peb needed none of that, just him standing, and a pretty girl on her knees. What did anything else matter, especially when the cost would go up twofold for all the extravagances?

"Hello?" Peb asked the alleyway as he stepped inside. Normally there'd be three or four girls there, eager to sell themselves to the men who stayed in the tavern. The night was still young, though, so perhaps they were elsewhere.

"Can I help you?" asked a soft voice, like tinkling glass. Squinting, Peb saw a petite woman farther in the shadows. Long brown hair curled around her neck, and she smiled at him with such delicate, pretty features.

"I think you can," he said, smiling. Gods, those eyes, just staring at them would have him done in no time. He'd be able to go charging ahead of Thren, feeling on top of the world as they tore Victor from his room and beat his face to a pulp. He reached into his pocket as she beckoned him closer.

"How much?" he asked, fearing the normal rates might not apply to someone so clearly of a higher class.

"Not much," the whore said, her eyes twinkling. "In fact, cute as you are, I might pay you."

She was just flattering him, he knew, but Peb liked hearing it anyway. His hand reached for the sash of his pants.

"That so?" he asked. "How much you think I'm worth?"

That smile darkened, and those delicate features suddenly seemed far less innocent.

"Two silver, and two gold."

Peb was too stunned to even move. By the time he saw the small crossbow, it was too late. She pulled the trigger, and the bolt thudded into his neck. He opened his mouth, but no sound came out. His stomach heaved, and he dropped, unable to maintain his balance. He tried to run, to scream, but his muscles ignored every command. Poison, he realized, his terror increasing. The bolt was poisoned.

"I know you can't move," the whore said, kneeling down beside him, covering the front of her brown dress with dirt. No longer did her voice sound like tinkling glass. Now it echoed of razors sliding against one another. "Maybe you think that means you won't feel anything. You're wrong. I just want you to know that. You'll feel every...single...thing."

A knife flashed before him, held aloft so he could see the sharp edge in the moonlight. Then it turned, and Peb felt tears run down the side of his face. The tip pressed beneath his right eye, slipped deeper. It cut through nerves, muscle, and then with a sickening plop, pulled free. With his remaining eye, he saw her holding aloft his severed eyeball, a thin, bloody strand of tissue still attached to the back. Satisfied, the whore put it into a pocket of her dress, then leaned forward, dagger leading, hungry for his remaining eye.

It was true.

He felt every bit of it.

CHAPTER

9

The hours passed, the sun setting and the moon rising, all while Haern watched the tavern. After Tarlak's departure, Lord Victor had remained inside. As night approached, more and more of his men returned, increasing their lord's protection while he slept. Haern shifted his weight back and forth so his legs never fell asleep. The tedium wore on him, but he was used to such things. Most nights he patrolled the city he saw nothing, and accomplished little.

But he knew tonight would not be one of those nights. The Hawks had drawn first blood, but someone else would come in for the kill. He had a sneaking suspicion that his father would elect himself the one to do it. Thren viewed himself as the king of the underworld, and in his mind only he should take down someone so arrogant as Victor.

"Come on," he whispered, glancing up and down the street from his spot. "I know you want him, now come and get him."

Opposite Victor's repurposed tavern were several businesses, including a smithy. In the recesses of the smith's doorway Haern waited, hunched over with a ratty blanket covering his body. He kept his hood off, for, amusingly enough, he was less likely to be noticed and recognized with his blond hair and blue eyes showing. Just a drunk, that's all he was, with his sabers hidden beneath a blanket and his cloaks bunched into a pillow to ease his back as he leaned against the door. From where he sat, he could see the main entrance to Victor's home, plus one of the sides. Based on what Tarlak had told him after placing the runes, the only possible way of entering was through the front door. The windows were too heavily boarded, the roof and walls solid, and Tarlak's runes ensured no magical means allowed anyone to bypass them.

A frontal attack then, where many of Victor's guards waited, armed and armored. No, there was only one person who would be mad enough to do it, and it was the one man who might succeed.

Haern closed his eyes, took a deep breath. Patience, he had to have patience. Thren would leave nothing to chance. He had to keep ready, to plan ahead. Cracking his eyes just enough that he'd still look asleep, he watched and waited. Minutes crawled by, turning into another hour. He shifted again, grimaced at the tingles that shot up his leg. Waited too long, leg asleep. He was getting nervous, and he knew why. Ever since faking his death during the Bloody Kensgold nine years ago, Haern had never crossed swords with his father. Yet if he was right about tonight, there was no avoiding that possibility. Growing up, Haern had known his father was one of the best in the world when it came to swordplay, certainly the best in Veldaren. That had been a long time ago, and now the thieves whispered that it was the Watcher who deserved that claim. But what if they were wrong?

Movement in the shadows forced his mind away from such worries.

There, thought Haern. A scout from the Spider Guild, peering from around the corner of a building far to his right. By his guess the scout could just barely see the guards at the doorway. Taking in positions, looking for patrols, confirming numbers. That was Thren's way. Haern wondered if his father had prepared for him as well, and shivered. A grown man, yet he still felt like a child when he compared himself to that stern, imposing figure. More than anything, he did not want to face him. Swallowing that fear down, he watched the scout, all while being careful to make no movement that might give away his presence.

After less than twenty seconds, the scout was gone. A hunch made Haern shift so he could watch the other way, and sure enough, another scout appeared along the rooftops. Checking the other direction, of course, as well as seeing if there was a patrol the first might have missed. No doubt they both saw the same thing: a well-boarded, protected tavern, the lone entrance guarded by four soldiers in armor. Two wielded swords, two others long spears. The scout vanished, and Haern shifted so he might more easily reach for his sabers. As an afterthought he touched the pendant of the Golden Mountain that hung beneath his shirt.

"Please help me, Ashhur," he whispered. "I have a feeling I'm going to need it. Oh, and protect Victor, if you think he's worth protecting."

That done, he readjusted so he was on his knees instead of his buttocks. Tilting his head to one side, he let his mouth drop, let his breathing slow. With a single eye he watched. Waited. But the attack didn't come. Haern felt his patience tested. Why not? Everything was ready. The scouts had checked. The guards at the front looked tired and bored. Why did he not see their approach?

The soft creaking of wood gave him his answer. Above him. The massed Spider Guild had traveled across the rooftops, and now overlooked the tavern, inspecting it just as he did. Suddenly uncertain, Haern lay there as the silence of the night was interrupted by the sound of crossbow strings. A deadly barrage of bolts sailed toward the four guards. The archers' aim was true, the bolts piercing throats and eyes. All four men dropped, unable to call out. The sound of their chain mail rattling was the only warning they gave to those inside.

Haern bit down a curse.

Ropes rolled down in front of him, and then the thieves descended. Haern kept perfectly still, hoping his presence might go unnoticed. Through a crack in his eyelids he counted their number. Twenty...thirty...forty...

Thren Felhorn landed before him, and Haern stopped counting. His father looked almost exactly as he remembered. His strong jaw, his coldly intelligent blue eyes, his reddish-blond hair cut short so it would not interfere with his hearing or vision. The only differences were the wrinkles, and the way his skin looked stretched and thin. It was a strange thing, realizing how much his father had aged, but peering up at him, Haern still felt like a child. For a brief moment of terror, he thought Thren might see his unhidden face and recognize his long-lost son. If Thren did turn and draw his short swords, Haern didn't know if he would be able to react in time to save himself.

The first of the thieves reached the door, and Thren followed after. Haern slowly exhaled. His hands were shaking, and as he sat up, his years of training steadied his breath and calmed his heart. This is what he'd expected, what he'd known would happen. In times past, Haern had stormed through the mansions of the Trifect, slaughtering mercenaries and thieves alike to bring about peace. He'd fought the most skillful of opponents, from the Wraith to the elven scoutmaster Dieredon. He would show no fear—not here, not now. The Spider Guild must fear him, not the other way around.

Should have kept Tarlak with me instead of searching for that Widow, Haern thought. One well-placed fireball and the entire fight would be over. With so many of the thieves' backs to him, it was tempting to rush into their ranks, but he knew Thren would not be so foolish as to leave such a blatant opening to attack. Instead Haern slunk to the side of the smithy, then ran to the back. Scrambling to the roof, he drew his swords and pulled his hood over his head, letting its magical darkness hide his features. Four men with crossbows remained on the rooftop, protecting the Spider Guild's rear flank. Haern crossed the worn shingles without a sound. Two were already dead before they knew he was there. Another fell to the hard stone below, blood gushing from his throat. The fourth managed a single scream before a saber took away his voice, and his life.

In the tense silence, that scream was enough. Standing to his full height, Haern held his swords out wide, let the Spider Guild see him there, looming, a promise of death in the dark night. The guards inside had started to shout, for several thieves had jammed thick iron crowbars against the hinges and begun jarring them loose. Those in the back turned, though, and they readied their weapons. There was no hiding their fear at his presence.

At least fifty on one, thought Haern.

Could be worse.

The door shook, men rammed against it, and then it broke. The Spider Guild rushed the opening, and from within the tavern Haern heard the sound of combat. He knew soldiers protected Victor, but how many? And would they hold? Below, a line of thieves remained, about ten left to protect their rear from the lurking Watcher. Haern smiled despite himself. Now that was better.

He leaped into the air, his cloaks trailing silently behind him. Sabers eager, he twirled so they could not guess what his direction would be upon landing. They'd cut in, try to bury him in sheer numbers. And he'd be ready. His feet touched the ground, and he dropped, rolling to help soak up his momentum. He felt his shoulder connect against a man's legs, and when the thief went down Haern pulled up, leaping again, avoiding frantic cuts. This time he was fully in control, parrying hits with vicious speed. Pirouetting on one foot, he lashed out, cutting down two nearby thieves.

More rushed in, but they made simple attacks, thrusts and chops that showed their lack of formal training. Most could only dream of training with the masters Thren had brought in from around the world every month. He'd wanted Haern to be his heir, his lord of the underworld. As the Spiders died around him, Haern knew himself the fulfillment of that destiny, in a way his father never could have anticipated. Parry, shift, counter, and another two fell. Spinning, he let his cloaks flare out, let them disguise his movements. One thief slashed only to miss, stabbing into gray cloth instead of flesh. Haern lunged at him, knowing him to be vulnerable. His sabers pierced the man's belly, and a twist sent the contents spilling.

The remaining men wanted no part of him, instead turning to flee. Haern let them, knowing he had bigger problems to face. Looking to the door, he saw the rest of the guild had managed to force themselves inside. He still heard combat, which was a good sign. As long as men were fighting, Victor had a chance.

When he reached the broken door, an eruption shook the ground, along with a bright flash that lit up the night. Haern struggled to keep his balance, then swore. A thunderclap followed, rumbling like an angry beast as high above the rooftop smoke billowed into the night sky.

"Damn it, Tarlak," said Haern. "Do you not know the meaning of the word *subtle?*"

The last bit of defense Tarlak had told Haern about was in Victor's room, which when activated would explode the wall outward, giving the lord a chance to escape. Obviously it had been triggered. No time left, Haern dashed through the door, and his recklessness nearly killed him. A sword thrust pierced the space before the entrance, shockingly fast. Yet Haern was also fast, collapsing to one knee as he twisted away. The tip of the blade cut across his chest, just a nick that would scar at worst. A faint spray of blood flecked across the ground as Haern continued his turn, bringing up his sabers in the process.

Thren stood before him, bent into a ready stance. He twirled a sword, not yet attacking, only staring. Behind him his guild-members battled a slew of guards making their stand atop the stairs. All around lay corpses of both Spiders and soldiers.

"This is no concern of yours," Thren said. "The man is a fool, and he threatens the balance you've killed so many to achieve."

"Fool or not, I'd rather keep him alive. I'll have no war in Veldaren, not again."

Thren shook his head, took a careful step forward.

"Victor brought the war, not us. If you want it to end, then Victor must die tonight. Stand down, Watcher."

Haern felt his pulse quicken, felt his breath catch in his throat.

"No," he said.

Thren leaped, closing the distance between them with the speed of a demon. Short swords stabbed in, their angles decep- tive. Only instinct kept Haern alive, his hands moving of their own accord. His sabers parried both aside, and a shifting of his feet made it so his shoulder met Thren's when they collided. His father was strong, but Haern kept his feet planted firmly, just long enough to halt Thren's momentum. Hoping for surprise, he rolled aside, toward Thren's back, and swung for his neck. Thren ducked the swing with ease.

This time they both rushed each other, their blades clashing together with a steady ringing of steel. Haern felt his nerves settle as he blocked and parried. Skilled as his father was, he was slower than Haern, and not as strong. Not by much, of course, but in a contest so close, even a little advantage was crucial.

"You can still flee," Haern said, his riposte cutting a thin line across Thren's shoulder. When Haern tried to follow it up, Thren fell back, his short swords batting aside every thrust.

"You're a puppet of the Trifect," Thren said, pulling his swords together and settling into another stance. "You won't defeat me. I'm what you'd become if they cut your strings."

Haern narrowed his gaze, the tips of his sabers pressed against the wood floor as he took in heavy gasps of air. Before their combat could resume, a thief rushed down the steps. The last of the guards downstairs were dead, and whatever fighting there was had continued higher up.

"Victor's made it to the street!" the thief cried out, as if oblivious that his guildmaster faced off against the Watcher.

Haern met his father's gaze, and a half-smile tugged at his lips.

They both sprinted for the door, Haern sliding to one leg just as he reached it. As he predicted, a dagger sailed over his head, thrown by Thren when he realized he could not keep pace. Leaping back to his feet, Haern ran on, desperate not to fail. A quick glance behind showed Thren at his heels, his own gray cloak billowing behind him. Together they rounded the corner, and saw the mess Tarlak's spell had created.

The entire side wall of the tavern was gone. The wood was blackened and burned along the edges, as if pushed out by a great fire. Rubble lay scattered across the street. Thieves had given chase, and Haern saw at least twenty. Ahead of them all was Lord Victor, a distant silver shape. No escort remained with him. Despite his lead, Haern knew the thieves would catch him, most of them younger and unburdened by armor.

"Just keep going," Haern breathed as he ran, knowing Thren followed dangerously close. He was faster than them all, knew how to maximize the push of every swing of his legs, but the moment he stopped to fight, Thren would come crashing in. Haern saw little hope, but it didn't matter. He ran on. Catching up to the tail end of the thieves, he slid close and swung. His saber hamstrung a man, toppling him head over heels while he screamed. Another stopped to strike, but Haern veered aside and continued past.

Too many ahead. The homes on either side flashed by in blurs. Haern's heels pounded against the hard stone of the street. His pulse thundered in his ears. When they caught Victor, they'd tear him apart, overwhelm him with...

The street exploded before him. Rocks, each the size of a man's fist, thudded into the homes. In its center swirled a pillar of fire that flared bright before dwindling. Smoke billowed from the crater that now separated Haern from Lord Victor. Over half of the thieves had been caught in the fire, their corpses now lying scattered about, their clothing aflame. The rest staggered aimlessly, bleeding from the ears. And then from the smoke emerged Deathmask. A pale gray mask covered his face, and hovering about his head, hiding his features like a dark cloud, was a swirl of ash. Fire danced from his fingertips.

"Now's not the time to be a hero," Deathmask said to them, pointing at the nearest Spider. Fire shot from his finger and bathed the man in flame. His screams did not last long, but were still terrible to hear. At the same time, a woman leaped from the rooftops, two daggers glowing a soft violet in her hands. She landed amid the stunned thieves, making short work of those who tried to defend themselves. Haern recognized her as Veliana, Deathmask's second-in-command. Not that he had many to command. Only two others were in his guild, twins...

He found them beside Victor in the distance. Haern feared they would hurt him, but from what he could see through the smoke, they only stood at his side, as if protecting him. Shaking his head, Haern turned around, realizing he had forgotten the threat of his father. If Thren had wanted, he could have borne down upon him, but instead he stood far back, the look of anger on his face chilling even to Haern.

"You have no one to blame," Thren said, meeting Haern's eye. "Whatever games we've played, consider them over."

He fled into the night, and Haern had no desire to chase after hearing those cryptic words. Sheathing his sabers, he neared the crater, its heat and smoke slowly fading. Deathmask crossed his arms over his chest. From the way his eyes twinkled, Haern had little doubt the dark-haired man was enjoying himself.

"Since when do thieves protect the lords who hunt them?" Haern called out as he approached.

"We have no fear of the hunt," Deathmask said, removing his mask. With a snap of his fingers, the ash fell to the street, revealing his features. He was a handsome man, his dark hair grown down to his neck, his tanned skin smooth and clean. Most noticeable were his eyes, the left a deep brown, the right colored red. "Besides, you know I enjoy a bit of chaos every now and then."

Veliana came to his side, her daggers still twirling in her dexterous fingers. Her dark hair was pulled into a ponytail. She might have been beautiful but for the wicked scar that ran from forehead to chin, cutting across her right eye and leaving it a bloody orb.

"You don't mind if we borrow him for a while, do you?" Veliana asked.

"Victor?" asked Haern. "Why?"

"Just somewhere safe," Deathmask said, giving Haern a wink. "Don't try to follow us. Besides, I think you have your own mess to clean up."

Deathmask nodded to the tavern that Victor had been using as a home. Haern glanced at it, saw the bodies and dwindling fire. When he looked back he realized the twins were gone, and Victor with them. Deathmask's smile grew.

"Don't worry, Watcher," he said. "We won't keep him long."

He and Veliana stepped into the crater, and smoke wafted over them. When it cleared they were gone. Haern took a deep breath, let it out. Whatever was going on, it was currently beyond his control. But it seemed the Ash Guild wasn't ready to see Lord Victor killed. At least not by someone other than themselves.

"Damn it all," Haern said, shaking his head. He looked to the fire, the bodies, and heard the screams of the injured who had yet to die. Far away a trumpet sounded, the call of the city guard arriving far too late. A rock settled deep in Haern's gut.

Whatever peace Veldaren had known died that night. Thren's look had promised war, and in time, decimated guild or not, he would have it. Saying a prayer for the entire city, Haern returned to Victor's place to wait for the rest of the Eschaton to arrive. Whatever their motivations, the Ash Guild could not be trusted. One way or another, Haern would find them before the night's end, and Tarlak knew many, many ways...

CHAPTER

 **10**

Zusa waited atop the eastern wall of the city, hidden in the recesses of a watchtower. Whenever a guard lazily wandered by, she clung to the stone ceiling and let him pass underneath without a clue to her presence. Then she'd drop down, return to the edge, and wait. It had been many years, but she knew she would recognize Daverik the moment he arrived. What she'd say to him—that she was far less certain of. Perhaps she'd just kill him. She wanted to. Almost needed to.

The night wore on, but she forced herself to be patient. She had given Daverik no specific location, for she didn't want his faceless to set up an ambush. If they tried following, she would spot their movements. No matter how good they might be at slinking through shadows, they were young, and Zusa was better.

"Are you a coward now?" Zusa wondered aloud as the night wore on. Daverik had been many things, but at least he had never been one to give in to fear. But it'd been over a decade since they'd lain in each other's arms. Perhaps she was naïve to think he had changed so little.

Distant thunder turned her eyes west. She saw hints of a fire, and a lot of smoke. Curiosity tugged at her to go, but she refused. No matter what, she would not have Daverik wander by unnoticed, left to return to the temple thinking that *she* was the coward. Wherever the fire was, she could tell it was nowhere near Alyssa's mansion, and that was enough to keep her still.

When he finally did show, she nearly missed him. Instead of priestly garb, he wore plain clothes, dull brown pants and a gray shirt. He carried no torch, the moonlight sufficient for him. While once his hair had fallen past his shoulders, now it was gone completely, his head smoothly shaved. Time had worn his features, hardening them, but when she cast a second glance while he passed beneath her, she saw the cheeks she'd kissed, the large lips that had kissed her in return.

The plain clothing was clearly a disguise, and she wondered whom it was really for, him or her.

"Daverik," she called out. As he turned she slid down the wall, silently landing in a crouch. Scanning the rooftops, she saw no sign of the other faceless. Good. Her attention turned to her former lover, who smiled at her and opened his arms.

"Katherine," he said, and the sound of his voice was the key to a vault of a hundred memories. "My god, Katherine, is it really you?"

She stood to her full height, pulling her shoulders back and turning her head to the side. Though the wrappings had originally been meant to hide her beauty, they also revealed her body's every curve. Let him see the woman she had become, she decided. Let him know what the priesthood had denied him for ten long years.

"Not Katherine," she said. "They took that name from me when they covered my face. They lashed it out of my soul with their whips and barbs. I am Zusa now."

A soft smile spread across his pale face. The moonlight added a blue tint to his green eyes. That she noticed it at all annoyed her.

"In all my memories, you will always be Katherine," he said. "But if I must, I will call you Zusa." He laughed, then shook his head in disbelief. "Even in Mordeina, I'd heard one of the faceless had revolted, and turned away from the order. I hoped it was you. You were never one for rules or limitations."

"Neither were you, or did the priesthood take that from you, convince you that every time we fucked it was my fault?"

That smile of his faded. He took a step toward her, and she recoiled.

"They tried," he said softly. "They said you seduced me, that your beauty was unveiled sin. At times I almost agreed. You are beautiful, Zusa, perhaps without equal. But what we did . . . what we had . . . I would never diminish it in such a way."

Such charming, honest words. Daverik had always known what to say to her, and she felt her old wounds bleeding anew. They'd been in each other's arms when the priests had discovered them. They'd needed no trial, no council, to confirm the obvious. While she watched, they'd lashed Daverik before the altar, let his blood run across the ancient stone. As for her, the order of the faceless awaited. They'd stripped her naked, and while Daverik watched, bound only her mouth and eyes with the wrappings that would become her ceremonial dress.

And when they carried her away, he'd said only two words,

whose meaning she had always feared, and which she had never forgotten.

Forgive me.

"Why are you here?" she asked, forcing a cold edge into her voice. Daverik was just a phantom from her past, a girlhood love. They'd both been so young, so foolish. "I thought you were banished from Veldaren."

"I was," Daverik said, glancing about. When he saw that they were still alone, he walked over to the wall and leaned his back against it, crossing his arms. "But I've made many friends during my time in the west, friends whose voices carry weight among our order. Given my loyalty over the past ten years, Luther has convinced the temple to give me one final task as penance. One final way to redeem my insult to our god."

"Your god," Zusa corrected. "I have no love for Karak."

This clearly pained Daverik, but he continued without remarking on it.

"The betrayal of the faceless has weighed on the priests in Mordeina. Though Pelorak initially refused, he finally accepted my return here, along with the reopening of the order. I am their teacher, their master."

"Why you?"

"Because they felt I would best understand their weaknesses, having fallen for them myself."

Zusa shook her head, and to show her opinion on the matter, she spit at his feet. His explanation sounded hollow, the reasoning unlike what she knew of the priesthood. He'd be forever branded as a man weak enough to give in to his passions. Why would they put women also believed to be weak into his care?

"The order should have remained dead and gone," she said. "How many women have you enslaved?"

"It is not enslavement…"

"I asked how many."

Daverik sighed. "Four. I doubt any are as skilled as you, but they're learning. Karak has blessed them greatly, and I think they might even surprise you with the gifts they possess."

Zusa smirked. "I'm sure I have a few surprises for them as well. Keep them far away from me, Daverik. The very sight of them sets my blood to boil. If you're wise you'll leave Veldaren immediately."

She turned to leave, but he reached out and grabbed her arm. Her free hand moved for her dagger, but their eyes met, and she saw the incredible force of will there. For a moment she remained still, lost in time, remembering a seventeen-year-old girl hiding in a dark alley with a pretty boy willing to touch her, kiss her, in ways the priesthood had forbidden.

"They say you work for Alyssa Gemcroft now," he said. "Is that true?"

"It is," she said, pulling her arm free. She wanted to hurt him, to shock him, and she didn't know why. "I am her sister, her protector. She loves me, and I her. Why do you ask?"

Daverik swallowed, and she could tell he was struggling to choose his words.

"These are dangerous times," he said. "I don't want to see you hurt. Lady Gemcroft is not safe from the coming storm. Things would be better for everyone if she were to become a friend of Karak."

"Is that a threat?"

"Only a warning," he said. "I wish I could do more."

She took three steps and leaped high above his head, to the rooftop of a nearby home. She landed without a sound, then spun to face him.

"You're a smooth liar," she said. "But I am no fool. Why did they really bring you to Veldaren?"

Daverik sighed and ran a hand across his bald head. "You say 'they' as if the priesthood were but a single entity. There are many factions within it, many unreconciled beliefs. I am here to prepare the faceless, for what, I cannot tell you. I knew you might be here when I was asked, I must admit. Knew I might find you. I hoped...I hoped we could talk. That you might offer me, offer us a second chance."

Zusa felt her neck flush with anger. "And if I refuse?"

He met her gaze, let her see the pain in his eyes. "You are seen by the temple as an abomination, a betrayal that stabs into the very heart of Karak. You know damn well what I'll be ordered to do should anyone know of our meeting."

The words were a dagger, but they did not surprise her, did not even make her flinch.

"And would you?" she asked him. "Would you try to kill me, Daverik?"

"My love, or my god. Do not make me choose, Katherine. I chose you a long time ago. I'm not sure I have the strength to do so again."

She let the shadows swirl around her, drawing them to her as if they were liquid and she the bottom of a well. "Did you not hear me before?" she asked. "Katherine's dead. My name is Zusa. Send your little girls after me if you must. I'll kill them all. But don't you dare bring Alyssa into this, or try to harm a single hair on her head. If you do, not even the walls of the temple will keep you safe from me."

She ran, just a swath of shadow in the night. Far behind she heard him call her name, this time the correct one.

"Zusa!"

She ran harder, faster. Whatever she'd expected, she felt a fool for expecting it. She and Daverik were no longer children. Many times she'd pondered how she'd react upon seeing him,

and now she knew. There'd be no slipping into a past of excitement and danger. There'd be no becoming the doomed, love-
sick lovers exploring the body of another for the very first time.
Now he was a shadow, a ghost, a deceitful creation of flesh and
memories. His very touch upon her arm had sent a mixture of
revulsion and excitement down her spine, and it was the revulsion that had been stronger.

Coming storm, she wondered as she ran. What had Daverik meant by that? What did he know that she did not? Did
the temple of Karak have plans for the city? And what did his
remarks about factions within the temple actually mean? She
felt trapped in a web, just one of many in the strands. But who
was the spider spinning in the center of it all?

She didn't know, but she must find out. Alyssa's life was in
danger. The city passed by her, a silent blur, and it was only
when she reached the Gemcroft mansion that she realized she
was being followed. Turning, she drew her daggers, but by then
they were already gone, the four faceless women vanishing into
the night like the ghosts they were.

"Don't you dare," Zusa whispered, standing at the closed
gate as she issued her threat, not just to the faceless but to the
entire city spread out before her. "You won't take her away from
me. None of you will."

In the distance she heard the roar of another explosion, and
as it rumbled, she felt as if it were the city's heartless, mocking
laughter.

When they pulled the black cloth from his face, Victor found
himself in what appeared to be a small cellar, the walls made
of uneven rock and lit by two torches in opposite corners. He
saw no windows, and no doors. His arms were bound behind

him, rough rope biting into his wrists. His ankles were tied with equal skill to the legs of the chair he sat in. Before him, looking far too amused to be harmless, were Deathmask and his Ash Guild.

"How have you enjoyed tonight's entertainment?" Deathmask asked, sitting across from him in the only other furniture Victor could see, a similarly old and worn chair. "I'm not sure about you, but killing Spiders always gives me a smile."

Beside him a woman crossed her arms and leaned against his side. From what he'd learned, her name was Veliana, his second-in-command.

"I'm not sure he's worth it," she said. Victor peered up at her. He decided there was more compassion and mercy in her bloodied eye than in the healthy one.

"Perhaps not," Victor said, trying to remain calm. "Though it'd help if I knew what value my life was being weighed against."

"Coin," said one of the twins lurking against the wall, their pale skin making them seem like ghosts in the dim light.

"Lots of coin," said the other.

"Right," Victor said, turning his attention to Deathmask, the clear leader of them all. If anyone was to decide his fate, it was he. "But as ransom, or bounty? Or did you lie to me earlier, and there actually is something my soldiers will soon dig up on your little guild?"

Deathmask scooted his chair closer, and his grin spread.

"You think you're sharp," he said. "You think your charm will keep you safe from what your soldiers cannot. But you've come to a city that eats men like you for supper. We spit your bones out in the gutters. At most, you're gristle to get stuck in our teeth. You aren't a white knight come to save us all, and the sooner you accept that, the sooner you and I might start to get along."

"You've never faced a man like me before."

Deathmask shook his head and wagged a finger at him. "You see, that's the thing...we have. I daresay you remind me most of Thren Felhorn. Oh, don't give me that look. You two are more alike than you'll ever admit. Same cockiness, same certainty that you'll live forever without meeting someone better. You know, it might even be true. But the problem is you keep acting like you're *special*. You keep thinking that there's something unique about you."

He slid even closer and raised a palm to the ceiling. Purple fire burst into existence in its center, and it swirled in an unfelt wind, burned on fuel that was not there.

"If I shoved this fire into your lungs," said Deathmask, "you'd scream like anyone else, you'd die like anyone else, and then your corpse would shit itself, just like every other man and woman who has ever lived and died on this joke of a world. When the worms are eating our bodies, there'll be no difference between you and me, not a one."

Victor took a deep breath, and was glad that the tight ropes holding him to the chair kept him from shaking. "I'm not afraid of you," he said. "Tell me what it is you want, or untie me and let me go."

Deathmask chuckled, and he clenched his fist, banishing the fire. "Do the ropes bother you so much? They're really for your own protection, not mine. I'd like you to listen without trying anything stupid, like escape. As for what I want? I want you safe and alive, that's what I want. Why else would I have saved you from Thren's men as they were about to hack you to pieces in the middle of Iron Road? But that's just a momentary gesture. If I want you to *stay* safe and alive, you need to start listening. If we work together, we'll both meet our goals, and you might even live long enough to see the end."

Victor tried to hide his revulsion and failed. He thought of his words to the Watcher and shook his head.

"I will not have you drag me down," he said. "No deals, no bribes, no sacrificing a shred of my intent. I know how you work, Deathmask. You can't defeat me, so you hope to make me like you."

"Can't defeat you?" Veliana asked. She grabbed his face in her hands and gave him an earful of her mocking laughter. "Can't defeat you? Look around, Victor. Instead of removing that mask over your head, we could have buried a dagger in your throat and been done with all this. In fact, that was my preferred method of handling your meddling in Veldaren. Use that mind of yours. Deathmask is the only reason you're alive, so stop spouting blind nonsense, and for once, listen to the words you're saying. You might surprise yourself."

She let go, pushing his head back hard enough to hurt the muscles in his neck. He felt his face flush, and he caught the twins snickering in the background. Pride wounded, he looked to the floor, forced himself to think. They were right, of course. His life was fully in their hands. But that didn't mean he had to surrender. It didn't mean he had to break.

"I will not die a hypocrite," he said softly. "I've come to Veldaren to cleanse it of your kind. I will not work with you to do it. It is a poor executioner who relies on the condemned to swing his own ax."

"Are you so sure?" Deathmask asked. "We now have a common enemy. Thren will never forgive me for what I've done, and you damn well know Thren is the biggest threat to this farce of yours you've set up. I say we take him down together. Such a lovely couple, the two of us, don't you agree?"

Despite their mocking, Victor was no fool. He knew what would happen if he declined their offer. So long as he was useful, Deathmask would keep him alive. The moment he stopped being useful, the moment he became more of a pain than an amusement, his life was over. Could he refuse? Was it right to let everything come crashing down, all because of his pride? Deathmask was right: if Thren died, the biggest threat to his entire campaign would be eliminated. The Ash Guild was dangerous, but it was also powerful, resourceful...

Meeting Deathmask's eye, he opened his mouth to answer, and that's when the wall to his left exploded. Rock and dust filled the cellar. The four members of the Ash Guild fell back to the far wall, drawing daggers and readying magic.

"I must say, Death, I'm rather disappointed in you," said Tarlak as he walked through the rubble and into the cellar. "Not a single protection spell against scrying?"

"I cast one on Victor the moment I took him," Deathmask said as purple fire danced about his fingers.

"Not on Victor," Tarlak said, grinning. "On *you*. But the night's late, and such a mistake can be forgiven for how tired I'm sure you are. I'll take your guest off your hands so you can rest. He's such a troublemaker, isn't he?"

More arrived through the hole in the wall, some Victor recognized, some he didn't. The Watcher was the first, his sabers drawn, his face hidden in shadow. With him was a priestess of Ashhur, the wizard's sister, Delysia. He'd met her briefly, when he first came to ask Tarlak to cast wards about his home. Last was a short, stocky man with a beard, clunking down behind the others in a full suit of plate mail. The four faced off against the Ash Guild, who almost looked eager for a fight—all but Deathmask, who just looked amused.

"Such a dramatic display," Deathmask said. "But truly unnecessary. Did I not tell your pet assassin he would be safe with me?"

The Watcher slipped closer, and with a few quick swings of his sabers cut Victor free from the chair. His back stung when he stood, but Victor was thrilled to be able to move. Glancing to the Ash Guild, he dipped his head low.

"Thank you for the hospitality," he said.

"Anytime," Deathmask said, still looking more amused than upset that the Eschaton had come to save him.

"Come see us again," said the twins in unison.

Victor stepped through the blasted hole in the wall and earth, climbing up to the surface. The priestess took his arm, asked him if he was injured. Shaking his head, Victor glanced back, saw the Watcher remaining behind. The assassin said something to Deathmask, then followed.

"Take me to my men," Victor said to Tarlak. "I must let them know I am safe and well."

"We'll do that for you," Tarlak said. "But for now, you're coming with us. Your home isn't safe."

"I know. Your spell left a gaping hole in the wall."

Tarlak glanced back at the cellar.

"Indeed. Seems to be my specialty tonight."

"Damn fools," said the shorter fellow in armor. "What were they trying to do?"

"They were saving my life," Victor said, remembering his flight down the street, thieves in pursuit.

"Doubt that," the man snorted.

"Quiet, Brug," Tarlak said. He stopped them all there in the middle of the street. Victor didn't know why, but the wizard was twirling his hands about in odd motions.

"Deathmask doesn't have an altruistic bone in his body," the Watcher said, joining them. "If he's interested in you, enough to keep you alive, it's probably far worse than if he'd never noticed you at all."

"Thanks for the comforting words," Victor muttered. "My home was attacked, at least fifteen of my men are dead, and a madman has plans for me he's unwilling to share."

"Don't forget Thren Felhorn wants you dead," Brug said. "That should be up there too."

Victor glared at Brug, who seemed not to care.

"Done," Tarlak said, and with the word, the air split before him like a torn painting, revealing a swirling blue beneath. Victor stepped back, stunned. The tear grew, swirling with an unnatural light, until it was the size of a man. Without hesitation Tarlak stepped through, vanishing instead of appearing on the other side. His sister followed, then Brug. Before Victor could step through, the Watcher grabbed his wrist and held him still.

"We risk our lives by helping you," he said. "Do you understand that?"

Victor nodded. "I do."

"Good. Never forget it."

He shoved Victor into the portal. Victor's vision was flooded with stars, gravity twirled and reversed, and then he was landing on cold, hard earth. His stomach heaved, and he vomited uncontrollably. As he gasped for air, he looked up to see a large tower where rolling green hills met an expansive forest. Tarlak stood before him, hand outstretched, a grin on his face.

"Welcome back to the Eschaton Tower," the wizard said. "Now that I've saved your life at least twice by my count, I think it's time we re-discuss my fee..."

CHAPTER

11

Antonil Copernus surveyed what was left of the bodies and shook his head.

"What's that put the death total at?" he asked Sergan, his most trusted friend. The man was a ruffian in soldier's armor, big features, dirty hair, and an even bigger ax across his back. He was a good man, though, disciplined, and always willing to tell Antonil the truth no matter how little he wanted to hear it.

"Not the best at numbers," Sergan said, turning to spit. "Think we're getting beyond what I can count. About fifteen or so of Victor's men dead in and about his home. Twenty gray cloaks in there with them. Three or four on the way to here, and now this..."

Sergan gestured to the crater in the street, the corpses scattered about, some killed by fire, some maimed by heavy blows. They lay stinking amid the worn stone rubble, starting to rot beneath the rising sun.

"How many more died when that—whatever it is— happened? Fifteen? Eighteen?"

"Lord Victor was a fool to think they'd let him go unpunished," Antonil said. "Which of these bodies do you think is him?"

Sergan squinted at a few nearby, frowned. "Not seeing any wearing fancy-enough clothes. Might still be alive and cowering under a rock somewhere, though I doubt it'll mean shit. His fool's quest is over. Once he's done wiping his ass, he'll take the first wagon out of Veldaren, I guarantee it. Question is, what do we do? Pretty obvious the Spider Guild is the one responsible for all this. Think we could have the king declare them all under arrest?"

"Perhaps, if we wanted to send them all into hiding and make all our lives miserable for the next ten years." Antonil knelt before one of the bodies, picked up a torn scrap of gray cloth, rubbed the coarse material between his fingers. "Who killed the Spider Guild, though? Don't see any of Victor's guards having made it this far."

"I don't know, but whoever it was was doing us a service."

Antonil let out a grim laugh.

"Don't let Thren hear you say that. I'd hate to have to find myself a new trainer for the guard."

More city guards arrived from the castle, wheeling a cart behind them. At Sergan's orders they began loading up the dead and shifting aside the larger stones to reopen the road for travel. They'd be at it for hours, all to clean up the mess the attack had caused. The sun was rising above the city wall, reminding Antonil how tired he was, and how long a day he had ahead of him.

Antonil watched his soldiers work with a pall cast over his mood. He'd known this was coming. It seemed everyone in Veldaren *but*

Victor had known. But expecting it and actually seeing the anger and power of the underworld rising up to strike were two different things. And lest they risk all-out warfare on the streets, Antonil could do nothing about it. It used to be that the easy money made the guilds soft, but that seemed no longer to be the case. The Watcher had been the one to keep the more troublesome in line, but this was beyond him. Perhaps it was beyond them all.

"Something bothering you, beyond the obvious?" Sergan asked, coming back from the crater.

"If necessary, we could raise an army to battle off kingdoms, perhaps even the wrath of the elves," Antonil said. "Yet we are powerless against these thieves. How? Why?"

"Once the worm gets in the apple, it's near impossible to get out," Sergan said, smacking Antonil on the shoulder. "Our walls don't work against this enemy. They've got no boundaries, no diplomats, no castles to take or crops to burn. Just men, sticky fingers, and a frightening amount of daggers. Much as I'd like to have every one of them thieves stretched out before me in an open battlefield, they ain't that stupid. So we'll do what we can, with what we've got to work with."

"They're killing everyone who talks to Victor's men," Antonil said, revealing what had weighed most heavily on his heart.

"Thought you were posting guards?"

"It isn't enough. It never seems to be enough. My numbers are stretched thin as it is."

Sergan shrugged. "You'll think of something. You always do. And besides, weren't you listening? Victor's going to be halfway to Ker by this afternoon, and all the way to Mordeina by nightfall. There won't be any more witnesses to protect. In a few days, it'll all die down to the quiet little insanity we've learned to live with lately."

Antonil chuckled. "Forgive me, Sergan, but I have my doubts."

The weathered man raised an eyebrow, spit again.

"Why's that?"

In answer, Antonil pointed to where Lord Victor approached with a large retinue of his men, their armor gleaming in the morning light. Antonil bowed at his arrival, and Victor responded in kind.

"Good to see you safe and well," Antonil said.

"I'm surprised myself," Victor said before gesturing to his men. "Whatever help you need, my soldiers are here to offer it. Much of this is my fault, and I won't leave you to clean it up alone. Once it's done, we can resume the investigations."

Antonil managed to keep the surprise from his face and voice, but only because of a lifetime of discipline.

"You're still to remain in Veldaren?"

Victor clapped Antonil on the shoulder.

"I don't scare that easily. We'll use more caution, of course, take things a bit slower now that we know what lengths they will go to."

Antonil had Sergan dole out orders, then asked Victor if he'd join him for a moment so they could talk privately.

"Something wrong?" Victor asked as they put their backs to their men and walked along the barren street. It'd still be half an hour before they'd reopen it to foot traffic, and the solitude allowed Antonil to speak his mind.

"It's the men and women you've been bringing in to testify," Antonil began. "I've tried posting guards, but many go into hiding, and even the ones I do protect have been killed. Often my guards die with them."

Victor nodded while listening, and Antonil saw the hidden anger and frustration.

"Casualties of war, Captain," the lord said, but he couldn't quite keep his dismissive tone from wavering.

"Your war, not theirs."

Victor sighed. "What do you want me to do, Antonil? I won't leave, not after all this. Would you have me render their deaths pointless?"

"I'd have there be no deaths at all. Conduct these talks in secret. Give shelter among your soldiers for those who request it. Once we've weakened the guilds, these measures won't be necessary, but until then…"

"Enough," Victor said, his sharp tone startling Antonil. The guard captain watched as Victor turned away for a moment and stared at the crater in the street and the bodies being loaded onto the cart.

"I thought I was prepared," Victor said, his voice softening. "I thought I could bear the burden. And I still will, Antonil. I will bear it. But it is far heavier than I ever imagined."

"It will get worse before it gets better," Antonil said.

"I know," Victor said, turning back to him. "I will do what I can to hide the identity of those we bring in, whatever good it will do. Your king has already agreed to let me use his castle, so I will question everyone there. As for those in fear for their lives…"

He gestured down the street, where work had already begun to repair the wall of Victor's repurposed tavern.

"There are many rooms within, as well as space on the floor. Bring them there, until there is no room left."

"Will it be safe?" Antonil asked, thinking of the attack only hours prior.

"From the outside, yes," Victor said. "I can promise you that. But inside…I don't know. I invite assassins in with every man and woman I give shelter. I pray you understand the risk I take, and hope I never have reason to regret it."

"I'll have my men keep an eye on your place as well," Antonil said. "Just ask, Victor, and I will help you, so long as it protects this city and the people in it."

"What of your king?"

Antonil felt the corner of his mouth twitch, the closest to a smile he'd allow. "What of him?"

Victor offered his hand, and Antonil clasped it. "I would have us be friends rather than enemies," Victor said. "But tonight has done me well. I know how strong we must be to succeed. Trust me. Last night will not happen again."

Antonil nodded, wished the man well. Still, when he left to join Sergan, he did so with a heavy heart. Something about the way Victor had spoken his vow made the hair on the back of his neck itch. After near death and failure, Victor didn't show doubt, but instead hardened his resolve. Yet what could he do to the thief guilds that would be any worse than what he already did now?

"What do we do with the dead Spiders?" Sergan asked at his arrival. "Hold them for a day at the castle, let family members come and see if they recognize them?"

Antonil chewed on his lower lip. "Bury them all in a common grave, not a name given for any," he said. "They're enemies of the peace, enemies of our king. They deserve no better."

"Might piss 'em off."

Antonil laughed, and he waved his arms at the wreckage about them. "Any worse than they are now? Bury them, and forget them. We have a lot of work to do, and not anywhere near enough time to do it."

Nathaniel hovered around his mother in the early part of the morning, but her mind was clearly elsewhere. His attempts at talking to her always ended abruptly, her answers terse and distracted. Henris, the scribe sitting beside her, seemed more important, his questions to be given more thought. Terrance was also there, looking nervous and incredibly young next to the wrinkled old scribe. He didn't speak much, and only when the scribe directly asked him something. Nathaniel tried being more persistent, until Alyssa looked up from the table in her study and snapped at him.

"Must I make up tasks to gain a moment of peace?"

Nathaniel flinched, but he'd listened to Lord Gandrem's words closely, and knew childish fits were not becoming to him. He grabbed his stump of a right arm, just a small chunk of bone and skin coming down from his shoulder. Nervous, he drummed his fingers atop the bone as he did when he needed to distract himself. Alyssa saw this and immediately softened.

"Come here, Nathan," she said.

He walked closer and leaned his head against his mother's stomach as she wrapped her arms about him.

"You've endured troubled times before," she said. "This is one of them. I haven't forgotten you, though. Tonight I'll fetch us a bard, and pay him to dazzle us with a dozen songs. We'll listen together, and when he finishes you can tell me which was your favorite. You'd like that, wouldn't you?"

He nodded, and she kissed his forehead. "Go play," she said. "Otherwise I'll have John find you something to do."

"He'll just make me practice with my sword," he said. "He knows it gets heavy."

"That just means you need to practice more, until it feels like a part of your arm."

"Milady, may I ask the source of these imports?" Henris asked, pointing to one of what seemed like a thousand pieces of parchment. Alyssa turned back to the man, and Nathaniel knew it was his sign to leave. He wanted to stay, to stomp his foot and demand attention, but he imagined the way John would react should he hear about such a display.

"Yes, Mother," Nathaniel said, even though he doubted she heard him. At least her promise about the bard was exciting. He loved listening to their stories, most of them anyway. Some dwelt on lords and ladies, and who was in love with whom. They bored him to tears. The ones about dragons, paladins, orcs, wolf-men, and other creatures of the Vile Wedge... those were the ones that kept him up far past his bedtime, wide-eyed in the lap of his mother. He especially loved hearing of the war between the gods, back during the creation of the world.

Nathaniel left the study so the adults could argue and bicker about money and paper, as John had once put it. Part of him felt sad knowing that fate awaited him when he got older. There'd be no charging into battle on a white horse as he dreamed. His missing arm alone ruined any chance of that. No, he'd bicker with old men and women, count coins until the moon was high, and trade things he did not have for things he would never see.

So much better the life the bards sang about.

While on his way to see Lord Gandrem, Nathaniel passed by the door to his grandmother's room. She must have seen him, for he heard her call his name. Rolling his eyes, Nathaniel turned around. He always felt awkward in his grandmother's presence. He didn't know her, had barely even heard of her until her sudden arrival, yet he was expected to act as if she were close family. It left him confused, unsure of how to act. And the way she looked at him, her eyes always watery even if she wasn't crying, made his stomach twist.

"Yes, Grandmother?" he asked, stepping into her room, which had been a guest bedroom mere weeks before. His grandmother lay in the center of the bed, as she often did.

Alyssa had said she had gone through many trials, and was left weak because of it. But she didn't seem weak to Nathaniel. Whenever he was alone with her her motions were quick, her words sharp, his grandmother a coiled spring wound up and eager to release.

"Please, just Melody," she said, shifting to the side so she might put her feet off the bed. She wore a thick homespun dress, the blue fabric clinging to her thin body. "Though it warms my heart to hear you say the word *grandmother*."

"Yes, ma'am."

She laughed as if this amused her, though he'd purposefully chosen not to call her Melody. "You look upset, dear," she said. "Is your mother still busy with that worm of Victor's?"

Despite himself he cracked a smile, thinking of Henris's scrunched-in face. "He doesn't look like a worm. He looks like one of the gophers groundskeeper Willis hates."

To his relief Melody laughed instead of getting upset at him for saying such a thing. "Watch your tongue in their presence," Melody said, gently easing herself off the bed. "But don't worry about me. I spent too much time in silence to care for tempered words and padded half-truths. I say if a man looks like a gopher, call him a gopher, don't you?"

Nathaniel nodded. He still felt awkward, but at least he could trust Melody to pay attention to him, and not care if he said something John would claim was "improper." His grandmother walked over to her expansive closet and opened the doors.

"Can you can keep a secret, Nathaniel?" she asked as she peered into its darkness.

"Yes, ma'am," he said. "Lord Gandrem says my word should be my bond, and to never break it."

"John's a smart man," Melody said. "And you should trust much of what he says. But I've spent a few afternoons with him, and he is lacking in knowledge of the gods. Tell me, Nathan, what do you know of Karak and Ashhur?"

As she asked this, she pulled a small wooden box from the far recesses of the closet. Nathaniel stepped closer, his curiosity too strong to resist. Her question itself, though, nearly deflated him. His teacher of numbers had been devoted to Ashhur, always telling Nathaniel lists of rules and expectations. It seemed nearly everything Nathaniel could do would make Ashhur sad for his doing it.

"My teacher made me memorize some things," Nathaniel reluctantly admitted.

"I don't mean prayers and sermons, Nathan. The gods are not figments, not boring lessons with names. They were real. They wielded blades, raised armies, and conquered the wild lands Dezrel used to be before their arrival."

Nathaniel's eyes widened. Now this was more like the bards' songs than the dry lecturing of his teacher. When Melody opened the box, his eyes widened farther, so much that he thought they'd bug out of his head. It was unlike anything he'd ever seen before. The base was a circle made of dark stone, with a soft indentation on either side. The center was almost like a bowl, but much too shallow. Lying in it were nine precious stones, each with a thin silver chain encircling it that attached to the base. The stones were all different: ruby, sapphire, emerald, topaz, even a couple he didn't recognize. Each one was the size of his thumb.

"When I was in the darkness, this was all I had to keep me company," she said. "Pull the curtains across the window, child. We must make it as dark in here as we can."

Nathaniel hurried to do as she said. Even accustomed to the lavish lifestyle of a house of the Trifect, he was still excited by the sheer wealth before him that Melody held. Whatever it was, it was certainly worth a fortune. That Leon would have allowed her to keep it was stunning. As he tugged on the curtains, he thought to ask her about her time spent imprisoned at Leon Connington's mansion, but dared not. Deep down he knew that he would not enjoy what he heard, and that it would involve things he was only starting to understand.

The curtains were long, and sewn thick, so that when Nathaniel returned to the closet, he had to hold his hand against the wall to guide him there until his eyes adjusted.

"Remember, Nathan," Melody said, "you must tell no one of this. This is a chrysarium, and is worth more than I could ever replace. I've long cherished it, so do not make me feel foolish for showing such a young child."

"I'm not so young," Nathaniel said, puffing out his chest. He caught a smile from her, just a crease in the shadows, and then she lifted the chrysarium. Her thumbs and palms pressed against the grooves on the sides, the rest of her fingers holding it from beneath. Melody's eyes closed, and he heard her whispering. The words were too low and quick for him to understand, but he felt something strange and foreign building in his chest. Panic struck him, and he wanted to flee, but before he could work up the nerve, the gems began to shine.

It was soft at first, just a flicker of color, like sparks of tinder on a fire not yet caught. The emerald shimmered, a deep glow growing in strength from the very center of the gem. Next was the ruby, its blood-red light swirling within, as if it were filled with a smoky liquid. One by one the rest lit up, their light growing in strength as his grandmother continued to pray. Nathaniel reached forward, pushed on by a compulsion to touch them, but a sudden fear overcame him. His hand dropped to his side.

"They shine by the power of my faith," Melody said, pausing for a moment to catch her breath. Even as she spoke, the glow began to fade. "Watch the center, Nathan, and open your heart to matters beyond this world. Let the spirit guide you, and you will see."

He didn't know what she meant, didn't understand what to do, or what the spirit was. But then she prayed again, louder, stronger. The gems shook in the chrysarium, flared bright, and then lifted in unison from the stone. They floated in the air, higher and higher, until the lengths of silver chain holding them stretched taut, halting their ascent. Nathaniel gaped, mouth open in wonder. So strange was this light. Though at times it was so bright that it hurt his eyes, it did not spread. The walls of the closet remained dark, and even when Nathaniel had brought his hand close to touch the gems, their light had not shone upon his skin. A strange hum filled his ears, though where it came from he did not know. It made his stomach tighten, but he could not stop it, could not leave.

In the center of the chrysarium, where it should have been brightest because of the gems, it was darker than anything he'd ever seen. *That is where the monsters live*, he thought, not knowing why. *That is where the stars hide.*

"Look deep," his grandmother instructed. Her voice was a songbird's over the din of a thunderstorm. Much as it frightened him, he looked inside, into the darkness, and therein he saw the first of his visions.

He saw a man crying in darkness, but when the man looked up, Nathaniel realized it was not a man but a woman. Her tears shone silver. Shadows turned, and another woman held her, her tears made of gold. Above them roared a lion, and from the creature's throat poured a thousand stars. They washed over the two, bathed them in light, and together they emerged as one being whose hands were stained with blood. Next came Veldaren, and he soared high above like a hawk. Below him the city burned, a hundred suns igniting within its depths. Nathaniel tried crying out, but he heard nothing of his voice, and was only dimly aware of his own body. Another vision, that of a hundred rows of wheat. They swayed in the wind, then withered and died as the moon rose. Reapers, their faces hidden by masks, collected the dead wheat, gathering it together in a great pile. When they set it aflame, Nathaniel felt the heat of it on his skin, felt sweat pour down his neck. The bonfire split, revealing a great canyon, its depths endless. Stomach churning, he spun about until he was standing on one side. On the other a great army gathered, muscular bodies of gray shadows dancing, lifting swords and axes high above their heads. And amid them, laughing, was a faceless man with eyes of fire.

"No more," Nathaniel begged as laughter filled his ears. "No more, no more, no more!"

Pain on the back of his head pulled him out, scattering the visions. He lay against the side of the closet, Melody cradling him. The chrysarium lay on the floor, looking like nothing out of the ordinary beyond the wealth of the gems.

"You poor boy," she whispered. "You poor, poor boy. I'm so sorry, I didn't know."

"It's all right," Nathaniel said, his voice coming out drowsy. His words were an immediate response, spoken from a desire to comfort her, for he knew something he'd done had frightened her. What was it? Laughter rang in his ears, and he felt his skin crawl.

"No, it isn't," she said. "The chrysarium always showed me pleasant images, fields of flowers and mountains in distant lands. I didn't know it would work so differently on one so young. I should have warned you, I should have made sure..."

She was crying, he realized.

"I'm fine, everything's fine," he said, standing so he might hug her. She kissed his cheek, and he felt her tears brush against his skin.

"Thank you," she said, wiping them away. "I only meant to show you something wonderful. I fear Karak thought to use you for some other purpose. I caught only glimpses, but you saw a vision, Nathaniel. You witnessed the future yet to come. You should feel honored, for few are blessed with such a gift. You truly are a special child."

Nathaniel didn't feel special, or blessed. He felt awkward again, and the darkness of the room only made it worse. Most frighteningly, she had spoken the name of the dark god, the god who had enslaved Zusa and sent his paladins to kill Nathaniel's mother.

"Karak?" he whispered, unable to keep the word choked down. "That was from Karak?"

She must have seen his fear, for she stroked his cheek with her bony fingers.

"Whatever you know of him, I assure you, it is wrong," his grandmother whispered back. "I could tell you stories of his greatness, his power and mercy. It is his love that let me endure the darkness, for it is in darkness that Karak is most comfortable. That is where we are at our lowest, our most humble and willing to hear his voice."

"But Karak is the Lion," Nathaniel said. "He's fire, and he eats sinners."

Melody's smile was so sweet, so condescending.

"My dear child," she said, "there is so much you must learn."

He didn't want to learn. He didn't want to be in that dark

room. He wanted away from the chrysarium, wanted that horrible laughter to stop echoing in his ears.

"I should go attend to my duties," he said, rushing over to pull aside the curtains. When the room flooded with light, he trembled. The warmth of it felt divine on his skin, and it chased away the last image in his mind of those terrible burning eyes.

"What duties are those?" Melody asked, slowly rising.

"Lord Gandrem will have plenty ready for me," he said, drumming his fingers across the bone of his stump. "Thank you, Grandmother."

She smiled. "Remember, it is our secret," she said. "And please, don't forget what you've seen. A vision from the gods should never be ignored, nor forgotten. And if you need to talk about it..."

"I will," he said, still in a hurry. He wanted out. Just out. Opening the door, he fled the room, eager to be back in John Gandrem's world of chores, duty, and learning. He'd had a taste of what it meant to deal with the divine, and suddenly the tales of the bards seemed far away from the truth.

Come that night, and the bard's arrival, Nathaniel cuddled with his mother, listening to stories of doomed lovers, wars between lords, and the fall of dragons. Only once did the bard, a portly fellow in red, try to sing of Karak and Ashhur. Nathaniel frowned, and begged his mother to make him tell a tale of monsters, princes, even thieves and murderers, anything else but that.

CHAPTER

 12

Haern ran, forfeiting the rooftops for faster travel upon the roads. He'd gotten caught up tracking what turned out to be a false lead, just a guildless street rat trying to steal in Spider territory. Not the Widow, as Haern had first hoped. The time wasted meant he might miss his chance to speak with Alan. Legs pumping, he raced toward the southern wall. Alan's patrols varied, but every eight days he made sure to swing by a long stretch of the south wall, where there was little to steal, and even fewer eyes to see. For the most part, that was the only place Alan felt safe enough to talk.

And they certainly had much to talk about.

Since the attack against Victor, the city had settled into an unstable peace, a held breath before the next catastrophe. Victor's work continued, a steady picking at the various thief guilds and their numbers. Through it all, the guilds remained quiet. Haern wanted to know what Alan knew, what Thren was thinking after such a vicious loss. That, and the Widow had struck again, another Spider found mutilated. Despite their best attempts, none of the Eschaton had been able to stop it. The rest of the city was catching on to the murders, and for most it was just a cruel joke.

"Another went to see the Widow," he'd heard a guard say, and the rest laughed as they picked up the body and pocketed the silver and gold. It was a lead Haern knew he should pursue, though the task was daunting. Systematically questioning every prostitute both within and surrounding the Spider Guild's territory would take countless hours...

He shook his head. Even then it didn't explain the dead child on the Gemcroft property. Perhaps a housemaid cast off for some reason, forced to work the streets for a living? Haern resolved to question Alyssa later as he climbed to the rooftops. Too close now to risk being spotted, even with the clouded sky hiding the moon and stars. Despite his numerous contacts, Alan was the only one within the Spider Guild willing to give information to the Watcher, so great was the fear Thren Felhorn inspired. The two previous members he'd contacted had died horribly as examples to the rest.

All the more reason to be careful, Haern told himself. He slowed down his run and forced himself to carefully observe his surroundings. Far better he miss speaking to Alan for a few more days than get the man killed by his carelessness.

The southern district was the poorest of them all, and against the wall were dozens of little shanties, homes made of thin wood that looked as if a stiff breeze could knock them over. For a few months King Edwin had tried to scatter them, but they always came back, the hungry and homeless too adept at fleeing, too desperate to fear his threats. Because of this, few thieves bothered to patrol the area. What was there to steal, or prevent another guild from stealing? With the night so deep, all there were asleep, all but Alan. With a leisurely stroll he passed them by. Only after a quick whistle from Haern did he turn about, heading toward a corridor where shadows were at their deepest.

"You spotted?" Alan asked as Haern dropped to the street before him.

"If someone had spotted me, do you think we'd be talking?"

Alan grunted. "Confident, aren't we? You have my coin?"

"Hopefully you have something more useful than last time," Haern said, tossing him another bag. Alan caught it, stashed it away, and then leaned against a wall.

"Depends on what you consider useful. You just pay me to sing, anyway. Not my fault if you don't like what you hear. By the way, never, ever come to me again during the day. I thought someone had spotted us, but since Thren isn't eating my heart for dinner, it looks like I got off easy."

Haern fingered his sabers, not any more eager than Alan to have their meeting last very long.

"I'll try to be more considerate for your safety," he said. "How's Thren handling the loss?"

"Terribly. He's planning something big against Victor, but he's not telling us what, other than it has something to do with the Trifect as well. I think this Widow—whoever it is—is starting to wear on him. Our numbers are thin as it is. We don't need some crazy whore killing even more of us. Shit, it's even making me a little nervous to do my rounds."

"Why'd the Ash Guild ruin your attack?"

Alan shrugged. "Grudge? Amusement? Maybe Deathmask was bored, I don't know. I find it a poor use of time trying to guess what that madman is thinking. Might as well go hunting ghosts, or searching for dragons."

Haern frowned. "Will Thren turn on the Ash Guild for it?"

Alan shook his head. "Not yet, not unless they provoke him again. Thren says that's what everyone wants, to have the guilds killing each other while Victor goes about picking off the remains. He ain't falling for the bait."

Haern figured it also might have something to do with the catastrophic casualties Thren would suffer if he tried storming the Ash Guild's territory. Deathmask was as dangerous as he was elusive. At best it'd be a waste of time. At worst a death sentence. Haern kept such thoughts to himself, pulling his hood low and preparing to leave.

"Should you learn anything of the Widow, anything at all, make sure I know," he said.

"I learn anything, you can be sure—shit, get down!"

Before the curse was even off his lips, Haern had seen the widening of Alan's eyes and begun to roll. Even then it was too late. A heavy weight struck the back of his head. Stomach lurching, he fell forward, fighting off the coming waves of darkness. His sabers drawn by instinct, he turned to face his foe.

Grayson followed Alan with the ease of a man who had shadowed others a thousand times before. It had been years since he walked the streets of Veldaren, but they came back to him like an old friend. When Thren Felhorn was first establishing his reputation, Grayson had been there at his side, the two a vicious team. Every rival learned to leave them be, with those slow to learn dying in painful, and creative, ways. As for this songbird, Alan, the man had only a fraction of Thren's talent at masking his movements, at sticking to the shadows with an almost unnatural awareness of the flickering of light across cloak and flesh.

Go sing your pretty song, thought Grayson. *I have my own bird to catch.*

By the time they reached the southern wall, Grayson had let the thief slink farther and farther ahead. The Watcher had told Alan they'd meet there, and unless their conversation lasted only seconds, Grayson knew he'd have time. But his presence couldn't be known. Skulking through alleys, he found a spot where he could watch Alan patrol the wall. At last they both heard a whistle. Together they headed for the same building, albeit from different angles. Finding a way up, Grayson climbed to the rooftops and carefully made his way to the alley. Though his weight was great, he knew how to space his steps, how to shift his body, so that no sound might alert the two below.

At last he reached the edge. He drew his short swords, crouched low. He saw the Watcher and Alan talking. A smile spread across his face. Given all the rumors, the borderline worship the man received all the way to Mordeina, surely it would not be so easy to kill him?

Grayson leaped, already disappointed, as Alan let out a frightened cry. But the Watcher was faster than he'd expected. Unable to slash with his swords, Grayson kicked out his leg as he fell. His heel connected with the back of the Watcher's head, sending him sprawling. Grayson landed roughly, unable to brace because of his kick. Alan took the brief respite to flee to the entrance of the alley, but he still remained nearby, watching. The Watcher spun to his feet, drawing his blades. As he did, he coughed out a thin line of bile.

"I know a concussion when I see one," Grayson said, settling into a combat stance. His two swords tilted, looking almost puny compared to his large frame. "You should be running."

"That so?" the Watcher asked. His voice was like a whisper, but Grayson heard it clear as day. Instincts told him it was magic, and the way shadows hid the Watcher's face, regardless of the direction of the light, hinted at the hood's being the source.

"Consider it friendly advice from an equal," said Grayson. "Assuming you live up to your reputation, that is."

He stepped in and slashed, careful to keep one blade back to block in case of a counter. The Watcher spun into action, and with dizzying speed slashed at his attacks. Grayson found himself retreating, his eyes widening to take in the sight. He could tell the man was off balance, but that didn't stop him from pressing hard, pushing Grayson to his limits to keep up the blocks. The sound of steel hitting steel rang in his ears. Grayson kept circling, countering only when the moment presented itself. A realization grew in the back of his mind, becoming stronger and stronger with every cut and parry. The fight melded into something familiar, something Grayson remembered all too well from many years ago.

The Watcher fought like Thren Felhorn.

Not exactly, of course, but the fluidity of movement, the constant motion, the ability to turn from the defensive to the attack within the blink of an eye...it was Thren. It had to be. His build was the same, his height, even the reach of his arms. But that didn't make one lick of sense.

"Why?" he asked as he forced himself closer. Reach should have been his advantage, given his longer arms, but he knew from a thousand spars with Thren that shrinking the man's room to maneuver easily outweighed any advantage as simple as reach. The Watcher batted his sabers left and right, then spun about so his cloak blocked his movements. No fool, Grayson fell back, ready for the attack, but it did not come. Instead the Watcher retreated, falling to one knee as he vomited a second time.

"What madness leads you to this?" Grayson asked, welcoming the reprieve himself. His chest ached, and his heart pounded in his chest. "Was it a ploy to save face? Did you need someone else to blame for ending your little war? Or do you like the idea of being paid twice to keep the peace?"

"What are you talking about?" the Watcher asked.

"Don't lie to me. Take off that hood and show me your damn face, Thren. I know it's you."

The way the Watcher's whole body shook, his shoulders bobbing up and down, made Grayson think the man had fallen into a seizure. And then the sound of laughter reached his ears.

"Thren?" asked the Watcher as he stood, his sabers hanging low at his sides. "You think I'm *Thren*? I don't know who you are, or what stupidity sends you after me, but if you think I am him, then you are a greater fool than I can possibly imagine."

Grayson tensed for another lunge.

"Last chance," he said. "Take off the hood, show me your face, and I'll let you live. Otherwise..."

More laughter, wild, almost mad.

"So perceptive," he said. "Yet so stupid. You want to remove my hood? Come cut it off my shoulders."

Grayson charged, his long arms swinging. This time the Watcher was not so fast, his footing not so sure. The effects of the blow to his head were starting to grow more prominent. Twice he slammed into a side of the alley, miscalculating the angle of a dodge. Grayson pressed on, hammering him with his swords. The Watcher had speed, but Grayson had strength to back up his own skill, and with every blow he saw his opponent growing weaker.

The Watcher knew it too, and his sudden reversal nearly gutted Grayson where he stood. Spinning again to set his cloaks in motion, the Watcher lashed out once, twice, to keep him at bay, and then lunged. If he'd been a hair faster, his sabers would have connected, but Grayson twisted at the last moment. He felt pain across his side, but it was only a mild wound to the flesh, not the vital organs the tip had been aiming for. Letting the pain fuel his motions, Grayson wove his swords in a complex series of attacks. The Watcher tried to parry, but Grayson kept shifting the angles, making it harder and harder. At last, when victory was apparent, the Watcher tried to flee. It was sudden, quick, but Grayson was ready for it.

Out went his foot, tripping him. The Watcher stumbled, struggling to regain his balance. Too late. Grayson's short sword pierced his cloak, his shirt, stabbed through ribs, lung, and then out his back. When he yanked it free, blood splattered across the street. The Watcher let out a gasp, kept stumbling. Grayson did not hurry, knowing such a wound was most certainly fatal.

"Your choice, remember," Grayson said, slowly stalking after. "But you never knew when you were beaten, did you? That's why you let your fight against the Trifect last until you were too weak to stop it. That's why you let Marion die..."

He'd expected the name of Thren's dead wife to elicit more emotion than it did, but then again, the man was clearly bleeding out before him. The Watcher continued limping, one hand along the wall, the other clutching his wound.

"Not...beaten...yet," he said, his voice sounding wet, strangled. He struck his hand against the wall, and a ring around his middle finger sparked with red light. Grayson tensed, expecting some sort of magical attack, but none came. When he started to relax was the moment the Watcher pulled a glass vial from a pocket hidden inside his cloak and flung it to the ground. Smoke exploded in all directions, thick enough to fill the alley. Grayson covered his eyes with his arm and swore. He knew the concoction, a fairly simple mixture any wizard could make and sell. He'd guarded his face quickly enough to avoid any of the burning sensations, but it would be a good thirty seconds before the smoke dissipated. Pushing through, he emerged on the far side. The Watcher was nowhere to be found.

"Die in private if you must," Grayson said, wiping a few stubborn tears from his eyes because of the smoke. "I wasn't going to mutilate your body. We're friends, remember?"

Back in the alley, Alan was gone as well. Grayson turned away, hardly caring. Whistling a tune, he traveled back to the Spider Guild's headquarters. The lone guard there saw him and wisely let him through. Grayson thought the place would be quiet, empty, but inside were over twenty men, drinking themselves into a stupor. Thren had canceled most of their patrols, he realized.

"Where's Thren?" he bellowed, interrupting their stories, their songs, and their games of chance. A few shot him looks, the rest unwilling to meet his gaze. "I said, where is Thren?"

"Here," Thren said, emerging from his private room. "What is so important that you must shout like a buffoon?"

No blood on his clothes, no wounds, not even a limp. Grayson grunted, surprised that he'd been so wrong.

"I killed him," Grayson said as Thren approached.

"Him?"

"The Watcher. He's dead."

For a moment total silence filled the tavern. Every man looked his way. Grayson saw the turmoil in Thren's eyes, saw the way he tightened the muscles in his body to carefully control his reaction.

"Are you certain?" he asked.

Grayson held up his short sword, still covered with blood. "Gutted front to back," he said. "Yeah. He's dead."

And with that the cheers began, calls for drinks and cries of celebration that were beautiful to Grayson's ears. And all the while, Thren glared, unwilling to show a shred of joy or gratitude.

"You're free of him," Grayson said. "Your slavery to the Trifect ends tonight if you wish it to. Or has the legendary thief grown afraid?"

"You've done what you wished," Thren said, just loud enough to be heard over the din. "When will you be returning to Mordeina?"

Grayson accepted an offered drink, downed half of it.

"I don't know, Thren," he said, grinning. "I'm the man who killed the Watcher. I feel like a bit of a hero. Maybe I should stick around, enjoy the rewards."

The two stared each other down. Grayson knew Thren was no fool, and could see the inevitable arrival of the Sun Guild signaled by Grayson's mere presence.

"You can't stop us," Grayson said softly.

"We'll see about that."

When he turned to leave, Thren grabbed his arm and held him. Grayson tensed, and shot the thief a cold glare.

"The Watcher's body," Thren asked. "Where is it?"

Grayson just gave him a smile.

"Just thought to be sure," Thren said. "It'd be terrible if he somehow survived. You'd truly look like a fool."

Grayson pulled himself free, marched for the door. Just by the exit, he noticed Alan drinking himself stupid at one of the tables. Alan's eyes met his, and the man jerked to his feet. Grayson stepped in his way, preventing him from escaping.

"In my guild you'd have your tongue cut out inch by inch, each piece shoved back down your throat until you drowned in blood," Grayson said, and he took a rapid step closer, startling the man. "But then again...this isn't my guild, is it?"

He laughed, shoved open the door to the outside. Lifting his arms to the moon, he let out a whoop, feeling so damn *alive*.

"The Watcher's dead!" he shouted. His deep voice echoed throughout the night. "Praise be, the Watcher's dead! We are free!"

He heard no cry in return, but he felt it flowing through the city's veins. Day was near, and when it arrived, they'd all listen, all wait to hear proof against the claim. But if none appeared, then come nightfall...

Four years of pent-up rage and vengeance would be unleashed across the city. This was everything he'd hoped for. Letting out another primal cry, he punched the air, his heart still pounding from the fight. The Watcher had been good, no question, but he'd been better. And if he was better, then nothing in Veldaren could stop them.

Not when the Suns came in from Mordeina, slipping through every crack and window. The city was ripe for the taking. Within days they would pluck it from the soft hands of the current guilds, and with an iron fist, show all of Dezrel who should truly be feared when the sun went down. It wasn't Thren. It wasn't the Watcher.

It was him.

CHAPTER

 13

When word reached Antonil, he pushed aside his morning meal and hurried to his room. A knot in his stomach, he put on his tunic with trembling hands. Over it went his armor; he needed the hard metal against his body to feel safe. If it was true...if the Watcher was dead...

He didn't want to think about it. Didn't want to acknowledge the cold truth. Victor had already stirred them into a frenzy. With the Watcher gone, his ability to keep the peace, whether it was symbolic or real, was over.

"Antonil," Sergan said, spotting him as he exited the castle.

"I have matters to attend to," Antonil said, not slowing.

"The king's looking for you," Sergan said. "He's talking about calling in soldiers from all corners of Dezrel, even leaving his throne to...sir, please, listen to me!"

"It sounds like Edwin needs comforting," Antonil said, spinning about and grabbing his friend by the shoulders. "Shame you weren't able to catch me before I left the castle."

Sergan swallowed, and his jaw clenched. "Understood, sir," he said.

In peace, and without escort, Antonil passed through the streets. He looked like any other guard, and earned himself hardly a second glance. Ears open, he listened to the conversations, the hushed whispers of the marketplace. All wondered the same thing. The Watcher was dead? What did that mean? A few were glad, and some blamed all the bloodshed on him, but most understood. Most remembered the chaos of Thren's decade-long personal war.

Antonil passed through the western gates of the city, then hooked off the beaten path. It wasn't often he went to the Eschaton Mercenaries, only when he needed to speak with the Watcher personally about something he'd done or witnessed. But this was something he had to know. Rumors and questions would not suffice, nor would he entrust this knowledge to a messenger. Eyes downcast, he approached their tower along the edge of the King's Forest. Pausing a moment before the door, he took a breath, then knocked.

"I am Sir Antonil, and I come to"—he hesitated a moment—"I come to speak with the Watcher."

The door opened halfway, and Tarlak peered out from within.

"You alone?" the wizard asked.

"I am."

"Good. Then come in."

Antonil stepped into the well-furnished bottom floor of the tower. A fire burned low in the fireplace. The blacksmith, Brug, sat beside it, a full mug of ale sitting ignored beside him as he stared into the fire. Both the priestess and the Watcher were gone.

"You must know why I am here," Antonil said as the door shut behind him.

"I know," Tarlak said as he headed toward the stairs. "Follow me."

On the fifth floor, Tarlak opened the door, and they stepped into the sparse room of the Watcher. He lay on his bed, pale, eyes closed, a blanket pulled all the way up to his neck. His hood was off, and Antonil looked upon his face. He was a handsome man, and that made his sickly look all the more noticeable. Beside his bed sat Delysia, dark circles under her eyes, her long red hair pulled back and slick with sweat. Blood covered her white robes.

"Try not to disturb him," the priestess said. "He needs his sleep."

"So he's alive?" Antonil asked, trying to keep his relief in check.

"Barely," Tarlak said, his voice low per Delysia's request. "We've been out the past few nights trying to find this Widow killer at Alyssa Gemcroft's expense. Last night Haern got himself in a fight. With whom, I have no idea. Throw a dart into a crowd and odds are high you'll hit someone who wants him dead."

It took Antonil a moment to realize the wizard had given him the Watcher's true name. Did that signify their trust, or how much Tarlak was truly worried for his friend? Of course Antonil had already seen his face...did his name really matter? He looked to the wounded man, repeated the name in his head. Haern...a simple, earthy name. For some reason he'd always imagined the Watcher coming from a line of kings or assassins. But carrying the name of poor farmers?

"How'd he survive?" Antonil asked. "Rumors are saying his killer watched him die."

"Who?" Tarlak asked, his voice rising. His fingers twitched, and they sparked with fire. "Who do they say it was?"

"His name is Grayson. I know little more than that."

Tarlak nodded, repeating the name as he looked down at Haern. "If you pull down his covers, you'll see burn marks around his middle finger. It was a ring I had Brug make for him. If he ever got in trouble, all he had to do was break the gem on top and I'd know where he was, sort of like a beacon. Found him hiding on a rooftop down in the southern district, bleeding like a stuck pig."

"How bad are his wounds?"

"They would have been fatal," Delysia said, slowly standing. She looked beyond exhausted. "Whoever this Grayson is, he was right to think him dead. He'd been stabbed through the side, pierced his lung so that it was filling up with blood. Something also hit the back of his head, and hard. If I hadn't been there, if I'd shown up even a minute later..."

She fell silent, looked back to where Haern lay asleep. Tarlak hugged her, kissed her forehead. "Sometimes it pays to have a priestess of Ashhur as a little sister," he said, forcing a smile.

Delysia smiled back, then took her seat once more at Haern's bedside. Tarlak grabbed Antonil by the arm and led him from the room.

"How long until he's better?" Antonil asked as the door shut behind them.

"Del's been praying at his side every few hours," Tarlak said. "She's a miracle worker, but this is taxing her far more than I'd like. By the time we found him, I honestly thought Haern was dead. It'll take two days, maybe three, before he's a shadow of his former self."

"That's two to three days too long," Antonil said as they returned to the bottom floor. "Everyone thinks this Grayson killed him. The truce between the guilds and the Trifect was already fraying. It is all but torn without him."

"What do you want me to do?" Tarlak asked, his temper flaring. "Prop him up with some rope and dance him about the rooftops? He's not leaving that bed. Announce to the city you've seen him, he's alive and well, and that you expect everything to go on as normal."

"They won't believe me, and you know it."

"Then get every soldier out into the streets, because tonight's going to be anarchy!"

"Will you two shut your traps?" Brug called from over by the fire. "Making it hard for a man to enjoy his drink."

Tarlak looked away as if ashamed. Antonil frowned, feeling similarly embarrassed.

"Forgive me," he said. "I only fear for the people I must protect."

"I understand," Tarlak said. "Whatever peace of mind this gives you, just know we'll be out there tonight, doing what we can. Just endure, and mitigate this. When Haern's fine and well, he'll come storming into the underworld like a demon-spawn of the Abyss, making every one of them cowardly buggers regret celebrating the Watcher's *death*."

Antonil nodded, giving the wizard a half-smile.

"You're a good man, Tarlak," he said. "I'll do what I can to make sure the king's treasury pays you well."

"Thought never crossed my mind," Tarlak said, giving him a wink. "Good luck, and pray to Ashhur we escape this madness unscathed."

Antonil bowed low, then stepped out. As the door shut behind him, he saw a strange woman sitting cross-legged just off the path. Her dress was plain, simple, but it looked poorly fitted, as if never worn by her before. She had olive skin and hair cut short. Two daggers twirled in her hands.

"Does he live?" she asked him.

Antonil's hand drifted to the hilt of his sword.

"Who?" he asked.

The woman stared at him, her head tilted to one side.

"Haern," she said at last. "I'm a friend."

Knowing his name had to mean something, Antonil decided, though he kept his hand on the hilt all the same.

"He's alive but hurt," he said. "I don't know how long until he recovers."

The woman nodded, stood. Her daggers slipped into her sash.

"I will try to quell the rumors," she said. "But it will not matter. They want to believe he's dead, even if for only a night. Blood will spill when the sun sets, Guard Captain. Do what you must to make it of the guilty, and not the innocent."

Lazily she stood and began walking toward the city. Antonil waited, not wanting to be near her as he traveled. Something about her wasn't quite right...

Shaking his head, he banished the thoughts and headed down the path, seeing no sign of her. Upon reaching the gates of Veldaren, he saluted the guards and denied their offer of an escort. Antonil was not yet ready to return to the castle. Instead he hurried to Victor's tavern, where he was allowed entrance with hardly a glance. Inside, Victor sat at a table, a map of Veldaren unrolled before him. Sef sat beside him, pointing at various districts and muttering. Upon Antonil's entrance they both stood.

"Forgive my intrusion," Antonil said. "I'm sure you've heard the talk of the day."

"We have," said Victor.

"I hate to do this, but my guards will not be enough. I don't know what coin I can guarantee, but..."

"Save your words," Victor said, sitting back down at the table. "My men will be out there, and I with them. We'll do everything we can to save this city. You won't be doing this alone."

"Thank you," Antonil said, feeling a brief glimmer of hope. Between the Eschaton, the city guard, and now Victor's men, they just might endure. "I am relieved to hear it."

"You shouldn't have doubted in the first place," Victor said. "Even if you never asked, I'd still be out there. I'm here for you, Antonil. For all of the city. By my life or death, we will see brighter days."

Antonil bowed low, convinced of the man's sincerity and honored by it.

"The Watcher is alive," he said before leaving. "We only need to buy him time."

"That's good news to hear," Victor said. "I feared his death would one day tear down everything, but I thought it many years in the distance. Shame on him for giving us such a scare. I'll have harsh words for him the next time we meet. I daresay I might even yell and call him selfish for nearly dying on us so early."

The lord grinned, and Antonil grinned back.

"Protect the peace," he said.

"You as well."

Antonil left, and with everything either prepared or set into motion, he went to the castle to endure his king's frightened rants and calls to action.

CHAPTER 14

Tarlak adjusted his hat, smoothed out his robes, and made sure his bag of spell components was fully stocked in case he needed some of his trickier spells. He took a deep breath, let it out, and then stepped into Haern's room. Delysia still sat at the edge of his bed, her red hair a rumpled mess. She saw him, straightened up.

"Are you leaving?" she asked.

"Sun's almost set. The party should start soon enough."

His sister nodded. "I'll get ready," she said.

Tarlak took another deep breath. This was the conversation he'd been dreading.

"You're not going," he said.

Delysia's eyes narrowed, and he saw her stubborn streak surfacing.

"I am not afraid," she said. "Nor am I helpless. You need all the help you can get tonight, and you know it. I will not sit idly by while you risk your lives."

"That's not it," Tarlak said, sitting down at the edge of Haern's bed. He gestured to Haern, who still slept. "You're needed here. If you get hurt, or captured, then his recovery will only take longer. Not sure how this happened, but right now Haern's the most important man in the city. We've got to get him up and stabbing people with the pointy end of those sabers."

He pulled off his hat, ran a hand through his hair.

"Besides, Sis, I'm already in over my head. Haern's the one who knows these people, who their leaders are, what they'll do. I just plan on roasting anyone who looks at me funny, and praying to Ashhur that I got a bad guy."

Delysia shifted so she sat beside him, and he wrapped his arm about her.

"I'm tired of this room," she said, letting out a laugh.

"I know. You don't look too good, either."

She elbowed him, and he mussed her hair in return. Their cheer was forced, and it died quickly. Tarlak looked to Haern, and he felt the weight of the night pressing on him.

"I think he'll wake soon," he said. "Someone should be here when he does, and I think he'll be happy that it's you. Let him know what's happening. He'll try to be stupid and leave the tower before he's ready, so don't let him sway you with his masculine charms."

Delysia kissed his cheek.

"I'll be praying for you," she said.

"Thanks. I'll need the help. And don't you worry. Me and Brug'll be back by dawn."

He waved good-bye, then climbed down the stairs to where Brug waited. The man was trying to adjust his plate mail, and grumbling all the while. Every movement he made rattled and creaked.

"Be hard to sneak up on them with you making a ruckus," Tarlak said, earning himself a glare.

"You see this armor?" Brug asked. "It's perfect. Made it myself. No dagger's slipping between these creases. Rather be last to the fight and live, than first and dead."

"With how much all that weighs, there won't be a fight left by the time you arrive anywhere."

Brug shrugged. "I'll still be alive. What's the problem?"

Tarlak chuckled. Couldn't argue with that.

"You ready?"

Brug gave his breastplate one more hard twist, then readied his punch daggers.

"Lead the way, magic pants, or are we taking a portal?"

"We're walking," Tarlak said. "I expect a long night ahead of us, and need to conserve every shred of energy."

Brug grunted. "Del not coming?"

"She's staying with Haern."

"So just you and me against the world, eh?" Brug asked, a cocky grin spreading across his face.

Tarlak nodded. "Looks like I'll have to rely on you to keep them off me. Must say, Brug, I think I miss Haern already."

Daverik hurried down the dark streets, his heart pounding in his chest. The sun's descent past the walls of the city was almost complete, and when it was, everything would erupt. The very air was thick with energy, a nervous excitement tinged with fury. For four years the Watcher had ruled over the city. Four years, and all its fear, all its resentment, was about to be released in an orgy of fire, theft, and murder.

It wasn't that Daverik was afraid of it, though. He was a priest of Karak, and his god's gifts were strong in him. No, he feared to miss his meeting, yet when he stumbled off Songbird Road past a shoemaker's shop he found that he was indeed too late.

"Damn it," he muttered, rubbing his chin. The temple was planning on keeping out of the upcoming festivities, but Daverik knew he could give orders to his faceless if he so desired. The question was, what path was the right one to take...

"You just missed him," said a deep voice, startling Daverik. He spun about to see Grayson leaning against the wall of the alley, mere feet away. Somehow Daverik had walked right past him without ever seeing him, something he knew should have been impossible; yet he also knew that with Grayson's skill he could have accomplished such a trick with ease.

"A shame," Daverik said. "Would you care to tell me what Laerek said?"

"About my actions tonight?" Grayson said, pushing off the wall. His hands rested comfortably on the hilts of his swords, dwarfing them with his giant fingers. "No, I won't tell you shit. But he did tell me what your part of tonight would be, just before he ran off to hide like he always does. Such a cowardly little bugger."

"Laerek has need of such caution," Daverik said, disliking the idea of such lowborn scum as Grayson criticizing a man like Laerek. "The goal we strive for is dangerous, and the lives of thousands rest on our hands."

"I don't give two shits about your goals," Grayson said. "I don't know them, don't want to know them. All I care about is that you do what you promised to do. The Sun Guild is taking over, and tonight will mark the beginning of the end for the piss-poor guilds that currently claim Veldaren."

"Exciting," Daverik said, his voice heavy with sarcasm. "But instead let us talk about what Laerek said my orders were to be."

"They're simple enough," Grayson said, pacing a few steps in the alley toward its exit. "I have need of your faceless. A party's going to take place in Alyssa Gemcroft's mansion, and I plan on playing host. They're to come with me, and help eliminate every last one of that miserable family line."

Daverik froze, thinking of Zusa and how she would react should Alyssa's life be in danger. Even worse, how she'd react upon seeing one of his faceless joining in the violence.

"No," he said.

"No?" asked Grayson. "Come now, we all have our orders, remember?"

"Your orders are wrong," Daverik said. "Alyssa was supposed to have time. Melody needs to..."

"And speaking of Melody," Grayson interrupted, "that's the other sticky measure. Your faceless are to ensure she doesn't die during all of the, well...excitement. Everyone else is fair game, but Melody needs out of there. I'm assuming she's important, at least to you or Laerek or whoever's actually running this game."

Daverik looked up and down the alley, frantically trying to think of a reason to deny the request. He didn't want Zusa's life in danger, and more important, he didn't want to perform such an obvious betrayal. If he was to awaken any dormant feelings she had for him, the worst thing he could do was piss her off... or get her killed.

"No," he said again. "I won't do it, Grayson. Your orders are wrong, or hasty, or unnecessary. My faceless are staying out of this."

It was as if a new man had come and replaced the old Grayson. His smile went dark, eyes malicious. His voice, already deep, went even deeper.

"No, they aren't," he said. "Alyssa has mercenaries, lots of them, and I expect both the city guard and that idiot Victor's men to be patrolling the streets. I need your faceless with me, need their particular talents to get past the walls. You have no say in this, no choice."

"You don't command me," Daverik said, wishing he could match the man's booming voice.

"Don't I?" Grayson asked, taking a step closer. His hands had drifted back down to his swords, his fingers curling around the metal.

"I am far from helpless," Daverik said, and dark fire smoldered across his hands. He met Grayson's eyes, saw the bitter amusement in them.

"You're not," said Grayson. "But are you faster?"

Daverik looked to the blades, back to his eyes, and then let the fire extinguish itself.

"They'll be there," he said, letting out a breath he hadn't known he'd been holding.

"Good man!" Grayson said, and suddenly he was charming again, all smiles and white teeth. "I knew I could count on you. Just trust Laerek to know what he's doing. He might be a young jittery bastard, but at least he's a man with a plan, right?"

Daverik had no desire for banter, and his face was locked in a frown as he made to leave, his mind racing for ways to somehow turn events to his desire, or even outright betray Grayson. But it seemed Grayson was no fool as to that either.

"And Daverik," he said, grabbing his shoulder. "Your little girls don't show up, then I go to the temple myself. Tell me, what would the rest of your fellow priests think if I tell them who you're working for? I'm thinking all these midnight visits wouldn't be necessary if they approved. Am I right?"

Daverik's glare was answer enough. The big man laughed, pushed him away.

"Get on out," he said. "There's not much time left, and I have a rabble to rouse."

"Have fun," Daverik muttered, rushing back toward the temple.

"Fun?" cried Grayson. "Trust me, my friend, if there is one thing I will be having tonight, it is wonderful, bountiful, obscene amounts of fun!"

His laughter followed Daverik out of the alley, into the street, and all the way to the temple entrance. Each and every step, mocking, always mocking.

CHAPTER 15

Haern felt the darkness peeling away into layers of dreams that came and went. Within were friends and foes, even those long dead. As the dreams faded, he realized he slumbered, and a pain in his head suddenly roared to life. Slowly he opened his eyes, almost regretting the return. His skull throbbed, and the pain in his side was frightening in its strength. He tried to remember where he was, what he was doing. He was on a rooftop, hiding from his unknown assailant. No, there weren't any stars, so where...

"Haern?"

He knew that voice. Something soft and warm took his hand, and he looked down. Delysia's hand. It was her face he saw next, tears in her eyes.

"Del," he said, and despite his pain, his exhaustion, he smiled. "You found me."

"My brother did, to be fair. How do you feel?"

"Like I was run through by a bull. Do you have any water?"

A moment later she handed him a glass. He tried to sit up, but the movement was unbearable. Carefully he lay back down and sipped the cold water. It felt divine on his parched throat.

"How long?" he asked, setting it aside.

"Almost a full day. You lost a lot of blood, as well as took a vicious hit to your head."

"Yeah," Haern said, the attack replaying in his mind. "I remember that. Felt like a horse kicked me. Could hardly see straight afterward. Where's Tarlak?"

He saw a shadow cross over her face.

"Don't worry about that right now. You need to rest."

Haern frowned. "Something wrong? Is he all right?"

She nodded, but still refused to say anything. He tried to think through his headache. He'd been bleeding, inches from death, by the time he fled from his attacker. What was the reason for the attack? Did the man work for the guilds, perhaps one of the three families of the Trifect? And what in blazes was Tarlak out there doing that worried Delysia so?

"Tarlak's not searching for the Widow," he said. "You'd tell me that. What's going on, Del?"

She dipped a washcloth in a basin at her feet, then wiped his forehead. The cold water felt glorious, and he tried to relax as she dipped it again, this time moving it across his neck.

"The man who attacked you," she said hesitantly. "His name is Grayson. He told all the guilds that he'd killed you, and they believed him."

Haern felt his blood chill.

"How bad is it out there?" he asked.

She shook her head, clenched her teeth. Into the basin went the washcloth.

"I can see the fires from the window," she said. "Beyond that... I don't know."

Haern curled his hands into fists. As his heart pounded, a bright light flashed across his eyes, and his headache intensified tenfold. He clenched his eyes shut, let out a gasp. Immediately Delysia's hands were upon his face, still cold from the water. He heard whispers of a prayer, and a distant ringing of an unearthly bell. Waiting out the pain, he focused on her touch, until at last her fingers pulled away, and the pain with them.

"I know you were stabbed deep," he heard her say. "But the blow to your head worries me more. I never saw this when at the temple, but I did hear of warriors who suffered symptoms such as yours. It can last for days, if not weeks or months. You need to rest. I'll do what I can, I promise."

The thought of enduring such headaches, of feeling that pain throbbing from the top of his head down to his feet for weeks, was horrifying. He remembered how when he was fighting Grayson his balance had consistently eluded him, and at times his vision had even gone blank. How could he be the Watcher under such a handicap? How could he tame the chaos Tarlak was out there struggling against while he lay there stricken?

"He was right," Haern said, his voice a harsh whisper. "Damn it, he was right."

"Who?" she asked.

"Victor. He said this would happen. He knew I'd fail like this one day. He knew it. I was a fool to think I could control them. To think I could do this forever."

A sudden cough hit him, and he turned to one side. Each sharp breath hurt, and he coughed louder, harder. He spit blood across his white sheets, the rest dribbling down his lip.

"Shit," Haern said, seeing it. He lay back down and closed his eyes as he felt the beginning of another headache forming. Tears swelled, and he was too sick to stop them. Delysia's cloth went back to work, cleaning away the blood, even dabbing at his tears.

"What am I doing?" he wondered aloud. "Was it ever right?"

"It isn't my place to tell you," Delysia said. "But I don't think you're a fool. I don't think you're a failure. You're allowed to err, Haern. No one would believe you human otherwise."

"And what if Tarlak dies out there tonight? Does that make me even more human?"

It was a cheap blow, but the worries were valid, and what weighed most heavily on his mind. It should be him out there bleeding and dying to protect the city. He'd given his life away as an orphaned child, sworn it while watching the Connington mansion burn years ago during the Bloody Kensgold. He could have kept killing. He could have continued his attempts to wipe them all out. But instead he'd forced peace. A fool's peace, the weight of it solely on his shoulders. And now it was breaking, and it seemed all the world had seen it coming.

"Stop this," Delysia said. Her voice was soft, wavering from the anger and determination behind it. "This isn't you. I didn't sit at your bedside praying so you could wallow in misery and doubt. I didn't do it because you are a fool, or I feared for my brother's safety."

"Then why?"

His eyes still closed, it took him a moment to realize what was happening. In answer, she knelt down over him, her hair cascading across his face, and then pressed her lips to his. He almost resisted, almost turned away, but could not. He kissed back, gently lifting a hand so he could touch her face. His mind whirled, too sick and tired to think of anything beyond the softness of her lips. When she pulled away, he finally dared open his eyes to look. She was tired, her eyes swollen and black from exhaustion, but through it all he saw a strength greater than his, and he clutched her hand tightly as if to never let it go.

"The world will continue without you," she told him. "People will kill, steal, bleed, and die, whether you live or not. Stop judging yourself by what you've done with your swords. If you would despair, remember those who love you. Let your life be judged by that instead."

"Do you love me, Delysia?" he whispered.

She met his eye, and he saw the hardness in her soften. She nodded, and he reached for her. She curled against his chest, and he let his hands surround her, let his face press against her hair as he kept his breathing controlled so he would not cough blood upon her. Together they lay there, not moving, not talking. The comfort of each other's presence was enough.

"I don't know if I can," Haern said after a time. "I've hurt everyone I loved. And I can't hurt you, Delysia. I could never live with myself if I did."

"I know," she whispered. "But I'll still be here. I always will be."

A memory came to him, from when they were just children, and he still in the care of his father. Together they'd met in secret on a rooftop, for Thren had denied him any knowledge of faith or love, all to make him the perfect killer. With Delysia, Haern had glimpsed a life with meaning, with purpose... only to have Thren shoot Delysia with an arrow, her bleeding body falling into his arms. That she'd survived at all was a miracle, a parting gift from another woman he'd loved before Thren had killed her. He thought of that moment, of how his cruel life had so vehemently rejected such a light as hers.

He couldn't bear the thought of it again. He couldn't hold her in his arms and watch her die. Whatever good in him existed would break. Did she know that? Did she understand?

"Let me sleep," he said.

Her fingers went to stroke his cheek, but hesitated just before. Before she could pull away, he leaned forward, forcing the touch, turning his face so she could cup him with her hand. She said nothing, only held him for a moment before leaving him alone in his room to sleep.

But instead of sleeping, he turned to one side and through the window watched the distant flicker of flame that spread throughout his beloved city, burning away like a hundred candles lit in memorial.

"These damn idiots have a funny way of celebrating," Brug muttered as he kicked a corpse that lay at his feet. Tarlak had to agree.

"Whatever they don't want, they're burning," Tarlak said, rubbing his throbbing temples. "Good thing they want nearly everything."

The two stood near the center of town, before a home with wrecked windows and a smashed-in door. Tarlak could only begin to guess why they'd chosen that particular place. The owner lay at the entrance, dragged out and throat cut. They'd arrived too late to do much of anything other than give the dead man vengeance. Three dead Wolves—just a fraction of the guilds roaming the night.

"It's all meager pickings," Brug said, wiping blood off his punch daggers. "Been out here for hours, and only small-time stuff. One of them's got to have something bigger planned. Maybe the Conningtons' place, or Alyssa's."

"Might not have anyplace big to hit," Tarlak said, walking aimlessly north. "Both have their places crawling with guards. It's the rest of the city that's vulnerable, but thankfully Victor and Antonil have their men running round like mad."

"Still a big city," Brug grumbled.

Tarlak shot his friend a look. "You sound disappointed."

Brug shrugged. "Was hoping to gut a bunch of thieves. Only seems fair, given what they did to Haern. Instead they'd rather set fires, burn down some stalls, and then run like cowards. Pathetic."

"Their kind tends to not be known for their bravery."

They followed the road, listening for sounds of combat and keeping their eyes open for signs of fire. Much as he might mock Brug for it, Tarlak understood how he felt. They'd expected far more chaos, a true call to arms in celebration of the Watcher's death. The night was half over, and all they'd seen had been little worse than the food riots they'd had in years prior.

"Maybe all the patrols are actually working," Tarlak said.

"Haven't seen anything by the Spider Guild," Brug said.

"Ash Guild tore them up pretty bad. They might be sitting this one out."

Brug laughed. "Yeah. I believe that."

Tarlak shrugged. "Can always hope, right?"

A deep explosion roared from near the castle, hard enough to shake the ground they stood upon. Brug tapped his daggers together.

"Nope."

They hurried north, passing wrecked stalls, broken windows, and dark alleys that all seemed filled with men and women lurking within the shadows. Tarlak couldn't help but feel like they were waiting for something, just stalling for the true celebration. If anything, perhaps they were wondering if the Watcher would appear and prove the rumors untrue. Every spreading fire, every theft unpunished, only confirmed his absence.

But then again, that explosion had been really loud...

They rushed faster, and Tarlak saw smoke billowing near the castle.

"Makes no sense," he muttered. "Why attack the castle?"

"Not the castle," Brug said, and that's when Tarlak realized what they'd done. Stepping out to the wide space before the castle, where Victor had held his interrogations, he found the area filled with rubble and dirt. Several guards lay about, all dead. The west side of the city's prison had been blown open, and Tarlak recognized a magical explosion when he saw one.

What could be more symbolic than freeing all captive members of the guilds from a prison?

Too much time had passed between the explosion and their arrival. Whatever combat had taken place was long over. Men in tattered clothes flooded out, a few armed and dressed in the colors of the Hawk Guild amid their ranks, revealing the guild responsible.

"With the guard scattered across the city, too few must have been here to stop them," Brug said, clearly nervous at seeing so many.

Tarlak nodded in agreement. He lifted his hands, let fire surround them.

"Stop as many as possible," he said.

"Will do."

Brug charged ahead, trusting his plate mail to keep him safe. The prisoners and Hawks were fleeing west, away from Brug's and Tarlak's road. Knowing he needed to slow them to have a chance, Tarlak hurled a ball of fire over their heads, detonating it in the road beyond. It set fire to the street, as well as a nearby home. Tarlak winced, but figured one more blaze wouldn't hurt the city too badly. He hoped. Their route cut off, the prisoners veered in various directions, many having to turn about and retrace their steps to find another road. Tarlak clapped his hands, and a bolt of lightning struck in their center, killing two. More important was the confusion the light and sound made, giving Brug his chance to reach them.

He barreled through their numbers, head low, helmet leading. He punched and kicked with wild abandon. Tarlak knew his friend was not the best of fighters, but what he lacked in skill he made up in eagerness and stupidity. He didn't try to block attacks, nor avoid blows, just let them hit his armor and slide off. Blood soon covered his punch daggers. The escaped prisoners fled, but the Hawks among them converged, daggers and short swords ready.

"Keep 'em busy," Tarlak shouted, hurling bolts of ice from his palms. They slammed into the thinning crowd, bowling over men and women and then freezing them to the ground. A glance behind showed a squad of soldiers rushing their way. Tarlak grinned, glad for the help. Brug wouldn't last much longer. With a few well-placed spells, he flung small stones at blinding speeds, striking the Hawks who surrounded him and knocking them unconscious or dead.

Then the soldiers were rushing past, the symbol on their tunics that of the Kane family. It seemed they were smart enough to realize who was friend and who was foe. Ignoring him and Brug, they spread out to chase down the thieves. Tarlak ended his casting, watched as the soldiers pulled two thieves off Brug, who, apart from a multitude of bruises, was no worse for wear.

One of the men gathered a group of five and then passed by, abandoning the chase, and Tarlak recognized his face well.

"Victor?" he asked.

Victor turned, hand on his sword until he realized who it was.

"The people here are in your debt," Victor said, saluting quickly before hurrying on.

"Wait," Tarlak said, falling in step. "What's going on? You need to help us find the escaped..."

"Alyssa Gemcroft's mansion is on fire," Victor said over his shoulder.

"What?"

"Riot broke out, completely surrounded their estate. I went for the castle first, for the king and his guard are of more importance. Time is not on our side, wizard, and unless you have a spell to turn it backward, this night will not end well. It's the thief war all over again. Gods damn it, I should have returned years earlier."

Tarlak glanced back, saw Brug hurrying to catch up. Sighing, the wizard began casting a spell.

"If you want to get there now, then come with me," he said as a portal ripped open before him. Without waiting for their answer, he stepped through, to see the chaos that had overtaken the Gemcroft mansion.

CHAPTER 16

Zusa watched from the window of their second-story room as the crowd gathered about their gates. Alyssa stood beside her, a cold expression on her face.

"Do they blame me for this?" she asked. "Have they not forgiven me for the chaos my mercenaries caused?"

"People have long memories when they are suffering," Zusa said, scanning the crowd. She could not hear their individual cries, but she spotted those who were the most vehement and shouting the loudest. A few wore guild colors, all the same.

"The Spider Guild is behind this," she said. "Thren is turning their fear to his own ends."

"It doesn't matter who is behind it," Melody said. She stood at the other set of windows in the room, Nathaniel at her side. "They won't harm us, no matter what. I know it."

"My guards will be enough," Alyssa said, and Zusa caught the way her eyes narrowed when she saw how Melody tightly clutched Nathaniel's hand in hers. "They once tried to burn my home to the ground. They failed, and they will fail again."

"Of course they will," Zusa said, kissing Alyssa's cheek. "You have me."

She pushed open the window and leaped through it, the cold wind blowing across her hair. Landing with a roll, she sprinted until she reached a tall oak tree. Climbing its limbs with ease, she neared the top and, hidden among the leaves, scanned the crowd anew, taking in numbers and weaponry. They were in the hundreds, far outnumbering Alyssa's house guards. They were poorly geared, though, very few wielding any sort of weaponry beyond a torch or a knife.

More worrisome, though, was how she saw more than just the Spider Guild's cloaks among them, lurking at the outer edges of the crowd. Hawks, Wolves, Serpents... it seemed every guild but the Ash had come to play. Many more foes might be hidden in the nearby homes and alleys, and could strike from any angle. So far the gate held, despite the throng that pressed against it. Torches could do little to the stone fence surrounding the estate. So long as they did not bring out ladders and rope, or find a way to...

"No," she whispered. "Daverik, no!"

She could not move, too stunned by the betrayal. Four faceless women leaped over the crowd, their gray cloaks billowing behind them. They sailed over the fence with ease, landing among the handful of guards at the gate. Three of the four formed a perimeter, cutting and slashing with their daggers. Shadows bled from their bodies, giving them an unearthly, terrifying image. The fourth slashed the lock with both blades. Black sparks fell to the ground. The women leaped away.

Just like that the gates were open, and the furious crowd poured in like a wave. The house guards closed the gap as quickly as they could, their shields locking together and their swords stabbing, but they would soon be overrun. Zusa knew she must help them, but there was no way she could. The four faceless had rushed the mansion, leaping at various windows and smashing through. She thought of them running through the halls, searching, their daggers eager to take away the life of those she loved.

"Damn it all," she swore as she leaped from the tree. Arms wide, she sailed across the yard, propelled forward with strength born of magic. Karak's magic, which she would turn against his blind, foolish servants. Alyssa had closed the window, but Zusa crossed her arms at the last moment and crashed right on through. Glass cut her skin, tore at her wrappings, but she ignored the pain. Rolling to a stop on one knee, she looked to Alyssa, saw the growing fear in her eyes.

"It's not lost," Zusa said, rising. "Not yet."

The door opened, but it was not a faceless, only Lord Gandrem in his polished armor. In his left hand he held a sharpened sword.

"Milady," he said, tilting his head toward Melody Gemcroft. "Might I have the honor of standing at your side and protecting you with my life?"

"It's only an honor if you keep her alive," Zusa said. "By the window, now."

"Window?"

"Do as she says," Alyssa said. Zusa was glad to see that Nathaniel was back at her side. John glanced between them, still clearly confused, but he accepted the order of his hostess. He stood before the window Zusa had smashed, his weapon drawn, and overlooked the fight below.

Putting her back to them, Zusa closed the door to the room and leaned her side against it. Closing her eyes, she focused her senses, listened for the slightest sound that might reveal the presence of the faceless. She heard screams from all about the mansion, servants and guards fighting, fleeing, dying. Getting closer.

From the other side, she heard a soft exhalation of air.

Zusa somersaulted as the door was kicked open. She was curling in midair when the faceless woman rushed in, searching. Melody screamed. Nathaniel cried out. Before the woman could attack, Zusa landed between her and Alyssa.

"Stay back!" she screamed at John, who had turned to help. "Stay at the window!"

The faceless lowered her body, tensed for a lunge. Zusa recognized those hazel eyes, that small wiry frame.

There's Ezra, thought Zusa. *Where are the others?*

Ezra leaped at Melody, but it was a feint, and she curled back in. Zusa met her charge, having fully expected it. She knew Ezra's hatred of her, knew that she would attack no one else while in her presence. Their daggers collided, engaged in a dance Zusa knew she would win as she had before. But if the previous defeat weighed on Ezra's mind, it didn't show, for she pressed her attack with an unexpected ferocity. Zusa parried twice, tried to knee her foe, but Ezra shifted aside. Zusa continued on, rolling until she hit the wall, then used it to kick off. They met again, their bodies contorted and twisted in ways only they, unarmored and limber, could accomplish. Steel rang against steel. They collided, elbowing, striking, each twisting to absorb the hits of the other as their daggers continued to dance, seeking an opening.

Zusa found it first. Her dagger slashed across Ezra's thigh. As the injured woman tried to retreat, Zusa somersaulted, foot catching the underside of her chin. Ezra's head snapped back and she fell, rolling on instinct to avoid any follow-up attacks.

When she came to her feet, blood spread across the wrappings of her face. She hesitated, and her eyes flicked once to the window. That was all Zusa needed.

She was halfway there when another faceless came leaping feet first through the shattered window. Lord Gandrem was unprepared for the attack, which caught him full in the chest. He stumbled back, but to his credit he kept swinging, his long blade forcing the new attacker to keep her distance. Zusa didn't slow her approach in the slightest, and when close enough she leaped, slamming into the other woman with her shoulder. Together they tumbled out the window, falling.

Still holding the other tight, Zusa closed her eyes. They were falling at night, toward a ground littered with a hundred shadows cast by the few torches of the mob. She'd done this before, but never at such a great distance, never with another...

Demanding the power, whether from Karak or herself, she focused on a corner of the room she'd just leaped from, where the shadows were deepest. Shadows were but doorways to her if she was strong enough, and instead of hitting the ground, she and her opponent fell right through. They reappeared in the room, falling from the corner. Zusa twisted so she landed on top, her daggers piercing the faceless woman through the breast and throat. Abandoning the blades so she could continue moving without slowing, she swept the feet out from Ezra, who had turned on John following her departure.

John, surprised as he looked, was still no fool. His sword stabbed down, but Ezra was too fast, spinning on her back. The stab missed, and with impressive strength, she pushed off in a backward somersault. Zusa kneed and kicked her, felt bones break, but still the woman made it past, crumpling at the door to the room.

And at that door appeared two more faceless, shadows rolling off them like water.

Zusa looked to her daggers, still embedded in the corpse.

"You will not win tonight," she said, shifting so she stood beside John, the two of them protecting Alyssa and her family.

"Karak has decreed you an enemy of the faith," Ezra said, standing with the help of the other two. Her hazel eyes glared with a feverish intensity. "Your fate is already sealed. Without your faith you are nothing."

"Strange for a god of order to ally with thieves and rioters," Alyssa said. "What have I done to earn your ire?"

They received no answer. The three faceless fanned out, forcing the group tighter against the window. Zusa reached out a hand to John, her eyes never leaving her foes. Ezra was the smallest, the other two taller, and with longer reach. One in particular looked almost gangly due to her height, and the way the wrappings pulled tight about her body. The third looked strong, her body heavier than the others'. So far none showed any impatience, instead slowly advancing, watching for any tricks or the first sign of an attack.

"Cut my palm," Zusa told John, who did so despite clearly not understanding why. As the blood poured across her hand, Zusa clutched her cloak. Her body ached from the blows she and Ezra had exchanged, but despite it she grinned.

"You think I am nothing?" she asked as her gray cloak turned the color of blood, the redness spreading like dye in a glass of water. "You think I must beg Karak for strength? Come, faceless. Come, slaves. I will show you what power I have."

In unison the three attacked, and Zusa met them head on. Clutching an edge of her cloak, she twisted and spun, weaving through their thrusts and slashes so that none could cut her deeply. Her cloak itself billowed and curled as if it were a sentient thing. Its edges hardened like steel whenever touched by the women's daggers. Zusa kicked to her left, spun low, then slammed both fists against Ezra's chest. The others tried to trap her, but she vaulted high, landing by the corpse of the one she'd killed. Yanking free her daggers, she leaped fully into the offensive. Her cloak was just another weapon, and it cut into their skin like razor wire. The faceless retreated, parried and dodged. Their blood covered the floor.

They all forgot John Gandrem, all but Zusa, who forced the heavyset faceless into a retreat his way. His sword pierced her back, punched out the other side. The woman convulsed on the blade, then dropped to the ground. The other two froze, and as if to mock them, Zusa knelt and tore the wrappings from the dead woman's face, revealing her round cheeks, her dimpled face draining of color, her green eyes locked open in death.

"Look at her!" Zusa screamed. "*Look* at her! Tell me why such a face must be hidden! Tell me why such a beauty must die! Is Karak so petty as to hate us all? Do you think the priests tell you his true word? You are fools, you are chained, now *leave my family alone!*"

Ezra and the tall faceless glared at her, and she wondered if they would attack. She wanted them emotional, wanted them to rush into battle unprepared against her so she could finish them forever. But instead they ran, and she could not tell if it was cowardice or wisdom that made them do so.

Zusa let them go, for she felt her strength ebbing and a headache growing deep in her forehead. With their absence, Zusa's cloak returned to its dull gray color, and she limped over to Alyssa. A dozen shallow cuts bled across her body.

"You're safe," Zusa said, and she smiled. Alyssa caught her when she leaned forward, and Zusa accepted the embrace.

The sound of combat continued unabated despite the emptiness of the room. Looking out the window, Zusa saw the house guards completely overwhelmed, only a small force holding fast at the crowded entryway before the mansion door. The rest were dead or had retreated all the way into the building. Windows were smashed in from all directions, and nothing could be done to stop the rioters from pouring in, looters rushing out with treasures in hand.

"The castle guard will arrive soon," John said, wiping blood from his sword. "Surely they will not allow…"

"The city is like it is because the city guard has allowed it," Melody said, stepping away so she too could watch from the window. "We will find no salvation from them."

Zusa pulled free of Alyssa's embrace, kissed her forehead. "Shut and bar the door," she said to John. Without waiting for a response, she leaped once more from the window. The many below were just unarmed men, angry, confused, whipped into a fury by the thief guilds. Despite this, she had no pity for them as she descended, a whirling tornado of blades. They trespassed upon land not theirs, seeking to take what had never belonged to them and snuff out the life of those she loved. Let them die. Let them bleed out upon the grass. And that is what they did, those who did not scatter in time. Life after life she ended, losing herself in the flow of combat.

They fled from her, unable to overwhelm her with numbers and unable to defeat her with their simple weaponry. Zusa cut a bloody swath toward the guards at the door, who, despite their many wounds, held firm.

"Go inside!" she screamed at them. "Protect those within. I will hold the door!"

None looked happy with the command, but they knew her closeness to Alyssa, and the danger her daggers possessed. When they retreated inside, only Zusa remained in the yard. Turning about, she stared down the rioters. Many had begun to flee, overwhelmed by the carnage strewn about the place. The house guards had done their work well. Men and women still rushed the mansion, but most avoided her, choosing to crawl through the glass of broken windows rather than challenge her blades. Zusa shook her head, almost disappointed, but at least the mansion would be safe. The remaining house guards could handle a few looters and...

"This city is in the throes of a new birth!" boomed a deep voice outside the complex. Zusa looked, saw a large man dressed in clothes outside the norms of Veldaren, a triangular hat on his head. His left ear glittered with many rings running up and down the cartilage. "That there is blood and pain should not only be expected, but welcome! Our slavery ends tonight. The Watcher is dead, and the disgusting truce of this land breaks. Destroy those who once pretended to be your lords."

As he spoke, men of all guilds gathered around him, having hidden in alleys and homes to watch the carnage while the hungry, frustrated, and destitute did their work for them. They were at least two hundred, perhaps more, and they brandished crossbows and daggers laced with poison. Zusa stood before them, her whole body trembling with every tired breath. Whoever the strange man was, Zusa marked him, let his face burn into her memory.

"Those who pass through those gates will die," Zusa cried back, pointing a dagger. Her voice seemed minuscule compared to that of the giant who led them. "Come, then, if you are so eager to enter the Abyss."

With so many against her, and the city guard nowhere in sight, they were not afraid. They rushed in, all but their leader, who remained back to watch. Zusa flung open the door and pressed her back against it, using it as a shield as the crossbow bolts came flying. They thudded like a heavy rain. Zusa closed her eyes, felt tears in them. Damn it, not like this. What they'd do to Alyssa, to Nathaniel...

When the footsteps were almost near, she kicked the door back open and charged, willing to bleed, to die, to keep them safe for just a minute more. But to her surprise, she was not alone. Landing before the door, his body shrouded in gray cloaks, was a man who should not have been able to leave his bed, let alone tear into the forces assembled against them.

"Haern?" Zusa asked in the brief pause before she rushed to join him. They were terribly outnumbered, but they moved through the ranks with blinding speed, taking advantage of the sudden doubt and terror the Watcher's presence inspired. He should have been dead. This was their night to celebrate his execution. To have him appear, sabers hungry, suddenly put every plan of theirs in doubt.

After about thirty died, their progress slowed. Shock turned to fury and desperation, and now it was Zusa's turn to retreat, weaving from side to side to avoid the occasional crossbow bolt. Instead of putting their backs to the door, she and the Watcher fled inside. Together they slammed it shut, needing the brief reprieve to catch their breath. Zusa looked to the Watcher, still unable to believe it. He looked similar, had a similar build and height, but something was wrong. Much of his face was hidden in the shadows of his hood, and even his grin had that same amused yet tired edge to it. His hands, she realized. They were older, more callused and scarred.

"Who are you?" she asked. "You can't be him."

"I am who I need to be," said the imposter. He kept his voice low, but it was rougher than Haern's whisper. "Or would you prefer to fight them alone?"

The barred door halted them only a moment. The remaining house guards had retreated farther into the house, most likely to the upper floors where they could narrow down the conflict to a few choke points at the stairs. This left the windows unguarded, and the thieves leaped through them in a sudden wave. Zusa took one side, the Watcher the other. She parried a clumsy thrust, kicked her shin against the man's groin, and then slashed out his throat as he doubled over. Two more neared, and she flung herself at them, her exhaustion increasing her recklessness. Both scored minor wounds, but she accepted them to cut both down, each of her daggers burying into a throat.

An explosion roared from the outside, and suddenly there were no more coming through the windows.

"What's going on?" Zusa asked, turning. The Watcher stood at a window, grinning.

"Not everyone is so willing to play along with Grayson's farce," he said.

Not understanding, she opened the door to look out.

Lord Victor fought at the entrance to the mansion grounds, a squad of his men surrounding him. Amid his group she saw the yellow robes of the wizard Tarlak. Powerful magic flew from his fingertips, bolts of lightning and boulders of ice slamming across the corpse-covered yard. The various guilds turned on them, hoping to bury them quickly, but then the Ash Guild arrived as well. Somehow they'd gotten over the wall, and they methodically moved through the yard, wiping out those who neared. Dark fire leaped from Deathmask's hands, and Veliana shredded terrified men with her daggers. Whirling about them were the twins, preventing anyone from flanking.

"Let's rub salt in their wounds," the Watcher said, rushing out. Zusa followed, and together they chased down thieves who knew not where to retreat, for they had enemies on all sides. Eventually they fled toward the gate, enduring Tarlak's assault so they might push back against Victor's men and dash for the safety of the dark streets.

The Watcher leaped to the wall and climbed up, balancing himself so he stood in the gaps between the spikes without harm. As the chaos died down, and men fled in all directions, the Watcher lorded over it all, let every eye look upon him. Zusa sheathed her daggers, the battle over. As the Ash Guild met up with Victor's men, the Watcher leaped to the street and vanished. Deathmask gave a mock salute, and then he too made his exit.

Zusa waited, feeling so tired that standing seemed a burden, as Victor made his approach.

"We are safe," she told him. "My thanks for your arrival."

"I don't know how you lived," Victor said, glancing about. "Gods, it reeks of shit and blood. You'd think we fought a war."

Hundreds of corpses, all throughout the yard and mansion. It would take months to clean it all, she knew, and to completely banish the odor.

"We did fight a war," Zusa said, looking up to the window to see Alyssa peering down. "But we won."

"If you say so," Tarlak said, his attention still drawn outward. She knew what he had to be thinking.

"It seems the Watcher is not dead after all," she said, baiting a response.

"Seems like it," Tarlak said, but she heard the doubt in his voice, the confusion. It was no ploy of his. Whoever the imposter was, the Eschaton were not involved. What did that mean?

"I must go to my mistress," Zusa said, bowing low.

"I should return to my patrols," Victor said. "Though I think the bulk of the trouble has passed. Give Alyssa my regards."

Tarlak tipped his hat, and then they trudged off with their soldiers, leaving Alyssa to deal with the mess. Zusa tried not to think about it. Entering through the door, she quickly scanned the mansion, looking upon the destruction. Paintings were slashed or stolen, furniture broken. Every shred of silver or gold, from the candles to the dinnerware, had been taken. The bodies of servants and guards lay in every room, side by side with thieves and looters.

At the foot of the stairs she found Alyssa, come to survey the damage.

"We'll rebuild, replace it all," Zusa offered. "Your loved ones survived. That is what matters."

Alyssa slowly wrapped her arms about her, leaned her head against her breast, and cried.

"Ten years," she whispered. "Gods help us, ten years."

"Not this time," Zusa said, stroking her hair. "Not this time."

It was shallow comfort, a weak promise, but right then she had little else to offer.

CHAPTER 17

Grayson knew he should be infuriated by the defeat, but he was far too amused. He'd gathered together men of all guilds, united with promises of the Watcher's death and a luxurious future. At each guild he'd been treated like a prince, and cheered with raised glasses despite its knowing so little about him. Only a rare few had glanced his way with untrusting eyes, realizing what the others did not. He was a fearsome man, and a thief, but a thief from a distant nation, one with foreign guilds.

Foreign guilds eyeing Veldaren with hungry mouths open.

"To the Watcher's killer," said one of the members of the Spider Guild as Grayson stepped into the guild's tavern, the man lifting his glass in a mocking toast. Grayson grinned at him, the look sapping away whatever cheer the man had.

"I stuck my sword through his gut and out his back," Grayson said. "Perhaps this Watcher of yours is a devil after all. No man lives through that."

The thief was smart enough to say nothing, only shrug and resume drinking. Still grinning, Grayson looked about the tavern, counting numbers. A pathetic remnant of what they'd been, especially compared to when he and Thren had been working together so many years ago. Hardly a merchant would quake at seeing the ragtag group of fifteen men drinking and bandaging wounds. Thren would recruit like mad to replace his numbers, but it would take time. With so much death and conflict, and so little coin in return, he'd gain only the desperate and delusional.

Now that he thought of it...

He found Thren drinking with a group of three in a far corner. Stealing a drink from the man who had mocked him, Grayson guzzled it down as he walked over to Thren's table, slamming his empty cup atop the hard wood. Three of them jumped, but not Thren.

"So how goes your night?" Grayson asked, grin spreading.

"As poorly as your ill-conceived plan," Thren said, leaning back and looking as if he had not a care in the world. He couldn't pull off the image completely, though. Thren was never much of a bluffer, Grayson knew, never had been and never would be. His eyes always gave him away. Too much intensity.

"That so?" Grayson glared down at the man opposite Thren, who glanced at his guildleader.

"Go check and see if any others have made it back, Martin," Thren said.

Martin shrugged and gave up his seat so Grayson could take it.

"I must say, I thought things would go differently," Grayson said, his elbows on the table. "With the rioters loosening up the guard, should've had easy pickings. Sadly, looks like the looters got the bulk, and we just shed the blood."

"Blood that shouldn't have been shed," Thren said, tilting his head slightly. His eyes narrowed. "You are no master here, no leader. Whatever your influence with the Suns, this is Veldaren, not Mordeina."

"Don't remember you forbidding it," Grayson said, and he laughed at the way Thren twitched. He was furious, Grayson could tell, but something kept him in check. Was it the way the attack had failed? Perhaps, but with his guild suffering such losses, that couldn't be enough. Had to be something more. Had to be...

"So where were you during all this?" Grayson asked, looking over to the bar and frowning when he realized he would have to fetch a drink himself. "With you at our side, I daresay we still might have broken through. Might have even taken down the Watcher."

Thren stared him in the eye, not moving, not answering. So smug. It was answer enough.

"Yeah, guess it's foolish of me to think you'd have helped," Grayson said, standing. "You couldn't kill the Watcher all these years, doubt you'd be able to now. Shit, you'd probably take his place if you could."

It was as direct a challenge as he could make without proof. Instead of rattling Thren, it only made him smile.

"You've attempted to usurp control of my guild," Thren said as the thief on either side of him stood and reached for his weapons. "You lied about killing the Watcher, and led my men to their deaths in a battle you had no stake in. You are no longer welcome in my home. Go elsewhere, old friend, for you cannot stay here."

Grayson's hand drifted to his sword. All about, the tavern had gone deathly quiet. Hopelessly outnumbered, Grayson knew he could not win, not then.

"You fear me a threat, yet cannot run, so you would banish me instead," he said. "You are a coward. You've never had the strength to face an opponent that might defeat you. Keep pretending you're strong. Keep pretending you're in control. That's what you did when Marion died. Why not continue?"

Thren was on his feet in a heartbeat, short swords drawn.

"Say it," he said, ice in his voice. "Say what you've always wanted to say, so I can kill you."

"Say what?" Grayson asked, purposefully putting his back to Thren and walking to the exit. "That you killed my sister? I would if it was true, but it ain't."

He stopped at the door, no one having the courage to get in his way. He looked over his shoulder, gave Thren one last smirk.

"She killed herself the day she married you."

The door slammed shut behind him, and Grayson laughed. It'd been so long, he'd forgotten how great it felt to raise the ire of one so focused and controlled. But his humor hid the scars that Grayson himself had nearly forgotten. His poor Marion, in love with that fool. Now she was dead, and both her sons as well. All because of Thren.

It would be such a pleasure killing him.

Entertaining the image of himself plunging his sword through Thren's throat, Grayson made his way toward the southern district. He might be late, but that was of little concern to him. The others would not leave. They'd need to hear how things had gone down. Whistling a tune, he cut through the alleys until he reached Songbird Road. Keeping an eye out for the stores, when he saw the shoemaker's place he stepped into the alley beside it, all smiles to the two men who waited there for him.

"Your women performed admirably," Grayson told Daverik,

who glared at him. "Granted, four went in, and only two came out, but they got my friends past the gates and that's all that really mattered."

"A foolish waste," Daverik said, turning to the other man there with them. "And an order that never should have been given."

The man was a young and scrawny priest named Laerek. He wore plain brown pants and a white shirt, the only thing revealing his priestly nature being the necklace of the Lion that hung around his neck. His face flushed red, and at Daverik's glare he looked away. Grayson shook his head, hardly able to believe he was stuck taking orders from such a pip-squeak. The man was twitchy, never able to sit still. During their meetings his eyes were always flitting to the exits, the windows above, the rooftops. Gods, he'd probably give the moon a sideways glance if he thought there might be people watching from atop its pale glow.

"I only follow the commands sent to me," Laerek said. "Commands you yourselves agreed to follow, so do not take your anger out on me."

"Come now," Grayson said, putting his arm around Laerek. The man flinched at the touch. "You shouldn't be upset. I'd say tonight went fairly well."

"Was Alyssa killed?" Laerek asked.

"Of course not," Daverik said. "Zusa protected her from my faceless, and then Victor arrived with the Eschaton. Together they chased away the rioters."

"Don't forget the Ash Guild," Grayson added.

"Indeed," Daverik said coldly. "Yet another foe my faceless would have better served removing."

"Please," Laerek said, pulling away from Grayson. "I know this is difficult, but you two knew the dangers when we started. Right now we must adapt to the situation at hand until

I receive new orders. Grayson, tell me, who now remains the largest threat to your guild's take-over?"

Grayson crossed his arms, pretended to think even though the question wasn't difficult in the slightest.

"I'll be bringing in the crimleaf next," he said. "Doing that puts us at our most vulnerable, and out of everyone that threatens my plan, the Ash Guild is the most dangerous. They're unpredictable, powerful, and led by a madman. Beyond that, there's Lord Victor, who's proving both persistent and meddlesome. Oh, and the Eschaton Mercenaries. They showed last night the danger they pose if left unchecked."

Laerek bobbed his head up and down.

"So be it then. I didn't want to, but I must. I must."

Something about his tone worried Grayson, so he refused to let the matter die.

"Must what?" he asked.

Laerek met his eyes, looked away.

"The Bloodcrafts are currently in my master's employ. They've been waiting just outside the city."

Grayson let out a whistle.

"You brought those crazy bastards all the way from Mordeina? Must be more desperate than I thought."

For once the young priest was able to look in his eyes. For once Grayson saw the fear that drove him to their clandestine meetings, the faith that gave him the nerve to withstand being in the presence of the Sun Guild's second-most notorious killer.

"What we do, we do not just for Veldaren," he said. "All the world will never know the debt they will owe to us three if we succeed."

Grayson shrugged. He had no idea what their little goals were, but so long as his Sun Guild got to move into the city and take away all the wealth and power of its thief guilds, he was happy to play along.

"And if we fail?" he asked, mostly out of amusement.

"Then the world suffers and dies in darkness," Laerek said. "The Bloodcrafts will take care of the Ash Guild and the Eschaton. What about Lord Victor?"

"Victor is a fool," Daverik said. "Let his little crusade burn out on its own. Someone from the guilds will do our job for us and slip a bit of poison into his drink. Besides, no matter how hard he pretends, he's a stranger to this city. It's people like the Ash, who know its darker secrets, that we must fear first."

"Very well," Laerek said. "Good night, gentlemen. Carry on as before, and meet me in six days."

"Wait," Daverik said, just as Grayson and Laerek were about to leave. Grayson paused, glanced behind him as the two priests talked.

"What of Alyssa and Zusa?" Daverik asked. "I needed more time with Zusa. She's not ready to listen yet, not willing to remember..."

Laerek let out a sigh.

"Moving against Lady Gemcroft was...premature. My own fault for deciding it would be best to remove her now, when it seemed certain Grayson could overthrow the mansion during the riot. My apologies, Daverik. I will give you and Melody more time."

"Thank you," Daverik said, dipping his head low. Laerek did so in return, then rushed off to go wherever it was he stayed in the city. Grayson waited until Daverik caught up with him, then bumped him with his shoulder.

"Worried about your girlfriend?" he asked, face all teeth and smiles.

"You're a vile man," Daverik said, shaking his head. "And you could never understand my worries."

"Understand them more than you'll ever realize," Grayson said, laughing. "It's you who will never understand how simple and common your little puppy love is. Let the bitch go, and find yourself a nice whore. Keep her at your side until you can't afford her no more, and then see how much clearer your head is afterward. You might realize you don't quite miss Zusa so much after all."

The very mention of the woman's name seemed to spark a fire in the priest, and the earned glare was all the more rewarding for it.

"Careful," said Daverik. "One day you will go too far."

"And one day I won't be working for Laerek back there," Grayson said. "Then we'll see who needs to be careful. Just between you and me...I don't think I'm the one who'll have to watch his step. Come then, the city will be mine, the Sun Guild claiming every shred of territory. And you, well, you'll have your four faceless. Oh, I'm sorry. Two."

Still laughing, he put his back to Daverik and strolled into the dark streets of Veldaren.

Gods damn it, he thought, what a wonderful, wonderful night.

CHAPTER

18

Victor looked upon his tavern and sighed with relief. He'd left only a token guard, and he'd fully expected it to be a burned heap come morning instead of safe and sound. His head ached, and his armor felt as if it weighed a thousand pounds, but the night was done, the sun had risen above the walls, and at last he might have some rest.

"Get men sleeping in shifts, all that you can," he told Sef. "We'll need to be rested for tonight. There's no guarantee this one will be any better than the last."

"Course it won't," Sef said. Victor thought to reprimand him for the lack of respect, then let it go. They were all exhausted, their nerves shot. Pulling off pieces of his armor, Victor strode into his tavern. Within were around thirty men and women, people given shelter for fear of the guilds. Overnight it'd been closer to a hundred crammed in there, but most had work to do and mouths to feed. Cowering all day wasn't an option.

A few looked his way, and he nodded to them in return. One in particular, a man with long dark hair, rose from his chair. Several of the guards reached for their weapons, but the man lifted his hands to show he was unarmed.

"A word with Victor," the man said. "I know things, things you'll pay a lot to know, but I speak only to him."

Two of the guards were on him then, each grabbing an arm. They looked to Victor, seeking confirmation one way or the other. Victor rubbed his eyes and stepped off the stairs leading to the upper floor. His boots thudded in the crowded tavern.

"Come over here, and tell me your name."

The guards brought him near. The man bowed low.

"I won't give you my name, not with so many near," he said. "But for the past six years, I have served Thren Felhorn and his Spider Guild."

Victor glanced at the people under his protection, all watching with rapt attention. He frowned.

"Check him thoroughly for weapons," he told his guards. "Then send him up."

They saluted, and without another word Victor climbed the stairs to his room. He'd planned to change completely, but instead only removed his outer armor, leaving on the inner padding despite its stinking of sweat and blood. The washbasin had been recently filled, steam rising from the top. He washed his hands and face, the warm water feeling divine on his skin. The water was a brown mixture by the time he was done, and his door opened.

"Well, we're alone," Victor said, still holding a washcloth. In its folds was a slender dagger, which he kept carefully hidden. "I assume this is when you try to kill me?"

"Not at all," said the man as the guards shut the door behind him. "Killing isn't something I'm good at. Talking, really, and listening. That's what I do. My name's Alan. Pleasure to meet you at last, Victor. You've caused quite a stir."

Victor chuckled. "I think others have caused greater. It wasn't my men who stormed Lady Gemcroft's mansion last night. No, I do believe that was you."

Alan shrugged. "I wasn't there myself. Told you, killing ain't my thing."

Victor didn't care if the man had been or not, and given how badly his bed was crying out for him, he had no desire to argue.

"Why are you here, Alan?" he asked. "My time is short, and my temper shorter. Speak your mind, and then begone."

Victor noticed Alan held a copper coin, kept it turning between his thumb and forefinger. A nervous tic, perhaps?

"I don't know what you've been hoping to accomplish," Alan said, "but I doubt last night was it. If Thren rallies the guilds, we're looking at another war. That's something I don't want, and, truth be told, most people don't want. But so long as everyone's scared of Thren, well, he'll bend people his way eventually. A few rants, a few murders, and everyone will be foaming at the mouth. He's good at that."

"Make your point, thief," Victor said, still holding the dagger tight.

"My point? Fill my pockets with enough silver, and I'll tell you where he is. Not just him, either. The entire guild. Everyone knows the Spider Guild is responsible for the attack on Alyssa's. You want to stop this now, before it gets out of hand? Then pay up, and make your move."

Victor frowned, tried to think through his exhaustion. The man was right... the Spider Guild was widely being blamed for the attack, and there didn't exist a parchment long enough to list all of Thren's crimes. He'd not made any significant move on Thren yet because he'd wanted to weaken his guild first. Letting them think he'd take only small-timers in a doomed crusade had bought him precious time to slowly whittle away at their strength. But now things had come to a head, and blood soaked the streets. When he first marched into the city, he'd sworn to never work with any thief, but with such possible gain for so little…

"Can you promise he'll be there?" Victor asked.

"You know I can't," Alan said. "But there's a good chance. You got the guts to take it?"

Victor felt his pride being challenged. The copper coin spun faster between Alan's fingers.

"I'll pay you thirty silver now, thirty after we verify…"

"No," Alan said, shaking his head. "All now, or nothing. To be honest, Victor, I don't trust you to let me be after you have what you need. You pay me, I talk, and then we never see each other again."

"And what prevents me from imprisoning you now, and torturing the information out of you?"

Alan smirked. "Because that'd take far too much time. Thren'll be on the move, and if he hears you've got someone from his guild being interrogated, he'll move that much faster. Besides, if you think you can make me sell you Thren by tossing me in a cell, well, you're a damn fool. Pay me, or watch Veldaren burn."

Victor rubbed the stubble growing on his face, then pushed a knuckle against his lips. At last he moved to the door, walking past Alan. If there was to be any attack, it would be now, but Alan just let him by. After a knock, the door opened, and the guard peered in.

"Bring me a bag of silver," Victor told him. "Sixty pieces, now hurry."

The guard snapped to attention. When the door shut again, Victor turned to the thief.

"Now what?" he asked.

"Isn't it obvious?" Alan said. "We wait."

And they did. Victor walked to his bed and set down the cloth and dagger. Alan paced before him, trying not to look nervous but seeming so anyway. Victor watched him at all times, still not trusting him. It burned his gut to pay for information that should have been given freely, but times were growing desperate.

Another knock, and then a guard entered holding a brown leather bag. Victor took it, then tossed it over to Alan.

"There," he said. "Now talk."

"Corner of Iron and Wheat," Alan said. "It's made to look like an inn—the Thirsty Mule. Everyone should be there, recovering from last night's debacle. Now be a man of your word, and let me pass."

Victor sat down on his bed, stretched his arms out at his sides.

"Go," he said. "But before you do...how do I know you don't lie?"

A faint smile tugged at the side of Alan's mouth.

"There's easier ways to make money than this, Victor. Safer, too. Go to the Thirsty Mule. You won't be disappointed."

Victor chuckled. His hand slipped inside the washcloth, grabbing the hilt of the dagger. With a burst of speed he caught Alan flat-footed, slamming him with his shoulder. Together they rammed against the door, the tip of Victor's dagger pressing against the thief's throat. Guards cried out from the other side, but Victor called them off with a word.

"Where is Thren?" Victor screamed into his face. His dagger pressed harder against flesh, threatening to pierce it at any moment. "Where is he really?"

"I told you where he is," Alan insisted.

Victor stared into his eyes, daring him to lie, to give the slightest twitch revealing his guilt.

"One last time," Victor said, his voice dropping. "Where… is… Thren?"

Alan met his gaze, and he leaned closer so that the dagger drew a drop of blood.

"Threaten all you want," he said. "My words aren't changing. He's there."

Victor let him go, then shouted another order to his guards. "Get him out of here," he said.

Alan was all too eager to oblige. With him gone, Victor tossed the dagger atop his dresser and then rubbed his eyes. Truth or lie… truth or lie?

"Form an escort," he said at last, exiting his room and kissing good-bye his morning of rest. "I need to speak with Antonil immediately."

Victor met Antonil in the castle courtyard, the guard captain looking as tired as Victor felt. All around them rushed servants, soldiers, and merchants, all trying to assess the damage from the previous night's carnage and do their best to recover. Already a line stretched from one of the doors of the castle, those seeking an audience with the king.

"Good to see you escaped last night unscathed," Antonil said. His clothes were clean but unkempt, as if he'd dressed in a hurry. No doubt he had been trying to sleep when he'd heard of Victor's request. As much as Victor tried to feel bad for him, he knew they had a job to do, and each of them understood the requirements of such dedication to his position.

"A shame the rest of the city cannot say the same," Victor said, clasping Antonil's hand in greeting. "Please, forgive me for interrupting your morning, but I must act soon, and I need the help of your guard."

A note of caution entered Antonil's words.

"Act on what?"

"I know where Thren is," Victor said. "Him, and most likely the rest of his guild."

Antonil turned away and swore.

"You realize what this will do," he said.

"I know."

"This isn't some minor thief or merchant. Thren has killed *kings* before."

"And yet still he lives," Victor said, crossing his arms.

Antonil frowned, but could not argue that point. Pacing a few steps in either direction, he mulled over the thought.

"What exactly do you want?" he asked at last.

"This is something in which we cannot fail, and therefore every precaution we can take, we take. Between your city guard and my soldiers, we can seal off a dozen streets, and surround his hideout with a wall of swords and spears. Last night was the end of whatever peace Veldaren has known. Thren will not let this pass."

"How do you know that? I heard nothing of Thren last night, nor did anyone report his actions to my guard."

Victor shook his head, hardly believing what he was hearing.

"The man is a thief, a criminal, and a madman who has terrorized this city for years. Every shred of history says he will take this opportunity to make things worse, and you want to argue about how in a single night no one happened to see him? What are you afraid of?"

"What am I afraid of?" Antonil stopped his pacing and stepped close. "You weren't here during that long decade. At times I could barely patrol the streets because we were too busy pulling corpses out of homes and gutters. I had to put men at every single window of the castle, for Edwin was convinced he'd have his throat slit in the night. No matter what the crime, I could not get men to talk to me, nor my guard to investigate thoroughly, for doing so would just result in more dead. Every night it took a little piece of me to convince this city that just maybe they could sleep well. And now I see the same chaos erupting before me, and you call me a coward for fearing you'll fan the flames instead of smothering them?"

Victor endured his rant, and as memories flashed before his eyes, he breathed in deeply to stop his fists from shaking.

"I saw far more than you think," he told the guard captain. "I know what Veldaren was like. But you misunderstand me. I am doing this regardless of what you say. All I ask for is your help. If I must, I will bear the burden on my shoulders alone."

"Damn it, man," Antonil said. "My men are exhausted. Was there not enough death last night?"

This time it was Victor who could not control his anger.

"Not enough?" he asked. "No, there wasn't enough. Murderers and thieves still live. They still hold the heart of this city in their hands, and even brave men quiver at the thought of what they might do. No, the dying must go on, the blood must continue to flow, until the guilty are the ones filling the graveyards, *not* the innocent. Now will you help me or not?"

Antonil swore again, clearly unhappy. Victor waited him out, let him fume and think. At last the guard captain met his gaze.

"It's all on you," he said at last. "If this burns us, I'll have Edwin banish you faster than you can blink. Have I made myself clear?"

"Clear as day," Victor said. "Though it saddens me how quickly you forget that I and my men were out there last night alongside yours."

"Since your arrival, this city has gone to the Abyss," Antonil said, shaking his head. "Forgive me for not being so sure you're more help than burden."

Victor swallowed down his frustration and pride. Time would be his judge, not a mere soldier, regardless of his rank.

"Keep your faith in me," he said, once more offering his hand to Antonil. "Our freedom is coming. Trust me."

Letting out a sigh, Antonil clasped his wrist, then stepped back.

"So," he said. "Where is that bastard hiding, anyway?"

CHAPTER 19

Thren leaned back in his seat, feet up on the table. He drank alone. Martin had come over to talk, but he'd waved him away. The rest of his guild had gone to various rooms of the inn to lick their wounds, rest their eyes, and sleep with their whores. He didn't blame them. Not that he'd ever find himself a whore. To have his desires overcome him so fully that he'd pay to have them satisfied? No, he had better discipline than that. Besides, Marion was fresh in his mind, and it would be an insult to her memory to bed another woman now.

"Do you miss me, Marion?" he asked the reflection in his glass. "Or do you watch me even now? How many tears have you shed?"

She'd been a stunning woman, her beauty almost exotic. While Grayson's parents had both borne the dark skin common to those in Ker, Marion's father had been a soldier from Neldar instead. She'd inherited his brown hair, and the color of her skin had softened so that no matter where she went she stood out, his beautiful angel with sapphire eyes. She'd been no stranger to the life of a thief, and behind her well-crafted act of tenderness and humility, there'd been a will of iron. Of all the women he'd met, she'd been the only one he fully respected. The one time he'd struck her, she'd slapped him right back.

"Never told you," he muttered. "I wasn't mad, not then. I just wanted to know how you'd react. By the gods, you were fire in a dress."

He'd had too much to drink, he knew. What had started as a celebration had settled into quiet reminiscence as the guild turned in one by one. Much as Thren didn't want to admit it, Grayson's comment had cut deep, but of course the man had known it would. Even though it'd been many years since their parting, few knew him better than his old friend.

Former friend, Thren thought, correcting himself. Things had changed since Marion's death. Even then he'd known Grayson would never forgive him. More than a decade later, he now had his proof. His wife was dead, and his sons were lost to him. What remained of her in this world was in Thren's and Grayson's memories. Staring into his glass, he felt his stomach twist. Had Grayson told the truth about the Watcher? Was he really dead? If he was, that was just one more piece of Marion gone from the world, forever denied to him.

Thren let out a bitter laugh. Grayson had killed his own nephew. Would he even believe it if Thren told him?

The door opened, and the look on the man's face upon entering was enough to startle Thren to his feet.

"What is it?" he asked as the thief shut the door. Through his alcohol-addled mind, Thren forced a name to match the face. Ricki. That was it.

"Something ain't right," Ricki said, his squished oval face

glancing about the empty cellar. "Where's everyone? We need to get out, now!"

"Calm yourself," Thren said, taking a step toward him. "Speak clearly, and tell me what is going on."

"City guard's closing off streets all around here," Ricki said, tugging at the collar of his shirt. "Was coming back from the market, spending what little I got from the Gemcrofts' place, you know? Just barely snuck past while they was setting up, yelling at people to get in their homes."

"You think they're coming for us?" Thren asked, struggling to believe it. How would they even know of their location, let alone have the guts to make a move?

"They ain't alone," Ricki said, pulling open the door. "I saw Victor's men gathering far up Iron Road. Don't take much to figure out what they're doing. Looks like someone decided to take us out."

That was enough to spur Thren to action. He pushed Ricki aside, dashed up the stairs, and burst into the proper rooms of the inn.

"Wake everyone," he yelled at the innkeeper. "Now! You too, Ricki!"

They rushed toward the rooms on both floors, hollering at the top of their lungs. Meanwhile Thren tightened his cloak about himself and pulled its hood over his head. The more he looked like every other thief the better. He was no fool. Victor had no interest in scum like Ricki, or even a more talented man like Martin. No, they wanted him. Of course they wanted him. Question was, how did they know? Who had sold out their location?

Men and women began stumbling down the stairs and into the main hall, most drunk or in a stupor.

"Ready your things," Thren yelled to them. "Our lives are in danger. Soldiers come with swords!"

This awoke a fire in them. The inn grew more chaotic, and amid that, Thren went back to the door and glanced down the street. In the far distance he saw squads of soldiers approaching. He had thirty seconds, perhaps a minute at most, before he was surrounded.

Thren ducked back inside, found what was left of his guild anxiously awaiting orders. He looked to them all, and feeling his insides harden into stone, he gave those orders.

"This is not the end of my guild," he told them. "But wherever you go, whoever of you lives through this, toss aside your cloak and colors. I know your names, your faces, and will forever remember your vows. Listen, and wait. The Reaper cannot take me, the guard cannot break me, and no whoreson of a noble will defeat me. Not now. Not ever."

He saw the shock in their eyes, the disbelief. But Thren could see the writing on the wall, whether it was carved into the stone or written with blood. Someone plotted against him. Perhaps it was Victor. Perhaps it was one of the Trifect. It might even be the Widow who killed his men and mocked him afterward. Whoever it was, he needed to be found and killed. The lesson of the Watcher weighed heavy on Thren's mind. Free of all ties, one man alone could accomplish so much if he had the strength and will to do it.

"Go, and await my return," he told them, and that one word broke the spell. The shattered remnants of his guild rushed to the doors, a few returning to their rooms to grab their things. Thren did not wait, nor did he make for a door. Instead he climbed the stairs, having prepared for such an event. His room was at the far back of the upper floor, and within he stood on the bed, using its height to push against the ceiling. One of the boards gave way, lifting to reveal a hole in the roof. Climbing up, Thren replaced the board, then slunk toward the roof's edge. From there he looked down and surveyed the forces arrayed against him.

It wasn't good. They'd brought at least a hundred armed men, if not more. Every which way he looked, there was a squad of six to ten guarding a street. No doubt more lurked in the alleyways closer to the inn. Only the rooftops remained open to him, and the crossbows the various soldiers held made him nervous. Crouching lower, he waited just a moment to see how the chaos played out. His former guildmembers fled in all directions, like rats abandoning a sinking ship. The squads closed in and, more worryingly, none gave chase. It was a perfect net, tightening. Those who tried to make it past were attacked, and Thren saw several shot dead with crossbow bolts.

And then Victor's main force reached the inn, many carrying torches. They didn't enter. They didn't try to flush anyone out. Instead they set it aflame.

"Oh shit," Thren muttered. Whatever time he'd had was over. He'd hoped to lurk, perhaps even hide on the rooftop until the search ended, but now he had no choice. Every way was guarded. In every direction he turned, he saw armed men waiting. One after another of his guild surrendered, those not fast enough to avoid the squads. Others dove into windows and forced open doors as soldiers chased after. Thren wished them well, then drew his swords.

Either they'd kill him, or he'd kill them. There would be no capture, not for him. The fire grew, the smoke of it reaching the ceiling and the heat of it warming the wood beneath his feet. Despite it all Thren pulled his hood lower and grinned. How long had it been since he truly faced a worthy opponent?

His senses were heightened, his vision given a sudden clarity. With Victor, Grayson and his Suns, and now the Widow, he finally had a plethora to choose from. Before, he'd only had the Watcher, and his presence had been a blanket across Thren's ambitions, smothering him.

Now the Watcher was dead, and the weakness in his heart had died with it. The city was once more an enemy, a thing to cow and break. His complacency had nearly killed him, but it was not too late. He was not too old to face this, not yet. A thousand soldiers might swarm the streets, but they would not catch him. His son had burned bright, and in his own way made him proud, but at last it had come to end.

Arms out, he descended upon a squad of four that circled his side of the inn. Two died before he even landed, one sword piercing a soldier's back, the other slashing out another's throat. When he hit the ground he kicked out the legs of the third. The fourth turned on him, and he cried out. "Here!"

That cry was the last word he ever spoke. Thren batted aside a hasty block and then shoved a short sword through his mouth. That done, he pulled it free and ran. Though the various alleys would be guarded, he knew they were still his best bet. In the main streets they could surround him, call in help when they realized who he was. Rushing a nearby home, he leaped through a window as crossbow bolts thudded against its side. His landing jarred his shoulder, but he rolled to his feet, almost amused by the terror he saw on the faces of the family living there.

Cutting through one room, he kicked open a back door, emerging into an alley. Three men hurried toward him, one with a raised crossbow. Thren rushed them, leaping to one side to prevent a clear shot. Catapulting himself into the air, he kicked off the wall, sailing over the soldiers while upside down. His sword lashed out, cutting the string of the cross-bow as the soldier tried to follow him with his aim. Landing, he spun, swords weaving so that the remaining men fell back, expecting an attack.

But it was just a feint, and before the group realized it, he was already running. Another squad moved to cut him off up ahead, but Thren used a heavy barrel as a stepladder, leaping to grab the edge of a roof. Momentum swung him higher as more crossbow bolts pierced the air all about him. Rolling onto the roof, he took a moment to gasp for air, then lumbered back to a stand.

His city. His life. He knew it all too well, far better than any soldier. Without slowing he ran for the edge of the roof, legs pumping, heart pounding. Leaping off, he sailed through the air, crashing down on an awning stretched out from a building on the opposite side of the street. The fabric tore, but slowed him enough before he landed hard on the wares of a petty jewel crafter.

Thren laughed, rolled off, laughed some more. Tossing aside his cloak, he vanished into the thick market crowd, leaving the soldiers and the burning wreckage of his guild far behind.

CHAPTER 20

Nathaniel did his best to help, but given his diminutive size, and the sheer amount of things being transported from their mansion to Lord Connington's, he was just a burden to those lifting and carrying. So instead he decided to entertain his mother, and keep her mind off whatever bothered her. As they rode together in the litter he sat beside her, wrapped in her arms, and asked a thousand questions.

Would there be any children there?

Who had been the first lord of the Connington family?

What did their family crest look like?

Where'd they gotten their money?

Would his things be all right?

Did they have any interesting pets?

"Dear, if you're nervous, you can just say so," Alyssa said as he continued to ramble, and she struggled to keep up with her answers. Nathaniel shrugged and grinned at his mother.

"I'm not nervous. You're nervous. I bet you've never slept anywhere but your room, but I stayed at Lord Gandrem's."

His mother laughed, and it made all of Nathaniel's world brighter with it.

"I was fostered at various homes when I was your age, and that includes Lord Gandrem's stuffy old rooms. But you're right, I am nervous. Would you be a gentleman and hold my hand, lest I faint?"

Nathaniel stood up straighter, put on his most serious face.

"Whatever you would require, milady."

She laughed again, and his face cracked into a smile. So long as his mother wasn't crying, he'd be all right. They'd be just fine. His mother was strong, deep down he knew that. Seeing her upset, seeing her afraid as Zusa fought against the other strange ladies, had been far more frightening to him than the chaotic looters gathered at the gates.

The litter stopped, and in through the window climbed Zusa, having ridden on the top. She ruffled Nathan's hair, then turned to his mother.

"We're here," she said. "And true to his word, there are many, many guards."

They stepped out, and it seemed an army of servants awaited them. His mother's servants met them, exchanging looks and words with each other in hushed, quick tones. Nathaniel watched them, feeling as if he saw a glimpse of a world he'd been sheltered from. Some handed over belongings, others followed guides inside, carrying bags and armloads of clothes, shoes, belts, jewel boxes, and dusty heirlooms. Burlier men carried heavy trunks, smaller women food and supplies for baking. It was a whirlwind of things to Nathan, a stunning amount all to keep him fed, keep him happy, keep him well. He thought of the simplified existence John Gandrem led in his castle and wondered what he might say to such a chaotic sight. But John had stayed behind so he might ride with Melody to their new temporary home. The thought made Nathaniel uneasy for some reason he couldn't identify.

"I'll speak with Stephen about arrangements," Alyssa said to Zusa. "See if you can find him a room."

Zusa frowned but did not object. She offered Nathaniel a hand. He stared at it. She wore plain clothes, as if she were a servant. Try as he might, he could not remember ever having touched her bare skin before, just her wrappings. Feeling the eyes of his mother upon him, he took it, nodded for Zusa to lead the way. He did his best to hide his surprise at how soft her hand was. His mother kissed his forehead, and then they were away, crossing the expansive yard surrounded by fences and weaving through the bustle of servants and guards.

Once inside, Zusa looked down both sides of the hallway and frowned.

"Stephen has little family," she said. "Surely there must be plenty of rooms worthy of a little prince such as you."

"I'm not a prince."

Zusa smirked at that.

"Given the wealth of your mother, you might as well be one, Nathan."

A few of the house servants hurried past them, but Zusa seemed reluctant to bother them. Instead she picked a direction, and together they traveled deeper into the mansion. Nathaniel stared at the walls, mesmerized by the many paintings. Some were of fields and mountains, crystal-blue streams running through green hills. Others were of grim men and women, dressed in fine clothing of times past, smiles seeming such a rarity in these people of wealth.

Nathaniel frowned. Maybe it was just the way they wanted to look, to be remembered. Why was it so wrong to be remembered laughing, to be thought of as kind?

Of course he knew what John would have said to that. Those with power had no time for games and smiles. Too many others might suffer for it.

"Anywhere is fine," Nathaniel said when he realized Zusa was still searching for a room he might use.

"For you, perhaps," Zusa said, stopping a moment so she could duck her head between large double doors opening into a vast room. "But I will be keeping an eye on you while we are here, and I would have you sleep somewhere safe."

"There's guards all over," Nathaniel said as she tugged on his hand. "Mother said Lord Stephen even hired extra. Why wouldn't we be safe?"

Zusa pulled free one of her daggers and then spun low so she could grab his neck with one hand and press the tip of her blade against his throat with the other. Nathaniel didn't react, too stunned and confused. There in the dim, long hallway they were alone, the mansion strangely silent.

"There are a hundred guards outside these walls," Zusa whispered to him. "But not a one could stop me from killing you this second. Guards don't mean safety. Walls don't mean safety. We are safe only when we are strong enough to protect ourselves, and right now you are but a child. Until you are grown, I must protect you as well as your mother."

She stood, let go of his neck.

"But you'll protect me," he said. "How is that any different than Stephen's guards?"

"I protect you because I am loyal to your mother," she said, putting away her dagger. "But who are Stephen's guards loyal to?"

"To...to Stephen, but that doesn't mean they'll let something bad happen to us."

Zusa shook her head. "Always know the loyalties of the hands you put your life in. You will one day be a lord of the Trifect, Nathan. You cannot rely on the honor and decency of men to stay alive."

"So I should trust no one?" he asked. It sounded like a cruel lesson of an even crueler world that would await him when he grew older. Zusa stared at him, and he saw a bit of her hard façade fade. She knelt again, put her hands on his shoulders.

"Trust those you love, and that love you in return," she said. "It will hurt more if they betray you, but at least you'll still know joy."

Zusa nodded toward a simple door that looked almost quaint compared to that of most of the rooms they'd passed. "In there. Let us see what we find."

She took his hand again, and they stepped into a fairly plain room, just a bed with a naked mattress, a dresser for clothes, and a washbasin with a mirror in the corner. Zusa looked about, analyzing things in a way Nathaniel doubted he would ever understand. She checked the window, the door, beneath the bed, and then nodded.

"I must look outside first, but I feel this will be safe," she said. "The door is sturdy, and you can bolt it from within. The window is high, but you should be able to crawl through and land outside without breaking any bones. Those unfamiliar to the mansion will not think to find you in such a small, unadorned room."

"There's also a lot of shadows near the ceiling," Nathaniel said, and his look made Zusa smile.

"There's that too. If you are ever afraid, trust me to be in the dark corners, always ready to save you. Now stay here. I'll fetch some servants to bring you your things."

She left him there, and he stood before the plain bed and tried to pretend the room was just like home. It wasn't. The bedknobs were carved into roaring lions, their paws lifted into the air, their mouths open and baring their fangs. He shivered, thinking of those four wooden creatures protecting him while he slept at night. Zusa's words continued to haunt him, and he closed his door, shut the bolt. The room was quiet, and dark. Nathaniel sat on the bed and drummed his fingers against his stump. Time ticked along, and finally, unable to stand anymore, he lurched to his feet, flung open the bolt, and began wandering the halls.

In many ways the mansion felt familiar, built in a similar style to his mother's. But the tiny differences in the color of the stone, the texture of the carpet, added up to something that was a constant reminder of his status as a visitor. A large woman passed him by, arms full of dirty sheets, and she gave him a glare. She said nothing, and didn't stop him, so he hurried along. The hallway came to an end at a plain door, similar to that of the room Nathaniel stayed in. The main difference was that a small image had been carved into the wood, though he couldn't quite make it out. A cat, perhaps?

Curious, he tested the doorknob, found it unlocked. Unable to stop himself, he pushed the door open and stepped inside.

It was a child's room, similar in size to Nathaniel's. The bed was smaller, the window lower. All about the floor were scattered toys, little animals carved out of wood, each the size of his fist. There were no paintings, no markings, and something about the place made his hair stand on end. Hurrying to leave, he rushed through the door and bumped into a man, his head driving into the man's stomach. As arms pushed him back, Nathaniel let out a yelp, convinced that Zusa's words had been prophetic, and that he was about to be murdered within walls surrounded by a hundred guards. But instead it was a well-dressed man, not much taller than he. The man was young, and had a softness to his face that immediately removed any of Nathaniel's initial fear of harm.

"I'm sorry if I startled you," the young man said. He looked him over, his eyes lingering on the stump of his arm. "You must be Alyssa's boy, right? Nathaniel?"

Nathaniel nodded, self-consciously clutching the stump with his other hand. "I am," he said.

"I'm Stephen. So glad to meet you."

Stephen? Nathaniel realized who stood before him and nearly panicked. Here was their host, kind as could be, and he'd plowed headfirst into the lord's stomach because he'd been spooked by a few old children's toys. Nathaniel fell to one knee and bowed his head.

"Milord, I am honored to meet you. Please, forgive my poor greeting."

He wanted to say it, and nearly did.

Oh, and please, please don't tell my mother.

"Nothing to forgive," Stephen said, tilting his head to one side and giving him a look over. "Now stand up. It seems you wandered off, and others were starting to worry."

Nathaniel felt his neck flush. Hardly ten minutes into their new home and he was already in trouble. Not a good start to the day.

"I didn't mean to scare anyone," he mumbled.

Stephen put a hand on Nathaniel's shoulder, guiding him back down the hall. "I'm sure you didn't. Your mother is just nervous, what with the attack on her mansion. Most understandable, really."

Right before they turned a corner, Melody stepped around, and she sighed with relief at seeing the two. "You shouldn't run off as if you were a little street urchin," she said, but her words felt perfunctory. Nathaniel caught her eyes stealing to Stephen. Was she trying to gauge his reaction, see if he was upset?

"He was only studying the layout of the house, as any smart child would do," Stephen said, smiling down at Nathaniel. "Isn't that right?"

Nathaniel couldn't nod his head in agreement fast enough. Stephen let go of his shoulder, and at Melody's approach he opened his arms so the two might embrace.

"It is good to see you again," Melody said. "And I have no doubt as to the boy's intelligence, though he could use a bit more sense. But I should be kind. Anyone graced with visions should be expected to have his head more often in the clouds than on where one foot goes after the other."

Stephen cocked his head at that. "Visions? Do you mean...?"

"With my chrysarium," Melody said, and there was a hint of pride in her voice. "Truly, I have never seen one so blessed. His mother has taught him little of faith, and never taken him to temple. I think the chrysarium awakened his soul with a hunger."

Something about this seemed off, and Nathaniel didn't like it at all. He kept hoping to see Zusa coming around the corner to join them, daggers in hand. They spoke of the chrysarium, and the visions, and it made his mouth dry and his testicles shrivel thinking of what he'd seen.

Stephen knelt down before him. A subtle change had overcome him, that youthful innocence replaced with something more, something Nathaniel didn't understand.

"What did you see?" he asked. "Did you see Veldaren?"

He swallowed. Melody and Stephen were on either side of him, blocking the hallway. He felt trapped, and worse, the vision was returning, dominating his sight against his will.

"I did," he said. "At least, I think it was."

"What of it? Did it bloom, or burn?"

"Burn."

Like a thousand suns, he thought, but did not say it. Melody and Stephen shared a worried look, and he saw his grandmother take Stephen's hand.

"He was so frightened," Melody said. "I think…"

Stephen seemed to get it immediately, and he turned once more to Nathaniel.

"You saw *him*, didn't you?" he asked. "The dark man with the eyes of fire?"

Terror gripped Nathaniel's heart. He didn't want to think of it, didn't want to remember it. Tears ran down the sides of his face.

"I did," he whispered.

Stephen wrapped his arms about him, pulled him close against his breast. "Shush now," he said, gently stroking his hair. "It's all right. You poor child, you haven't slept well since, have you? I'll pray for you so that you can."

Stephen stood, and again he and his grandmother shared a lingering moment.

"We're almost out of time," he said. "It won't be long until the prophet makes his move. I'm not sure we'll be able to…"

He stopped as Alyssa came around the corner. "Nathan?" she said, and Stephen moved away so he could run to her. He wrapped his arm around her leg, felt her gently stroke his forehead. "Nathan, are you crying?"

"He felt guilty for running off," Stephen said. "I think he feared he embarrassed you because of it, or that I might be upset, which I can assure you I am not. My home is his now, as it is yours, until everything can be made right."

The eyes, thought Nathaniel, unable to stop the memory.

The tears had been of silver and gold, his face a shadow, but the eyes... the eyes...

The eyes of fire burned, focused on Veldaren, their essence consumed with fury and craving destruction. More and more gathered under the shadow's banner, and the silver tears fell like rain across the city. He heard a child crying, crying...

By the time the vision ended and he came to, he was lying on his back, his mother kneeling over him. All he could say was the same thing, over and over.

"I'm sorry. I'm sorry. I'm so sorry."

"I would not worry about it," Melody said later that day, both she and Alyssa holding thin glasses filled with wine. They relaxed in a private den of Stephen's mansion, free from the bustle of the servants and the movers and the private guards.

"It's hard not to," Alyssa said, thinking of the way Nathaniel had collapsed amid his crying. It still gave her shivers.

"Your son watched rioters gather at the gates, determined to kill him," Melody insisted. "And then he witnessed the slaughter as it unfolded. To go through all that, and then suffer the stress of moving into a new home, however temporarily? It is a lot for a boy his age. He just had a fit, that's all."

Perhaps, thought Alyssa, but she'd never seen Nathaniel act in such a way. He was always a quiet, thoughtful boy, not prone to crying or hysteria. Still, it had indeed been a rather awful week...

"I pray you are right," she said, wishing to put the moment out of her mind.

"Indeed," said her mother, "but to whom should you pray?"

At first Alyssa tried to laugh it off, gesturing with her glass. "To whichever god will listen," she said, feeling slightly uncomfortable.

Melody leaned forward in her red leather chair, a sudden eagerness coming over her. "The gods are not playthings we should cast our whims upon, Alyssa. They are real, they are powerful, and their intervention will always come with a cost. I asked whom you prayed to. It is not a question I ask lightly."

That slight discomfort became nearly unbearable. Alyssa focused on her drink, preferring that to the wide-eyed look of her mother. The gods...what did Alyssa know of the gods? Nothing.

Well, perhaps nothing...

"I do not pray to either of the brother gods," she said. "I know not enough of Ashhur for it to be honest or wise. As for Karak"—she shook her head—"I do know of him. I've heard enough stories of his servants to last a lifetime."

"Stories?" asked Melody, leaning back in her chair. "What stories? From whom?"

"Zusa once served in the temple," Alyssa said. "For daring to sleep with another man, she was stripped naked, beaten, and forced into servitude. Many years ago, when I first met her, we were also chased by a man in dark plate mail. One of Karak's paladins. He would have dragged me back to Veldaren, to a dungeon or to my death, I do not know. Zusa protected me from him, saved me from such a fate."

"What you know of Karak is twisted," Melody said, shaking her head. "The priests here, you must understand, they do not follow the right path. They do not understand the old ways..."

"And I don't care," Alyssa said, finally setting down her drink and looking her mother in the eye. "If you want me to pray to Karak, then you will be sorely disappointed. Pray to him yourself. In Zusa I have seen all I need to see of the perverse ugliness at the heart of your lion god."

Melody looked away, then rose from her chair.

"Forgive me," she said. "It is a bad time to discuss such things, and I am a poor vessel in my attempts."

"You're forgiven," Alyssa said, but she had to force out the words. For some reason she felt absolutely furious.

"I'll go see if our things are unpacked," her mother said, heading for the door.

"Mother," Alyssa said, stopping her before she could leave. "Never bring this up to me again."

"You're a grown woman," Melody said. "I understand."

"Nathaniel too."

Melody winced as if someone had pinched her neck.

"Of course. He is your son to raise."

She left, the door shutting hard behind her. Alyssa looked to the door, to her glass, and then on an impulse flung it into the fire. The shattering of the glass did little to improve her mood, sadly. Slowly she rubbed her temples, wishing she could erase all of the past two weeks, wishing she could go back to her simple life of her and Nathaniel, slowly growing older together as she prepared him to succeed her. Why did everything have to change, and so fast?

When someone knocked on the door, she wanted to yell for them to leave her be, but better manners prevailed.

"Yes?" she asked.

The door crept open, revealing Terrance Gemling's ashen face.

"My lady," he said. "I . . . there's something I must talk to you about."

"Then come in and talk," she told him. "It seems today is a day for me to listen to awkward talks."

Terrance clearly didn't understand, but he stepped inside, closed the door behind him, and then stood there. Alyssa gave him a look, then gestured to the chair before him.

"Sit," she said. "You'll just get on my nerves if you hover there by the door. Or must you prepare yourself for a fast retreat?"

She was trying to calm him down, but instead it seemed to make him all the more nervous. He started to talk, stammered, then stopped so he could sit down in the chair. Taking a deep breath, he put his hands to his face and slowly exhaled. Alyssa could hardly believe what she was seeing. He looked ready to cry. He was a bright man, and good with numbers, but before her was a shocking reminder of just how young he was.

"Terrance," she asked. "What is it? What's wrong?"

"I take full responsibility for this," he blurted. "If you wish, I'll go right now to the king and demand all punishments to be on my head."

Zusa's warning echoed in Alyssa's mind, and immediately she knew what it was that bothered him.

"What did you do?" she asked quietly.

He was crying fully now, and that made it difficult to understand him.

"My father's always insisted it was never a concern, and countless other lords get away with it. The gold we mint at our mines in Tyneham, and the taxes we're to pay on it... the numbers of what we've minted I've always kept low by depositing portions of it in John Gandrem's treasury in Felwood on the wagons' trips south."

Alyssa felt a chill spread through her chest.

"I take it the coin is later sent to us by John under the guise of something else?" she asked.

Terrance meekly nodded. "Gifts or payments for materials he never receives," the young man said.

Terrance hung his head as if preparing himself for the executioner's ax. Which, in truth, wasn't far off. Alyssa wanted to reprimand him, but that'd come later. He was a good man, and she'd trusted him for years now to manage her wealth. Compared to her previous adviser, Bertram, he was a genius. Plus, Bertram had attempted to stab Alyssa to death, whereas Terrance worshipped the ground she walked on. It was her own fault for not keeping a closer eye on things. She had very little doubt that what Terrance described was done by hundreds of others. Only hundreds of others didn't have a madman with an agenda poring over their every transaction page by page.

"Will Henris discover this?" she asked.

Terrance shrugged his shoulders. "I don't know. I've always kept a second set of books with the real amounts, and when Henris first arrived I kept him distracted, then destroyed the other books that night. But there's still the shipping records from John's castle. Henris is staying with Victor now, and those records are with him. I've disguised the gold as best I could on them, but if Henris looks closely..."

His voice trailed off. Alyssa swallowed, and despite the bitter irony, she said it anyway.

"Then we'll have to pray he doesn't take a closer look, won't we?"

CHAPTER

21

Haern woke to the sound of scraping steel. He bolted upward in his bed and immediately regretted it. A moment of vertigo doubled him over, and he coughed and heaved as his insides twisted. Beside him Brug sat up in his chair, dagger and whetstone in hand.

"Easy there," Brug said, reaching over and pushing Haern back down onto the bed. Haern lacked the strength to resist, and he slowed his breathing so his heartbeat might return to normal.

"Where's Delysia?" Haern asked.

Brug lifted an eyebrow at him and let out a grunt. "Forced her to take a rest," he said. "Been at your side nearly all night. It's midday now, in case you can't tell. You were out all morning."

Haern remembered the fires he'd seen, the chaos unfurling at his supposed death.

"How'd everything go?" he asked.

Brug scraped the stone across his blade. "Well…"

He began talking, and Haern listened. He heard of the

smaller fires, the delay, and then of the larger attack on the dungeon. Haern shook his head at this, thinking of so many he'd put away managing to escape. It seemed the guilds were not just eager to celebrate, but wanted to wipe away every shred of his accomplishments in a single night.

"It was all just a feint, though," Brug said, putting down one dagger and grabbing the other. "The real fight was at Alyssa Gemcroft's. I'd say you should have been there, but from what my eyes were seeing, you already were."

Haern frowned, confused. "What do you mean?"

"I mean someone dressed up as you, grabbed similar swords, and went to town killing thieves to protect the Gemcroft mansion. Saw him, or you, or whatever, fighting alongside that Zusa girl who's always protecting Alyssa. He was damn good too. Might have fooled me if I hadn't seen the gaping hole in your chest earlier that morning. Not even Delysia can get someone up and running just a day after that."

Haern lay down and closed his eyes to think. Someone had impersonated him, but why? The obvious reason was to convince the town he was not, in fact, dead. But who benefited most? Who had the skill, and the physical ability, to so closely imitate him? It was a small list indeed, and none of the names made any sense.

"What of the fight?" he asked, trying to pull his mind back to other matters.

Brug shrugged. "Was just a huge mob for the most part. Plenty died, but at least a good chunk were thieves as well."

"Which guild?"

Brug scratched at his beard. "Now that I think of it...all of 'em. Alyssa must have pissed someone off good. Grudge from letting all those mercenaries loose, perhaps?"

It was possible, but didn't feel right.

"Thren's the only one who's been able to unite the guilds before," Haern said. "I wouldn't doubt he'd hold a grudge, but this feels too similar to the failed attack during the Bloody Kensgold. He would have learned from that. And this may sound crazy, but I think he likes things as they are. That's why he attacked Victor."

"He attacked Victor because Victor was taking down his men and cutting off their heads."

"Small-timers, minor thieves. He didn't like Victor threatening the delicate balance I've created."

Brug grunted, rocked his chair back and forth.

"You're starting to sound like that hit on your head really got to you worse than we thought. Listen to yourself. Are you saying Thren *likes* having you lord over the underworld? Why? Next you'll be saying that it was him pretending to be you last night."

Haern gave him a look, and Brug closed his eyes and rubbed his eyelids with his thick, callused fingers.

"Really? You actually think he did? If that's the case, then I don't know what's going on in Veldaren anymore. Everyone's losing their damn minds, you included."

Haern laughed. "Be useful, and get me something to eat."

As Brug left the room, muttering to himself, Haern closed his eyes and tried to relax. He felt the beginnings of another headache coming along, and if it was anything like the last, it'd be crippling. Shifting from side to side, he tested his wounds. The skin was tightening up, though when he lifted the bandages he found his stab wound was now a deep purple scar. Rocking back and forth didn't seem to strain it too badly, though it did make his muscles ache. Worse was how his balance still felt off. Even that slight motion sent his stomach looping.

Not too frightening, a foe who keeps vomiting mid-fight, thought Haern.

Brug returned carrying a small tray of food, and it was more cruelty than kindness. The smell was divine, and Haern's mouth watered, but his stomach heaved, and he turned to the side of his bed so he could vomit. No blood in it this time, so he tried to console himself with that fact.

"Thought it looked pretty good myself," Brug said, glancing down at the plate of carrots and beef. "Perhaps just some ale for now?"

Haern looked at the offered mug.

"Why not," he said. At least it would get rid of the foul taste in his mouth. He took a few swallows, just enough to clear his throat. Brug put the tray down beside his bed and settled back down in the chair.

"Tarlak said he's hearing some bizarre rumors coming in from the city," Brug said. "Looks like Victor moved against the Spider Guild. Those he caught are all claiming the same thing: Spider Guild's been disbanded, and Thren's vanished."

Haern lowered his drink, and his mouth opened and closed as his mind feebly attempted to make sense of what he'd heard.

"You can't be serious," he said dumbly.

"I'm not much for joking, Haern. I'm starting to think you might be right about Thren pretending he was you, because let's face it, he's completely falling apart."

Haern pressed his palms against his forehead. "What now?" Brug asked.

"Headache," Haern said, slowly breathing in and out. "Feels like someone stuck a knife in my brain, and every few minutes they can't help but give it a good twist."

"Del said that hit to your head was a nasty one. What smacked you, anyway? A brick?"

"A foot."

Brug snorted. "I'm not sure I want to meet the guy who did

it, then," he said, stealing Haern's mug and downing a third of it. "What's his heel made of, stone?"

The confrontation with the mysterious man came back to Haern, much as he didn't want it to. His attacker had shown no guild affiliations, at least not in any way Haern recognized. He'd been a giant man, dark-skinned, incredibly fast for his size...

"Can't stay like this," Haern said. "Still in the dark about too much. The Spider Guild's disbandment proves that. I need to find out what's going on. I need to know who's playing us all like fools."

Run, run little spider...

"You aren't going anywhere as is," Brug said. "At least give yourself another night to..."

Haern caught Brug glancing out the window, and whatever he saw gave him pause.

"What is it?"

He shifted in bed so he could look out. From his window in the tower they could both see the pathway stretching toward them from Veldaren. Walking alone on that path was a man, his lanky form wrapped in a thick red leather coat. A wide-brimmed hat colored crimson hung low over his face. Across his back, easily visible despite the hundreds of yards between them, was an enormous two-handed sword. A red ribbon fluttered from the hilt in a soft breeze.

"Friend of yours?" Brug asked.

Haern shook his head. "Perhaps he knows Tarlak?"

Something about the way he moved made both of them uneasy. The fashion of both the hat and the coat suggested he was an outsider, from far from Veldaren. Brug fetched his daggers, then moved to the door.

"Stay here," he said. "I'll find out what's going on."

Haern chuckled as the door closed.

Stay here?

He pushed himself out of bed, clutching the wall to keep his balance. Vertigo came over him a second time, but he fought through it. He'd been trained better than this, he thought, taught to overpower far greater. His father had supplied him with tutors, teachers, masters of both mind and body. So what if a man the size of an ox had nearly caved in his skull? He was still stronger.

All that determination still felt small compared to the pain in his temples, and it did nothing to reduce the obnoxious white glare that seemed to come off everything. But he forced it away, thrust it into the corners of his mind, let it ache but not distract. He found his shirt lying beside the bed, a hole still in it where he'd been stabbed. He put it on, then grabbed his cloak as well, tying it over his shoulders and then pulling the hood over his head. As the shadows covered his face, he felt his tension ease. No matter the injury, no matter all that had happened, he was still the Watcher. He was greater than this.

A glance out the window showed the man was almost to the tower. So far he had not drawn his blade. At the shorter distance, Haern could see strange markings tattooed across his neck and hands. Set into the hilt of his sword was an enormous crystal, clear as water. Haern could only guess its worth, but the estimate was staggering. Stopping just shy of the path to the door, the man looked up at the window, right at Haern. A wide smile spread across his face, which was half covered by lanky strands of blond hair. That smile was like an icicle to the eye.

"Eschaton!" the man shouted. His voice tore through the quiet afternoon, and it was strangely high-pitched. "I am Nicholas Bloodcraft, and I have come to kill all of you. If you surrender now, your death will be merciful, a swift, painless beheading. If not..."

Before the man could even finish, the door to the tower opened, and Tarlak stepped out, fire burning on his hands.

"Consider this my counterproposal," Tarlak said. A ball of fire shot from his palm, directly for Nicholas. Haern tensed, convinced it would not be so easy. The strange man pulled his sword off his back and held it blade-downward, the hilt raised before his chest. Mere feet away from him, the fireball suddenly winked out of existence, without even a hint of smoke. Tarlak hurled a second ball of fire, and it vanished in the same way.

Haern grabbed his sabers from beside the window as Tarlak lifted his hat and scratched his head.

"Huh."

Tarlak slammed the door shut after rushing back inside. Nicholas calmly approached the tower, sword still drawn, grin still from ear to ear. Haern pushed away from the window and staggered toward the stairs. The man was a professional, there was no doubt about that. Worse, he looked to be the perfect counter to their mercenaries. If Delysia and Tarlak could not use their magic, that left only Brug...

Haern shoved his door open, pausing a moment to tighten the bandages about his chest. No, Brug would not be able to handle someone of that skill. His talents lay in smithing, not combat. Haern had to get down there. He had to hurry. Step after step, each one jolting him with pain. The sabers in his hands shook, and he felt sweat start to cover the leather of the hilts. Had to hurry. Had to be stronger.

The door smashed open as Haern reached the bottom step. Nicholas's massive sword cleaved it in two, a feat that should have been impossible. Besides the enchantments Tarlak had placed upon it, the wood itself was incredibly thick. But Haern's mind's feeble protests changed nothing as the man stepped inside, red coat billowing as dusty air poured into the tower. Brug stood guard opposite him, Tarlak and Delysia behind.

"You're not welcome here," Brug said, clanging his two punch daggers together. He wore his plate mail, though Haern wondered how useful it'd be against a blade that could chop an oak door in half.

"Least he was polite enough to knock," Tarlak said, ice swirling in his palm.

Nicholas lifted his sword with a single hand and pointed it at the three.

"Last chance," he said. "Not that I mind the gore, or a good fight, but this won't be any competition. Won't be any *fun*. Kneel down, offer me your necks, and you'll die easy."

Haern saw more tattoos on his hand, swirling lines like arcane runes. They shone a soft blue, pulsing along with the man's heartbeat. Everything about Nicholas screamed danger, but those runes told Haern to expect more than the humanly possible from his opponent. Well, that and the split door.

"The only one dying today is you," Brug said, stomping his feet. "Just try it, come on, come on!"

Haern slipped farther into the room, hugging the wall. Brug was trying to be a distraction, he knew, doing everything he could to hide Haern's approach. Just a few feet closer and he could lunge.

Nicholas whirled, and his sword stretched out, the tip aimed for Haern's throat.

"And you," he said. "Shouldn't you be dead?"

Brug leaped forward, bellowing. Nicholas spun, his blade cutting through the air with unnatural speed. Both Brug's daggers were smacked aside, and he had to pull back to avoid having his head lopped off. Haern rushed to his friend's aid before

Nicholas could finish him. His sabers stabbed in, and when Nicholas pulled his sword close to his chest to parry, Haern pressed the attack, weaving a continuous assault so the man would have no chance to counter. A mindless roar flowed out of his mouth, a primal cry to overwhelm the pain as blood dripped down his leg from reopened wounds.

But his foe was too good. When Brug made to stab him in the back, he pretended to turn to block, then flung himself at Haern, who had to twist to shift his aim. The twist hurt too much, and he let out a gasp as his vision turned white. Only instincts kept him falling back, kept his sabers up to push aside the killing chop.

"Get back!" Tarlak yelled, and both Haern and Brug obliged, flinging themselves away. Lances of ice crossed the room, points deadly sharp. Nicholas turned to face him, his sword spinning in his grasp so the hilt neared his face. The lances vanished amid a subtle flash of the crystal within the hilt. But that was not all of the attack. Delysia cried out the name of her god, and from her out-turned palms shone a brilliant flash of white. Nicholas swore, and he turned away, rubbing his eyes.

Brug came barreling in, all clattering plate mail. He slammed headfirst into Nicholas, but instead of bowling the man over, Brug let out a cry as he bounced to the side. His helmet was dented as if he'd struck stone. Up went Nicholas's sword, ready for the kill. Another flash of light from Delysia, but he squinted and shifted his head so it did not blind him. That half-second delay was enough, though. Haern stretched to his limits, his sabers piercing through the man's coat and into flesh. The leather was thick and heavy, rendering the cut a shallow flesh wound. Worn out as he was, Haern did not have the strength to force it deeper. Blood dripped to the floor as

Nicholas clenched his teeth and brought his full fury to bear on Haern.

"I'm glad you are alive," he said, swinging his sword in wide arcs so Haern had to remain back. A bolt of fire shot in from Tarlak, but it winked out of existence, not even giving Nicholas pause. "At least you make this interesting. You even made me bleed."

Haern ducked underneath a swing, then tried to roll to one side. Nicholas predicted the maneuver, and Haern screamed as a heavy boot slammed into his stomach. His old wound tore, and it was like being stabbed all over again. He tried to move, to keep going, but his body convulsed against his wishes, doubling over amid his cries of pain. Nicholas's sword lifted, but a heavy brick slammed into his shoulder before he could swing. Startled, Nicholas fell back as two more flew in, one striking his sword, the other his chest.

"Don't like magic, eh?" Tarlak said, still hiding on the far side of the room. "How about something more real?"

More stones dislodged themselves from the walls, held in the wizard's mental grip. They flew at Nicholas, and though the magic propelling them died when nearing the man, that did not remove the natural momentum of the stone. Nicholas dove from side to side, flinging his sword about to block. Upon reaching a wall he leaped into it and kicked off into a dive straight at the wizard.

And that's when Tarlak lifted the couch into the air and swatted Nicholas with it as if he were a bug.

"Need some help here," Tarlak shouted as he flung more chairs and stones at Nicholas. Haern saw that the wizard was losing strength, each projectile considerably slower than the last. Struggling to his feet, he staggered into a run. Nicholas caught one of the slower stones, flung it straight back at Tarlak. It struck his forehead, and with a soft gasp the wizard slumped against the wall, blood trickling down his face and neck. Haern ignored it, couldn't afford to worry about the fate of his friend. Pushing through the wall of agony, he thrust for Nicholas's stomach.

Too slow. Nicholas parried the sabers, then stepped in so that his elbow collided with Haern's throat. He fell gasping, and the hard stone below him jarred his bleeding side further.

"I see why your band caused so much trouble for my employer," Nicholas said, standing over him. Blood dripped from his cut side, and his tattooed skin was a mess of bruises. "But not any longer."

He jerked forward, then collapsed to his knees as Brug's daggers pierced his back in a flurry of punches.

"Why—"

Brug shoved his daggers together into Nicholas's lower back.

"—does everyone—"

Twisted them left, then right.

"—always—"

Yanking them free, he clubbed Nicholas across the head.

"—ignore me?"

Nicholas collapsed to the ground in a dead heap. Brug stood over him, his whole body shuddering as he gasped in. He kicked the corpse with his armored foot.

"Stupid bastard," grumbled Brug.

Haern laughed where he lay, despite the pain it caused. Delysia was soon there, holy light shining on her hands.

"You're an angel, Del," Haern said, nearly delirious from the pain.

"I'm all right," Tarlak said, staggering to his feet, having to hold on to an upended couch beside him to stay balanced. With glazed eyes he looked about the room, the overturned bookshelves, the broken couches, then grunted. "We need a new door."

"Who was that?" Delysia asked as healing light poured into Haern's wounds. Haern did his best to relax, and he let his sabers go limp in his hands.

"Nicholas Bloodcraft," Haern mumbled. "He said it pretty clearly."

"You know that's not what I meant."

"But that's all that matters," Tarlak said, walking unsteadily about his tower, inspecting the damage both he and Nicholas had caused. "The Bloodcrafts are a fabled bunch of mercenaries from Mordeina. They're ruthless, powerful, and apparently have terrible taste in fashion."

"You mean there's more than one like him?" Brug asked, giving the corpse another kick for good measure.

Delysia kissed Haern on the cheek, then went to her brother. When she tried to inspect the growing bruise on his forehead, he gently pushed her away.

"I'll be fine," he said. "And yeah, there's more than one. If what I've heard is true, there's always five."

Haern scooted until he could sit with his back against a wall. Leaning his head against the cold stone, he watched as Tarlak knelt beside the corpse and inspected the sword. With a frown he grabbed the crystal in the hilt and carefully twisted it until it broke free. When he lifted it up, Haern saw that it had turned gray.

"A damn expensive enchantment," Tarlak said, peering at it. "Banishes all magic in the area, at least until the crystal's thoroughly filled." He looked at Nicholas's body, and after a thought, pulled off the cloak, then removed his shirt as well. Tattooed all across the body were hundreds of runes, some still shining a soft blue, others faded down to just black ink. Noticing this, Tarlak grunted.

"Let's see, strength, more strength, speed, a few blade enchantments, here's one for balance...these tattoos were impervious to the effects of the crystal. He banished all magic about him except for his own."

"Clever," said Haern.

"I'd call it cheating," Tarlak muttered.

"Will the others be like him?" Delysia asked, cleaning Haern's blood from her hands.

"I don't know," Tarlak said. "But someone wants us dead, and they brought out the best. We need to be careful. If there's more Bloodcrafts here, we're all in severe danger."

"If they're here, why aren't they...well, here?" asked Brug.

"Again, I don't know." Tarlak chuckled. "But we might not be their only target in Veldaren. If so, I feel bad for the other sorry bastards they're after."

"Wonderful," Haern said, closing his eyes. It suddenly felt like a perfect time for him to sleep, his chest pain ebbing away and his headaches returning. The last thing he wanted to think about was more frighteningly powerful men running about the city, not to mention whoever had brought the expensive mercenaries to bear against them.

"Just...wonderful."

CHAPTER 22

Half a mile outside the walls of Veldaren, Grayson inspected his three wagons, particularly their cargo. All around him were gathered his fellow Suns, thirty in all. Each man and woman sported at least two earrings in their left ear, for he would consider no less for such an important job. The first few days would be crucial, and not a time for amateurs.

"Not sure I've ever seen so much leaf in one place," said Boggs, the hefty man in charge of operations in Grayson's absence. He scratched at the dark stubble on his face, then sniffed. "How much we charging per pinch? Four silver? Five?"

"One," Grayson said as he hopped down from the last of the wagons, inspection complete. Several others scoffed at that, and Boggs shook his head.

"That's insane. This trip to Veldaren will cost us a fortune."

"One silver on the first day," Grayson repeated. "Two after that, until all of the crimleaf is gone. The Trifect won't be able to match, and neither will any of the guilds. We're spending money now to make it all back later. Consider it an investment."

"Don't understand why we need to go through all this," said Pierce. He was a thinner man, and often complained, but his ear was full of rings and he'd proven himself an adept killer for the Suns. "You hear what they say back home? Every guild here's weak, full of pussies too frightened to go after a coin purse lying on open ground. If we want territory, I say we just take it, and anyone who gives a shit can die."

"I give a shit, Pierce," Grayson said, grinning at the man. "You gonna kill me?"

"Only if I get to take your earrings afterward."

Grayson laughed. "We'll have our share of killing, and pay no attention to the rumors you've heard. Even with their balls chopped off, the thieves here are dangerous. But we'll be better, won't we? We'll kill everyone we need to kill, but for now, no reason to fight. When the money starts running dry, the underworld will turn to us. It's only a matter of time before the other guilds crumble. Now ready up the oxen. I want us at the gates before the midday trade is done."

"Get 'em harnessed!" Boggs shouted.

The thieves scattered about, gathering the few supplies they'd broken out for their rest and preparing the wagons to move. Grayson hopped into the front-most wagon and leaned back in the seat, hands behind his head.

"Think it'll be easy getting through the gates?" Boggs asked, taking a seat beside him and grabbing the reins. Grayson fingered the medallion in his pocket, then shrugged.

"We'll find out," he said. "No reason to panic until then."

"Never a bad thing to be prepared," Tracy said, hopping up to join them as the wagon shuddered into motion. Tracy was Boggs's half sister, and far more pleasant to look at. Her brown hair was tied into a tight ponytail, clearly showing her seven dangling earrings as she took a seat behind them.

"If the guards give us trouble, just show them your tits," Grayson said.

"And if they're not into that?" she asked, flashing him a wide smile.

"Then I'll show them my dick. Hardly complicated."

Boggs let out a laugh, and Grayson shot him a look. "Care to share, Boggs?"

"Don't you see?" Boggs asked. "We're the most dangerous men Veldaren's seen in ages, and they're going to let us through their walls because of some tits and a dick?"

"Don't forget a little help from on high," Grayson said, pulling the medallion from his pocket by its bronze chain.

"Just seems shameful," Boggs said. "Shouldn't we be climbing over walls at night or something?"

Tracy kicked him in the back with her heel, the hilt of the knife hidden in her boot jamming him hard in the kidney. "Just shut up and steer."

"Yes, Sister."

They followed the road through the shallow hills, enduring the jostle of the wagons. Grayson lay back so his eyes were free of the sun and did his best to relax. Getting through the gates would be trickier than he let on, and a crucial part of their plan. In the nation of Neldar, the Trifect had arranged so that only they were allowed to grow and sell crimleaf, the drug of choice for the lowborn. This had allowed the price to rise by gross amounts, yet in the west, where the Trifect's influence was far lesser, the simple leaf could be grown in abundance by any farmer regardless of station.

So the guilds in Veldaren had taken the natural course: they bought absurd amounts of crimleaf from the west and smuggled it east. They then undercut the Trifect's sellers, but only a little, given the trouble they went to to get it past the guards and walls. It was that easy coin that fueled much of the thief guilds, Grayson knew. It was that easy coin he wanted to disrupt, if not permanently take away.

But that meant getting into the city with their wagons untouched.

"Remember," Grayson said, sitting up as the walls of Veldaren grew closer. "You keep your mouths shut and let me do the talking. Don't want anything to draw attention to us."

"Not our first time smuggling," Tracy said.

"And all things considered, I'd prefer it not to be our last, either," Boggs said. "Guards are crawling everywhere. Well, Grayson, I hope you're right about your little helper on high."

Grayson grunted. He hoped he was right as well.

The wagons approached the west side entrance, the portcullis open for the daytime traffic. Boggs stopped the lead wagon at the behest of two guards who approached with hands raised.

"Been here before?" asked the first, an older man with his gray hair mostly hidden behind his helmet.

"Can't say we have," Grayson said.

"Need you to register your cargo, as well as pay a fee if you're not with the merchant's guild. I'll let you know the tariff once I look it over."

"Not sure that's necessary," Grayson said, leaning closer to the guard. He lifted the medallion, given to him by Laerek to ensure entrance to the city without incident. The guard's eyes widened upon his seeing it, and he glanced about.

"Back to your post," he said to the other. The man looked unsure, but did as he was told.

"You're asking a lot," the guard said when they were alone. "We allow the temple to bring in supplies as necessary, but three wagons? And you've yet to tell me what you carry."

"What I carry is of no concern to you," Grayson said, reaching into his pocket. He'd worried the priests of Karak might not have enough sway to get his men and crimleaf through. But of course power wasn't the only way to get what one wanted in the world...

"This, however," he said, tossing a bag of coins at the guard, who caught it. "I think this is what will most interest you."

The guard opened it, saw the gold within. The yellow sparkled in his eyes. Closing it, he pocketed the bag and then nodded.

"I'll still need to inspect it," he said. Grayson motioned to the others so they knew to leave him be. The guard climbed into the back of each wagon, giving only cursory glances and not once opening a crate. After the third, he returned to the front.

"Your tariff plus merchant fee is seventeen silver," he said. "Going rate for such low-quality wheat."

"You heard him," Grayson told Boggs. "Pay the man for our wheat."

Boggs grumbled but pulled the demanded coin from his own pocket. That done, the guard waved them through, then went back to his station to hand over the tariff.

"So much for your help from on high," Tracy said as the wagons rolled forward.

"We're through, and untouched," Grayson said. "That we had to grease the wheels a little shouldn't be much of a surprise."

"Just preferred we used your grease instead of mine," Boggs muttered. "Where to now?"

"Head south. I already have a contact there waiting. Once

we've claimed the hearts of the city's most poor and desperate, and established our territory, we'll worry about moving north."

The quality of the roads steadily deteriorated as they traveled deeper into the southern district, the neglect apparent with potholes and even gaps where the brick had been covered with long swaths of dirt in halfhearted attempts to smooth out the passage. The wagons slowed, and the jostling increased. Grayson saw Pierce hop out of the second wagon and come running. At first he thought him just tired of the rough ride, but that turned out not to be the case.

"We got a tail," he said, walking beside them.

"To be expected," Grayson said. "I doubt too many merchants travel this far south. Did you catch which guild?"

"I don't know them well enough to say for sure," Pierce said, shaking his head.

"Just keep your eyes open," Grayson said. "And don't let them know we see them."

Pierce nodded. "They're running 'long the rooftops," he said. "Watch them if you can."

He returned to the second wagon. Grayson leaned back, imitating his relaxed position of earlier. As he did, he looked to the rooftops, trying to see out of the corners of his eyes who shadowed them.

"Any of them a threat?" Boggs asked as they shifted to one side to avoid a nasty stretch of mud.

"Not really," Grayson said. "Spider Guild's in ruins, which just leaves the Ash Guild as any real danger. But if that's who's tailing us, well, they might have a tail of their own soon..."

They continued until they reached their contact, one of the few merchants still maintaining a presence in the far south of Veldaren. He was an overweight man, sweaty and with his shirt overstuffed with his own fat.

"Afternoon, Billick," Grayson said as they stopped the wagons in front of his shop.

"I assume no guards followed you?" Billick asked, furtive eyes bouncing among the wagons.

"Guards?" Grayson asked, hopping down from his seat at the front. "No, guards are the least of our problems, my friend. Where can we store our merchandise?"

"Space for everything," Billick said, gesturing toward the open door to his shop. "Carry it in, and put it in the back room."

"You heard him!" Grayson roared, amused at how the fat man jumped at the volume of his voice. One by one the wagons were unloaded, his Suns lugging the crates into their place of storage for their time in Veldaren.

"I won't be handling any of it," Billick said as he watched. "You know that, right? Don't tell me what it is, and don't make me sell it. I'll let you get it in, and I'll let any of you Suns get it out. Just make sure the pay is on time."

"Good man," Grayson said, smirking at him. "So brave, so noble. You'll get your pay. Just keep an eye on our wares. I don't take kindly to those who help themselves to what isn't theirs."

Billick got the message, and he nodded fast enough to make the fat of his neck bounce.

"I have business elsewhere," he said. "Shop's all yours for the rest of the day. I won't come back until morning."

Once the crates were stored, Grayson gathered his men and began handing out smaller bags.

"One silver per pinch," he told them. "Stay close, and stay together. No one's sold crimleaf this cheap for decades, so let them come to you. And I'll drag back to Mordeina in a bag anyone I hear of charging more and pocketing the top."

The men began to scatter, each eager for his first step in taking over the streets of Veldaren.

"Pierce," Grayson called out, stopping the man.

"Yeah?"

Grayson grinned at him.

"Go find someone in a different guild, don't care which, or how old they are. Just find someone, and then gut them. I want to send a message that we aren't to be messed with, understood? So make it brutal."

Pierce's grin was from ear to ear.

"That I can do," he said, twirling a dagger in his hand.

"Good. Go get to work."

As the rest scattered in groups, only Boggs and Tracy remained behind.

"Not many places to stash three wagons," Boggs said, climbing up into the first.

"We aren't leaving for a while," Grayson said, glancing up and down the street. "Should be an inn nearby desperate enough for coin to let us hole up all three for a few months. At worst we can sell them at market."

"Come on, lovely sister," Boggs said as Tracy climbed up to join him. "Let us find some clean, comfortable beds for our companions."

Tracy snickered. "So not too much lice in them, then?"

Before they could move out, the back two wheels of the wagon exploded, and with a loud bang the wood hit the ground. The oxen jostled, startled, but Boggs kept them calm.

"The fuck?" Boggs asked, looking back. Tracy hopped down to take a look, but Grayson could already tell what had happened. Smoke rose from a magical fire that burned out into nothing. Grayson drew his swords as a man in a gray cloth mask approached from down the street. Ash swirled about his face, hiding his dark features. Grayson recognized him from the failed attack on Alyssa's mansion. He gripped his swords tighter.

"Grayson..." Tracy said, also seeing him, but Grayson raised a hand, gesturing for her to remain calm.

"Well, now," Grayson said, approaching the intruder in a way that positioned him nearer to the first wagon, and therefore cover. "This is a surprise."

"Perhaps," said Deathmask. "But *your* arrival isn't. I've been expecting one of the guilds from Mordeina to arrive for years. Honestly, your delay proved irritating."

Grayson let out a laugh.

"No more than your interference. What is it you want? If you're here to protect your territory, you might as well give up now. Our money, leaf, and coin are pouring in from Mordeina like a flood. You won't stop us."

"I've stopped you twice already," Deathmask said, crossing his arms. "I stopped you when you sent mobs and thieves after Alyssa Gemcroft's mansion. Or have you already forgotten the fun my guild had on that night?"

Of course Grayson hadn't, but he kept his smile going, kept hoping whatever conflict he faced he could resolve without a fight.

"You were an inconvenience, nothing more," Grayson said. "But I only count one time you've stopped us."

The strange wizard gestured to the broken wagon.

"I consider that number two. But the biggest one that matters is number three...but I don't mean to stop you. Not unless I must. Your Sun Guild may think it can move into Veldaren easily, but they'll encounter resistance soon enough, and not just from me. The guilds won't go down quietly, not unless things change. Not unless you have my help."

"I can't decide if you underestimate us, or overestimate your own worth," Grayson said. "Speak plainly, wizard."

"I am no wizard," Deathmask said, and Grayson was surprised to see the anger glowing in those mismatched eyes. "And my offer is plain enough, even for you. Let me help your guild take over the city, every single brick and stone. In return you split your profits with me, and give me a portion of the city to remain under my direct control."

"Is that so?" Grayson asked, honestly intrigued. "How much of a split would that be?"

"What else would a split be? Half."

Grayson's curiosity died amid his laughter. "Do you think I need you so badly that I'd sacrifice a fortune for a victory I'm already certain to win? Show some intelligence. Besides, my master won't share power, not with the likes of you. He's decided to make Veldaren his, and nothing will prevent it."

The ash swirling around Deathmask's face slowed, grew thicker.

"I am no fool, Grayson. The guilds are crumbling, dying to both you and Victor. I can help finish them off, show you where to shove your sword. What I ask for isn't much, not when you consider that every coin you take from Veldaren is a coin you didn't have the day before. But don't think your takeover of these streets is inevitable. Not when Thren still stalks the city. Not while I'm still alive."

"Well," Grayson said. "I guess we should take care of that, shouldn't we?"

Fire was already surrounding Deathmask's hands before Grayson rolled to the side, using the wagon as cover. The expected attack from the wizard came, a burst of fire that consumed where he'd stood. It was slow, though, and more flash than heat. He was being played with, Grayson realized, as he leaned his back against the wagon.

"Doesn't have to go like this," Deathmask said, his voice drawing nearer. "We could be partners, and work together."

"Bullshit!" Grayson shouted, his mind elsewhere. Tracy had rolled from the wagon to the door of the shop, hidden from Deathmask's view. Boggs crouched just above Grayson within the broken wagon. Grayson held up three fingers to Tracy, counting them down. At one, they leaped out, but Deathmask was no longer alone. Men—twins, by the looks of it—stood before him, each holding a pair of daggers. Grayson slid, and he swung his arm to knock Tracy down as well. Four daggers sailed above them, hitting nothing.

"Back," Grayson said as he turned and ran, sheathing a sword so he could grab Tracy by the arm. No spells gave chase like he thought. Instead, with a few words from Deathmask, his wagons caught fire one by one, burning as if doused with barrels of lantern fuel. Tracy let out a cry for her brother, but amid the smoke Grayson could not tell if he escaped or not.

They ran for the door, but instead of their finding safety in the shop, a woman with a wicked scar across her right eye blocked the way in, bearing the colors of the Ash Guild. She held a dagger in her hand, and it glowed with purple fire.

"Running away?" she asked. "Hardly fits your reputation, Grayson."

"I think it does," Deathmask said, calmly walking toward them. Ash circled his head faster and faster, his smile hidden behind cloth yet clearly visible in his eyes. "Arrogance? Shortsightedness? Sun Guild, through and through. The four of us have held our territory for years against all challengers, Grayson, yet you think to brush us aside like children?"

Boggs fell from the back of the nearest wagon, coughing and hacking. Tracy tensed, and Grayson could tell she wanted to go to him. His hands and face were black from the ash, but his burns didn't seem too severe. Far more worrisome were the twins, who hurried to his location.

"Still breathing," said the first.

"Just barely," said the second.

Deathmask stepped closer and closer. Grayson could almost reach him with a lunge, but the man looked unafraid, as if he actually believed he was the dread ghoul he appeared to be. The scarred woman seemed far more tense, and she kept her dagger at the ready.

"Don't you dare lay a finger on him," Grayson said to the twins.

"Or what?" they asked in unison.

In answer, Grayson flung himself at the woman, catching her across the face with his fist. As she fell back he tried to stab, but she was faster than he expected. Instead of fleeing farther, she dove to the ground, narrowly avoiding the downward thrust that should have skewered her. Continuing, she joined the twins, who stepped before her protectively. The woman fumed, but Deathmask only chuckled.

"How is the burned friend of theirs?" he asked as Grayson and Tracy stood there, still tense. They could flee into the shop, but that way was a dead end. If they wanted to escape, it had to be through the streets. Grayson had fought spellcasters before, and he knew he'd be pressing his luck trying to avoid their attacks in open space for any length of time.

"He looks like he's seen better days," the woman said, lifting Boggs up with both hands, her dagger pressed against his chest. Boggs let out a gasp at her touch.

"A shame," said Deathmask. "Veliana, if you'd so kindly put him out of his misery."

The woman was only too happy to oblige. Before Grayson could think of what to do, Veliana pulled her dagger back, spun it, and jammed it through Boggs's throat. Tracy let out a choked cry, part horror, part fury. Veliana dumped the body on the street, retrieved her dagger, and then burned away the blood with more purple fire. The twins shifted apart, just outside sword reach, blocking off the other side of the street. Only the shop remained, and for some reason Grayson felt he was being herded inside.

"All that smoke will be attracting attention soon," Deathmask said, still maddeningly calm.

Glancing behind him, Grayson realized most of his merchandise was still inside the shop. If he was trapped inside, and the Ash Guild summoned the city guard, then they'd be out their lives, and their coin. Worse, their guild's intentions would be revealed to the king's men. Deathmask didn't want to just kill Grayson. He wanted to humiliate him, and make life far more difficult for the rest of the Sun Guild should they attempt to move in on the city.

"You bastard," Tracy said, tears in her eyes. "I'll kill you, I promise it."

"Shouldn't make promises you won't keep," Veliana said.

"Last chance," Deathmask said. "Partners, or the executioner's ax. Your choice."

"Tracy," Grayson said as movement across the rooftops caught his eye. "You do exactly as I say, you understand?"

She nodded. Lowering his swords, Grayson stood to his full height, delaying as long as possible. He had to time it just right, just when the attack hit...

"I guess I have little choice," he said. "But I'm thinking I'd much rather have you dead."

Spinning about, he leaped into the door of the shop, smashing it open with his shoulder. Tracy followed without hesitation. Barging in, they flung themselves to the side, avoiding another barrage of daggers. Grayson rolled onto his back, swords up to fend off an attack that didn't come.

Explosions of fire rocked the street, and they weren't from Deathmask. Shrapnel from the wagons clacked against the side of the shop, and a long plank shattered a window. Tracy crouched low to the floor, stunned by the sudden barrage of combat.

"We should go help kill..."

"No," Grayson said. "Either they'll live or they'll die. I'm not foolish enough to step in the middle."

The ringing of steel on steel intensified. From the window Grayson heard a roar of wind, and then what sounded like a battering ram slamming into a castle gate.

"Who's out there?" Tracy asked, stunned.

In answer Grayson only shook his head.

In less than a minute, the combat was over. Holding his swords at the ready, Grayson made his way to the door and stepped out to survey the wreckage. Their wagons were ruined, each one exploded into pieces. Three of the nearby buildings burned, and a fourth had a gaping hole in its front, from what, he could only guess. There were no other bodies on the ground besides Boggs. Tracy rushed over to her brother, cradling his head in her hands. Tears flowed down her face, but only for a moment.

"What happened here?" she asked as she calmly removed the rings from his ear.

"Saw their coat for just an instant, but the damage is enough to answer," Grayson said, putting away his swords. "Still think it was a mistake to hire them, but at least they saved our asses instead of getting in the way."

"What are you talking about?"

"The Bloodcrafts," Grayson said. "If the Ash Guild lives through this, it'll be a miracle."

Tracy paled at the name. "We need to check on the rest," she said. "The Ash Guild might not have been the only one to…"

"No," Grayson said, offering her his hand. "We need to move, now. The city guard will be here any second, and we can't risk them finding our cache. We'll take whatever we can carry and then hide."

Tracy nodded, pocketed the last of Boggs's earrings. She kissed his burned forehead and then whispered into his ear.

"I'm sorry."

She took Grayson's hand and stood. Inside the shop they gathered every bag they could, and as the first of many arrived to investigate the destruction, the two ducked into the nearest alley and lost themselves in the darker parts of the city.

CHAPTER 23

Zusa was in her room when Alyssa found her.

"What are you doing?" Alyssa asked. Zusa ignored her, instead continuing to put on her wrappings inch by inch. Lifting one arm, she began circling them across her breast, around her sides, and then back again. Loop after loop after loop....

Alyssa grabbed her hands, forcing her to stop. "Look at me," she said. "Zusa..."

"I have to go," Zusa said, gently taking Alyssa's hands in hers, then pulling herself free so she might continue to dress.

"Go? Go where? I need you here. You know that. Whoever it is...this Widow...she followed us here. She's *here*. And you're to leave me?"

Zusa turned her back to Alyssa, not wanting to see the worry in her eyes. It was dark now, but in the waning hours of daylight they'd found another body, this one dumped against the walls of the Connington estate, a crossbow bolt still stuck in her chest. It had been one of the servants left behind to care for Alyssa's mansion while it was repaired. Her eyes had been removed, coins replacing them. The rhyme had mocked Alyssa directly yet again.

tongue of gold, eyes of silver
run, run gemcroft whore
from the widow's quiver

Stephen had sent the guards into a frenzy of searching, furious that such a thing had been done without their noticing. Zusa, though, had only stared as the walls closed in around her. She'd calmly walked to her room, stripped naked, sharpened her daggers, and then begun to dress.

"I only do what I must," Zusa said.

"Don't lie to me," Alyssa said. "I need you here. My son needs you here. Without your protection, we might..."

"Don't you understand?" Zusa said, whirling to face her. "*That* is why I go. It doesn't matter how closely I guard you, you're still vulnerable. The threat lurks, and I must find it."

"No," Alyssa said, crossing her arms. "This Widow is just some sick fuck with a crossbow. Whoever it is can't be better than you."

"It's not the Widow," Zusa said, shaking her head. "That was only a reminder of the threats made against us. It's the other faceless. They're just like me, Alyssa. No matter how many guards you surround yourself with, or how diligent I remain, they can still find you. When I sleep, or am separate from you for only a moment. Walls mean nothing, and shadows are just doors..."

Alyssa stepped closer, put a hand against Zusa's cheek. "You stopped them before. You can stop them again."

"They were foolish, and revealed themselves before they attacked. They won't be so proud again. For whatever reason, Karak's servants want you dead. Don't you understand how dangerous a position that is? They are powerful, and they are relentless. If I don't do something now, if I don't find out why, then I can't keep you safe. And I won't let that happen. I won't lose you. I won't lose Nathan."

Alyssa pulled back her hand, put it against her own breast. "So you'll run off and get yourself killed instead?"

Tears were forming in Alyssa's eyes. Zusa hardened her heart as best she could against them as she continued to dress. "Far better me than you," she whispered.

Alyssa kissed her cheek, then wrapped her arms about her. Zusa tilted her head, just the slightest opening, enough for Alyssa to press her face against her neck and let her tears wet Zusa's skin.

"With everyone else I must be strong," said Alyssa. "With everyone else I must be a lie. Don't you dare leave me alone. You come back, understand me? You come back."

Zusa gently pushed her away, then kissed her on the forehead. "Help me put on my cloak," she said.

That done, Zusa went to the door, put her hand on the wood.

"Alyssa," she said, trying to find the words. "I want you to know..."

"Whatever it is you think you should say, don't," Alyssa said, and her face hardened along with her resolve. "You're coming back, remember?"

Zusa smiled at her. "Of course, my mistress," she said, then vanished into the corridors of the mansion. She wove through them like a ghost, slipped through the courtyard without being seen by the guards, and then vaulted over the fence. She could only hope the other faceless would not attack in her absence. She'd searched the grounds for hours before leaving, but there was no way to know for certain. It was a gamble, but one she had to take.

She'd made Daverik a promise: if he came after Alyssa and her family, then nothing would protect him. It was a promise she had every intention of keeping. She kept to the streets, needing speed more than anything. Her strike had to come before the temple decided to act again. The mob had failed to accomplish its goal, and her daggers had protected Alyssa from the faceless. Two failures…it would be too much to expect a third.

Zusa slowed as she neared the temple. To most it would have appeared to be a large, well-furnished private mansion, but those who knew how to look, who had bent the knee to Karak, saw differently. They saw a great temple cut from black marble, the path to it lined with stone. Statues of lions roared from atop various pillars, their teeth sharp, their eyes always watching. Zusa remembered her final day within it, the day she'd been stripped and banished. The faceless, unworthy of Karak's presence, were boarded elsewhere. Zusa had been tempted to seek out the faceless where they slept, but they were just puppets, not the real threat. Even with their deaths, more would come. Priests, perhaps, or dark paladins. She had to find the reason for Karak's ire, and see if she could somehow defuse it.

With a running leap she sailed over the fence. Drawing her daggers in midair, she landed with a quiet whisper of bending grass and sliding dirt. In the silence of the night, she let out a single prayer, a soft blasphemy against the temple she was about to enter.

"I have seen no love from you, Ashhur," she breathed. "But I ask for it now. Help me kill him. Help me save my family."

The wind blew, and she took that for her answer. Like an uncoiling serpent she moved, a sudden burst without pause or doubt. She knew the layout of the temple, knew where there'd be guards, priests, young disciples, and servingwomen. They would not have changed a thing over the ten years she'd been gone, she knew. Karak was not fond of change, especially when it came to his most devout followers. Her feet barely touched the grass as she ran, gathering momentum. It was suicide, she knew, to attack the temple head on, even at night, with her prey unprepared. Suicide.

Her grin spread.

At full speed she leaped feet-first toward the door of the temple. The entryway was dark, with nothing but the stars to give it light. Eyes closed, she focused, thought of the inner chambers. They'd be lit with torches, but not the door, deep in the entryway. Her feet did not touch wood, but passed right on through. She emerged on the other side, and her daggers lashed out, cutting the necks of two guards positioned inside. As they fell behind her, she landed on the soft carpet and tucked into a roll to preserve her momentum. Pulling out, she raced between the pews, toward the great statue of Karak at the end of the gathering hall. It was that altar they'd bled Daverik upon. She felt an impulse to kneel before the imposing statue that towered so greatly above her, but she fought it down. That wasn't her god anymore.

To the left was a door into the greater complex, where the priests slept. It was there she'd find Daverik's room, and with any luck she'd get the answers she needed. Upon reaching the door she slammed into it with her shoulders, blasting it inward. Entering a hallway, she lunged, extending her body to its fullest as a priest turned from his seat beneath a flickering torch, an old tome in his lap. The words of a spell were on his lips as the tip of her dagger pierced his throat, silencing him. Her shoulder absorbed the impact of her landing, and then she rolled past, pulling her dagger free along the way. Blood gushed across the carpet.

So far, so good, but Zusa knew she'd been lucky. The slightest cry of warning and everything would become much, much harder.

Still running, she passed silently through the hall, her cloak a ghost of cloth following after. She tried to think of where Daverik might be staying. There had been no man teaching them last time; instead a fellow faceless, Eliora, had been their trainer and spiritual leader. That meant Daverik would have no official room prepared for him, such as there was for the high priest.

At an intersection she peered around the corner, looking left and right. She caught sight of a man changing candles as he moved down the hall. She waited until his back was to her before approaching. Her left arm pressed against his mouth, the other shoving a dagger through his back and into his heart. As he shuddered, she let him drop, then glanced about. Too many rooms. She couldn't just open doors at random. Where would Daverik be?

He was new there, she decided, little more than a guest. And guests were given a specific place, the rooms far more ornate, the intricate paintings exaggerating the power and importance of the priesthood. Urging herself on, she glanced back, wondering how long until someone found a body. Not long. She had to move faster.

At the guest room she stopped and pressed her ear to the door. She heard no movement, no sign of life within. But it was dark, and Daverik would most likely be asleep. Gently she grabbed the doorknob and started to twist.

The door was flung open with explosive force, knocking her backward. As she hit the opposite wall, she rolled, narrowly avoiding a kick from a faceless woman. Zusa's daggers flashed out, parrying stabs, and then she was running down the hall, back toward the entrance. Curses screamed in her mind. When another faceless stepped in her way, shadows curling off her body like smoke, Zusa knew this for what it was.

A trap laid out just for her.

"You won't stop me!" she cried, leaping at her foe. They collided in a mess of limbs and daggers, lashing and stabbing, neither able to score a solid blow. Pulling herself free, Zusa dropped to her back, flattening beneath a hurled dagger from the other. Hoping to gain some distance, she ran again, but doors started opening, and she heard the deep thrumming of a bell located in the bowels of the temple, alerting all to her presence. One man tried to jump in her way, but she slammed right into him, her knees blasting him to the ground, her daggers ending the spell he'd tried to cast. Another, this one a priestess, remained in her doorway, and at Zusa's passing she hurled a bolt of red lightning. The power arced through Zusa's body, and she screamed her agony away.

The spell slowed her movement, and a foot swept beneath her. Falling, she raised her daggers, just barely blocking Ezra's downward strike. Pushing her away, she rolled to her knees. A bolt of shadow flew from the hand of another priest rushing to join them from farther ahead. She dodged it, along with his follow-up, but then the priestess caught her with a shadow bolt of her own. It slammed into Zusa's body, bruising flesh and sapping her strength. This time Zusa gave no scream, unable to muster the strength.

The two faceless women flanked her, each blocking an entrance, as more and more priests and priestesses gathered. Zusa kept weaving from side to side, struggling to breathe through the pain. She saw no way out, but it didn't matter. She'd die fighting, and would not die alone.

"Attack me, cowards!" she screamed, ignoring the pain it caused. Instead they fell back, and furious, she flung herself toward a group. Her daggers plunged and stabbed, but she could not connect. Lightning and shadow swelled against her, forming a wall she could not penetrate. Its very touch jolted her limbs. The faceless women both chose that moment to attack, kicking her with their long legs. One took the air from her lungs, the other connecting with her kidneys. Gasping, Zusa collapsed to the cold floor, unable to stand. A dagger slipped around her neck and pressed against her throat.

"Don't kill her!"

With dazed eyes Zusa looked up to see Daverik pushing through the crowd. He knelt before her, put a hand against her forehead. Whoever held the dagger backed away.

"You poor thing," Daverik said, softly stroking her short hair. "You poor, foolish thing. Take her."

Something hard struck the back of her head, and then came darkness.

The first thing Zusa noticed when she came to was the sound of running water. It was constant, and close, as if a river ran in the same room. The second was how her hands and legs were bound with chains, the metal on the inside sharp and jagged so that the slightest movement drew blood.

"Open your eyes, little doll," whispered a sweet voice. When Zusa did she saw an older man standing over her. His face was wrinkled and free of any facial hair. His eyes were a pale blue, and when he smiled his serpent's smile, it was without teeth. He wore the robes of a priest, but instead of black they were a deep red.

"Who are you?" she asked.

"Does the little doll not remember me? I am Vrashka. I was

there when you were banished, and your little boy beaten. I held the whip."

Despite the years, she did indeed remember. More so, she remembered the name of Vrashka, Pelorak's favorite and most ruthless torturer.

"I know you," Zusa said, looking beyond him to take in her surroundings. She was in a small stone cell, poorly lit. The temple's prison, of course. She sat on the floor, her arms and legs manacled to the wall. The only thing she did not recognize, or understand, was that constant sound of water. "Just a sick old man."

"It's been a long time," Vrashka said, stepping back and crossing his arms over his chest so he could look down at her. "I have gotten older, yes I have, little doll. But I have also gotten wiser, too. Do you see this?"

He stepped aside, revealing the source of the water. It was a strange sight, as if a stalactite had grown from the stone ceiling. Stretching a foot downward, it stopped, its tip hollow so that water might run out in a constant stream. It fell into a small spiral cut into the floor, causing the water to swirl before dropping into a hole, going how far down below, Zusa did not know. Perhaps to the depths of the world, perhaps all the way into the Abyss where it could trickle on Karak's head.

"Am I supposed to be afraid of water?" Zusa asked, hoping to keep him talking. She felt her strength returning, and where she was manacled there were many shadows. The chains would not hold her, not for long.

Vrashka chuckled, and the sound made her skin crawl.

"You have poor imagination, girl. You do not understand where you are, or what we have. Daverik made this himself. I know what you think, that you will slip into the shadows."

He reached into his robe, pulled out one of her daggers, and cast it on the floor mere feet away.

"Take it," he said, smiling. "Slip through the shadows, grab it, and cut my throat. You can do that, can't you, little doll?"

She smiled back, then pulled in the power, demanded it, stole it with the strength of her soul. Falling backward, she expected the familiar cold feeling, but instead something grabbed her. She felt like a bird trapped in a thunderstorm. Her body became a distant thing, and lost in horror she watched her vision be pulled toward the swirling water. It was so thin, like a single thread of silk. Before her eyes it grew larger, larger, and then her whole form was swirling with it, down into the void, a boat doomed in a maelstrom. Colors faded, only the water retaining vibrancy, shining a brighter and brighter blue that made her entire body ache. Panic settled in, and she yearned for her body, to pull out from the shadows.

And then she was back in her manacles, gasping for air. Vrashka bent down and grabbed her dagger.

"Does she understand now?" he asked. "Your magic will not work here, nor that of any priest. It will be lost into the funnel, the holy water taking in every bit of Karak's power. You will not escape us, little doll. You are ours now, to be made pure over the crawling years."

He knelt before her and pressed the dagger against the skin of her breast.

"And I say years, because I know you are stubborn. I know you will resist. Much time, much effort, but I have little else to do at my age. You wear the wrappings of your order, but in your heart you blaspheme against Karak. You expose your face to the world, and in doing so spit in the eye of our god."

He withdrew the dagger and walked over to the door. Beside it was a small bag, and he pulled out a set of sewing needles. When he turned back to her, his pale blue eyes were feverish.

"Whatever you came here for, you failed. Think on that as I do my needlework."

The chains held her as he took her hand in his and uncurled her fist. She tried to tense, but he held her firm with surprising strength. She wanted to struggle further, but the inner surfaces of the manacles were sharp and filled with barbs. Doing so would only cause her pain.

Taking a needle in his mouth, Vrashka softly ran a finger along her fingertip.

"Even old as I am, it is never too old to learn," he said. "I spent time with Leon's gentle touchers years ago, did you know that? You will soon. They are masters, artists. I hope my needlework can begin to compare."

There were many hooks along the wall, and he looped the chains holding her arm through one so that it held her tight. Teeth gritted, she tried not to let out a cry, even when he jammed the first needle underneath the fingernail of her forefinger.

"Karak is not my god," she said, struggling to keep her voice firm. "I will not repent."

He smiled at her.

"Perhaps. But I have many needles."

One after another they were jammed into her skin. Each was worse than the one before, and she cried out in agony after the seventh. Leaving them in, he moved on to her other hand. Even more slender needles pierced underneath her fingernails, tearing the soft skin. Tears ran down her face, but he asked no questions, and made no demands. Time became meaningless. All she could think of was Alyssa, and Nathaniel, but their memories were poison, for she was trapped in a prison, which meant they would soon suffer death, or, even worse, join her there in the pits of the temple.

"The gentle touchers are artists," Vrashka said, stepping back to observe his work. "So careful, so clever. They view whips and daggers as crude toys for children. It is a mark of disdain for any of them to leave a bruise."

Zusa kept her head low, not caring to look at him or acknowledge his words. Her hands shook uncontrollably, and she felt blood trickling down her wrists. As he crept closer, she shut her eyes, tried to imagine herself far, far away. His rough hands grabbed her face, forced her to look up at him.

"Such beautiful eyes," he said, staring into them. "But you do not need them anymore, just a tongue to pray, and knees to confess upon."

He was reaching for another needle when the door opened, and Daverik stepped inside. Zusa stared at him amid her delirium, the man just a blurred figure outlined with light from a distant torch.

"I would have a word with her," he said.

Vrashka stepped back, bowing low.

"Of course," he said. "She is yours to convert. But it will take time, and I have only started to break her."

"She might still see reason," Daverik said, not looking at her. Vrashka bowed again, then stepped out. As the door closed, the priest noticed the needles still in her fingers and frowned.

"I warned you," he said. "Now keep still."

"Not sure I can," she said. She felt his hand close around hers, pinning it to the wall. One by one he removed the needles, dropping them into a bloody pail Vrashka had brought with him. Switching to the other hand, he worked in silence. Zusa kept her eyes downcast, let her mind focus on the pain as the needles slid out from within her fingertips. When he was done, he sat opposite her and pushed aside Vrashka's bag. Tension filled the room, broken only by the soft trickle of water.

"You set a trap for me," Zusa said.

"Not a trap, just protection. I thought you might come for me after what happened at Alyssa's mansion."

Zusa shook her head, feeling like a stupid child. Her warning had been clear, so of course Daverik had planned for her arrival. Eyes still downcast, she wondered if she had anything to say to him, but found herself strangely empty inside.

"They want you executed," Daverik said. He paused a moment, as if waiting to see if she would respond. She didn't.

"I'm not sure I can stop them," he continued. "You killed two of my faceless, and you have blasphemed against Karak for many years now by showing your face after abandoning the order. You also fought against one of our paladins sent to retrieve you in the early days of your betrayal."

"His name was Ethric," she said. "I killed him in a river, cut out his throat, and then left him there so the fish could eat his flesh. He'd been sent to kill me, not return me to the temple. We did as we were told, as we have always done, and were branded outcasts for it. But that's what Karak does, isn't it? He finds ways to punish his faithful should they ever be an inconvenience to his temple. Our lives are nothing to him."

"You're wrong," Daverik said. "Karak showed you forgiveness. He gave you a chance to repent, to make right the wrongs…"

"What wrongs?" She laughed. "Our love wasn't wrong. It wasn't sin. It was just against the rules. It complicated things, made people worry. But you were lashed, and I imprisoned, and now you come here to remake the order that took me from you. You're a disgrace."

"They didn't take you from me," he said.

It felt as if a fever had overcome her, and she laughed again. Her hands were giant throbs of pain, and she could not feel her individual fingers.

"They didn't? Then who?"

"It was me," Daverik said, and he looked away as if ashamed. "I told them of our affair."

The last words he'd spoken to her echoed in her head.

I'm sorry...

"You bastard," she whispered. "You damned, stupid bastard. Why? Why would you do that to us?"

"Because we would have been caught," Daverik said, standing so he might pace. His eyes never met hers. "Because it was only a matter of time. And because it was wrong. I neglected prayers, I stopped paying attention in services. I only thought about you, cared about you. When I should have been meditating, I was thinking of seeing you, imagining what I might do the next time we..."

He stopped himself. Frustrated, he struck the wall with his fist. Zusa wanted to feel fury, to feel betrayal, but instead she saw the torment deep within her former lover and knew what had brought him back.

"You came to Veldaren for me," she said. "Just for me."

He looked to the door, nodded his head. "Every single night since, I've lain down in my bed and felt guilt for what I did. I thought it would get better. I thought the certainty of my faith would prove what really mattered, and that in time, with separation, I'd know without a doubt I'd been right. But it never happened. That I was asked to train the new faceless is a cruel joke, Zusa, but I agreed to do it for you. You can come back. We can be together. Perhaps not as we were, but I'd still see you, still be able to hear your voice."

He breathed in deeply, then let it out in a sigh.

"My decision cost you your faith in Karak. I have committed no greater crime than that."

Zusa's anger had been softening, but those last words were worse than Vrashka's needles.

"Are you really still so blind?" she asked. "You carry guilt not for my torment, but because I turned my back on Karak?"

"What could be a worse crime?" he asked. "To see you lost to the fires of the Abyss..."

He approached her, knelt before her so they might see eye to eye. His hand gently stroked her cheek, brushing away tears.

"Come back to me," he whispered. "I don't want to lose you, not again, and not forever."

He looked so young then, so much like the boy she'd loved. His face was leaning ever closer. Shackled, helpless, she could not stop him as his lips closed around hers. Her insides twisted and curled with turmoil. She felt fury at his foolishness, yet hope that he might free her. She felt sick at his desires, that he could find beauty in her while she was captive and tortured, yet at the same time it was so easy to slip back into the past, to escape from her cell into memories of him and her, young, foolish, and clumsy as they sneaked into each other's rooms late at night. She felt pain, sorrow, and betrayal.

Her lips did not kiss him back. When he tried to kiss her again, she turned to the side and steeled her gaze at the wall.

"You're a cruel, evil man," she whispered.

"You don't mean that."

"I do. You were a fool, a naïve child to have done what you did. But that was then. For you to still think it now, to kiss my naked face while begging me to have it covered, shows just how sick your mind has become."

His whole body tensed, and for a moment she thought he would strike her. But he did not. Instead he stood and went to the door so he could lean his back against it.

"I told you Alyssa was in danger," he said. "That she still lives is a miracle, but it won't be long before her death. It's inevitable,

Zusa. You should know that. We are the servants of Karak, and we will not be swayed."

"What has she done to you?"

"I'm sure if we dug into her past we'd find sins, but that isn't what matters. I told you to make her a friend of Karak, but your stubbornness struck you as always. Dangerous times are coming, and we must prepare Veldaren for the prophet's arrival. The world will suffer dearly if we fail."

"The prophet?" Zusa asked. She wanted to laugh, and would have had she not been so exhausted. "You speak of phantoms from the past, of a man long dead. You would kill us, make us all suffer, because of bedtime stories about Karak's first priest?"

Daverik slowly shook his head. "I'm sorry," he said. "Good night, Zusa. I'll buy you some time before Vrashka returns, claim that I'm giving you a day or two to think on my request. Come back to the order, and all will be forgiven."

"They won't let me come back," Zusa said as he opened the door. "You know that. What would stop me from leaving once I am free of the temple? What would keep me chained and bound to the faceless? The moment I accept myself into the faceless is the moment I die. But that's what you want, isn't it? At least my soul would be saved."

She could not deny the hurt she saw in Daverik's eyes at her words.

"Someone will bring you food in a few hours," he said. "Rest well."

The door closed, plummeting her into darkness. The water glowed a soft blue, yet it cast no light about the room. The sight of it made her head hurt and her stomach twist, so she closed her eyes, shifted her arms as much as she could given the constraint of the manacles, and tried to sleep.

CHAPTER 24

One after another died to the executioner's ax, and the sight slowly calmed Victor's nerves. The deal he'd made with the thief Alan had left a bad taste in his mouth. The results, however, were undeniable. The Spider Guild was all but crushed, except for one niggling detail that kept Victor pacing everywhere he went. Somehow, Thren Felhorn had escaped. The one person who mattered, and he had gotten through their lines.

"It's been a good day," said Sef, joining him there in the shadow of the castle as the sun began to fall.

"Could have gone better," Victor said, nodding toward the executioner's block. "Thren should be up there, bound and gagged."

"We'll have his head hanging from the city gates soon enough," Sef said. "But the whole city's buzzing about it. People are far more willing to talk to our men now, their lips loosening. I think after last night everyone expected a war, for something like what happened before. But instead they got a bunch of dead thieves and their symbolic leader broken and in hiding."

"So what you're saying," Victor said, finally cracking a smile, "is that it was a good day?"

"That's correct, sir."

Victor laughed. "Was there something you needed?"

Sef nodded. "His Majesty's adviser is ready to speak with you. He said he'd meet you in his chambers in the castle to discuss your request."

"Tell Gerand I'll be there shortly," Victor said, turning back to the platform. "There's still a few more awaiting the ax."

Sef bowed low.

"Of course. Enjoy your show."

Thieves, murderers, and lowborn thugs trudged up the steps, their crimes labeled, categorized, and proven to the necessary extent. Then came the ax. For Victor it wasn't enjoyable, and truthfully he would have been disturbed to feel that way upon seeing another man die. No, as the ax fell, and the head separated from the neck, he felt his city taking one tiny step closer to peace. It carried the same satisfaction as pulling a tick from a dog, or yanking a weed from a garden. A sick, immoral life was snuffed out. It would commit no more crimes, frighten no more innocents, and take no more lives.

Step by step. Up the stairs, before the executioner, and then the chopping block. Step by step.

When it was done, Victor went into the king's castle and trudged up the stairs to Gerand's room. He knocked on the door, and was quickly let in. Gerand's room was a tidy place, well furnished for its small size. Taking a seat at his desk, Gerand motioned for Victor to sit in the only other chair, which he did. It was overly stuffed, and far from comfortable.

"I thank you for coming to see me so late," Gerand said.

"I should be thanking you for not making me wait another day," Victor said. Gerand smiled at the comment, but he didn't look amused. It was almost like a trained response to anyone attempting wit.

"I've gone over your request," Gerand said, leaning back in his chair. "And while your results are impressive, and the costs you listed for hiring your soldiers fair, I am not sure the king's treasury is ready to pay just yet."

"Why is that?" Victor asked. "Have I not crushed the strongest, most dangerous guild in your city's history? Surely that is worth a partial advance on the compensation I was promised."

"Perhaps." Gerand tapped his fingers together, collected his thoughts. "You see, Victor, while His Majesty might be rash and willing to agree to things without much thought, I try to be a bit more... patient. I like to peer deeper into things, and I've done so with your family. I know who you've done business with, every trader and every merchant."

Victor's eyes narrowed. "Is that so?"

"It is. When the king's adviser comes calling, people tend to talk. No one wants to let things become... unpleasant. And since you've given me the costs of training and hiring your men, it was a simple matter to compare that to what I learned of your wheat trade. Do you know what I found out?"

"What is that, adviser?"

Gerand breathed in deep, wrapped his fingers together. His face was emotionless, a well-controlled mask to hide whatever it was he felt.

"You're broke, Victor. You can't afford your own army."

The words sent a chill down Victor's spine, but he did his best to hide it, just as Gerand hid his own emotions.

"That's preposterous," he said.

"Is it?" asked Gerand, his eyebrows lifting. "Your lands are not large, and such skilled men as yours are not cheap, especially for the danger they face and the time you've committed them to. Perhaps a few you've promised a pittance of land, but you don't have much to give. Others are loyal to your house, but sworn men like that are few and far between, especially for such an average family line as the Kanes. Even if you've been saving for the past five years or so, which I honestly believe you have, within a few weeks your men will want another portion of their pay and you simply won't have it. Which of course brings us to your request for an advance."

Gerand leaned back, clearly giving Victor an opportunity to speak. Victor tried to think, to know what was expected of him.

"What I've done has helped this city," he said, deciding to be honest in his appeal. "You have to know this. After everything I've accomplished, surely His Majesty can issue in good faith a portion..."

Gerand waved a hand, interrupting him.

"His Majesty will do as I say in this, so long as I convince him he'll sleep safer at night. I am the one you must convince, so direct your arguments to me. What makes you think I should trust you with such wealth?"

"You've seen my men combing the streets. You've seen the scum I've brought to your judges. Even the Trifect has opened its books to me. For what reason would you doubt me?"

"Stay calm, friend," Gerand said, rising from his seat. "I have no time for anger or personal insult. And forgive my manners...would you care for a drink?"

The adviser poured them each a glass of wine, and Victor accepted his reluctantly. Once Gerand had taken a sip, Victor did so as well. It was a fine vintage, and despite himself Victor drank half the glass.

"So you wonder why I should doubt you, after all I've seen," Gerand said, setting his glass beside him on his desk. "That is exactly the point. I've seen you driven to put your life in danger, risking every shred of your wealth to hire and train men to accomplish this fanatical quest. I can only imagine how many moneylenders are eyeing your wheat fields even as we speak. Yet what I don't know is *why*. What could possibly push you to such lengths?"

"Why does my reason matter so long as my motives are pure?" Victor asked.

"Are they pure? I don't know. You see, it matters because I do not like entrusting the streets to a madman, and to me you carry the look of a madman. It sparkles in your eyes. Sane men do not do what you've done, especially out of altruism. I'm sorry, that is something I feel in my gut. So tell me something I can believe, that will convince me to open the treasury to you, and I will do so."

"You don't trust someone to give everything, to sweat and bleed for others," Victor said. "You are a sad, bitter man if that is true. But if you don't trust that, then what of vengeance, Gerand? Is that something you can trust?"

"Perhaps."

"Then know that what I do, I do for the honor of my parents. I do to avenge my childhood. The crimes these guilds have committed against me are loathsome, and if you have looked into me as you say, then you know what they did to my parents. It should never have happened, never, and I will do whatever it takes to break every person involved and lay their corpses before the memory of my mother and father."

Victor crossed his arms, and he felt like one awaiting judgment.

"So tell me," he said. "Am I still a madman?"

Gerand chuckled. "Perhaps, but if you are, you're a madman I can understand. I will give you the advance you requested, plus half over. But I want you to remember something, Victor. If you are wise, you'll listen well. If you accomplish what you desire, if you keep breaking the guilds one by one, then I'll make sure your men remain paid, in secret, and quietly, so none will know of His Majesty's involvement. But if you fail, then I'll suddenly discover how you attempted to defraud the castle, and lied about your wealth in the vain hope of having our treasury pay for your ill-conceived crusade. In short, either they hang, or you do. Have I made myself clear?"

Victor swallowed down both saliva and his pride, then nodded. "I do," he said.

Gerand waved a dismissive hand. "Good. Now go. I'll send the gold sometime in the next few days, once it's clear this peace will actually last."

Victor stood and bowed to the adviser. "You are most gracious," he said, each word like a bee sting on his tongue.

"You can hate me if you wish, but you shouldn't," Gerand said, sensing his frustration. "I'm your friend in this. I have no love for these guilds either. They've threatened my life plenty, even in this very room. But my friendship extends only so far as your usefulness. I have faith in you, and hope that you're the right madman to create something good in Veldaren. Besides, with the Watcher dead, someone needs to inspire fear in the hearts of thieves."

Victor chuckled. "He's not dead," he said.

Gerand shrugged. "Then we'll have two madmen spilling the blood of the underworld instead of one. Try to get along."

*   *   *

They had the bar to themselves, just as Carson Bloodcraft preferred. He sat facing the door, his back to the wall. No one would sneak up on him. A fool might try to prevent his exit, thinking him trapped, but such a fool was no threat to him. Just an inconvenience at best. Given how young the night was, the tavern should have been teeming with activity, but some coins and a few simple words had changed that.

"I think we might have underestimated our foes," Carson said, pushing powder into his long-stemmed pipe. It was the finest leaf available in Mordeina, and he'd brought it with him all the way across the continent to Veldaren.

"Just their tenacity for survival," said Nora Bloodcraft, his wife. She sat opposite him, trusting him to alert her to any threat. Unlike his short dark hair, she had beautiful blond hair tied into a tight ponytail that ran across her neck, down her chest, and to her waist. They both wore crimson coats made of the finest leather and then stained to identify their mercenary band. Nora, seeing his pipe full, leaned forward and snapped her fingers. The leaf smoldered and began to smoke. Leaning back, Carson drew in a long breath and sighed.

"Need to ration this better," he said, looking down at his pouch. He'd used too much on the trip over. Last thing he needed was to go bartering for whatever shit they grew in Neldar. "And perhaps you're right. The Ash Guild presents no greater threat than we thought, but their ability to survive is admirable. They seem to lack any pride or honor, at least when it comes to fleeing a fight."

"What does pride or honor matter?" asked Joanna, their only daughter. She had just celebrated her seventeenth birthday, and while she had her mother's blond hair, she kept it cut short around the neck. She too wore a long red coat, and sat to the side of the two of them, able to keep an eye on the door leading down to the cellar. "Pride and honor would only get the Ash Guild killed. They're smarter than that."

"It's our own fault for trusting that weasel Laerek," said Percy Bloodcraft, carrying four drinks from the barkeep, who stood behind the bar, skin pale, hands shaking. They'd told him only once to leave them be, and made it clear what might happen if he did not. The chubby fellow kept glancing at the door, where the bodies of two men lay, both having been foolish enough to ignore the Bloodcrafts' request for privacy. One had bled out from a gash running from belly to throat. The other's face was a charred husk, with faint flecks of white bone showing.

Percy sat beside Joanna, put down the drinks, and then leaned back in his chair. He had no biological relation to the other three, but like all members of the Bloodcraft Mercenaries since their creation, Percy had been adopted into the family once his skills had proven suitable. He looked like nothing but bone and hair, but he was fast. Hidden in the folds of his crimson coat were dozens of knives of all sizes, and he could make each one fly like a bird on the wind. His hair was a soft brown, the only thing beautiful about him.

"We're new to this city," Carson said, ignoring the drink set before him. "We must make do with the information we are given."

"Sure thing, Father, but wouldn't it make more sense to doubt everything instead?"

Carson and Nora were not much older than Percy, but he'd taken to calling them Mother and Father ever since joining the Bloodcrafts. Something about it amused him, perhaps how it managed to get underneath Carson's skin.

"With how our day has gone?" Nora said, tasting her drink

and then frowning at it. "Perhaps it would. The Ash Guild avoided our ambush without casualty. Even worse...where is Nicholas?"

"Nicholas is dead," Percy said, smirking. "You know it, I know it, we all do. I told you I should have gone with him."

"His abilities were a perfect counter to the Eschaton," Carson said, breathing in more from the pipe. "The Ash Guild was more of an unknown, and posed the greater risk."

"Well, it looks like you calculated wrong."

Nora shook her head. "That, or the Watcher still lives. If his rumors are to be believed, he could have achieved victory. Surely it took someone of his skill with a blade to kill Nicholas."

"Laerek assured us the man was dead," Joanna said, her eyes locked on her drink. She'd barely had a sip of it, yet her attention rarely left her reflection in the liquid. To Carson it seemed she was bored with anything and everything that didn't involve making a man suffer in pain.

"That he did," Carson said. "I might have to have a word with him. His poor information has cost us dearly."

"If the Watcher killed Nicholas, then we need to hunt him down and return the favor," Percy said, leaning forward in his seat and drumming the table with his fingers. Carson saw the eagerness there, and it amused him greatly.

"There's little word on who he is, or who his loved ones are," Carson said. "All anyone knows is that he works for the Eschaton Mercenaries."

Percy shrugged.

Joanna dipped her finger into her drink, lifted it out, and then sucked off the cheap wine.

"They talk," she said, fingernail still scratching against her teeth. "They always talk."

The door opened. Carson leaned to the side, the better to

see past his wife. It was a woman, slender, with long brown hair that curled down around her shoulders. Her dress was plain but clean, and of a soft blue.

"Miss," the barkeep said. "Please, you should go..."

"No men here to buy a whore," Percy said, glancing back and seeing her. "That's what we got Joanna for. Go on your way."

The woman stepped around the two mutilated bodies, seeming unfazed by them. Carson narrowed his eyes, and then he began to laugh.

"My, my," he said. "I think we've found our Widow."

The woman did not sit at their table, but the one beside it, as if uncomfortable with their presence. She kept her hair low over her face, and when she talked, it was in a strained whisper that Carson had to struggle to hear.

"Laerek said I could find you here," she said.

"Well, that's the first thing Laerek's been right about so far," Percy said, but he was the only one to laugh.

"The city seems to know *you* well," Nora said. Carson could tell his wife was examining her closely, trying to reach an opinion of some sort. He trusted her ability to read someone, and when their talk was done, he'd listen well to what she had to say. "Yet I wonder why. All you've done is kill a few members of a guild. Others do it all the time. Why are you so special to Laerek, or to us?"

"People die all the time," the strange woman said. "I give the city something to remember, to both fear and enjoy."

"What's your real name?" Carson asked, putting aside his pipe.

"I'm the Widow, of course, and that is the only name I will tell you."

The woman smiled, and something about it unsettled Carson's stomach. He shifted in his seat, and his hand reached for the sword strapped to his belt.

"Keep your secrets, then," Nora said. "But why are you here? What business do you have with us?"

"I'm here to help you," she said.

Percy laughed, and even Carson had to fight to keep down a chuckle. "Is that so?" he asked. "Who are you to help *us*? And help us do what, exactly?"

"I know this city," the Widow said. "Know it far better than you. I've seen its gross underbelly, know its scabs and scars. If you want, I can draw the Watcher out. You'll have a clean shot, all of you. All I ask is that you do me a favor as well."

"And what is that?" Carson asked.

"Kill Lord Victor Kane at the same time. They'll be together, and vulnerable. All you need to do is...well, do what your kind does best."

Carson looked to the other two. Nora's nod showed that her gut told her the Widow was to be believed. Percy merely shrugged. "It's either the Watcher, or finishing off the Ash," he said. "We need to stick together no matter who we go after."

Carson nodded, but Percy's remark about trusting no one still echoed in his head. He looked to this strange, nameless woman, then gestured for her to continue.

"Go ahead," he said. "Let's hear your plan."

When she was done, and Carson had agreed to the plan, he ushered away the Widow, who left without a word. The four Bloodcrafts looked to one another, waiting for the first to speak.

"Well," Percy said at last. "To say it's a gamble is to be kind."

"A gamble in our favor, though," Nora said. "And though she is steeped in dishonesty, I believe that she believes in her plan."

"So we throw in with the gamble," said Carson, leaning forward toward Joanna. "But that doesn't mean we can't adjust things even more in our favor."

Joanna swirled her finger along the top of her cup. "What are you thinking?" she asked him.

"I'm thinking," he said, grinning, "that two traps might be better than one. How would you like a shot at the Watcher with those pretty little daggers of yours?"

Her blue eyes flicked upward at last, and he saw hunger sparkle in her irises.

"I'd like that," she said. "I'd like that very much."

CHAPTER

25

The first night was terrible, but Nathaniel managed. Several times he woke up thinking he'd heard a noise, or that he'd seen movement in the shadows.

"Zusa?" he called out each time, squinting to see. Always nothing, but he couldn't help but think monsters lurked within the dark corners of his room. Normally he told himself it was Zusa, but this time he knew it wasn't. She'd left. Somehow, by the way his mother had kissed him good night, he knew she was gone. The night crawled along, until at long last daylight met his tired eyes.

The day came and went, Nathaniel sleepwalking through most of it. At one point he fell asleep at the table, his uneaten food beside his face. One of the servant women scolded him harshly for that, and he was able to offer only the most meager of apologies. All the while he waited for Zusa's return. And waited. The servants whispered of how the previous night had been far safer, and that Victor was winning over the city. Nathaniel knew this should have made his mother happier, but it did not.

Night came again, and Zusa still hadn't returned. Nathaniel once more tried to sleep alone in his room, but this time he heard monsters scratching inside the walls, and every shadow bore a blade. He squeezed his eyes shut and pushed his face into a pillow, but then they were all around him, stepping closer, mouths drooling, claws reaching. Zusa wasn't there to protect him. His mother's guards weren't about to rescue him. It took all his courage to pull down his blankets and look, and no matter how many times he saw his room empty, he knew without a doubt they were there.

At last he got up and left. He felt like a thief sneaking through the dark halls, but at each corner stood a house guard, looking somber and dangerous in the lantern light. They watched him as he passed, and it made his skin crawl. At his mother's room, he stopped and gently pushed open the door with his arm.

"Mother?" he called out. Then louder, "Mother?"

"I'm here, Nathan," she said, and he saw a feminine form lean up from the pillows.

Nathaniel curled his shoulders together, and he grabbed his stump with his other hand, as if he were cold.

"I'm scared," he said. The question within was implicit, and his mother heard it well.

"Come here," she said. "The bed's big enough."

He climbed up and then crawled forward until he reached the top. His mother's arms wrapped about him as he curled against her and laid his head on a pillow. Immediately he felt his fears ebbing, and his exhaustion clawed at him with pent-up fury.

"Getting too big for this," Alyssa said as she moved to give him room.

"I'm sorry."

She kissed the back of his neck to show she wasn't angry. Nathaniel shifted and slid his legs underneath the blanket.

"Mom...when is Zusa coming back?"

For a long while she did not answer.

"I don't know," she said at last. Nathaniel closed his eyes, glad to be safe from the monsters, glad that he could rest. Still, the question nagged at him.

"She is coming back, isn't she?" he asked.

An even longer pause. His mother sniffed, and he realized she was crying. It made his stomach queasy, and he pulled himself into a tighter ball to fight the uncomfortable feeling growing in his chest.

"I hope so," his mother said. He felt her fingers brush against his face, lovingly touching his features with her fingertips. "Gods, I hope so."

He didn't know what to say, but he wanted to comfort her. He wanted to make her feel better.

"I hope so too," he said.

He closed his eyes and slept. Come the morning, he awoke to find himself alone in the bed. Feeling embarrassed, he slid out from the blankets and hurried back to his room to change. On his way there, he passed by his grandmother's room. The door was cracked open, and he heard voices from within. The past two nights had left him wary, and something about the hushed tones made him slow. Pressing against the wall, he peered inside to see Lord Gandrem talking with his grandmother. Melody sat on the bed, and he could just barely see her hands as they gestured along with her words. John stood before her, arms crossed. His face was turned away, so Nathaniel could not read his expression.

"I cannot leave my lands unprotected," John was saying. "Surely between Stephen and your daughter, the house guards are sufficient."

"They aren't," Melody insisted. "Alyssa lost so many, and has yet to rehire, instead focusing on repairing her mansion. She puts her faith in that strange woman, Zusa. I don't trust her, John. I just don't. And Stephen's guards are loyal only to him."

John sighed and looked away, right toward the door. Nathaniel's breath caught in his throat, and he pulled back and pressed himself tighter against the wall. Counting to five before peering in again, he saw his grandmother had stood and put her arms around John's waist.

"My lands are tame, and my steward is a good man, and runs my affairs well," John said. Nathaniel could hear weakness in his voice, a bending of his will toward Melody. "Are you really so sure we need more men to protect us? What of Lord Victor? They say Victor has done much to make the city safer."

"I'm scared, John," Melody said, pressing tighter against him. "I came back from such a dark place. I don't want to be scared anymore. Victor can't be everywhere, and those thieves are like rabid dogs. You saw what they did to our mansion. They'll come again. They'll come, with torches, with daggers, with...with..."

She buried her face in his neck, and as she shuddered, John wrapped his arms about her.

"I just want to feel safe," she said. "Is that so terrible of me?"

"Of course not," John said. "I'll send for my footmen. They'll stay until all of this business in Veldaren settles down."

In response Melody kissed him on the mouth. It was quick, skittish, almost afraid.

"Thank you," she said, burying herself in his chest. "Thank you."

Nathaniel ran, scared and confused and wanting to see no more.

Thren watched as the men and women gathered about the entrance to the alley, all thin and meager-looking. They surrounded the hooded figure, who kept looking for guards as he took in silver and gave out his crimleaf. As if guards would come to the southern district. They were too busy in the north and west, protecting the trade and homes of the wealthy. No guards, Thren knew. No control. The Suns had come into the lawless anarchy of the slums, and it was time they paid for it.

He kept his walk lumbering, as if he were just another overworked member of the city barely staving off hunger. He'd discarded his guild colors and instead wrapped a thin coat about him. It was dark brown, stained, and had many holes, but it hid the swords strapped at his waist, which was all that mattered.

There were three men still buying when Thren joined them, lurking at their backs.

"Shit, man, wasn't it just one silver?" argued the closest. His eyes were bloodshot, and lice crawled in his hair.

"It's two now," said the Sun thief. "Don't act all pissed off, either. You know you still can't get it cheaper elsewhere, not by a mile."

"I wouldn't buy from him," Thren said, stepping closer.

"Piss off, and mind your own," the thief said, glaring. "My leaf's good, and my prices fair."

"That's not why," Thren said, taking another step. "It's just not wise to buy from a dead man."

He leaped forward, short sword drawn. It rammed into the

man's stomach. A twist and a yank sent his innards spilling out across the ground. Two of the three other men fled, while the third made a desperate lunge for the falling bag of crimleaf. A single well-placed kick knocked the man out, leaving him sprawling beside the corpse. Cleaning his blade, Thren then sheathed it and knelt down to grab the bag.

"Save your coin for food," he said to the unconscious man, spitting on his chest.

Leaf pocketed, he ran back into the alley, hooked a right, and then emerged into heavier traffic, where he allowed himself to slow. One by one he'd been taking out the Sun pushers, always on the lookout for the ones who strayed too far from the rest, or were too foolish to have others with them for protection. It was slow work, but he'd killed five so far. In a few more days, he'd have another five.

And by then another fifty Suns might have moved in from the west. He shook his head. It was a losing battle, perhaps, but he'd still fight it until he knew of a way to really hurt Grayson. Out of instinct he traveled toward his old territory, now claimed by three separate guilds. Not that he was surprised. With the city turning wilder by the hour, such a vacancy would never last long. A thought hit him, an image of other guilds using his former base as their own, and it stirred an anger in his chest. Heading that way, he found the old tavern, now shuttered and closed down after Victor's raid. The upper levels had been ruined by the fire, but what of the underground portion?

It was a risk doing it in daylight, but he went ahead anyway. What did caution matter, now that his guild was disbanded? He opened the door to the stairs downward and found everything dark. Sighing with relief, he stepped farther in, grabbing a lantern hanging from the side. He checked it for oil, found a little, and then nodded. From a gap in the wall he pulled out some flint, and after a few sparks had the lantern lit. Holding it aloft, he stepped down into his former headquarters.

Everything was in disarray. Tables were overturned, chairs broken. Guards had torn it apart in their search. The small slanted windows near the ceiling were covered with cloth, and one by one Thren yanked them off, letting in more light. At first he was confused as to why the guards would have covered them, and then he saw the lone upright table in the center.

"No," he whispered, feeling his fury rise. "Damn it, how dare you do this now?"

One of his former members lay on the table, arms and legs spread wide. An arrow protruded from his chest. Carrying the lantern over, Thren felt stones turn in his gut as the light glinted off silver coins in the man's eyes. Alan, Thren realized. His name was Alan. After the raid, all the captured Spider guildmembers had been questioned and brought before judges. Those who turned on others had been spared the ax and sent away. Alan must have been one of them.

Pulling open his mouth, Thren found the two gold coins, there as always. Lifting the lantern, he looked at the opposite wall for the message.

gold and silver
silver and gold
where are you spider
where are you thren

It was written not once, not twice, but a dozen times all along the walls. Over and over the message was repeated, mostly just that final line.

Checking the body, Thren found a slit across Alan's neck, no doubt where this madman had gotten the necessary amount of blood. And Thren knew for certain it was a madman. Unlike in the streets, he, or she, had had time in the basement, and they'd indulged themselves with the display. Everywhere he cast his lantern light he saw the message, and it left no question as to whom it'd been intended for.

Where are you spider? Where are you Thren?

The killings had nothing to do with his guild, nothing to do with power or territory. Someone wanted him to suffer. Whatever vendetta they had, it was personal.

"I'm here!" Thren shouted, kicking the table so it slid a foot, rocking the body atop it. "You want me, here I am! Think you'll take my eyes? Think you'll shove gold coins down my throat? Here! Right here!"

Childish outburst out of the way, Thren forced himself to calm down, to think. If the Widow had taken his or her time, then so could he. First he needed more light than the little coming in through the windows. Most of their things had been ransacked, but he found a discarded skin with a bit more oil in it. He refilled the lantern, set it to burning brighter. That done, he dug through the scattered mess in the supply room, scavenging a few candles that he lit and placed about. That done, he began his investigation.

He started with the body, looking it over for any sort of clue. He found no sign of clothing, no dropped personal items. Moving on to the floor, he looked, but again found little. Too much tramping about by guards, too much activity prior to their arrival. Next he scanned the messages, each one. He read them all, to see if they said the same thing. He looked for any hint to the mind-set of the Widow, even something as basic as whether the man or woman wrote with the right or left hand.

On the sixth message he checked he at last found his clue. Pressed against the wall and held there by dried blood was a long strand of brown hair. Thren pulled it free and then wrapped it around his finger. At least he had a color to go on, and, given its length, he leaned toward the Widow's being a woman. A flash of thought, and he grinned. No, he had far more than that. Returning to Alan's body, he took the silver and gold before rushing out.

The Council of Mages' presence was weak in Veldaren, but it did have a few members. They were unanimously unimpressive, failures at mastering the craft. Thren viewed them as little more than charlatans, taking the coin of others and offering petty fortunes and trinkets in return. One such charlatan, however, had been useful. In what felt like an age past, a wizard had been a member of the Spider Guild. It was his shop Thren went to, the hair still tightly wrapped around his finger.

Inside was cramped, with hardly room for three men to stand side by side. The fat wizard sat on a stool, only a table separating him from the door. A few odds and ends hung from the walls, and behind the wizard was a shelf full of jars, each containing a strange organ or insect. From experience Thren knew few of them were necessary for spells; the rest were kept there for looks.

"Welcome, welcome," said the wizard. Most of his clothing was simple, dull browns and grays, but he wore a thin green robe over it, no doubt meant to impress the simpletons. Thren snorted at the sight.

"Hello, Cregon," Thren said. "How has business fared since you tossed aside your cloak?"

Cregon leaned closer, and then his eyes widened as he realized who was before him.

"Y-y-you let me go willingly," he stammered. "And I know my protection money's not been consistent, but business comes and goes..."

"Drop it," Thren said, taking a seat opposite the wizard. "If I wanted you dead, I'd just kill you. I have a use for your talents."

"Talents?" Cregon asked. He was already sweating. The sight of it disgusted Thren. Sure, he'd been useful, but he'd let the man go just because he couldn't stand the sight of his bloated self. "Talents, of course. Whatever you need, I'm sure I can help. What spell would you like? Or do you need some sort of enchantment?"

"I need a scrying spell," Thren said.

Cregon licked his lips. "Who is it? If they're unknown to me, I'll need a drawing or strongly personal object to see them."

"I don't know who he or she is, and don't care about their name or what they're doing. I just need to know where to find them."

Cregon nodded, but Thren could tell he was starting to worry. "That's better, but still not cheap, nor easy. Do you have anything of theirs?"

In answer, Thren tossed the silver and gold he'd taken from Alan's body, then put the strand of hair atop it. "That's for the cost, and that's for the spell," Thren explained. "Just a location."

Cregon pocketed the coins, then grabbed the hair. He frowned at it as he wrapped it twice around his beefy hand. "Not a lot to go on," he said. "But I think I can manage. Is this person important to you in some way?"

Thren chuckled. "You might say that. It's a woman, I believe, and I want her dead. But to do that, I need to find her."

Cregon nodded, the movement shaking his fat jowls. "Of course, of course. Just wait a moment. I'll see what I can do."

He put his hands over the hair, closed his eyes, and began murmuring the spidery words of magic. Thren waited, wise enough not to interrupt such an incantation. A soft light surrounded Cregon's fingers, and then it plunged into the hair. It shimmered yellow, then faded. Cregon frowned.

"What is it?" Thren asked.

"I found her," he said, "But it's somewhere dark. Not a building...I don't know. It's outside the city, though, not far from the wall."

"Not good enough, Cregon. I need to know where to look."

"I'm telling you! It's just beyond the west wall, little bit off the road into the city. I can't tell you how to get there when *there* is nothing. Maybe it's a camp..."

Thren stood, and his hand fell to the hilt of a short sword. "Can you find the way?" he asked. Cregon's eyes widened, and he nodded. "Good. Then close up shop. You're leading me there."

Cregon locked the door to his store, pocketed the key, and then hurried off. Thren followed, lurking a few feet behind him.

"Pick up the pace," Thren told him, rolling his eyes. The man looked like a pregnant sow trying to waddle on two legs. "I don't want this Widow to move before we get there."

"The Widow?" Cregon asked, glancing behind him. "*That's* who we're looking for?"

"It is. Now move."

Cregon hurried faster, huffing and puffing as they made for the west gate. A few passing by recognized him and said hello, and the wizard tipped his hat in return. At the gate the guards waved him on without a word. Thren followed, looking like a poor commoner and hardly earning a second glance.

"How far?" Thren asked as they traveled the road.

"Not far," Cregon said, very much out of breath. "Not…" He swallowed. "Not far."

A quarter mile from the city Cregon turned sharply off the path. Realizing where they traveled, Thren quietly drew his short swords, thinking the wizard was leading him into a trap. Cregon stopped just short, and gestured before him.

"In there," he said. "I'm sure of it."

He'd taken them to a pauper's graveyard, where the city guards buried the nameless dead without a single copper in their possession to buy them a gravestone or marker.

"This Widow is still alive," Thren said. "You've made a mistake. You must have."

"No mistake," Cregon said. "I assure you, she must be here."

Thren pointed a short sword toward the graveyard. "Then find her."

Cregon held the fist with the hair to his lips, and he closed his eyes. After a few whispers, he opened them. "Follow me."

Near the far corner he stopped, and with his heel he made a small X. "Right here," he said.

Thren wanted to believe the wizard was lying to him, but he'd always been a coward, and the fear in his eyes was genuine. Surely he'd made a mistake, but Cregon appeared convinced otherwise.

"Go on back to your shop," he said. "Leave me be."

Cregon was more than happy to oblige. When he trundled off, Thren remained, staring at the mark in the dirt. At last he returned to the city and swiped a trowel small enough to hide underneath his thin coat. Once more he walked to the graveyard, and, without a care for time, he began to dig. The day passed by, hour by hour, as he unearthed the grave. At last he hit bone, and then started digging around it. By the time the woman's skull was revealed, the sun had begun to set. Exhausted, he sat back and viewed the results of his work.

The body had been buried at least a year to his untrained eye. The dead woman still had her teeth, and her fingernails. As for her hair, though...

He broke the skull free and lifted it up to the waning light. All across the bare skull he saw tiny marks, scratches as if from a small blade.

"A wig," Thren said, tossing the skull back into the shallow grave. "What is it you hide, Widow? Who are you really?"

Still, he had a few clues now, however meager. Standing, he kicked dirt into the grave until the body was covered, then looked back to Veldaren. Her lanterns were starting to twinkle into existence one by one. There had been a time when Thren considered Veldaren his city, all his. How far had he fallen to be outside it, digging up a poor woman's corpse while the rest of the guilds and the Trifect plotted and maneuvered? Hands clenched into fists, he stabbed the trowel into the earth to serve as a burial marker. Alone he walked toward the road.

Veldaren would be his city again. He swore it. Once he had his vengeance, once he knew who was out there pulling the strings of puppets, he would retake his city brick by brick.

My city.

The thought put a grim smile on his face. For a while he'd accepted that the city was no longer his, but instead his son's. That was over. The rumors of the Watcher's survival meant nothing to him, for he'd started them, acting out the sham in a failed attempt to shame Grayson in the eyes of the underworld. But Victor's arrival had shifted things beyond his control, had made it so Grayson needed only to watch as Thren's guild was broken.

Darkness settled across the land as he walked his path. He'd take it all back. He'd rebuild, fight for it with every last measure of his skill. He would find victory.

And if he couldn't, then he'd burn it all to the ground.

CHAPTER

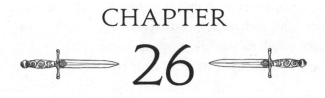 26

Victor stepped inside his makeshift home and let out a sigh of relief. Another day over, another twelve gone to the executioner's blade. The light was fading as the sun dipped below the walls of the city, but inside was well lit, and crowded with families still seeking refuge from the vengeance of the thief guilds.

"Where's your guard?" Sef asked, sitting at the bar, where Victor joined him. "You did have a guard, right?"

"What business of yours is that?" Victor asked, accepting the drink Sef slid over to him.

"My business is to keep you alive, and to kill the rats of Veldaren. So far I think I'm doing better at one than the other."

Victor shrugged. "The streets have grown calmer. You know that."

Sef rolled his eyes. "So no escort, then?" At Victor's chuckle, Sef shook his head. "Going to get your damn self killed, Victor. I thought you'd learned better."

"Lay off. I am no helpless child."

Sef stroked his beard, a habit Victor recognized well. It meant Sef was growing frustrated with him.

"Our foes aren't so helpless either. But if you want to go about trusting only your sword arm, then go right ahead."

Victor stood, patted Sef on the shoulder.

"You know the gods have a better fate for me than dying to some soulless vagabond. Stay safe on your patrols tonight."

Sef grunted. "Thought you said the city had grown calmer."

Victor grinned at him as he headed for the stairs.

"Did I? But my advisers insist the world is still a dangerous place, and I feel it best to listen."

"Bastard."

Victor waved without looking. At the top of the stairs were the two guards watching his room, to ensure no one entered during his absence. Victor nodded at them, then waited for his door to be unlocked.

"Sleep well, milord," said one as he pushed the door wide.

"That's the hope."

As Victor removed his armor, he glanced at the far wall, which was now bare wood without painting or decoration. The carpenters he'd hired had rebuilt it at an impressive pace, repairing the gaping hole Tarlak's spell had left. Victor chuckled. Next time he'd make sure he learned all the details of any spells that that wizard placed for his protection. He'd expected a few planks to fall loose, or some magical porthole of sorts to open up. When the wall had exploded as if a dragon had let loose its rage against it, he'd nearly soiled his armor. Of course it was his own fault for expecting subtlety from a wizard who dressed in bright yellow.

After checking underneath his bed, Victor climbed in, lay down, and tried to sleep. Try as he might, sleep would not come. Tossing and turning, he felt time crawling along. The sounds from the tavern below quieted as those under his protection settled in as well. That helped, but only a little. Sleep had grown steadily rarer during his time in Veldaren. The faces of the men who had died that day flashed before his eyes, and they joined the ghostly choir that wailed in his head. They all had something different to say, some plea or explanation, when they knelt before the chopping block. It was as if they could never admit they'd done their wrongs for themselves, to satisfy their own greed and lust. They cried of children, mothers, families, debts, mistakes made, and long-forgotten histories they always insisted they regretted.

Victor tossed and turned, tossed and turned. Perhaps he needed to have the executioners use a gag on them. The only other option was to not be present, but he refused. He might not swing the blade, but he was the reason for their deaths, and his pride demanded he be in their presence. Cowardly hiding might make it easier, but that was the last thing he wanted. He wanted it to be hard. He wanted every death to weigh on him, despite what he showed others. The final moment, when there was no one left to give to the executioner's ax, would be that much sweeter for it.

The night dragged on. Victor's thoughts turned to his parents, to brighter memories in his childhood. Lost in them, he almost didn't hear the soft clink of armor hitting the floor. Almost. Victor tensed, not once doubting his instincts and the danger they cried. It might just have been his guard shifting positions, but it didn't sound right. It almost sounded as if a guard had chosen to sit down, something one of his guards would never, ever do.

His sword was beside him on the floor, just within reach. Trying to make little noise, he reached down and lifted it still in its scabbard. As the door crept open a crack, he managed to slide it underneath his blankets. Victor half-closed his eyes so that his intruder might believe him asleep. With the smallest movements possible, he held the hilt with one hand and pulled the scabbard down with the other. Didn't want to let them know, didn't want to scare them off, especially if there was more than one.

The door opened wider. Victor clenched his jaw to prevent any giveaway. *Stay calm*, he told himself. *Just wait.* Still, he quickened his pace with the scabbard. The blade of his sword was halfway exposed, but it'd be cumbersome to use in the cramped quarters. Stupid, stupid, why hadn't he just kept his dagger with him instead?

Two men stepped inside, each one carrying a small blade. Victor choked down his fury at his guards for letting such things pass by their scrutiny. They'd slacked on their precautions because of how many came and went, he had no doubt. Victor waited until they stepped all the way in, and were just starting to move to opposite sides of his bed, before he struck. In a single motion he freed his sword from his scabbard and flung aside the blankets, giving him freedom of movement.

If the men were surprised, they showed no sign of it. Victor lashed out with his sword, a long arc that had far more reach than they did with their daggers. The one on the right tried to block, but he lacked both the strength and the weapon to do it. Victor's sword bounced off, angling higher so it hit the man's neck instead of his chest. It struck his neck bones with a wet chop. Victor tried to swing back to the other side, to where the second thief was lunging, but his blade had caught between two vertebrae. Panicking, Victor let go and fell back, narrowly avoiding a slash. He rolled away and off the bed, trying to gain some distance.

"There's no hope for you," the assassin said, his voice a whisper.

The crossbow bolt thudding into his neck seemed to say otherwise. The assassin slumped to the bed and bled out on the sheets as Victor scrambled to his feet. A third man stood at the door, miniature crossbow at his side. He was an older man, and wore the plain browns of a commoner. Plenty of scars lined his face, and calluses his hands.

"Friend," the man said when Victor reached for his sword.

"That so?" Victor asked, putting a foot on the dead man's head so he could yank his blade free. "Then who are you, friend?"

"No lie, milord. I'm here to help. My name's Gart. Antonil put me here to protect you."

The light was dim, but Victor saw Gart pull down his shirt, revealing a city guard's tunic underneath as proof.

"Antonil's keeping his eye on me, is that it?" Victor asked.

"You expressed concern about the families staying here. He thought it best to help keep an eye on them." Gart nodded at the two bodies. "Caught them sneaking toward the stairs when they thought everyone asleep. Killed the guards at the stairs by your door. Real pros."

Victor used his heel to roll over the one at his feet, then looked him over.

"Any idea the guild?" Victor asked.

"Not really. Not like they'd have been foolish enough to send people with colors or tattoos identifying them."

It made sense, but was still frustrating. Standing, he looked to Gart and frowned at the crossbow. "How'd you sneak that past my guards?"

Gart stood up straight. "I told them it was with the authority of the king, and that they were to tell no one, not even you. If it makes you feel better, your men were most displeased, and I feared they might inform you despite my warnings."

Victor felt his anger growing. Not only had two men come into his place of safety and nearly killed him, but Antonil was spying on him as well, and hiding things from him?

"It's no longer safe here," Victor said, grabbing his armor. "I told Antonil bringing in civilians would put me at risk. I told him! They will not stay here, not any longer. And much as I owe you, Gart, I still resent that your presence was kept hidden from me."

"Just following my orders, milord."

"I know. It's those orders I plan on questioning."

Armor on, sword buckled to his waist, Victor stepped into the hall. His guards lay slumped against the wall, throats opened and tunics stained with blood. Victor closed their eyes with his fingers, offered a silent word of thanks to the men who had given their lives to protect him. And then he was moving on, Gart in tow.

"Summon your guard, and have them clean up this mess," Victor told him. "After that, start gathering the people here and bring them to the castle. If Antonil wants them kept safe, and wants to position men in secret to guard them, then let him take responsibility for them in full. I need no more assassins in my bedchambers."

"Milord, I'm not sure if I should do that until..."

Victor spun on him while still halfway down the stairs.

"I will speak with Antonil myself, and I assure you, I will not have my request denied. Take them to the castle. Do you understand me?"

The older man nodded. "As you wish, milord."

They continued down the stairs to where the commoners slept all across the floor. Victor navigated around, and then he and Gart stepped out into the night. Four men stood guard at the door, and they saluted when they realized it was he.

"City guard will soon arrive," Victor told them. "Help them in any way you can."

He started toward the castle unescorted. One of his men called out after him. "Milord..."

Victor glared, silencing his comment. Gart followed him a little ways, then stopped. "Nearest guard station is this way," he said, gesturing east.

"I will be at the castle," Victor said, not slowing. "Safe travels."

Gart didn't look happy, but he left anyway. Victor knew he was being proud, but he didn't care. He was a skilled fighter, and he wore his shining armor. Piss on anyone who thought him vulnerable. The scum of the city needed to catch him sleeping in his bedclothes to even have a chance. Marching down the quiet night streets, he made his way toward the center of the city, then hooked north toward the castle. Only a few times did he see signs of life, those of taverns burning their midnight oil to fill the poor and destitute with enough alcohol to forget their dreary lives. Victor both pitied them and despised them. They'd be either fodder for thieves or new recruits. Once their lives continued to fall apart. Once they lost enough to believe they could never replace it without taking by force.

Several times he thought he saw someone following him out of the corner of his eye, a gray blur of a strange cloak along the rooftops. When he glanced back, it was always gone. He shook his head.

"Are you there, Watcher?" he whispered. "Do you follow me?"

He heard no answer, and he sighed. It might have been good to talk with the man, to see if he'd made any progress in his own private search for the Widow, or in combating the ruthless guilds. But, snubbed, he continued on north, toward the castle, to ensure Guard Captain Antonil would never again think it his right to spy on a lord of the realm.

Haern couldn't begin to guess what stupidity was leading Victor to walk the streets of Veldaren at night without any escort. Pride? Arrogance? Delusion? Whatever it was, it kept Haern skulking along the rooftops, a careful eye on both him and the ground below. Did it matter that Victor carried a sword? All it'd take was a single man with a crossbow to bring him down.

The wood beneath his boots should have creaked due to his weight, but magic placed within the soles by Tarlak kept his landings soft as he leaped across the alleys. Victor was picking up the pace, and Haern couldn't decide whether that was good or bad. Good because it got him to safety faster. Bad because it meant Haern had to hurry, and couldn't scout ahead as carefully as he wished. That, and the running wasn't exactly kind on his body. While not fully recovered from the wounds given to him by both Grayson and Nicholas Bloodcraft, he still felt well enough to be out in the night. Tarlak and Delysia, however, had strongly disagreed. His compromise had been to keep an eye on Victor's home while the rest of the Eschaton scoured the city in hopes of catching the Widow in another murder.

Victor, of course, was supposed to have remained in bed like a sane man, not rush through the main streets, sticking out like a damn bonfire in the middle of a snowstorm.

"Where are you headed?" he whispered aloud as he paused, just slightly ahead of the man on the street. "To the castle? Or to…"

An innate sense of wrongness flooded him, and in response he leaped off the side of the building, spun in air, and caught its side with both hands. Immediately he flung himself back up, drawing his blades and kicking forward. He caught his mysterious attacker square in the chest with his boots, blasting him backward.

Except that the hood of her red coat fell backward, and he saw that it wasn't a *he*, but a *she*. The girl had short blond hair, fierce blue eyes, and a glare to her that was chilling despite her obvious youth. In each hand she wielded a thin dagger so sharp its edge seemed to shine. She crouched on one knee, breathing heavily from the blow to her chest.

"Bloodcraft?" Haern asked, seeing the coat.

The girl smiled at him. "Joanna," she said.

She stood erect, daggers twirling in her hands. Haern refused to focus on her fingers, instead waiting for the tensing of the muscles in her legs, the shifting of her feet, to reveal the timing of her lunge. The moment she moved, he was ready, curling aside so she could not trap him against the ledge of the rooftop. Her daggers snaked in, but he had reach on her. His sabers sliced in a circle, the maneuver designed to sweep aside both her daggers and leave her right side vulnerable.

Except that when his sabers should have made contact, when he should have heard a familiar ring of steel, instead they passed straight through as if the daggers were not there.

Her momentum continued, and in a panic Haern kicked with his leg, forcing her to twist to avoid it. In that split second he dropped to the ground and rolled as her daggers stabbed the air above him. Pulling out of the roll, he found himself with no reprieve, for Joanna was already after him, the daggers in her hands dancing. Dancing, and it was a dance he couldn't be partner to...

"What's the matter?" Joanna asked, slowly stalking him, each movement like the step of a feline predator. "We're still playing the same game you've always played. I've just changed the rules."

She lunged again, and he pushed aside any reflex to parry or block. He had reach on her, and despite his inability to parry her daggers, he *could* still go for her wrists. His sabers curled in again, but the girl was ready, contorting her body so that she twisted both hands out of the way, then thrust downward with her left hand.

This time he couldn't stop her. The dagger sank into his shoulder, and she followed it up with a knee to his stomach. Agony flooded him, her knee striking close to the wound Grayson had given him. Before her blade could sink in farther he stabbed toward her stomach, forcing her to dance away. Blood, his blood, flecked across the rooftop. Her dagger, now glistening with red, she held before her face, just between her eyes.

"You're bleeding," she said. "Now it's just a matter of time."

Time, thought Haern. With each passing moment, Lord Victor was getting farther away. Tarlak had mentioned there were always five Bloodcrafts, and while one was dead, and he fought against another, that still left three to go after the man while he was vulnerable…

Joanna lifted her daggers, and as they shimmered the blood on one of them suddenly fell from the blade like rain, leaving the surface perfectly smooth. Shoving the pain into a far corner of his mind, Haern settled into a stance, and he stared into the girl's blue eyes.

"You live by forcing a fight your opponents have little practice in," he said. "But how well do those daggers work when on defense?"

Before she could respond he leaped at her, sabers slashing. She pulled back, but he was too fast, his reach too great. Up came her daggers, and he saw the sheen about them fade just before they made contact. The block was only partially effective, for Haern was much stronger and had all the momentum. As she stumbled back he continued, weaving his blades into patterns he knew by heart. At first he'd been thrown off by an inability to guide the duel, to use his parries and thrusts to position her weapons where he wanted them. But there was another way to control a fight.

Every cut, every thrust, he ensured would be fatal. She twisted and shifted, showing a flexibility and speed that rivaled Zusa's. Each time, she tried to find a gap in his routine, a moment's breath for her to counter. He refused to give it to her, pushing his speed to its limit, casting aside all his fear so he might strike all the more aggressively.

The glare in her eyes had been replaced with fear. She wanted to run, but he would not let her. Twice now the Bloodcrafts had threatened his life, and out there Lord Victor might already be dead. When Joanna turned to leap, he extended his arms, having already predicted this long before she even realized she meant to do it. In went the tips of his sabers, piercing her coat and slicing through flesh. The girl let out a scream, and despite his own pain, his own bleeding, Haern felt a tug of regret.

Joanna rolled across the rooftop, coming to a halt just beside the edge. She left a streak of blood across the dirty wood. Slowly Haern approached, unsure if his attack had been fatal. She knelt on her hands and knees, struggling to rise as blood dripped down the sides of her coat.

"Please," she whispered. "Please, don't kill me."

She rolled onto her back, let her weapons drop from limp fingers. Haern stood before her, weapons shaking in his own hands.

"My father," she insisted, staring up at him with those blue eyes. "He made me...he made me do it. Made me a killer. Please don't, please, please..."

For the shortest moment he hesitated, and that was all Joanna needed. Her right hand grabbed the blade beside her, and curling forward she lunged with all her strength, the tip of the dagger aimed for his stomach. So close, so fast, Haern knew he could not parry it away. Instead he dropped the sword from one hand as he fell to one knee, and just before the blade could pierce his chest he caught her wrist. His arm tensed as he struggled against her, and it was not long before she wilted. Her skin had grown pale, and he realized just how much blood had pooled beneath her.

"Damn you," she said, slumping back to the rooftop. "At least you could have...could have let me k..."

He released her hand, let it fall beside her. The dagger fell from limp fingers. Haern picked up his swords, sheathed them both. Touching a ring on his forefinger, he twisted the thin yellow stone atop it, just slightly, then brought it to his lips.

"To me, Tar," he whispered to it. "Victor's in danger."

That done, he glanced back at the body of Joanna, swallowed down the lump in his throat, and then ran toward the castle, praying he was not too late.

CHAPTER 27

As Victor passed by a row of homes, not much more than a quarter mile from the castle, he heard a soft voice call out to him.

"Sir?"

He slowed and glanced to his left. A disheveled woman leaned against the side of a home at the entrance to an alley. Bruises covered her face, and there was blood in her long brown hair.

"Miss?" he asked, taking a step toward her.

"They're taking everything," she said, starting to cry as she limped closer. "Please, they...they...please help. They're in my home..."

Victor saw her torn clothes and felt his anger grow.

"How many?" he asked, drawing his sword. "And have they gone far?"

"They're still back there," the woman said. "Please, sir, don't. There's two of them. I need the guard, help me find the guard."

"Just stay here," Victor said, hurrying past her. "I'll bring you justice."

"I'm not sure you can, Victor."

Victor stopped cold in his tracks at her words. He didn't want to believe it, but there was no other way. Slowly he looked back and saw a crossbow in the woman's hands. Her delicate lips were pulled into a smile.

"Justice," she sneered, pulling the trigger. "What do you know of justice?"

Stupid, thought Victor as the bolt hit his side, just below the curve of his breastplate. *Proud and stupid.*

He took a single faltering step, then collapsed to his knees. He felt his muscles going limp, his armor heavier than he could carry. His sword fell from his hand as he rolled onto his side, only his eyes able to move. With mounting dread and disappointment, he watched the woman approach, her smile growing. There was no doubt as to who she was. He tried to whisper the word, to call her the Widow as was proper, but his lips would not cooperate. Victor thought of the other bodies, of their missing eyes, and the messages written along the walls. Dimly he wondered if she wrote the message first or last, and whether he'd still be alive to watch her writing with his own blood.

"I know you can't move," she said, kneeling down beside him. From within the folds of her dress she pulled out a knife, its sharp edge reflecting the starlight. "You might think you won't feel it, but I assure you, you will. You'll..."

A gray shape descended upon her, and she let out a cry as a heel slammed against her chest. Her momentum carried her until she hit a wall, just beside the door to a lightless home. Victor felt hope stir in his chest.

The Watcher loomed over him, sabers drawn. "I've found you," he said to the Widow. "About damn time."

Instead of showing fear, the woman started laughing, the sound of it chilling. "No, Watcher," she said. "I've found you."

The door blasted open, and out rushed a man in a long red coat. He had short dark hair, and he wielded an ornate blade in one hand. He crashed into the Watcher, his sword a blur. Their combat continued behind Victor's head, and he could not watch, only listen to the shockingly loud clash of steel. From where he lay, he saw two more on the rooftop of the home, both wearing similar red coats. One leaped to the ground, just a wiry thing who barely filled out his outfit. The air pulled the coat open in the fall, and Victor saw dozens of small throwing knives. The man threw several as he fell, a vicious barrage. Victor heard them clink and ping against the wall and ground. He could only hope none had hit flesh.

Still, outnumbered and surprised, could the Watcher fight off so many?

It appeared he could, at least for the moment, as their fight returned to his line of sight. The Watcher was a twisting confusion of cloak and blade, his sabers fending off the advance of the man with the sword. He kept flinging himself from side to side, his motions nearly impossible to predict, as was evident by the daggers thrown by the other man in chase. Each one missed by inches.

Amid the chaos, Victor watched the Widow flee deeper into the alley, desiring no part of it. Victor wanted to scream out his fury at seeing her escape, but he could do nothing, not even lift his fingers.

As if the two on the ground were not enough, the third up top suddenly clapped her hands, and just like that the alley filled with fire. It burst along the walls, feeding on nothing.

Victor's eyes watered, for he could not squint against the sudden barrage of light and heat. The Watcher went on the offensive, crashing into close quarters with the swordsman. The man with the daggers closed as well, wielding them instead of throwing them. The skill on display took Victor's breath away. He'd thought himself capable. He'd thought he could handle any foe. But what he saw wasn't human. More fire burst around the alley, roping the Watcher in. So far none had scored a solid hit, but Victor could sense the Watcher's desperation.

Ice lashed across the fire, and white light bathed the woman upon the rooftops, eliciting a shriek of pain. Victor's hope increased tenfold.

The Eschaton had arrived.

Victor tried to follow, but so much was going on, and he couldn't shift, couldn't look. The dagger thrower turned on Brug, who came barreling in decked out in his thick plate. Daggers flew and bounced off, unable to penetrate. The Watcher upped his intensity, his sabers twirling as they battled outside his line of vision. Meanwhile spells flew through the air, ice and lightning crashing together as Delysia and Tarlak exchanged attacks with the woman on the rooftop. The sound was deafening, magic shook the walls of the homes, and amid it all Victor felt so helpless, so insignificant.

The battle split, traveling deeper into the alley as well as back out into the main street. Victor had no idea who was on the offensive and who was in flight. He could only lie there, waiting and hoping, as he found himself suddenly alone.

When he felt the touch of a woman's hand against his face, he feared it was the Widow, but then he looked up into Delysia's beautiful green eyes. Blood matted her red hair to her face, but the wound looked superficial.

"Can you not move?" she asked.

He looked from left to right with his eyes by way of answer. "I will see what I can do."

She reached down and pulled the bolt from his side. The pain was intense, but did not last long. Her hand touched the wound, and he heard a soft ringing in his ears, slowly growing stronger, as she whispered words to a prayer he could not understand. When it faded he felt a fire flood through his veins, followed by the tingling sensation of a waking limb. With the feeling all across his body, he grimaced, nearly overwhelmed.

A soft flutter of cloaks signaled the arrival of the Watcher.

"Two fled, but it might be a feint to try to isolate Tarlak," he said. "How is he?"

"I'm fine," Victor said, his tongue feeling thick.

"Get him to safety," Delysia said, standing. "I can't lift him."

"Are you sure?"

The priestess nodded. "I'll find Brug and my brother. They'll need me in case you're right. For now, take him somewhere safe until he can recover."

"City…guard," Victor said, sounding slurred, as if he were drunk.

"You saw what those people can do," Haern said, putting his arms around Victor. "You think a few guards will protect you from that?"

A good point, however frightening. The Watcher pulled him to his feet and began carrying him deeper into the alley.

"Where…are we going?" Victor asked, grimacing against the overwhelming sensations. It was as if a thousand wasps stung his exposed skin. The Watcher's touch was like fire.

"To be honest," said the Watcher, "I don't have a clue. But anywhere's better than here."

Victor felt his legs regaining strength, and he worked them as best he could so they might move faster. The Watcher's eyes constantly scanned the environment about them, both rooftop and street. If one of the attackers returned, they'd be in a sore spot for sure. After a moment he shook his head, then pulled them back around.

"Never mind," he said. "I have a better idea."

The Watcher carried him to the building that the attackers had been hiding inside, pulling him in through the busted door. Inside was a meager home. Bodies lay about, brutally slaughtered. Victor let out a gasp at the sight. Even children, cut down and left to die, all so the attackers might wait in ambush. The Watcher said nothing about it, but the rage rolled off him like a physical presence.

"Who are they?" Victor asked as the Watcher pulled him into the next room, where only a single body, that of a woman, lay facedown on the floor.

"A family in the wrong place at the wrong time," was his bitter response.

"I mean their murderers."

The Watcher helped him sit in a corner, then turned to the woman's body. "They're a group of mercenaries known as the Bloodcrafts," the Watcher said. "Now give me a moment."

The Watcher dragged the body out to be with the others, then came back in and leaned against the opposite wall. Victor studied him, finally noticing the blood soaking into his shirt at his side, plus more from his shoulder.

"Are you hurt?" he asked.

"It's an old wound," the Watcher said. He shifted so that the blood was hidden by a cloak. "Well, the worst one is, anyway. Forget it. I can endure worse. What of you?"

"Starting to feel like myself. A child could probably beat me at fisticuffs, though."

The Watcher looked back at the door, and Victor could tell

he wanted to be with his friends. Victor's guilt grew. A trap sprung, an innocent family dead, the Eschaton fighting, perhaps even dying, and all for what reason?

When the Watcher turned on him suddenly, his guilt magnified tenfold.

"Why are you here?" he asked. "You've driven this city insane, infected it with your own madness. What's going on, Victor? Attempts on my life, yours, the Trifect...is it all worth it? For your pride? Your attempts at power? I had this city under *control*."

"Control?" Victor laughed. "Control? If you say so, but that's not what I saw."

"What do you know of Veldaren? You're an outsider, some foreign-born..."

"No!" Victor shook his head, and he forced himself to sit up. "No, this is my home, Watcher. I was born here, raised here. It was the thief war that drove my family out. It destroyed everything we had, Watcher, *everything*. You know nothing, and I won't dare let you disgrace me so."

The Watcher fell silent, and he resumed scanning outside the building, as if unwilling to speak. The silence wore on Victor, and when the Watcher returned to the room, he did his best to push away his anger.

"I don't know how old you were," Victor said, gesturing toward his hidden face. "For all I know you were a child, or an elderly man even then. Do you remember when the thief war started? That first night was the worst. The Trifect had bargained and bartered for months, trying to establish certain boundaries—rules of engagement, you might say. They were fools to have done so, and because of that, all of Veldaren paid the cost. My mother and father heard of Leon's failed attempt to kill Thren, and they knew everything was about to go to pieces. We tried to flee, the three of us, our belongings crammed into a coach."

Victor sighed, and a shudder ran through him. "The streets were chaos," he said. "Every single guild rose up, determined to shock and cow the city into submission. Mercenaries ran about with orders to kill anyone they caught looting or vandalizing. I watched from the window of our coach. Buildings aflame, people screaming. And they hated us for it, the lowborn folk of this city. I didn't understand it then, but I do now. We had failed them. With all our wealth, all our power, we had failed to prevent the carnage. My family is no part of the Trifect, but we had dealings with them, we visited their homes and we basked in the light of their coin. To Veldaren we were just like them. They blocked our horses, flung stones, and screamed a thousand curses as we tried to flee."

The Watcher shifted, pulling his cloak tighter about him. "I was just a child, but I do remember," he said. "It was on that night my older brother died."

Victor grunted, rubbed his eyes with his forefinger and thumb. "Nearly everyone lost someone that day, and the commoners released that anger upon us. I still remember my father pulling me back from the window, telling me to ignore them. 'That isn't them,' he told me. 'That is their fear talking, their sorrow, their anguish. Don't hate them for it. We are as much to blame as they.'"

"A noble man," said the Watcher.

"A kind man," Victor said. "Gentle. Compassionate. Scared the shit out of me sitting across from him in that coach and seeing the fear in his eyes. They...the mob surrounded us. I saw the thieves among them, those damn cloaks. Even now they wear them without fear. Arrows hit the sides of the coach, along with rocks. I still thought we would push through. Our driver, he just urged the horses on. I remember the first person we hit, the sound I heard as the wheel crushed bone..."

Victor felt his memories threatening to overwhelm him, and for once he was too tired to fight them away. His tears swelled, and he let them fall. What did it matter if the Watcher saw weakness, after all that had happened?

"I *still* thought we'd make it out safely," he said. "But then they killed the horses. That was when I knew. My mother was crying, but my father, he never hesitated. He grabbed my shirt and tore it, then yanked the boots off my feet. I didn't understand, but he knew what was to happen. He knew. And then he struck me, again and again, until I bled across my clothes. I was too stunned to respond. He did it all so I could hide. I could be just one of the mob. Right before they tore off the doors, he had me crawl through a small window in the back and then roll to the ground. I thought they'd notice, but there were too many people, all focused on the doors. Without a single copper to my name, I ran. I didn't look back. Those thieves...those bastards...do you realize what they did to me? It isn't the coin. It isn't even the murder."

He smashed his fists against the floor, pressed his head against the wall.

"My last memory of my father is of him *striking* me!"

The Watcher had remained silent throughout, and he let Victor calm himself, let him sit there with his fists shaking.

"How did you survive?" he at last asked.

"I left Veldaren," Victor said. "Walked on bare feet north. Begged for food whenever I met strangers, and hitched rides with a few who seemed kindly. When I reached our family's castle, I walked into the court, muddy-faced and bleeding feet, and announced my presence."

Victor shook his head. "You ask why I do this? You ask what

madness drives me? That is it. I want revenge for everything the guilds took from me. I had to flee my childhood home while the beaten corpses of my parents were stripped naked, robbed of every possession, and then left to rot beside our dead horses."

He wiped away his tears, and as he did, he chuckled. "Do you know the worst part?" he asked. "The greatest insult? I found out Thren used our mansion as his home when he discovered it was vacant. For years he tunneled out holes and boarded up windows, and that scum lived and slept in the bed of my father. And when he left, he burned it all down to the last brick and board. That's when I knew. That's when I swore to come back, to make every man bearing the colors of a guild tremble in fear of my name. Day after day I trained. My family is not the wealthiest, but I saved money like a tightfisted miser. This is my purpose. This is how I will honor the memory of my parents. Before I die, I will rid my beloved city of the rats and vultures that have done nothing but destroy."

The Watcher stood over him, staring, thinking. Something burdened him greatly, but Victor could only guess at what.

"I understand more than you can possibly believe," he said. "I am sorry for the loss of your parents, and your home."

Victor closed his eyes and shook his head. "It doesn't matter, not anymore. What I saw out there...I am nothing to you, to your kind. I thought Veldaren full of thieves, cowards, men with daggers and poison and little else. But I was wrong. Now I see the monsters. How can I stop men who summon fire with a wave of their hand? How can I hunt down those who move faster than my eyes can follow, whose skill borders on that of gods? I've done nothing but throw stones into a cave, and at last I've woken the beasts within it. I'm a fool, Watcher, a damn fool."

"No," the Watcher said, kneeling down before him and grabbing his shoulders. His blue eyes pierced the magical darkness of his hood. "You are what we need. You can be where I cannot, you can fill the streets with a hundred men while I am but one. One man can be stopped, but a hundred? A thousand? You told me I would inspire fear from the shadows, yet you would be the light to banish all shadows. You still can. Be stronger than them. Be stronger than any of us. Prove to Veldaren that you can stand against the darkness, without mask or cloak, and live. Can you do that for me, Victor?"

Victor took a deep breath, and he thought of his mother and father, sitting opposite him in the coach as the mob surrounded them. No one should be that afraid, he decided. Not ever again.

"I will," he said. "Forgive my moment of doubt."

The Watcher grinned. "Good. Continue on as you have. As for me, well…"

A change came over the Watcher, hardening those blue eyes. A chill swept through Victor as he realized he saw what others must see when the cloaked man descended from the rooftops, sabers drawn, fury in his every movement.

"I'll handle the monsters."

CHAPTER

28

Melody ran her hands along John Gandrem's chest, touching the soft silk of his shirt. She lay in his arms atop her extravagant bed, the silken sheets smooth beneath her. They were both fully clothed.

"Are you sure you are fine?" John asked her, brushing his hands through her hair.

"I believe so," she said. "Please, just kiss me first..."

He did so, his lips rough, his facial hair brushing against her skin. Closing her eyes, she tried to slip into the rhythm, to remember what it meant to be embraced by a man who was strong, and kind, and caring. As she did, he kissed the top of her head, rubbed her neck and her shoulders, then drifted his hands downward. When his callused fingers touched her breasts she let out a cry, and immediately the hands were gone.

"I'm sorry," she heard him say, but despite it she sensed the frustration. Melody felt her lower lip quiver.

"No, it's fine," she said. "It's..."

Such a beautiful dove you are, Melody...

She sat up, pushing aside the blankets and wrapping her arms around her knees. John let out a sigh, and he slid his legs off the bed and put his back to her.

"I don't know what that sick bastard Leon did to you," he said. "I have a feeling I'll never know. If you need time, though, I'll give it to you. It's only what you deserve."

She grabbed his shoulder when he turned to go. He was stronger than any would guess, still muscular, and at her touch she felt him tighten.

"You are far better than I deserve," she said, kissing his shoulder, his neck. "When the time comes, when I...am ready, I will let you know. Thank you, John. You are a good man, a kind man."

He left her room, and the moment he was gone she slid off the bed, moved to the door, and flung the lock shut. A silent sob escaped her lips as she pressed her forehead against the cold wood.

Karak help her, soon she'd have to give John something more than a fleeting touch of her lips against his. But even those kisses flooded her with thoughts of Leon, of his touch, never entering her, only wanting her there like some idol he could touch himself to, something to spill his seed on as she lay imprisoned, helpless, chained.

"I need you, John," she whispered. "You're a good man. A good man."

She prayed he stayed so good, so willing to wait as she pushed through her pain. The world was dark, and her friends few.

Turning toward her closet, she walked across the padded carpet until she knelt inside and retrieved her chrysarium from its hiding place. Its touch helped soothe her worries, and she smiled as she closed her eyes. Putting it on her bed, she went to her windows. They'd shut the curtains when John entered, but she wanted them thicker still, wanted not even the moonlight to filter in. A spare sheet did the trick, hung over the curtain rods. That done, she returned to her bed, and in the darkness touched the sides of the chrysarium.

"Karak," she said, breathing the word like a charm.

Immediately the gems lit up, beginning to rock as the magic flooded into them. Eyes locked on the center, she watched as the gems lifted to the farthest extent of their thin silver chains. Prayers left her lips, simple ones, adulations to the beloved Lion. A warmth flooded her, the feeling of her god's presence. It was that feeling that had kept her sane through the years, the chrysarium the only gift Leon had allowed her to keep. In the darkness she'd seen visions, distant beauty, even glimpses of the friends and family she'd known.

It wasn't until she'd been freed from the prison that she'd fully discovered the chrysarium's true power.

"Laerek," she whispered when Karak's power filled her like a river.

The colors bled out of the gems and into the center of the chrysarium, shifting, molding, becoming a shape with a face. The young priest startled, and she saw his small form look up to her, right into her own eyes.

"Melody," he said, and then the miniature version of him bowed low. "I am glad to see you are still safe and well."

"Fear not for my safety," she whispered to him, crouching down closer. "It is you who must be careful."

"And I am," Laerek said. "I assure you, I am."

His voice was tinny, the pitch not quite right. Limitations of the chrysarium, she knew, but the ability to converse with someone so far away was a godsend. She didn't quite know what it was Laerek saw when he talked to her, and she'd been afraid to ask. Did he see a smaller version of herself? Perhaps a vision of her full form, hovering in the air above him? Or was she nothing but an image in his mind's eye?

"Any word from Luther?" she asked, deciding not to let the conversation run any longer than necessary. The longer she used the chrysarium, the greater the headache afterward.

"Indeed," he said. "I received his letter just this morning."

"And?"

Laerek looked left and right, his hands rubbing together to show his nervousness.

"Have you made any progress with your daughter about her faith, or lack thereof?"

Melody let out a sigh. This was it, of course, the one conversation she'd been dreading. Part of her wanted to lie, but she would not demean herself so in the eyes of her god.

"The outcast Zusa has been with her for too long," she admitted. "Alyssa will not turn to Karak, barring a miracle. The priests here in Veldaren have done little to persuade her, either. The Lion will find no home here, not without much work on my part."

"Is it only a matter of time?"

Melody shook her head. "It is a matter of years, not months or days."

Laerek crossed his arms, and however it was he saw her, he refused to look her in the eye. "Then forgive me, Melody, but my orders are clear. We do not have years. We may not even have months. If Alyssa will not bow to the faith, and allow us the use of her resources, then it is time for the Gemcroft family to find itself a new leader."

Melody felt a shadow fall across her heart. For the briefest moment Laerek's color faded, the gems starting to dim.

Karak be with me, she begged, her fingers tightly clutching the sides of the chrysarium.

"Would you have me imprison her?" she asked, daring to hope.

Laerek finally looked back into her eye. "We cannot take that risk. The Widow I hear of...she is still under your control, yes?"

Melody nodded. "For now."

"Then have the Widow kill Alyssa. No one will ask questions, and if they do, the answers they find will never lead back to you."

Slowly Melody breathed in, and slowly she exhaled. The gems lifted, and Laerek's skin glowed once more with a vibrancy that was beautiful to behold.

"Karak orders, and I obey," she said. "Tomorrow night I will relay your orders to the Widow. With Alyssa's death, taking over the household will be of little difficulty, especially with Lord Gandrem at my side."

Laerek's head bobbed up and down, rapidly, like a bird's.

"Good. Good. I'm glad things go well for you."

"Yes, so well, the execution of my own daughter."

Laerek opened his mouth to speak, but he had no words. Melody pulled her hands away from the chrysarium. The gems fell into the dark stone bowl with a clatter, and with tears in her eyes she stared at the fading afterimage in the darkness. Tears slipped down her face, and she didn't bother to fight them. She was too old for losing battles such as that.

"Your fault," she whispered, thinking of Maynard's cold smile, his ungentle hands. "This is all your fault. You drove me to him. He listened. You never did."

It was her affair that had brought Maynard's wrath upon her, her affair that had sent her into the bowels of Leon's prison, denied the fate of death her husband had been promised, instead left to suffer and rot. And now, because of a near decade of absence, her daughter had grown up denied the wisdom of her deity, denied the proof of his love. Alyssa's heart was hardened, and now she would suffer greatly for it.

"Damn you, Maynard," she whispered. "I hope you burn in the deepest pit of Karak's purifying flames."

She returned the chrysarium to her closet, then lay on her bed, wanting to at least attempt to fall asleep before the headache could come in force. It was a race she knew she'd lose, but she had to try. When the throbbing in her temples came, she pushed her face into the pillow, let her tears wash it, as she prayed and prayed.

"Thy will," she whispered. "Thy will, not mine, not mine, thy will, thy will…"

By thy will, the death of her daughter. By the will of the Lion, her household would be made clean.

Haern spent the day in the guise of a commoner named Jamie. As he wandered he kept his smile big, his eyes wide. Just a blabbermouth, that's all he was, a man eager to hear a good tale or two to tell later that night, and through the telling become a bit more important than he was in reality. And given the excitement of the past few days, he garnered hardly even a raised eyebrow from the target of his inquiries.

"Heard anything about them Bloodcrafts?" Haern asked as he sat before the bar of a tavern, the tenth one he'd visited that day.

"I've heard plenty," said the barkeep, not even bothering to look at him as he talked. His back was to Haern, and he was pouring him a drink of the cheapest alcohol they had. Haern accepted it with a smile on his face. The barkeep remembered what he'd order without asking? How flattering.

"Is that so?" Haern asked, sitting up straighter in his chair.

"Indeed," said the barkeep, a tough-looking man without any hair. "I doubt a word of it's true though, Jamie. People just like to tell tales."

"As do I!" said Haern. "But more than anything, I'd like to meet them. Oh, I won't talk to them or nothing, just want to catch a glimpse. Think they wear red like everyone says? And that they're all taller than a horse?"

"Red horses in coats would stand out fast," said a man beside him, laughing into his cup.

"So you have seen them," Haern said, the dumbest smile he could manage on his face.

"Aye, I seen 'em," the man said.

"No you haven't, Turl," the barkeep said. "Not if you want to keep drinking in my bar, you haven't."

Haern raised an eyebrow, but the man next to him shook his head.

"Never mind then," he said, taking another drink.

"Well," Haern said, downing half his beer and then tossing a few pieces of copper on the bar. "You hear something, you let Jamie Blue hear about it, right? I might even pay a bit, if it keeps being this hard to catch a glimpse of those bastards before they head back to Mordeina."

"Right," said the barkeep, though his tone showed he'd more likely sell a drink to the man in the moon than give information to Haern.

Interesting...

At the door to the place, Haern stopped a moment, leaning with his arms crossed as he thought. Going from tavern to tavern didn't seem to be as fruitful as he'd hoped. People liked to talk, but the moment the Bloodcrafts came up, they were willing to share only the wildest of rumors. Not that he blamed them. The reputation of the mercenaries was fierce, and no one wanted to cross them. At least not without something to gain.

A boy stepped out of the door, barely older than twelve. He refused to look at Haern, instead walking the opposite way. Yet the second he was beyond sight of the door, he turned back around and beckoned for Haern to follow.

Even more interesting...

Just beside the tavern was the thinnest of gaps between it and a small bakery shop. The boy put his back to the tavern, crossed his arms.

"Make it worth my while," he said.

Haern didn't dare ask about what. He pulled out three silver coins and dropped them into the boy's hands. His eyes widened at the sight of such wealth, and then he quickly pocketed them.

"Behind me," he said. "Highest window and on the left. My pa would kill me if he knew I told you, so don't tell anyone."

"It's not your pa you have to worry about," Haern said, and the chill of his voice seemed to convey to the boy the seriousness of his position. Nodding, he turned back around and rushed into the tavern.

Looking up at the window, Haern smiled, only this time it wasn't part of an act. At last he knew something about the Bloodcrafts.

"I've found you," he whispered as he made his way back to the tower.

Twice now they had been the ambushers, attacking the Eschaton when they were weak or unprepared.

It was time that changed.

CHAPTER

29

Zusa had no measure of time, nothing to go on beyond when they fed her. Twice a small boy adorned in gray robes arrived and gently spooned gruel into her mouth. As for drink, a young girl came bearing water every few hours or so. Every time it was a different girl, and Zusa looked upon them with pity. How many might soon hide their beautiful faces beneath rags and wrappings? She felt herself weakening, felt her muscles tightening and her back aching constantly. So far Vrashka had not returned, Daverik's promise appearing to have been true. But her time was almost up.

The door creaked open, and she stirred from her daydreams of life and freedom at the Gemcroft mansion. As if to confirm her fears, Daverik stepped inside, and he looked vaguely worried.

"Are you well?" he asked her, crossing the room.

"A cruel question to ask a woman in chains," Zusa said.

"Perhaps. I have stretched my influence to its limits, Zusa. I can protect you no longer. What is your answer? Will you return to Karak's bosom? Will you embrace the faith once more?"

Zusa shook her head. "You know I won't. What is there for me, Daverik?"

In answer, he knelt before her and brushed her face with his hand.

"There's me," he said. "There's a life free of imprisonment and torture. Can that not mean something?"

"The temple's laws will keep you from me."

"Temple laws can be changed."

Zusa laughed. "Is that what you tell yourself?"

He shifted closer, leaning so close that she felt his breath on her neck. His hands brushed her arms, her sides, her breasts. His cheek pressed against hers as he whispered.

"It doesn't matter. Come back to me, Katherine..."

She knew what he was trying to do. His lips pressed against her neck as he cupped her face. He was trying to reignite a distant flame, a flame that for him had never died. Yet that flame had long died for her, for it'd been nothing more than teenage lust and excitement. Now, as his hands roamed, she felt only disgust. It was one thing for him to touch her in a distant alley, a secret meeting between long-lost lovers... but here? While manacles held her wrists to a wall? While her whole body ached from the imprisonment, and she sat in her own piss and shit?

"Katherine's dead," she said, pulling away from him as best she could. "You killed her when you betrayed her to the priests, remember?"

He stood, and she saw the haunting memory in his eyes.

"I know," he said. "I guess I'm a fool to still believe otherwise."

Daverik walked toward the door, stopping just beside the strange flow of water falling from ceiling to floor.

"I learned this enchantment while in Mordeina," he said, observing its flow. "At the time I thought it would be useful should any of my own faceless go rogue. Never once did I think I would use it against *you*. This stream…it's a marvelous gift, so thin, so slender, yet wielding such power. In many ways it is like you, Zusa. Only I fear it is you, and not this stream, that will break before the night's end."

He left without waiting for a response. Zusa finally allowed herself to relax, and with his departure she damned him for hurting her so, damned him for the tears that started to flow. Hardly a minute later, the door reopened.

She expected her elderly torturer, but instead one of the faceless entered. From what she could tell, it was not Ezra, but the other. Her body was too thin, too tall. The woman said nothing, only stepped around the stream of water falling from ceiling to floor so she might stand before Zusa with her arms crossed. She tilted her head to one side, staring, analyzing Zusa as she might a strange animal.

"Like what you see?" Zusa asked, grinning despite her exhaustion.

The other woman slapped her, then knelt down so they might see eye to eye. Carefully she removed the thin white cloth over her eyes, then pulled back the wrappings of her face, revealing her blond hair and beautiful face. Her blue eyes stared into Zusa's, and they held a frightening intensity.

"Who are you?" Zusa asked when her visitor still said nothing.

"Deborah," she said.

"And who were you before you were Deborah?"

The woman shook her head.

"That name, that person, is lost and gone. I will not speak it to you."

Zusa shrugged her shoulders as best she could given the chains about her.

"If you insist."

Deborah shifted, their faces so close to one another. She continued to study Zusa, looking over her dark eyes, skin, and hair.

"Why did you reveal your face?" Deborah finally asked. "Why did you turn against our god?"

Zusa smirked at her visitor. "Are you having trouble with your faith, Deborah?"

Deborah grabbed her neck, shoved her against the wall, and held her there.

"You know nothing of me, Zusa, so do not insult me."

"I know you wouldn't ask if it were not so," Zusa said with what little breath she could manage.

The hand about her throat released its grip, and Deborah shifted a step backward.

"Do not question my devotion. I merely wish to know what it is that broke you, so I might better protect my own faith. Why...what made you decide to turn away?"

At this Zusa laughed, laughed until she could hardly breathe. Deborah struck her twice, but it did nothing to remove her dark amusement.

"You want to know why I left?" she asked. "Why I abandoned Karak? I followed the orders given to me, to find and protect Alyssa Gemcroft, years ago. But then Pelorak decided we were an insult to his temple and sent a dark paladin to kill us while he called us blasphemous and unworthy of forgiveness. I did nothing, Deborah. None of us did. We simply awoke one day to find Karak's followers arrayed against us faceless. I never *decided.* My beloved friends died, until I was alone and lost. I never abandoned Karak. Karak and his temple abandoned me. The same will happen to you, Deborah. You'll spend your life told you are shameful and weak, until one day you pull the cloth from your face, look into a mirror, and wonder what is so sinful about that beautiful blond hair, so terrible about those icy blue eyes..."

Deborah struck her with a trembling hand.

"They warned me not to listen," she said, unable to hide the fury in her voice. "I should have paid heed to those warnings. You are beyond redemption. Beyond reason. Never could I have guessed how foul a snake you are."

"I can see it in your eyes," said Zusa, straining against her chains so she was mere inches from Deborah. "Deep down, you believe every single word I've said. Every. Single. Word."

Deborah struck her with her fists, again and again. Zusa's face swelled, and blood welled on her tongue. She kept her jaw clenched tight and let Deborah burn out her fury. When her grin didn't falter, Deborah finally reached for her dagger and pressed it against Zusa's throat.

"I will cut the blasphemous tongue from your mouth," she said. "I'll burn it on Karak's altar while I sing psalms of praise. You are a sick, broken thing, and it shames me to think you were once of my order. Open your mouth."

Zusa shook her head. In response, Deborah struck her with the hilt of her dagger. The metal rattled her teeth, and she tasted more blood as a single tooth jarred loose. Zusa bit down hard, tearing the tooth free with a crack.

"I said open your mouth," Deborah said, the tip of her dagger once more poking against her neck.

After slowly filling her lungs with air, Zusa spit the combination of tooth, blood, and saliva. It arced over Deborah's head, through the air, and then broke the stream of water Daverik had created. Deborah had only the briefest moment to realize it before Zusa flung herself backward. The entire room was awash with shadows, and this time when Zusa fell through the wall, nothing stole her away, nothing pulled her into the swirling depths of the Abyss. She emerged on the other side of the room, free of the manacles.

Deborah's back was still to her, and she turned far too late. Zusa rolled once, then leaped, her heel slamming the other woman's head forward. It hit the wall with a loud crack. Blood dripped down as her body collapsed to the hard stone. Zusa knelt for a moment, catching her breath, and then checked Deborah's pulse. Still there, however faint. Despite the danger, Zusa kept her calm. Slowly she removed Deborah's wrappings, then used them to replace her own. Feeling far cleaner, far more human, she took Deborah's daggers, then spit a glob of blood onto Deborah's pale, naked breasts.

"I'll let you live," she said. "Because one day you will see just how right I was."

The stream of water had resumed, and standing close to it made Zusa felt strangely empty. Glancing about, she found her tooth, then jammed it into the hole in the ceiling. Water continued to trickle down, but it was different somehow, lacking the proper hue. Zusa felt immediately better, though still physically weak. Her food and water had been rare, her movement limited. Holding the daggers made her fingers ache after the torture they'd taken, so that she had to grip them tighter for fear of losing control. It'd take a few days before she felt like her old self...

The door cracked open, without knock or warning given.

"How is my little doll?" Vrashka asked as he stepped inside. He froze at the macabre sight before him, and Zusa gave him no time to recover. She grabbed him while simultaneously kicking the door shut. With ease she flung him against the wall, a hand against his mouth to muffle his frightened scream.

"This *little doll* is leaving," Zusa whispered into his ear as she pressed a dagger against his belly. "I suggest you stay calm, and answer me quietly and truthfully if you want to live. You understand?"

Vrashka nodded. If he was frightened, he didn't show it. Zusa couldn't help but be begrudgingly impressed.

"How many guards are outside the door?" she asked, then slowly pulled back her hand.

"None," he said.

She sliced a gash across his forehead, the shallow cut bleeding profusely.

"Every lie you tell me, I cut lower," she whispered. "Soon it will be your eyes, then your nose. Don't make me reach your neck. How many guards?"

"None at the door," Vrashka said, eyes closed against the blood that ran down into them. "There's only one exit from the prison, up the hall. That's where the guards are. I did not lie, little doll, I swear."

"My name is Zusa, not doll," she said, cutting across his eyebrows. "How many guards at the exit?"

It took a moment for the old man to gather his breath. "Five," he said. "There are always five."

"Is it night or day?"

"The sun has just set. The temple is settling down for bed, my...Zusa."

Zusa clasped a hand over his mouth, tried to think. If it was night, her escape would be far easier. Her prison was deep underground, she knew, with no other exit besides the one with the guards. Five armored men would be difficult, especially given how weak she felt, but perhaps she might catch them off guard...

But escape was not the only thing on her mind.

"Where is Daverik?" she asked. "Is he in his room?"

The old man shook his head.

"I passed him on my way down. He said he felt unwell, and needed fresh air. He was hiding something, I could sense it. Looked troubled. Did you say something to him, little doll? Did you make him doubt himself?"

She tried to cut across both his eyes, but her dagger caught on the bridge of his nose so only one was split in half. When she pulled it free, Vrashka screamed, and her hand did little to muffle the noise. Knowing time was short, Zusa hoped that the scream, if heard, would be mistaken for hers instead of his. Blood was pouring from his face now, and Vrashka's strength drained with it. Despite all the pain he must have felt, he bore a smile on his face.

"You...you make me sad," he said when she flung him to the floor. "You could have withstood so much. Breaking you would have been my greatest accomplishment. Even the gentle touchers would have been proud."

He stared up at her with his lone eye, and she could tell he expected her to take his life. She almost obliged, but something about the sick satisfaction on his face turned her stomach. It was as if he viewed dying to her as a privilege.

"You'd never have broken me," she said, grabbing the handle of her cell door. "But I broke you in seconds."

"You'll be back," Vrashka said, laughing as she left. "You'll still be mine, little..."

She flung a dagger through the air, straight through his

remaining eye. Walking over to it, she yanked it out and shook off the eyeball.

"Stupid bastard," she said. "You could have lived."

Taking a deep breath, she ran out of the cell, hooked a right, and then charged straight down the corridor. There were only four cells, with each door on her right. From what she could tell, she'd been put in the farthest from the stairs. At the far edge of the stone corridor was the exit Vrashka had spoken of. Five men stood guard, each with a lion painted across the front of his armor. They wielded a combination of short spears and swords, and four scrambled at the sight of her to form a defensive line. The fifth rushed up the stairs, no doubt to signal an alarm. Zusa sprinted faster, her breaths blasting in and out of her lungs.

"Halt!" one screamed.

Laughing at his cluelessness, she launched into the air, her body twisting like a dancer's. Spears and swords pierced the gaps between her arms and legs, catching nothing. Zusa shoved one dagger through a neck, and the other she rammed into the stomach of the man she crashed into. Together they fell, a heap of arms and legs. She rolled free in a heartbeat, spinning so the nearest guard's downward stab hit stone instead of flesh. Her heel caught his jaw, her left arm parried a desperate thrust, and then she was running up the stairs after the fifth, leaving the confused rest behind.

He in his heavy armor, she in her wrappings, there was no chance, not for him. Her daggers pierced his back before he could open the thick door at the top. Pushing the body behind her, she let it roll and tumble as an obstacle to the others chasing after. The door was not locked, and she flew through it. Beside the door was a heavy bar, and she wedged it into the nailed handles on either side of the entrance. The dungeon sealed, she had time now, perhaps enough to escape.

For a moment she forced her exhausted mind to think of the layout, to piece together where she was. The dungeon was located near the back of the temple. She stood in a short hallway, one way leading toward storage for various supplies and dried foods. The other went toward the barracks. Fists pounded on the opposite side of the door behind her, but she laughed at their helplessness. The temple was dark, quiet. Getting in might have proved difficult, especially with a trap laid for her. But getting out?

She ran, nothing but a shadow. She slipped through the barracks, with only a single young priest walking the halls. He never saw her coming. Her dagger cut his throat, and her hand muffled his dying gasp. On she ran until she reached the grand worship hall. Peeking out from a door, she saw three men kneeling in prayer at the statue of Karak, his enormous presence bathed in purple fire. Zusa thought to kill them, but escape was her priority now, not vengeance. Crawling along the floor, she slipped through the pews, careful to make not a sound.

Two guards watched the door, spears in hand. When she reached the final pew, she sprinted out, deriving sick pleasure at the stunned look on the guards' faces at her sudden appearance. In such close quarters, the spears were useless against her daggers. She cut them down, kicked open the door, and then rolled to avoid the bolts of shadow that leaped from the hands of the three priests who had been at prayer.

Now that she was in open air, nothing would stop her. She ran across the courtyard, vaulted over the gates, and then left the temple far behind.

Zusa wanted to return to Alyssa, ached to be in a place she

could call home, but did not. Vrashka had said Daverik felt unwell, and sought fresh air. Zusa knew there was more to it than that. With her balance teetering, she ran, weaving from side to side through the street as if she were intoxicated. Her stomach ached, her tongue thirsted for water, but on she went, until at last she reached the secluded gap by the wall where they'd first met.

Just as she thought, Daverik was there, leaning against the wall with his arms crossed. Instead of his robes, he wore the plain clothes he'd had on when first meeting her.

"I hope you didn't kill too many," he said, smiling at her arrival.

"Why?" she asked. "Why tell me how to escape?"

Daverik shook his head.

"It saddens me you have to ask. Do you think I lie to you, Zusa? That my feelings are false? I traveled across the entire continent to see you once again. I have slept with nightmares of our last moments together for ten long years. To see you beaten, humiliated, tortured into submission..." He sighed. "You know I can't do that. No matter the blasphemy you might speak. No matter how hardened your heart is against me. And you were right, Zusa. Even if you came back, they'd kill you. I can't accept that. I won't. They're wrong about that, wrong about you, and I will stop them."

Zusa bit back her retort, unwilling to spit in the face of the man who had helped her escape.

"What is going on?" she asked. "What role does the temple play in all this?"

"The temple has nothing to do with this, Zusa. To be honest, most of the priests here in Veldaren turn my stomach."

"Then who?" she asked. "Who is behind all this?"

Daverik uncrossed his arms, and he looked to the sky so he might stare at the stars when he spoke.

"I agreed to come here as a favor to an old friend, someone who'd been in a similar situation to my own when I was banished from Veldaren for our indiscretions. He has a contact here, a young man named Laerek who came with me from Mordeina. He was to meet with me tonight, very soon, but I'm tempted not to go. This role as taskmaster over the faceless is not one I cherish."

Zusa clutched her daggers tight, and had to fight back her excitement at finally having a name, a person to hunt.

"Tell me where he is," she said.

Daverik shook his head. "Not yet, Zusa. Things are not quite that simple. You have a choice to make first, and it is one I fear you won't be willing to make."

Something about the sudden shift in his tone made her throat clench.

"What do you mean?"

"It's simple," he said, pulling his gaze back down from the stars to her. "If you come with me, we can flee the city tonight, hide where not even the temple can find us. I'll leave all gods and kings behind. No one will know, no one will have reason to think you didn't vanish into hiding back at Alyssa's."

He took a step toward her, reaching out a hand.

"We can be together," he said. "I know I erred revealing our love to the priests. I know I was a fool to feel guilt and shame. Please, this is all I know to do to make up for it."

"Is that all you have to offer me?" Zusa asked. She thought of herself in her filth, him kissing her neck. Thought of how oblivious he'd been to her situation. She was just a memory to him, a perfect memory...

"You're insane," she told him. "You're a sick man unable to let go of the past. We aren't in love, Daverik. Perhaps once, but that love died a decade ago. It's time you open your damn eyes and see that."

She saw his anger building, an almost childish denial of the truth.

"You've only forgotten! It will take time, but time we will have. We were our firsts, Katherine. Surely no flame has burned brighter for you than me."

"I won't leave Alyssa and Nathan," she said. "They're my family now. You're only a bad memory."

Daverik let out a bitter laugh, and he tensed as if to strike her, but then suddenly his entire body went slack.

"I know," he said, defeat in his voice. "I'd hoped otherwise, but I know. I'm sorry, Katherine. If you'd only said yes, I'd have never told you. I'd have spared you the heartache."

Zusa felt her heart begin to race as her mind immediately went to the most dire of assumptions.

"What do you mean?" she asked.

More of that horrible bitter laughter.

"I am not the only one to meet with Laerek tonight," said Daverik. "The Widow was to meet him as well, but only after."

Her racing heart stopped. Her stomach clenched.

"After what?" she asked.

"After killing Alyssa Gemcroft."

Zusa flung herself at him, grabbing his neck so she might slam him against the wall.

"Why?" she screamed. "What have we done to deserve this?"

"I am not the one you should be angry with," Daverik said, clutching at her wrists. "I didn't set this in motion. We gave Alyssa a chance to turn to Karak, but she refused, and do you know why? Because of you. Because of everything you told her about our god. Her death is on your hands, Katherine, not mine."

"My name is Zusa!" she screamed, kicking him in the stomach. The man doubled over, coughing. Coughing, and laughing.

"There is no time," he told her. "The Widow is just a puppet, a minor player in all this. Alyssa is already dead. But I'll tell you where to find Laerek. You can go, take your vengeance, and then at last we can be together."

Zusa's grip tightened, and she almost strangled the life from her former lover.

"Don't be a fool," he said in a raspy voice, fighting to breathe through her grasp. "Kill the one responsible, then come with me. We'll leave this all behind. You'll never feel pain again, not like this. Don't go back. You don't want to see it."

"No," she said, letting him go. "You're a child, Daverik, just a child. You've never understood me, and you never will."

With every last bit of strength she ran toward the Connington mansion, daggers at the ready, long cloak billowing.

Daverik watched her go, and his heart ached worse than his sore neck. He loved her, so much he loved her, but time and trials had changed her, warped her into something he only vaguely recognized.

"Such a shame," he whispered.

He heard Ezra land behind him, quiet as a cat landing on padded feet.

"She still will not accept you, will she?" she asked.

Daverik shook his head. "Zusa is too far gone, and whatever love she has for me is not enough to bring her back."

He looked over his shoulder, saw Ezra drawing her daggers. Daverik once more thought of the softness of Zusa's skin, the way his lips had brushed her neck, and then cast aside the sinful memories so he might give his faceless her order.

"She'll interfere if she can," he said. "Kill her, and if the Widow fails, then kill Alyssa as well."

Ezra stepped closer, rubbing her wrapped face against his shoulder while peering up at him.

"You risked much for an old love," she said. "Deborah barely lives, and there are others in the temple not so lucky."

"The dead go to Karak, their souls claimed and protected," Daverik snapped. "Zusa is greater than any of them, yet she will burn, only burn. I had to try."

Ezra smirked as she stepped away to give chase. "Tell me," she said. "Would you have risked for my soul as you have for hers?"

He could not answer, and he felt his neck flush with the shame.

"I thought not," Ezra said. "Dangerous games, Daverik. You play such dangerous games..."

She ran, to murder the only woman Daverik had ever loved. The act was just, of course, a necessary fate for a woman who had blasphemed against Karak for so long. But he would find no comfort in it, no solace.

"Forgive me," he told the night. "Perhaps, after an eternity, I might one day hold your body against mine. But I've given you enough chances. I wash my hands of this. Your fault, not mine, dear Katherine..."

CHAPTER

 30

Stephen Connington stepped into the tiny room, holding a candle to give himself light. As he'd hoped, she was already waiting for him there.

"Mother," he said, seeing her sitting against the wall, surrounded by little toys carved out of wood.

"I'm here, child," Melody said.

Stephen went to her, curling up in her arms as he closed his eyes. He was getting too big for it, he knew, but he did so anyway. With his eyes closed, he was once more lost in darkness, lost in a past he'd thought he'd escaped. Sadly, it seemed he never would.

"Do you think Father loved me?" he asked.

"You know he did."

He thought of the years of darkness between months of light, of the beatings and the hunger, followed by Leon's lips on his neck.

"Do I?" Stephen asked.

He'd been a bastard of Leon's, birthed by a lowly servant girl who had aroused his father's rare sexual lust. Melody was not his mother, not by blood, no matter how much he might wish it were true. There'd been times Leon had treated him well, had laughed and told him stories as they walked through the mansion. Other times, though...other times...

"He told you he loved you, didn't he?" Melody asked, stirring him from his thoughts.

His father's voice echoed in his head, distorted over time so he couldn't be sure if the love he heard in it existed or not.

You know they would kill you, Stephen. They don't think you're good enough to be one of them, to take over everything I've built. They want someone pulled from a prissy noble lady's cunt instead. But you're my daughter, you hear me? You never forget it. My blood. So don't you worry when I put you down there. It's for your safety, Stephen. Your safety.

No matter the love he felt from his father, those long months spent in the cell had worn on him, bathing him in darkness as he grew up isolated and alone. But then, when he was almost six, an angel had been delivered to him. It was his mother, the true mother who owned his heart. Melody had been placed in the cell adjacent to his. The first he'd ever known of her was the songs she sang to pass the time. In that deep darkness, that voice had carried him, given him comfort so he could sleep without crying.

"Alyssa's supposed to be next," Stephen said. "Laerek insists on it, but only after you tell me it's too late for her."

"I know," Melody said, gently stroking his hair. Not his real hair, but the long wig he'd put on prior to entering. He still remembered the night he'd taken it, hidden in shadows while watching the whores pass. Oh, some didn't ask for money, might have even claimed they were proper women, noble ladies or faithful wives. But that's not what they were. His father had made that clear.

All women are whores, Stephen, even you. It's in their blood, and it's stronger than anything else in this world. That's why you shouldn't feel bad. It's not your fault. You just can't help it, always looking at me like you do. But you're my daughter, my precious little daughter. Now come here and sit on my lap.

Stephen had sliced the woman's beautiful brown hair off at the scalp, all while the venom of the brown widow spider kept her paralyzed. She'd been unable to move, but he'd seen the screams in her eyes when he finally pulled the last of it free. It was her beauty, he knew. She hated to lose her beauty, to see someone stronger, someone more deserving, take it away.

"Are you sure you don't mind?" Stephen asked. "You were so mad last time I threatened her."

Melody's careful stroking of his head paused, and he felt his muscles tense. He hated when she did that, one of those subtle things that gave away her worry.

"She is indeed my daughter," Melody said, her bony fingers tightening around his shoulders, making him feel like a disobedient child. "But some things are more powerful than blood, Stephen. Faith. That's what matters. Our beloved god must be saved, he must be served, and Alyssa has refused. It's not her fault, though. My child she once was, but now she's *Maynard's* daughter. After he sold me to your father, there was no way for me to pray with her, to raise her as she should be raised. Now her head is filled with the same doubt and sin her father always had."

Stephen felt fury burn bright in his chest. Of course it was Maynard Gemcroft's fault. Leon had made that quite clear. Stephen had come to his father multiple times during his rare moments of freedom to leave his cell and roam the mansion. Whenever he asked for Melody to be released, he was given the same answer.

If Maynard finds out, he'll kill me. She's supposed to be dead, Stephen. You know what dead means, right? It means not walking around talking to my servants, being seen by guests, eating food cooked by women with more mouths than sense. I love her dearly, but down there she has to stay if you want her to survive.

For five long years he'd asked, until the Bloody Kensgold came. He'd been in his cell, not allowed to join the festivities, when the thieves had come and set the mansion ablaze. The smoke had been thick as the building burned above them. The heat had swelled, and Stephen had huddled by the floor, sobbing in terror. Melody had kept him calm, singing through the noise and chaos, her voice echoing across the stone to give him comfort. Anytime he woke in the night, heart gripped with horror, he still recalled those songs. Deep underground, they'd survived while the rest of the mansion collapsed.

It'd taken two days, but at last they'd been dug free. Stephen still remembered staggering out into the light, stinking of filth, his body drained and dying for a drink of water. He'd reached for his father, only to have Leon take a step back, his nose crinkling in disgust. That was when Stephen realized just how ugly he was, how wretched the body he inhabited. When his mother had been pulled out, it was she he'd held, she he'd pulled close against his body.

"I was never his son," Stephen whispered. "He called me daughter, and every time it was a lie."

"Hush now," Melody said, putting a hand against his cheek and forcing him to look up at her. "You can't help how you were born, so don't blame yourself. Your father was a troubled man, but he loved you. He loved *us*. Never doubt that."

He nodded, then tugged at her shirt. "May I?" he asked. "If you must."

She unbuttoned her blouse, then pulled free a breast. Stephen latched onto it with his lips, rubbed across the nipple with his tongue, and then began to suck. No milk came out, but he was long past needing that physical nourishment. It was the attention he needed, the soothing sensation of being cradled by his mother. He suckled for a while, felt his nerves gradually ease. He was anxious about killing Alyssa, he knew. It was that bodyguard of hers, that heathen woman Zusa. Laerek had assured him she was imprisoned at the temple, but he knew enough of Zusa to worry. When he killed Alyssa, he'd have to make it quick, not enjoy it like the others.

But Laerek had made him another promise, one that still got his blood racing when he thought of it.

"Laerek said he'll have Thren ready for me soon," he said, releasing Melody's nipple and then pressing his face against her breast. "He was given orders to leave him alive, just so I can kill him. I can't wait, Mother, I can't..."

She stroked his face, and he heard her chuckle as if he'd said something amusing.

"You shouldn't let him trouble you so," she said.

Stephen shook his head. "How can you say that? You loved Father, too, didn't you?"

"Of course." Said with hesitation, and it worried him further.

"And he killed him, Mother! Thren killed him!"

Stephen had just taken power a little over a year ago, his right as firstborn son finally acknowledged despite his having been discovered within Leon's cells. The longtime adviser Potts had vouched for his blood relationship, despite clearly preferring he not take over the family enterprise. Upon receiving his power, the first thing he'd done was march down into the cells and free Melody, his beloved mother. For a year they'd let her recover, keeping her hidden from any who might desire to harm her while she regained her strength. During that time she'd written many letters, and one of those letters had brought the young Laerek to his home.

"Do you know who killed your father?" the priest had asked.

Stephen had not been told, so he'd been left to rumors. "I assume it was the Watcher," he'd replied. "Is that not what the whispers say?"

Laerek had shaken his head, and given him such a condescending smirk. "A man in gray, wielding matching blades, came into your father's home, slew his guards, and then executed him without mercy. He'd brought a companion with him, who died, unable to escape. Ask your house guards. Ask Potts. It took time, but they found men able to identify him. His name was Senke, a longtime member of the Spider Guild. The Watcher didn't kill your father, Stephen. Thren Felhorn did."

Stephen had had nothing to say to that. He'd given no thought to Leon's murder, only to maintaining his power. Melody had stayed at his side, teaching him the ways of high society, guiding him through the pitfalls that might have ensnared him. But upon learning this, upon receiving the name of the man who'd killed his father, Stephen had grown focused, felt his mind narrowing in like a razor's edge. Thren had to die. The man had killed his father. Thren, and everyone loyal to him, had to die.

Yet now it seemed Melody held so little interest in Thren's death.

"Why do you not hate him as much as I?" he asked her. His face in her cleavage, he inhaled deeply, the smell of her sweat and sex so familiar to him. "You told me Laerek was right, that

Thren was guilty. You sent me after them, praised me when I killed his Spiders…"

Melody gently pushed him back, and before he could protest, she fully clothed herself. "You aren't mature enough to understand the truth," she said, a stern edge overcoming her voice.

"I rule the Connington family now. I am no child, now tell me why!"

She gave him a look he'd always hated, one that made his insides squirm and his hands twist behind his back.

"I sent you after Thren because you're sick," she told him. "You were killing women, innocent women. I know you, baby, I know you can't help it…but I could shape it. I could point your weaknesses toward something good, something pure. Thren and his Spider Guild deserved to die, needed to die. The end of days will be upon us if we do not prepare Veldaren for the prophet's arrival. My child, my sweet child, I only wanted to protect you. I only wanted you to do Karak's will, and to stop hiding in here amid your darkness and your toys."

Tears grew in his eyes, and he fought to keep his voice under control.

"Please don't be mad at me," he said. "I will. I promise I will. I'll kill her just like Laerek told me to."

Melody took his chin in her fingers, tilted him close, and kissed his forehead several times. "Make it quick," she said. "No torture. No cruelty. Can you do that for me? I love her still, but she cannot rule the Gemcroft household anymore. Her lack of faith endangers us all, as well as poor Nathaniel's soul. I love you, Stephen. Now go do what must be done."

Behind her was a closet, and carefully he stood and pulled it open. Inside was a crossbow loaded with a single arrow, its tip coated with poison. All prepared and ready for him with his mother's loving hands. He took it, smiled at her.

"I'll make you happy," he said. "I owe you so much. I'm not sure I can ever repay you."

Now holding the candle, Melody lifted it to her face so the light shone across her smile. "You're my beloved child," she said. "The one Karak gave to me when Maynard stole Alyssa away from me because of his stubborn pride. You have nothing to repay me for."

Stephen reached for the door, and as he pulled it open, Melody called his name.

"Stephen," she said. "Remember, nothing must happen to Nathaniel. Karak has blessed him for a reason. Once he is free of Alyssa's influence, his gift will blossom like a flower, and we must do whatever we can to nourish it. He is no threat to my ascension."

Crossbow shaking in his sweaty hand, Stephen nodded to his mother. "I will be good," he said. "I promise I will."

He left, shut the door behind him, and then hurried down the hall to where Alyssa slept.

Victor leaned against the back wall behind his tavern, arms crossed, body covered with shining armor. His fingers drummed the hilt of his sword, but he forced himself to remain calm and leave it sheathed. Gathered together, in both the tavern and two nearby streets, were the bulk of his forces. They were all equally impatient, but Victor had no choice, much as it left a foul taste in his mouth. In his pocket was a note written by the enigmatic man, its message simple yet perplexing.

Victor, it read. *I will come shortly after sunset, alone and unarmed. We must talk, and we must act. I know the Bloodcrafts tried to kill you, and I know who brought the Bloodcrafts here. If you want revenge, now will be your chance. It's time you sprinkled*

Ash upon your head instead of trying so damn hard to scatter it upon the wind.

At first Victor had wanted to throw it on the fire. He'd come home after the Bloodcrafts' attempt on his life, his feet and hands still tingling from the poison the Widow had used against him. It'd been early morning, the Watcher having kept guard over him for most of the night before he deemed it safe for them to leave. Upon arriving at his tavern, he'd found Sef pitching a fit, half his men scouring the city for him. And then to top it all off, when Victor went to his room he found the note tucked neatly under his pillow.

Better a note than a knife, Victor had thought, deciding not to burn the note. For once he felt like a stranger to the city, the stranger he truly was. Deathmask knew something about the people who'd attacked him, and whatever it was, he wanted to know it himself. And so he'd slept much of the day, eaten a small meal upon awakening, and then readied his men for the meeting.

"He's not going to show," Sef muttered, pacing back and forth before Victor. "He just wants us *here* so he can go kill and rob someone *there*!"

He punctuated the word with a vague gesture to the rest of the city. Victor shook his head.

"The man plays games," he said, "but my gut says this time he's ready to stop playing. Whatever he wants, we listen. And he'll show, Sef. I assure you of that."

True to his word, Deathmask arrived twenty minutes after sunset. He walked alone, his face unclouded by ash or cloth. His smile was wide, and it unnerved Victor further.

"I'm here, and my men ready," Victor said. "What is of such great importance? Or do you plan on kidnapping me a second time?"

Deathmask bowed low in greeting. "Forgive me if I inconvenienced you," he said. When he pulled up from his bow, there was a sparkle in his red eye. "And I have no intention of taking you against your will. No, I hope that this time you'll come with me willingly, and with all your soldiers too."

"What are you talking about? Speak plainly."

Deathmask looked to be in no hurry, and he calmly paced before Victor, tapping his lips with a finger.

"I'm sure you know much of Veldaren's guilds, but what about elsewhere? Say...Mordeina?"

Victor shook his head. "I must profess ignorance in this."

"And other things as well," Deathmask said, grin growing. "But then let me remove your ignorance. There is a guild in Mordeina known as the Suns. Over the past few years they've spread their influence, first into Ker, then Omn, and now they've set their eye on Neldar. They're coming here, into Veldaren, so they might strike at the heart of this nation before branching out like a disease."

Victor frowned, not liking what he was hearing. "Are you afraid of losing some profit, thief?" he asked.

"Don't be naïve. Veldaren is already spiraling out of control, and the Suns will destroy things completely. They won't rest until every guild, mine included, is wiped out."

"So far I don't see much reason to hate them."

A bit of amusement left Deathmask's eyes.

"Enough, Victor. You know as well as I that the guilds here are weak. The midnight executions had stopped...well, before you came back, anyway. All the poisoning and assassinations have calmed. The Trifect pay us their sum, we sell drugs and women and take paltry sums of protection money. It's a balance, a nice one really, like the one Thren should have kept fourteen years ago instead of letting his greed cause the thief war in the first place. Point is, what we have is acceptable. These guilds here, they're guilds you know, guilds you can manipulate and control. But not the Suns. This is not some distant threat, nor someone that will bow to the Trifect or pay heed to the Watcher. They've come to conquer...and they're already within our walls."

Information he'd received the day before suddenly clicked, and Victor felt a pit grow in his stomach.

"The cheap crimleaf," he said. "I've heard of the bottoming out of prices. The new dealer...that's them, isn't it?"

"They've started with crimleaf," Deathmask said. "But they'll soon bring other leaves and powders far worse. Have your men not found the bodies all across the southern district? War's begun, so far silent but for their hiring of the Bloodcrafts. Each day the Sun Guild's numbers grow, and not just from the west. Members of Veldaren's guilds can sense the coming tide, and they're abandoning their old allegiances for the new. When every single street in this city bears the mark of the Sun, what hope do you think you have to accomplish your goal? You'll face a united force, one you can't strike at, for its money and wealth come not from here, but from far to the west. They'll attack anyone they wish, and make no treaties until they accomplish their goal of domination. They're your twin, Victor, only instead of freeing Veldaren they'd have it enslaved. And your stubborn pride may very well let them win."

Victor shifted, leaning more of his weight against the wall. He tried to think, to understand what it meant. Slowly he was bleeding the guilds dry of both members and coin. He might succeed, too, but only a fool would think someone else wouldn't try to fill the void. If the Suns were as dangerous as Deathmask claimed...

He looked up at the thief. "What is it you desire of me?" he asked.

Deathmask pulled a cloth from his pocket and tied it across his face. "Help me," he said, his other hand pulling out a handful of ash. "Swallow your pride, and send your soldiers flooding into the Suns' newly acquired territory. We'll crush them here, now, before they gain more than a foothold. I know where they're hiding, and I can lead your men right to them."

With a wave of a hand, the ash scattered about Deathmask's face, then hovered there, hiding his features.

"The city is mine," he said. "But I am a kinder lord than the Suns will ever be, and unlike them, I possess a sense of humor. Do not doubt your decision, not in this."

Victor closed his eyes, thought of the carnage he'd seen the day prior while being protected by the Eschaton. The Bloodcrafts were the worst of everything, men and women with strength that made his own armored soldiers look like children by comparison. The amount of dead he could pin on those mercenaries alone was significant. And if the Sun Guild was willing to bring in such reckless murderers...

"You're sure the Sun Guild hired the Bloodcrafts?" he asked.

"I'm sure of it," said Deathmask. "If not for them, I'd have already crushed their initial push into the city."

Victor shook his head. Veldaren was already in dire shape, but the Sun Guild's arrival only threatened to ruin everything he'd begun. Crushing the current guilds, only to allow them to be replaced... what sense did that make?

With a sigh he looked to Deathmask, watched the ash swirl around his face. Deathmask was one of the monsters, men who wielded power far greater than they deserved. But Victor now faced many such men, and as the guilds grew desperate, whom else would they turn to? Perhaps, to succeed, he needed his own stable of monsters...

"I'll help you," he said. "But know that I will watch you closely, and do this only for the good of the city."

"The good of the city." Deathmask chuckled. "How quaint."

He whistled, and the rest of his guild appeared from farther up the street, approaching in their similar colors.

Monsters, thought Victor as they gathered. *You said you'd protect me from the monsters, Watcher. But what if I turn the monsters on each other, and let them slay themselves?*

"Ready your men," Deathmask said. "It's time for a slaughter."

Victor left without a word, trying to not think about the company he kept, or about the bloodshed to commence. The peace at the end was all that mattered, he told himself. The final victory. The safe streets and unviolated homes.

"Milord?" asked Sef at his return to the tavern's rear alley.

"Prepare our men to move out," he said.

"Milord, something troubles you, I can tell. What..."

"I said prepare them to move out!"

Sef took a step back, then bowed low. "Forgive me," he said.

Victor sighed, put a hand on the man's shoulder. "No," he said. "You've done much for me, and now I must ask for more. Prepare them all. A new threat has entered our city, and we must crush it while we still have the chance."

Sef tensed as the Ash Guild came around the corner of the tavern, weapons drawn and shimmering with magic. Victor shook his head and motioned for his soldiers to stand down.

"I do this with a heavy heart," he said, pointing to Deathmask. "But it must be done. Follow this man's lead. Once more into the underworld we go."

Beneath the ash and cloth, Deathmask's smile grew.

CHAPTER

31

Earlier that morning, Haern met with the rest of the Eschaton Mercenaries on the bottom floor of their tower and outlined his plan. It went about as well as he'd expected.

"You've got to be kidding," Tarlak said, shaking his head. "That Nicholas guy alone nearly killed all of us, and it took everything we had to chase them off during their last ambush. Now you want to go charging into a fight with them head on?"

Haern shrugged. "If we're going to fight, I'd rather us be the ones doing the ambushing. Or would you prefer we wait for them to come to our tower while we sleep, or assault me when I'm alone upon the rooftops?"

"They've made their intentions clear," Delysia said, taking her brother's hand. "They'll kill us no matter what it takes. You saw the bodies. How many innocents they killed."

"I say we do it," Brug said, hopping up from his chair. "I'll get my armor."

"You're in agreement with this insane scheme too?" Tarlak asked.

Brug shrugged. "What? I killed one of them already. Nothing says I can't do it again."

Haern grinned at his friend. "That's more like it," he said. "So what will it be, Tarlak? Ready for us to go on the offensive for once?"

Tarlak lifted his hat and scratched the back of his head. "That means I'll have to face that one lady throwing all the fire, won't I?"

"Probably."

"Fine." A devilish grin spread over his face, removing his pout. "But this time I'm not going in blind. Come on, Brug, I'll need your help with this."

Over the day they prepared, and then, before nightfall, Haern led them back to the tavern. He felt confident the Bloodcrafts were like most thieves, sleeping during the day and going out at night. And if not, well, then the Eschaton would catch them sleeping. Hardly the most honorable kill, thought Haern, but he'd dealt worse punishments than that.

The tavern was at the corner of Iron, a major trade route heading north to south through Veldaren, and Raven, a far smaller dirt road that jutted off into the remnants of homes, most of which had been shuttered as the wealth traveled steadily north over the past decade. Haern watched the entrance from an alley on the opposite side of Iron. This gave him a wide view of the tavern, as well as the positions of the rest of the Eschaton.

Tarlak waited atop the baker's shop beside the tavern. Haern could not see him, for he'd cast a lengthy spell of invisibility upon himself before climbing up. The wizard directly faced the windows of the room in question, and precautions were necessary for such close proximity. Brug and Delysia were up Raven Street, so that if anyone fled away from Tarlak and Haern they'd be there to intercept. No exits went unwatched, no pathways unprotected. None of them liked the potential for collateral damage, but the ambush was set, and at least no innocent families would be butchered, as when the Bloodcrafts had prepared their own ambush.

Time passed, and Haern felt his nerves start to fray. Slowly the sun fell behind the wall.

"Come on," Haern whispered. "Come on, come on."

The sky turned red, then purple, and then at last the stars winked into existence one by one. Still no sign. With every passing moment, Haern knew something was wrong. No doubt the rest of his friends were as anxious as he. Maybe he should call the ambush off, or try to sneak into the Bloodcrafts' room to confirm...

It was only instinct that saved him. He saw a flash of something high above, a shadow that didn't feel quite right, and without thinking he dove to the side. Down fell a man in a red leather coat, long sword slamming the ground where he'd been. Haern pulled out of his roll, sabers drawn, but his attacker remained back. Surprise gone, he seemed in no hurry.

"Hello, Watcher," said the man. He was middle-aged, handsome, with dark hair cut short. Haern tensed. He'd crossed swords with him once already, and been stunned by his near-inhuman speed.

"I'd greet you in return," Haern said, "but I don't know your name."

The man grinned. "Carson Bloodcraft. Consider me honored to meet you a second time. Few have the skill to match blades against me and live."

"I could say the same."

Carson chuckled. "Indeed. Let me make this quick, Watcher.

We knew you'd come for us after our last ambush, and we have prepared one of our own. We know where your friends are, all of them. Yes, even the wizard foolish enough to think we couldn't see through a simple invisibility spell. With but a signal, they'll attack."

The man was too confident, the tone of his voice and pull of his smile too consistent. No lie. Tarlak, Delysia, Brug... they were all in danger.

"What do you want?" Haern asked, subtly tightening the muscles in his legs for a leap. "Do you wish to mock me before you try to kill me?"

Carson shook his head. "Our mission is to eliminate you as a threat, Watcher. This can be done a lot of ways. But you see, your mercenaries killed two of our members, which leaves us with some openings. Your skill is incredible. With your reputation and your abilities, you'd make a fine addition to the Bloodcrafts."

Carson stood, held his sword out to the side. Something sparkled in his brown eyes, and it made Haern's head ache.

"What do you say to that? Leave this pathetic group you serve. Whatever coin they pay you, I promise we can increase it tenfold. They only hold you back."

Haern took a single step, just enough to shift his weight so he might leap with greater speed. Carson saw it, and he held his sword before his chest.

"If you agree, we'll leave the rest of your group alive. Decline, well... you're still a threat needing to be dealt with. Make a choice, Watcher, but do us both a favor... make the intelligent one. You're too good to be weighed down with petty morality and friendships."

Despite the danger, Haern let out a laugh. "You think I do this for the coin?" he asked. "You damn fool. Give your signal. We'll see who dies tonight."

It was a bold bluster, a way to keep the fear for his friends hidden. He had to trust them, trust his own ability to finish off Carson in time to help the others. Carson shook his head, looking disappointed.

"Despite the loss of such potential, I'm glad you refuse," he said. Something about his voice changed, as if he were suddenly hurrying his words. "You killed my daughter, Watcher. I'll make sure you suffer greatly for that."

His free hand lifted, and when he made to snap his fingers Haern lunged at him, sabers leading. Sword a blur, Carson parried both to the side, then shifted so his elbow slammed into Haern's chest as he came crashing in. Breath lost, Haern swung twice in a futile attempt to keep the man on the defensive while he fell back, gasping for air. Carson parried the swings with ease, holding his sword with a single hand. His movements showed no slowing, no panic. He didn't even look as if he were breathing hard.

He can't be that good, Haern thought, trying to decide his next attack pattern. *I've fought Thren, the Wraith, Dieredon... he can't be greater than them.*

During his indecision, Carson snapped his fingers, then winked.

"Time for some fun," he said, again in that clipped, rapid speech, and then on the other side of the street the roof of the bakery erupted in flame. Before Haern could react, Carson stepped in, sword slashing. Haern blocked, a fraction of a second away from missing. He kept his swords out wide, using the only advantage he had. No matter where Carson thrust or slashed, Haern had a blade ready, just a flick of a wrist away from parrying. Not that it mattered. Carson thrust, looped his sword around, thrust again. When Haern tried to parry the second thrust, Carson batted both sabers aside as if Haern were a child. The tip of his sword continued unabated, piercing Haern's shoulder.

Rolling away before it could punch deeper, Haern fell to one knee, fighting off the urge to clutch the wound with a hand. His sabers shook in his grip as blood ran down the front of his shirt.

How? Haern wondered. *How can he be that fast?*

Carson stepped closer, and in desperation Haern employed his most skillful delay. Spinning, he grabbed his cloaks and flung them into the air, turning faster and faster so that his movements were a blur, the location of his hands and swords undecipherable to any but the most skilled. It should have worked, but Carson only shook his head as if disappointed. Something felt wrong. Haern noticed it just before Carson attacked, undeterred by his cloakdance. The cloaks were hanging lower than they should have, seemingly falling faster than usual, unable to maintain momentum.

Flinging himself back, Haern realized what was wrong. It wasn't that Carson was moving faster. It was that he was moving *slower.* While the magic affected him, it did nothing to the cloaks. All his senses were dulled, delayed. The rapid speech, he realized. Even his hearing was affected. The delay didn't appear to be great, just enough to sap away his greatest advantage.

Carson stalked closer, unworried about Haern's sudden retreat. And why would he be? Could Haern get away while running as if pushing through molasses? Forcing himself to stay calm, he continued his backward retreat. High above, smoke blotted out the stars, the result of the fire that continued to burn. Heavy concussion sounds rocked the building. It sounded like Tarlak was still alive, but for how long?

"Have you given up already?" Carson asked, steadily approaching. "You've yet to make me break a sweat. You fought so well earlier…what happened, Watcher? To think you beat Joanna is insulting."

What *had* happened? He'd fought Carson and the dagger thrower simultaneously. Yes, he'd been pushed to the limit, but still he'd endured. What was different now? What slowed him so?

"Come," Carson said. "Look me in the eye so I can see your fear as you die."

The eye…

Haern stared into those brown orbs, and again he felt an ache grow in his forehead. Tarlak's words echoed in his ears.

I'd call it cheating…

Something about Carson's gaze, be it spell or hypnotism, was digging into him, pooling in his mind. Haern looked down, forced himself to watch Carson's hands and hands only. Normally he might read a man's face to gauge his tension, to watch for tells and signs of impatience. But not now. Gaze low, Haern breathed in deep. He didn't know how the spell or hypnotism worked, or how long it might last, but he had to endure until the effects waned. The first time he and Carson had fought, Haern had had his attention split between two opponents, no doubt weakening the effect. If he could survive then, he could survive now. He had to.

Carson stepped close, and he repeatedly thrust for Haern's chest, pulling back every time Haern tried to parry. Haern watched, more and more aware of the sluggishness of his reactions. He felt robbed of speed, robbed of strength.

"What's the matter, Watcher?" Carson asked. Haern noticed the strange, hurried aspect of his voice was not quite so prominent.

Haern gave no answer, only grinned.

It seemed Carson suddenly realized the shift. He pushed his attack, this time without mockery, no longer playing with him.

Haern kept his eyes down, watching only Carson's hands and the movements of his feet. Carson was a viper, trying to mesmerize his prey with his gaze. But Haern was no mouse.

No, he'd been raised a Spider.

From side to side he shifted, avoiding thrusts, smashing aside cuts. Carson tried to step in and strike him with a fist, but Haern ducked underneath, whirling so his cloaks hid his movements. This time when he stood he counterattacked, the tip of his saber slashing open a bleeding wound across Carson's cheek.

Much as he wanted to enjoy the shock and fear in Carson's eyes, Haern pulled his hood lower across his face and stared at the ground.

"What's the matter, Bloodcraft?" Haern asked. "Aren't you going to kill me?"

In his childhood, during the years of training by Thren's hired tutors, Haern had spent several months learning how to fight in pure darkness. He knew how to predict the most common sword placements, how to listen for the movement of feet, the intake of air that marked an attack. In his mind's eye he could visualize where Carson stood, and from their fights he now had a feel for his favored routines. The man was good, but he was used to having speed on his side. He'd never been pushed to his limits.

But Haern had fought so much better. He'd met his own limits, and surpassed them.

Eyes closed, he lashed out, and the sound of metal on metal brought a smile to his face. He pressed forward, his sabers whirling so that he could control the placement of Carson's sword, forcing his defenses and countering his attempts to pull close. His speed had returned in full. His strength was back.

He thought of the rest of his friends, battling for their lives, and he would not fail them.

"Have you lost your nerve?" Haern asked, so close to Carson that he could smell the sweat and blood on him.

"You haven't beaten me yet, you—"

His words confirmed his location, and more important, how Carson was falling back to gain distance. It was all Haern needed.

He lunged, one saber thrusting, the other swinging wide to parry the desperate counterthrust he knew Carson would try. Metal hit metal, and then his thrusting blade met resistance, just for a moment. Blood poured across Haern's hand, and he felt the closeness of Carson's body to his. Only then did Haern open his eyes to see Carson gasping for air, a saber piercing his chest and coming out of his back.

"Look me in the eye," Haern whispered. "The fear you see is your own."

Carson opened his mouth to speak, but he could only cough blood. He slipped back, and Haern yanked free his saber. Carson collapsed, mouth still moving, eyes still locked on Haern's. The ornate blade fell from his hand and clattered upon the hard stone.

The ground shook, and Haern brought his attention to the other battles still raging.

"Hold on, Tar," he whispered. "I'm coming."

Tarlak sat on his rear, legs folded underneath him, as he leaned his chin against his palm and watched the inn. So far an hour had passed, yet they saw no sign of life or movement through the windows.

Some ambush, he thought. *I think I'll be killing myself from boredom before the night is over. The Bloodcrafts will win by default.*

He sat at the very edge of the bakery's rooftop, and he kept bouncing his attention between the windows and the alley beneath him. There was always the possibility they were out during the day, and would return sometime soon. He knew he had to be ready, but still...

"Boooored," Tarlak muttered.

He leaned back to stretch, and as he did, he caught sight of a woman on the roof of the inn, her slender frame dwarfed by the red leather coat she wore. Tarlak froze in mid-stretch, wondering where in the world she'd come from. She was looking right at him.

"Uh, hello?" he said.

She lifted her palm toward him, and fire leaped from it as if it were the gullet of a dragon. Tarlak flung himself onto his back, crossed his arms, and enacted a protection spell. The fire swarmed around him, bathing the rooftop, but it did not touch his skin. The strength to keep the protection going weighed on Tarlak, and the spell of invisibility around him vanished, not that it was doing much good. When the fire subsided, Tarlak rolled to his knees, then pushed to his feet.

"Not bad," he said, wiping some ash off his yellow robe. "My turn."

Shards of ice flew from his hands, their points deadly sharp. A dozen shattered across the rooftop of the inn, each one missing its mark as the woman dove from side to side, faster than Tarlak could adjust. Without slowing she ran for the edge, and when Tarlak hurled a bolt of lightning, she vaulted into the air, over the blast, and across the thin gap between the two buildings. Before landing she crossed her arms, and another wave of fire lashed out, as if she were the center of a great explosion. Tarlak braced himself, once more summoning a protection spell. The fire hit, and this time he felt the heat of it on his skin. He gritted his teeth, poured more of his strength into his spell.

When the woman landed, she pressed her palms together, and the burst of fire was tremendous. But Tarlak had had enough.

"Remember this?" he said, pulling the sword hilt from his pocket. The crystal on it flared to life, and all about him the fire died as if it had never existed.

"You have Nicholas's sword," she said.

At the woman's shocked expression, Tarlak grinned. "Just the hilt," he said, twirling it in his fingers. He'd had Brug remove the blade, and then, over the course of a few hours, he'd replenished the magic in the crystal, turning it back to clear. "I must say, I thought it cheating. Shame Nicholas died before I could tell him so."

The woman rushed him, abandoning the fire. Tarlak took a step back, but she was faster, and her kick connected with his midsection. He gasped as the air was blasted from his lungs. She swiped at the sword hilt, but he clung to it as if his life depended upon it. She unleashed a flurry of punches, half of which he failed to dodge. Her fists struck his face, his chest, and when he collapsed onto his back she fell on top of him. Tarlak tensed every muscle in his body as she put his head into a lock, her slender arms choking him tighter and tighter.

"What good is that sword if you can't cast either, you damn fool?" she asked, driving her knees into his stomach so she might apply more pressure on his neck. The hand holding the hilt was caught by her legs, but his other was free, and he pressed it against her chest in a futile attempt to push her off. As the arm of his robe fell back, he saw her eyes go wide when she caught sight of the blue tattoo glowing across his wrist.

"I can cheat too," Tarlak gasped as her panicked grip loosened.

The magic within the tattoo activated, flowing through his hand and into her chest. It was a solid force, like an invisible battering ram blasting her entire body, and it hit with a tremendous boom. Her head arched back, her arms flailed, and Tarlak winced at the sound of a dozen breaking bones. Her body flew several feet back, landing in a sprawl atop the roof. Tarlak stood, tossed the sword hilt aside, and rubbed his bruised neck.

"Think I might have overdone it," he muttered. He glanced at the tattoo, which was already fading from his skin. His entire arm ached, and it itched where the ink had been.

Never again, he swore.

Haern leaped up to the rooftop, landing silently mere feet away from the body. He was bleeding at the shoulder, but seemed otherwise fine.

"Dead," he said, letting out a curse. "Need someone alive."

He turned and leaped back off, toward the alley where Brug and Delysia had been waiting. Tarlak rushed after, and he peered off the rooftop to see where the fight continued below.

Brug stood protectively before Delysia, hunched over with several daggers sticking out from the creases of his armor. He still held his punch daggers, and he kept them up at the ready. Behind him Delysia cast a barrage of spells, blinding and disorienting their opponent, the rail-thin and final member of the Bloodcrafts.

"Come on," Brug was saying. "You can do better than this!"

The Bloodcraft seemed to agree. He flung several more daggers, but Brug kept in his way. Most bounced off his thick plate mail, except for the one that sailed wide, missing because of a blinding white light that flared from Delysia's hand. Tarlak shook his head, relieved the two could fight as such an odd but effective pair.

The man pulled out several more daggers, and through rapidly blinking eyelids tried to find a way around, to get close without enduring the priestess's barrage or Brug's daggers. He apparently saw none, and then his chance was gone. Haern emerged from the shadows behind him, striking him hard on the back of the head with the hilt of a saber. The man dropped, his body going limp.

Tarlak cast a spell to slow his own fall, then stepped off the roof and gently floated down. When his feet touched ground, he crossed his arms and glared at Haern.

"Some ambush," he said.

Haern shrugged. "At least we won."

Despite Delysia's insistence, Brug marched over to Haern and smacked him in the chest with a mailed glove.

"I had him," he said, clearly unhappy.

Haern lifted an eyebrow. "Sorry?"

"Get over here," Delysia said, grabbing Brug's shoulder. "You're bleeding all over the place."

Tarlak gestured toward the last Bloodcraft as his sister pulled Brug away so she could remove the knives and work her healing magic. "What do we do with him?" he asked.

Haern sheathed a saber, then tapped the unconscious man with the other. "We get some answers," he said. "I want to know who hired them."

Tarlak frowned. "Think he'll talk?"

A dark edge entered Haern's eyes, and Tarlak didn't like it one bit.

"Get Delysia out of here—Brug too," his friend said. "I don't want them to see this. And yes. He'll talk."

Tarlak put a hand on Haern's shoulder. "Be careful," he said. "He's no threat to me."

"That's not what I meant."

Haern looked away, sighed. "I know. But someone wants us dead, and I intend to find out who. If it comes between this man's life, and all of yours..."

"Just be careful," Tarlak said, turning to the others. "Now let's go home. And Ashhur help us, you really are bleeding everywhere, Brug..."

CHAPTER

 32

Thren lurked at the edge of the newly acquired Sun territory, watching the people come and go. Night had just fallen, but deep in the southern district it seemed a new life blossomed, ignorant of the light. Men and women were flocking to the new guild, Thren knew. He'd even watched several adopting the four-pointed star and casting aside their cloaks. Very little ceremony or fanfare. He'd done his best to cull their numbers, but it was beyond controlling now. With the promise of coin, trade, power, and the overthrow of the Trifect...what did the rest of the guilds have to offer against that?

"Tread lightly," Thren whispered to himself as he watched yet another man throw off his cloak. How many of his own Spiders might now be with the Suns? And when he put out his call, would they come to him, or dare hope they might go unpunished?

Thren chuckled. Of course they'd ignore him. Loyalty was

bought with power. There was a changing of the guard in the underworld, and until something happened to shake everyone's confidence in the Suns, none would dare return to his side. Which is why Thren lurked, hidden beside a building where there was no light so he could watch and wait. Only one thing could slow down the Suns, at least in his mind. Just one.

Killing Grayson.

To do that, he needed to know where the man was hiding, where he'd chosen to set up his base. So far he'd been patient, not wanting Grayson to even know he was being hunted, at least by Thren. The other guilds would no doubt also want Grayson dead, but they'd be hesitant about out-and-out warfare. Thren knew their leaders, knew how cowardly they were deep down in their black hearts. They'd want to know if they could make alliances first, if they could grab hold of the Suns' rise and use it to reestablish their own dominance in the city. They didn't realize the fire they played with. Didn't realize that when all was said and done, Grayson had no intention of letting any guild other than his own operate within the walls of Veldaren.

Thren tensed, the sight before him jarring him from his thoughts. One of the original members of the Suns who had come with Grayson from Mordeina was meeting with two others at the street corner. He passed them a bag, no doubt of some cheap crimleaf, and then whispered a few words. Thren watched to see if he'd return in the direction he'd come from, or move elsewhere, and then prepared to follow. When the man continued, Thren slipped in behind him, just a shadow in the street.

The Sun walked as if in no hurry, then suddenly burst into a run, hooking a sharp left into an alley. Thren chuckled, and he calmly drew his swords. He'd been spotted, which meant the man was skilled. That he'd given away this knowledge by running meant he was overconfident, and hasty. Someone skilled enough to notice Thren wouldn't panic so easily, nor be spooked by a simple tail. Which meant the man wasn't actually running.

It meant an ambush, one Thren willingly entered.

Six steps into the alley, Thren spun, sword slashing. As he'd thought, the Sun member had crouched behind a barrel at the entrance, then leaped out with dagger ready. Thren batted it aside, stepped closer, and then thrust. To his surprise, the man managed to pull back in time to parry. Skilled indeed, but not enough. Thren flung himself at him with the ferocity of a wild animal. He had the man trapped against the wall, and with the greater reach of his blades, had every advantage.

Ten seconds later the daggers fell from bleeding hands. Thren pressed the tip of his sword against the man's neck.

"Your name?" he asked.

"Pierce," said the thin man.

"Well, Pierce," said Thren, "how much pain do you wish to feel?"

The man licked his lips as if he were facing a trick question. "Little as necessary," he said.

"A wise answer. Tell me where Grayson is, and that is what you'll receive."

"Only a dead man turns on Grayson," Pierce said.

Thren pressed his blade tighter against Pierce's neck. "You are a dead man," he said. "But that's not what matters. That's not the question. The question was, and still is...how much pain do you wish to feel?"

Finally he saw a hint of true fear in Pierce's eyes. "You can't do shit to me," he said. "You do, and you'll get it back ten times worse. Veldaren's our city now. Go back to whatever guild you serve and tell them that."

Thren laughed. "I *am* my guild," he said. "I am Thren Felhorn, and I serve none but myself."

There it was. The fear he wanted. His smile grew.

It took a few minutes, but he got his answers.

Roark's Oddities wasn't too far away, and he knew the shop well. The man was a notorious cheat, and he showed no loyalty to any guild. Because of that everyone liked him, and everyone used him to deal stolen goods. With him, gold was all that mattered, which meant you knew exactly how far to trust him. Thren grinned at the thought. It looked as if Roark had found a partnership worth far too much to turn down.

Before Thren pulled the last of his intestines out of his stomach, Pierce had said they only used Roark's place to store their goods, since their first safe house, Billick's, had been burned to the ground. They weren't staying there themselves, but Thren had a feeling Grayson would always be nearby. His take-over of Veldaren depended on his product. He wouldn't leave it unguarded. Thren approached cautiously, watching for any inquisitive pairs of eyes. He couldn't rely on cloaks and colors anymore. With so much in flux, anyone could be a snitch.

When he was at the top of the road leading down to Roark's, and almost within sight of the store, Thren heard the first of the horns. He stopped, confused as to what it meant. When a second sounded, farther away, he realized what it was, but could hardly believe it.

"What madness is this?" he wondered aloud.

Troops marched into the southern district, coordinating their movements with the blasts of the trumpets. It couldn't be the city guard, at least not alone. The king was too cowardly for that. Only one person made sense, and given the audacity that man had already shown, Thren knew he shouldn't be as surprised as he was.

Victor was coming to play.

Thren rushed toward Roark's. He wouldn't let Victor get

Grayson. That was his kill, his chance to send a message west to the guilds in Mordeina. They would never fear Victor, no matter how many men he had. He was still an outside lord, a man not of their world. No matter how brightly he shone, he would never find them all in the shadows. For it to matter, Thren had to be the executioner.

Sounds of combat reached his ears, first quiet, then gradually louder. The marching of feet soon followed. Screams, scattered and few, accompanied the progressive movement south. As Thren ran he saw Suns joining him on the street, all fleeing to the same place. Thren drew his swords, stabbed a man beside him wearing their colors. Without losing a step he shifted to the side, overtaking a fleeing woman. She sprawled headfirst into the dirt after he slashed out her heel.

At the doors of Roark's Oddities, several men were dispersing as a squad of ten armored men turned the corner. One of the soldiers lifted a horn to his lips and blew. Thren hooked a right, finding the alley occupied by a man furiously pulling at a scrap of cloth sewn onto the sleeve of his shirt that identified his guild allegiance.

"Having second thoughts?" he asked the dirty man, grinning. Thren cut out his throat before he could answer, his fingers still in the hole he'd torn in the fabric. Glancing from side to side, Thren gauged the cramped distance between the two buildings, decided them close enough. He leaped from wall to wall, constantly kicking himself higher so that on the third kick he landed atop the building directly adjacent to Roark's. As he'd expected, Grayson was up there, surveying the movement of the troops. Thren knew well how he felt, for he'd done the same when Victor stormed his headquarters. But how had Victor discovered Grayson's place?

A black fire gave him his answer, rising up from the ground

toward the rooftop. Grayson dropped to his stomach, avoiding Deathmask's attack. Glancing over the edge of the roof, Thren saw the Ash guildmaster leading a squad of six armored soldiers, Victor at his side. Grayson looked up from where he lay, saw Thren watching. His lips were grinning, but his eyes promised death. Thren grinned right back. The two were about to be kindred spirits in their homelessness. Grayson, as if imagining his thoughts, only shook his head in disagreement.

Thren turned and ran, still shaking off surprise that Victor would ally himself with someone as unpredictable as Deathmask and his Ash Guild. On the only safe path out he raced across the rooftops toward the edge of the sweeping net Victor had created. And sure enough, when he glanced back, Grayson was in pursuit. They understood each other well, knew neither would settle for capture by the meddlesome lord. They had a score to settle. Behind them smoke billowed into the air as Roark's shop went up in flames, burning away the last of the Sun's leaf.

Thren ran, ran, leaping over the gaps between buildings without slowing in the slightest. His short swords grew heavy in his hands as he held them. Grayson had often defeated him when they sparred, and he'd near-fatally wounded his son as well. What hope did Thren have that now would end any way other than with his death?

Digging in his heels, Thren came to a halt, spinning on Grayson like a deer turning on a chasing wolf. He'd made a promise, sworn his vows. He was Thren Felhorn. How could he lay claim to a city yet fear to fight one making similar claims? He would not let Grayson be right. No running, not from this. Standing firm, he held his swords together in an X, eyes locked on the giant man barreling toward him. Let death come for him if it must, but it would not find him a coward.

They crashed together, Grayson's weight and momentum pushing Thren back. In the light of the stars, upon the rooftops, the two battled. Thren constantly circled, refusing to give Grayson a chance to bring his full strength to bear. The ringing of their swords was a song, and the battle felt so comfortable, so familiar, that only the pounding of his heart in his ears assured him that it was not some old training match, not some unimportant spar.

"This stops nothing," Grayson said, hammering at Thren's defenses. His short swords, dwarfed by his enormous arms, moved with both speed and unmatched power. "Veldaren is ours."

Thren dove underneath a swipe, circled to his left, then slashed upward at Grayson's side. One sword he parried, but the other cut into flesh. It was a minor wound, like a bee stinging a bull, but it angered Grayson nonetheless.

"It's mine, Grayson!" Thren shouted as he retreated once more, leaping back and forth in the constrained limits of their chosen place of battle. "Veldaren, its people, its fear...mine, and I do not share!"

"Liar! Wretch!" Grayson continued, showing no impatience despite Thren's stalling tactic. He knew better than to give Thren any sort of edge. When Thren fell too far back, Grayson took the moment to catch his breath and rebalance himself before slowly approaching. "You've lost that title, that respect. The Watcher took it from you. I fought him, Thren. He died, and at my hand. You could have killed him at any time, yet you never did. You coward..."

Thren stood there, hunched low, ready to spring into an attack at any time. Grayson shifted his feet, ready to meet it.

"Coward?" Thren asked. "Is that so?"

"All this time you let him live. Why?"

Thren's grin spread from ear to ear, and despite his exhaustion, despite his inability to score more than a single scratch on his opponent, he laughed.

"Because he's my son," he said.

Grayson froze, just for a moment, as he realized all that meant. "Your son?" he asked.

"Marion's son," Thren said. "Your blood as well as mine, you damn fool. The Watcher and I are two sides of a single coin. Every man, woman, and child of this city fears one of us. Together we own the night. You are nothing to him, nothing to me. Come, Grayson. Let's see which of us still lives come the dawn."

Thren leaped at him, every ounce of his speed sending him flying toward the giant man. Once more their swords clashed, but Grayson's mind was overcome for just a moment, unable to maintain the balance needed against such an opponent. Thren had cried his tears for Marion, and he'd long since buried her in his heart. Grayson's wounds, though, they'd stayed fresh, and because of it new ones slashed across his chest as Thren pressed harder and harder. He felt rage boiling in his veins, and it gave him strength. Looping closer, he slashed through Grayson's left wrist, severing tendons. The blade dropped to the ground. Thren hammered the other, staying close, denying Grayson the chance to flee. The other blade fell, its hilt soaked with blood as Thren hacked into his arm.

Grayson tried to sweep out his feet with a kick, but Thren leaped into the air, his knee catching Grayson's forehead. The man fell back, and Thren stabbed through his side, the blade puncturing the roof so it held him there like a stake. Grayson screamed, and he pulled against the blade. Another stab, this one through the shoulder, kept him down.

Thren leaned close, so they were mere inches apart.

"Who is he?" he asked. "Your arrival was not coincidence. You've spit in my face, and for that you'll die, but first you'll tell me who."

"What are you talking about?" Grayson asked, still struggling against the two blades. Thren had made sure neither punched through a vital organ, wanting to control Grayson's death, to have it be exactly when he desired it.

"The one mocking me," he said. "The one who has killed my members, taken their eyes, and left rhymes written in blood. The Widow. Tell me who it is."

"I don't know," Grayson said. He reached toward Thren with a shaking hand, and despite his wounds, tried to grab his neck to strangle him. Thren admired his dedication, but had no time for that. He released the hilts of his swords, grabbed Grayson's wrists, and held him down.

"You lie."

"I was never told his name."

Thren's eyes narrowed. "Told by who?"

Grayson shook his head, and he laughed despite his pain.

"It's all a game, Thren, and I played along because it suited us well. His name's Laerek, a priest of Karak."

It made no sense, but Thren detected no lie. "A priest?" he asked. "What have I done to them that Karak's followers would hate me?"

Another laugh. "I don't know, and I don't give a shit. Laerek helped us get into the city, all so we'd help him with something later. It was too tempting to say no."

Thren grabbed Grayson's neck with a hand and pushed his head down. "Tell me where to find him."

"Are you going to kill me?"

Thren swallowed, and then he nodded. "Yeah. I will."

Grayson let out a soft sigh. His dark skin was turning pale, yet he kept total control of his voice.

"So be it. He'll be waiting for me in an alley off Songbird Road, by that shoemaker's place."

Thren again sensed no lie. He stood, and his hand closed around the hilt of one of his swords.

"Thren," Grayson said, and for the first time his voice wavered.

"Yes?"

Grayson grinned darkly. "The Sun Guild doesn't die with me. You know that. The Darkhand will be here soon. Whatever life you have now, cherish it. Once he arrives, your time is done."

Thren knelt down beside him so he could whisper in his dying friend's ear.

"Let him come. This student has long ago surpassed his teacher."

Thren stood, yanked the blade free, spun it around, and then slashed open Grayson's throat. His body convulsed for a moment as blood spilled across his neck and chest, and then he lay still. Thren stood over him, breathing heavily, and despite himself, he felt tears run down his face.

"You loved Marion more than I," he told the corpse. "A shame it cost you so."

He yanked the other sword free, not bothering to clean off the blood. He still had work to do.

"Laerek," Thren whispered as trumpets sounded, the raid on the Sun Guild nearing its end.

CHAPTER

33

Alyssa tossed and turned, but she could not sleep. Zusa had still not returned, and with the sun long ago set she felt her hope dwindling. With every creak of a board she sat up in bed, looking to see if Zusa was opening the door or climbing down from the ceiling. Always nothing. She'd give so much to have the faceless woman climb into her bed, to wrap her arms around Alyssa and tell her everything was well, everything was safe. Despite her wealth, Alyssa could not buy the one thing she so desperately needed.

Still feeling anxious, she at last gave up on sleep and slipped out of bed. She threw a robe over her thin nightgown and stepped out into the hallways. It was dark despite the many candles. Something gnawed at her tired mind, but she couldn't place what it was. Even more impatient, she hurried to Nathaniel's room. If she was stuck awake, at least it'd be with her son. Seeing him asleep, and at peace, was often what it took to reassure her troubled mind that all was well. She'd done it plenty when he was a newborn, and though it felt weak to do so now that he was older, she didn't care. Reaching his door, she again felt that gnawing fear, an awareness that she was missing something both troubling and obvious.

Opening the door to her son's room, she stepped inside, and was surprised to find that he was still awake.

"Mom?"

His head tilted higher, and he clearly looked relieved. Two candles burned in a candelabra hooked to the opposite wall, filling the room with yellow light.

"Is something wrong?" she asked, sitting down beside his bed. He sat up, which revealed the stump of his arm. It was scabbed over, with several spots bleeding from his picking at it. Nathaniel seemed oblivious, just scratching repeatedly with his hand as he shuddered and looked away. Alyssa felt the worry in her gut strengthen.

"I don't want to sleep," he said.

"You know you need to. I can see how tired you are."

"It's not that," he said. "I...I don't want to dream. I keep seeing him, and I don't want to anymore."

"Him?" Alyssa frowned. "What do you mean?"

He looked feverish, yet when she touched his face, he was bathed in a cold sweat.

"Every time I dream, I see him laughing," he said. "Veldaren's burning, and he laughs."

Alyssa kissed his forehead, then gently pushed him onto his back. Tucking him in, she tried to hide her own fears. Nathaniel had had night terrors before, particularly after he'd lost his arm, and it took a year for them to go away. Yet this seemed different. He'd never really been aware of what frightened him back then, why he'd awaken screaming.

"How long have you had these dreams?" she asked, trying to sound more tired than worried.

"Ever since Grandmother showed me the chrysarium."

Alyssa forced herself not to frown. Chrysarium? What in Karak's name was a chrysarium? It sounded like something a wizard might conjure up. That her mother had exposed him to it without checking with her first immediately made her angry.

"Honey, what did Grandmother show you?"

He shrank into the bed, scratched harder at the stump of his arm.

"She made me promise not to tell."

"You can tell me. You know that. You can always tell me everything."

She reached down and grabbed his hand to stop the picking.

"Tell me," she said, letting a little of her earnestness come through.

"I saw visions," he said. "Grandmother said they were from Karak, and it meant I was special. But I don't want them, they're horrible, and they won't let me sleep!"

Alyssa swallowed, and a hundred things she might scream at Melody ran through her mind.

"Listen to me, Nathan," she said. "They're just visions. They can't hurt you, and they don't mean anything. I want you to lie here and relax. You don't have to sleep if you don't want to. I'm going to talk to Melody and find out what happened. If she did something, maybe she can fix this."

"But she'll be asleep."

A dry smile stretched across Alyssa's lips.

"Then I'll wake her."

She kissed his cheek, then stood. When she reached his door, she stopped, for she heard shuffling on the other side. For some reason her heart froze, and she remained perfectly still as the sound slowly faded away. Door open a crack, she peered through and saw a young woman with dark brown hair heading down the hall. Alyssa frowned. She didn't look like a servant, nor was she dressed like one, yet Alyssa could not place her despite their time in the mansion.

"Nathan," she whispered, turning back to her son. "When I step out, I want you to lock the door, all right? No questions, and don't open it for anyone but me, you understand?"

With that she entered the hall, and then waited until she heard the rattle of his lock. Satisfied, she hurried in the opposite direction from the unknown woman, coming upon Stephen's room, the door slightly ajar. Was the woman a prostitute, perhaps? Not that she cared to judge Stephen's actions, but it seemed odd the guards would not escort her...

And then it hit her, the obvious fear that had gnawed at the back of her mind. The guards. There should have been guards stationed all around the home, at her door, Nathaniel's, and especially Stephen's. But there were none. A chill spread through her veins. Why were there no guards?

Her instincts were to run to her son, but his door was locked, and she'd checked it the first night he'd stayed in there alone. It'd take a solid beating by grown men to break the bolt. Swallowing the instinct down, she instead slipped into Stephen's room. Always before it had been locked and guarded. She'd assumed this was because of well-founded fear of assassins. Now, though...

Inside she found a room similar to her own, well furnished and with an enormous bed in the center, its lavender curtains pulled back. Moonlight streamed in through three windows, faintly illuminating the room in a soft blue. The bed itself was empty. In the far corner she saw a door, also open. Yellow light shone from within, flickering from an unseen candle. Curious, she walked toward the door, glad her feet were bare. On the thick carpet, she made hardly a sound with her passing. Stopping just before the entrance, she drew a deep breath, and prayed it was nothing, all a strange misunderstanding. There'd be nothing within but clothes, finery, maybe some old armor...

Alyssa stepped inside.

Three candles in a golden candelabra rested atop a small stool. On either side of her, covering the walls of what appeared to be an extraordinarily large closet, were portraits of Leon Connington, painted in various styles and with varying skill. She recognized them well, for they'd decorated the walls upon her visits before Leon had been killed by the Watcher. She remembered Zusa remarking upon their absence, and the implied dislike the son might have for the father. But there in that room she knew it was the reverse, a clandestine reverence for the man whose eyes glowered down from all corners.

Every instinct of warning fired off in her mind. The mansion was no longer safe for her. Turning to leave, she stopped, for on the ground, nearly hidden from the light of the candles, was a jar. The mere sight of it twisted her stomach, despite her being unable to identify the contents within. With shaking hands she knelt down, grabbed it, and lifted it up to the candlelight. It was made of thick, clear glass. Swirling within a syrupy liquid of some kind were over a dozen naked eyeballs.

It took all her control to hold back her scream. The jar fell from her hands and landed with a dull thud on the carpet. Alyssa left it there and rushed for the door. They had to flee. Even the wild streets at night would feel safer than the enclosed walls of the Connington mansion. Before exiting she had the presence of mind to stop and check the hall. From the crack in the door she saw the approach of the same unknown woman... except now she wasn't quite so unknown. Alyssa recognized those eyes, the softness of the nose and chin...

It can't be him, she thought, but knew it was. She ducked behind the door. Was he coming back to his room? She had no blade, no weapon, and none appeared to be in his room. In her indecision she tensed, waiting for the door to press open. It did not. Holding her breath, Alyssa once more peered out through the door and saw that he'd continued. She could see the small crossbow in his hand, pressed against his side as he walked. Sticking her head out, she could just barely see her own door down the hall, and sure enough, Stephen slowly pushed it open and slid inside without making a sound.

The moment he vanished within, Alyssa ran, once more thankful for the bareness of her feet. When Stephen found her room empty there was only one place he'd think to go, and it was the one place she had to beat him to.

At the door to Nathaniel's room, she stopped, knocked twice (the noise seeming unbearably loud), and then waited for a sound of movement.

"It's me, your mother," she said, not waiting for him to ask. "Unlock the door, now!"

He did, and she shoved it open hard enough to send him staggering backward. Stepping inside, she spun, shut it, and then pressed in the bolt. That done, she grabbed Nathaniel, held him against her, and wondered what in all of Dezrel she could possibly do now.

"Mom?" he asked when she said nothing, only held him.

"Shush," she said, blowing out the candles to plunge the room into darkness. "Don't make a noise."

He nodded.

The two backed away, slowly, as if a monster lurked on the other side of the door. One did, except it wasn't a creature of legend or fireside tales. This one was real, its venom deadly, its appetite sick and deranged.

The doorknob turned. Alyssa's breath caught in her throat, and she put a hand over Nathaniel's mouth. The door pressed inward, just a fraction, before the bolt caught it. There was a pause, and then the knob returned to its resting position. Two knocks followed.

"Nathan?" she heard Stephen ask from the other side. His voice was gentle, as if he were embarrassed to impose. "Nathaniel, it's me, Stephen. Are you awake? I need to tell you something about your mother."

She clutched her son tighter.

"Nathaniel?" More knocks, heavier. His voice took on a firmer edge. "Nathaniel, I said open the door. This is important."

Alyssa's mind raced. There was the window, but it was fairly high, and only Nathaniel could fit through it. She held little doubt that after her death, Nathan's would follow. Guards crawled along the outside. Could her son escape, especially without her help? She didn't think so. She commanded a presence, an implied threat of house-against-house warfare. Nathaniel was a small boy with a severed arm, born of a disgraced father. His disappearance would bother no one.

But would Stephen hurt Nathaniel if he wasn't certain about her own fate? It was a horrible gamble, but she saw no other way.

"Listen," she whispered into her son's ear, desperately praying that Stephen would not hear through the door. "My life depends on you. Get in bed, and pretend you've had a nightmare. No matter what, I am not here, you understand me? I'm not here."

He nodded. She kissed his forehead as Stephen banged on the door.

"Nathaniel! Open the door this instant!"

Though her son was small, his bed was still plenty big, and Alyssa crawled underneath and backed as far as she could against the wall. Despite every logical part of her telling her this was her best hope to survive, she still felt a horrible guilt smothering her, crushing her chest. If Stephen did something to Nathaniel while she hid under his bed like a damn child...

No time. Taking in a breath, she held it as Nathaniel undid the bolt. The door opened, and she heard footsteps as Stephen entered.

"I'm sorry," she heard her son say. "I was scared, I had...why are you dressed like that?"

A pause before the answer. "I, um, it's just a game, Nathaniel. A game adults play. Is your mother in here?"

"I was hoping you were her," Nathaniel said. "I keep dreaming of him, of that horrible man..."

A good lie, thought Alyssa, especially off the cuff. Should they get out of this alive, she knew she'd have to watch him more carefully.

Stephen stepped farther into the room. She could see his feet from where she hid, and for some reason it horrified her to see a shaven leg in a high-heeled shoe. Was it just a disguise, or something more? Did she truly know so little of the man whose house she'd been living in? And what was the reason for his hatred of her household, and of the Spider Guild?

"I thought I heard whispering," Stephen said. "Was that you?"

"I...was praying."

"Praying? To who, Nathan?"

He seemed to have no answer. Stephen continued farther into the room, out of her sight. The closet door opened, shut. Still she waited. The lighting was incredibly poor, just what little moonlight came in through the curtained window. Perhaps in the darkness, he would not see...

Stephen knelt before the bed. Her whole world froze. He was

looking right at her. Everything about him was solid black, just a feminine shape peering underneath the bed. Alyssa didn't move, didn't breathe, didn't even dare think. She felt like a rabbit cornered by a wolf. And then, after a few agonizing seconds, he stood.

"Just checking for monsters," he said to her son. Slowly she let out a breath as tears ran down her face.

"Is it safe?" Nathaniel asked as Stephen headed for the door.

"No monsters," Stephen said. "Go back to bed. Oh, and Nathan... if you're to pray, pray to Karak. He's the true god of this world. You're old enough to be accountable for such things now."

"Yes, milord."

Another pause, and then the door shut. Alyssa clutched the carpet with her fingers, trying to push away her lingering terror. Her son sat on the bed, his feet dangling off. Rolling out, she got to her knees and wrapped her arms about him. She was still embracing him when the door reopened, and Stephen stepped inside, a terrible smile on his painted face. Alyssa froze, too stunned to act. Something so simple, so stupid, had cost her terribly.

Nathaniel hadn't relocked the door.

"Hello, Alyssa," Stephen said, lifting the crossbow.

Zusa flew through the streets, legs pumping and head bobbing with her gasps. Too much, she thought, she was pushing herself too much. She'd undergone hunger and torture, her right hand mostly numb as it clutched her dagger, yet she dared not waste a precious second resting, or recapturing her breath. A hundred images flashed through her mind, and every one of them was too painful to dwell on for long. She saw Alyssa lying on her bed, or the floor, or out in the garden of the estate, her eyes open but empty, silver coins staring up at the stars.

Through it all, Daverik's words echoed in her head. The Widow had a meeting, but only after.

After killing Alyssa Gemcroft.

She ran, and prayed to any god other than Karak to let her beloved Alyssa be safe, and Nathaniel as well. She'd promised him she'd always be there in the shadows to protect him. What if it wasn't just Alyssa she found with eyes of silver, and a tongue of gold...

Zusa stumbled, her concentration broken by such night-marish daydreaming. The empty streets spun before her, and she landed on her shoulder hard enough to elicit a cry of pain. Lying there, tears swelling, she saw a shape flying through the air behind her, solid darkness but for the faint gray of the cloak trailing after.

No pause, no hesitation. Zusa rolled to her right, her cloak wrapping about her upper body. Ezra landed, her knee and dagger striking where Zusa should have been. Zusa kicked at Ezra's legs, but the woman leaped over, diving toward her with both daggers leading. Zusa's arms trapped by her thick cloak, she pushed the fabric outward. Ezra's daggers punched through it, but the handguards snagged when Zusa twisted and shoved to the side. Again she kicked, this time connecting with Ezra's midsection. The faceless woman fell back so she might regain her balance. Zusa staggered to her feet, let her ragged cloak unfurl about her.

"Did Daverik decide it was time for me to die?" Zusa asked.

"He still loves you," Ezra said, crouching down as she circled, looking like a strange animal ready for the pounce. Even her eyes were wide and wild behind the thin white cloth upon her face. "But even he knows that the loyalty of our faith must come before those we love."

"Some faith," Zusa said, grinning to hide her exhaustion and worry. "Is that what they told you when they stripped you naked and forced you into the faceless? Loyalty before love?"

Ezra thrust, but pulled back when Zusa moved to block. Another thrust, this one equally prepared for. Ezra was testing for an opening, gauging Zusa's reaction speed. Zusa felt her nerves fraying. She didn't have time for this.

"You don't deserve his love," Ezra said.

"You're wrong," Zusa said. "He doesn't deserve mine."

She took the offensive, and was surprised when Ezra did not move to block. Instead she remained still, even when the daggers closed in on her neck. But Zusa did not cut flesh. Instead her daggers moved right through, as if hitting a mirage. From behind her she heard laughter, and spun to find Ezra there, twirling her daggers in mockery.

"I have Karak's blessing," she said. "Behold his gift."

As Zusa watched, Ezra's form grew still, then blinked away, just an afterimage. It was like staring too long at the sun, seeing something burned into the eye that wasn't actually there. Zusa tensed for an attack, but could only guess where it would come from.

"I prayed," Ezra said, off to her left. Zusa spun, but again there was just an afterimage that quickly vanished. When Ezra spoke again, she was on the right. "All night I prayed for the strength to defeat you. And now I have it."

The image of her shifted, and suddenly she was mere inches away, leering at Zusa.

"I can move faster than the eye," she told Zusa, laughing. "What hope have you now?"

Zusa swung at her, and their daggers connected. For a moment it was a familiar dance, a giving and taking of position that Zusa knew she could easily win. But when she tried to finish her opponent, to thrust through an opening to pierce Ezra's heart, Ezra's form turned blurry, and then she was ten feet away down the street.

"Damn it," Zusa whispered. She didn't have time for this, but she had to remain calm, had to think. Slowly Ezra approached, reeking of confidence.

"Will you always run?" Zusa asked her. "Stand and fight, and stop using Karak's gift as an excuse to hide your cowardice."

Ezra shook her head, still walking toward her. Every slow footstep ate away another second, any one perhaps the difference between life and death for Alyssa. And Ezra knew it, too. Zusa could see it in the mocking glint in the woman's eyes, in the exaggerated swish of her thin hips.

Zusa flung herself forward, a rash attack that Ezra would expect from her. With her skill, it might have been enough to overwhelm Ezra, but Zusa had something else in mind. At the last moment, just before their daggers clashed, she dove to the side, making a run toward the mansion. Ezra spun, and Zusa trusted her to react on instinct, to believe Zusa frantically running toward her loved ones.

A mere two steps toward the mansion, Zusa flipped her left dagger so the blade faced downward in her fist, then dug her heels in so she might fling herself backward. It was a blind stab, a gamble, as her dagger thrust through her own cloak. Ezra collided with her, caught unaware of the sudden change in her direction. The blade of the dagger punched through cloth, flesh, then belly. Ezra gasped, her upper body collapsing against Zusa, her head on her shoulder. Zusa twisted, keeping the position awkward and their bodies entangled so Ezra could not thrust.

"Zusa..." gasped Ezra as her body shivered.

"You should have listened," Zusa said, pulling her dagger free. "You could have found freedom. You could have prevented this."

When she pushed away, the other woman had nothing to lean against, and no strength of her own to stand. Zusa ran on, leaving Ezra to die alone, slumped over in the dirt and darkness.

CHAPTER

34

Alyssa lay on the floor of Nathaniel's room, slowly breathing in and out as blood trickled down the side of her chest to the carpet. The small bolt had caught her right breast, and with each breath it flared with pain. Despite every desire to move, to scream and fight, she could do nothing, immobilized by the poison coursing through her veins.

"Don't cry, Nathan," Stephen said, a second bolt readied in the crossbow and aimed straight at him. "I know you're young, but you're a bright child, a wise child. I think you're ready for this, ready to see the ugly truth behind the lies of this world."

A tear ran down Alyssa's face. She could see her son crouched on his bed, struggling not to cry. His entire body quivered with fear. A fresh wave of seething hatred flushed through Alyssa, and she tried to stand, to move her disobedient limbs. Still nothing.

"Don't hurt her," she heard her son whimper.

"Shush now," Stephen said, lowering the crossbow. Odd as it was, it seemed as if he meant the comforting words he spoke. "I didn't say this would be easy. But this must be done. It *must*. Do you love your grandmother, Nathan?"

Nathaniel glanced at her, their eyes meeting. The terror there was so deep, but he was still fighting, still trying to think of what to do and what to say. She'd never felt more proud, and her heart ached with the thought that she'd never see what type of man he'd become.

"Yes," he said.

"I love her too," Stephen said. He straddled Alyssa's waist while on his knees. The crossbow he placed beside him, and from his pocket he pulled out a slender knife. He leaned close to Alyssa, peering down at her with heavily painted eyes. The wig hung loose from his head, and at such a close distance, she could see flakes of dead flesh.

"I love her more than your mother does," he continued. "More than anyone ever has. Yet do you know what your grandfather did? Do you know what he put her through?"

Alyssa thought of the story she'd been told, of Maynard giving Melody over to Leon's gentle touchers. She tried to make the connection, to understand.

"You don't know," Stephen whispered, leaning closer so that their noses touched. "You're trying, but you don't know. Leon loved her, just like I loved her, but he couldn't do anything. How'd you put it? Your father would have killed my father if he'd found out? Such a sick man. Sick! And do you know what's worse, Nathan?"

He glanced at her son.

"Your grandfather paid for your grandmother to be tortured. Paid like she was just another common whore needing to be put in her place. Do you know how much he paid?"

Alyssa's terror deepened. She knew the amount, knew it before the words even left Stephen's lips.

"Two gold, and two silver."

The knife slipped closer, pressing against the underside of her left eye. Panic flushed her mind, but she couldn't move, couldn't move...

She looked to her son, knew it was the last time she'd ever see him.

The knife pushed in, twisted, cut. The pain was white-hot, and she felt tears and blood pour down her face. With a plop the eye came free, and Stephen held it in his soft, delicate hand. Nathaniel let out a cry, and Stephen whirled on him with a fury.

"You watch!" he cried. "Damn you, you little child, you watch! They left me in darkness when I was your age, just like they left her. I had to listen to her screams as they tortured her, sticking her with their pins like it was all a game."

"Mom," Nathaniel said, face red, nose and eyes running. She wanted to go to him, wanted to hold him. But Stephen was not yet done.

"Darkness," he said, turning back. He was speaking to her now, not her son. He twisted the bolt back and forth in her chest, just to make sure it still hurt. "Years and years in darkness, always alone but for Melody's beautiful songs. You don't deserve her, not now, not ever. She'll be mine, just mine."

In went the knife. Her vision swirled with a brief rainbow of colors that slowly drained away, becoming nothing but black streaked with orange and red that throbbed with the beating of her heart and the horrible spikes of pain. Drool spread down her lips as she struggled to speak, to say anything, as she heard Nathaniel's sobs.

Hot breath blew against her ear.

"I should leave you like this," Stephen whispered. "Put you in my dungeon to rot. I still have my gentle touchers. They could spend years on you, years without running out of new ways to..."

Alyssa heard a gasp, followed by a heavy thud.

"You bastard!" Stephen cried.

It was too horrible, not knowing what was happening. Had Nathaniel attacked Stephen? She heard a sharp intake of air, and then something hit a wall.

"How dare you strike me?" Stephen asked. Her son had defended her, it had to be.

"Don't," she pleaded. The words came out a slurred moan, but it seemed to steal Stephen's attention back to her.

"Don't?" he asked. "Don't what? Your son struck me, woman. Blessed as he is, I think he needs to learn his place."

"I'll scream," she heard Nathaniel say.

"Scream, and I cut your throat to silence it. Your choice."

If Lord Gandrem heard, or Melody, what would happen? Would he kill them, or would they talk him down? Alyssa didn't know, didn't want to know, but it seemed her son was braver than that. He let out a single bloodcurdling scream, at such a high pitch and volume that it pierced the night like a siren.

"Damn it, stop!" Stephen said. She waited for the killing blow, but before it came, something heavy blasted open the door, and then Stephen let out a cry. An object, perhaps a body, slammed against a wall. She heard the sound of metal, then a cracking of a bone.

"How dare you?" she heard Zusa ask. "Where is Laerek? Where is your master hiding?"

Stephen let out a moan, and it ended abruptly with a wet smack.

"Where!"

"He...he's waiting for me by Eddleton's."

"What street?"

"Songbird!" Stephen cried.

Alyssa heard crying, and then she felt a soft hand take hers. It trembled. Despite the poison, she gently curled her fingers about it, the weakest support she could offer. Nathaniel's face pressed against her chest, then lifted back, no doubt as he realized how close he was to the arrow still embedded there.

With an abruptness that startled her, Stephen's cries came to a halt.

"Alyssa," she heard Zusa say, and then wrapped hands touched her face. "I'm sorry, I'm so sorry. I never should have left you."

"Zusa," Alyssa managed to say, but that was it.

Lips kissed hers, and then out came the arrow. Her scream was a pathetic whisper of air exiting her lungs.

More movement at the door, plus a surprised gasp.

"What insanity is this?" asked John's booming voice. "Oh gods...Alyssa! Stephen!"

"You're safe now," Zusa whispered hurriedly into her ear. "He's dead, but one monster still runs loose. I have to find him. Please understand, I have to."

Zusa left her. More voices, more people, cries for a priest or a healer. Nathaniel stayed pressed against her through it all. At some point Melody arrived, her sharp feminine cry easily discernible.

"Stephen!" she heard Melody say. "Alyssa! Oh you dear, you poor dear..."

Nathaniel clutched her tighter. Despite the soothing words, and her mother's hand brushing against her forehead while she whispered comfort, all Alyssa could think of was Zusa's absence, and how it had been Stephen's name Melody cried first upon seeing the bloody carnage, not hers.

Haern dragged the unconscious Bloodcraft through the alleys, knowing it would only be a matter of time before the city guard arrived to investigate the noise and chaos that had been their battle. And despite his trust in Antonil, Haern didn't want the city guard to be the ones to discover the name he sought. No, he wanted that for himself. Whoever it was had made things personal in attacking the Eschaton, and he'd deal with them personally in return.

At last he reached a nice secluded spot tucked against the outer wall of the city. There'd be no patrols, and anyone who heard screams would be wise enough to keep the matter to themselves. Haern propped the man against the wall, then opened up his red coat to see the rows of leather loops for holding knives, half of them empty. Removing the rest of them, Haern cut strips of the coat into lengths, then bound the man's hands and feet. The throwing knives he left in a pile nearby, having every intention of using them if the need presented itself. Ready, he started slapping the man's face and pinching his nose to disrupt his breathing. It took a bit, but at last he awoke, gasping for air.

"Where the fuck am I?" the man asked.

Haern drew a saber and smacked him across the face with the flat side.

"I'm asking the questions," he said. "Let's start with your name."

"Percy," the man said. "And that's the only question you get an answer to."

Haern grabbed him by the throat and slammed his head against the wall. "For your sake, I'd hope not," he said.

Percy grinned at him despite the blood that dripped down his neck. "You think you can frighten me?" he asked. "You got Veldaren fooled, but you won't be fooling us. You're nothing."

"Us?" Haern asked. "There's no 'us,' not anymore. The rest of your group is dead. You're the last."

This seemed to shake him a little, but not much. Percy bit his lip, then turned and spit. "Such a shame. We had a nice thing going."

Haern narrowed his eyes. "Who hired you to kill us? I want a name, and where to find him."

Percy shook his head. "Can't do it. If I'm to have any work as a mercenary after this, it can't be with the reputation of a snitch. Bad enough a bunch of pussies like you beat us."

"Work as a mercenary?" Haern asked, leaning in closer. "You think I'll let you live?"

"If you don't, what reason have I to talk?"

In answer, Haern grabbed one of the throwing knives and jammed it into Percy's leg. Percy winced, but held down his scream.

"You think you can break me?" he asked after gathering his strength. "I don't think it's in you. Too soft."

A second knife, an inch higher up the leg. This time Percy did scream, but not for long.

"You," he said, laughing despite being out of breath. "You think this will work? I'll bleed out too quick. Don't have much"—he winced as Haern jammed in a third—"practice at this, do you?"

"Tell me his name," Haern said, grabbing Percy by the shirt and pulling him close. He'd frightened others before, often with just the intensity in his eyes, but this man seemed to be close bedfellows with pain and fear.

"You try to act the monster," Percy said, spitting in Haern's face. "But I grew up with monsters. I know who they are, how to smell 'em. You're not a monster. Thren is. Carson was. But you?" Another laugh. "You've killed so many, Watcher, yet you've somehow prevented it from changing you. Why? You think it makes you a better pers—"

Haern jammed his saber into Percy's stomach, then twisted it. The moment he removed the blade, blood would gush out, along with intestines.

"Now..." Percy said, slumping against the wall. "Now that's the monster. Were you hiding it, Watcher? How...adorable..."

"Tell me where," Haern said.

"His name's Laerek," Percy said. "One of Karak's priests. He'll be..."

He launched into a coughing fit, each cough weaker than the last. His skin was turning pale. Haern felt sick in his stomach realizing how far he'd gone. The man might die before giving him more than a name, all because he'd lost control. All because he'd wanted, for whatever reason, to prove that he could be the monster Percy doubted he could be.

"Down on Songbird," Percy said. "He's...at...shop..."

More coughing. His eyes had turned glassy. Too much blood lost, Haern knew.

"Damn it," he whispered. "Tell me where, quickly!"

Percy shook his head. "Pull out the sword," he said. "And go look for yourself."

Haern yanked it free. Blood gushed out, and as it did, Percy's body began convulsing in his death throes. Haern watched, feeling strangely guilty for the act. At last, when all life was gone, he sheathed his sabers and then ran. Songbird was about a mile long. There were only so many shops on it, but it'd take a lot of time to search them all. Still, time he had, at least to try.

Starting at the southern edge of the road, he followed it

north, his mind racing. Why would a priest hire the Blood-crafts to kill the Eschaton? That a priest of Karak would want them dead wasn't much of a stretch, and Tarlak tended to be meddlesome when it came to their darker affairs, but there had to have been some specific reason.

As Haern ran, he checked each shop, those of bakers, jewelers, smiths, makers of cloth and wool. Most were dark, and their doors locked. Feeling his desperation grow, he continued, until he heard a man scream from an alley behind him. Spinning about, Haern rushed into it, only to come to a halt.

Thren Felhorn was there, swords drawn. Lying at his feet was a priest wearing the black robes of Karak. So far he was alive, but his face was covered with blood. Haern realized why when Thren tossed the man's severed ear onto his chest.

"I said talk," Thren told him.

"Laerek," Hearn said, grabbing his father's attention. "This man's name is Laerek, isn't it?"

Thren looked up, and his expression was one Haern could not read. Was it one of anger, or amusement?

"It is," Thren said. "Do ghosts have business with him as well?"

So far he'd made no overtly threatening motions, but he still held his swords, which was enough to make him incredibly dangerous. Haern slowly stepped farther into the alley with his weapons drawn.

"I'm no ghost, and no dead man, despite what rumors you might have heard," Haern said, making sure his hood was pulled low to hide his face in its magical shadows. "This man hired mercenaries to kill me and my friends. I want to know why."

Laerek refused to look his way. He was a thin man with a

long nose, and now missing an ear. Thren kicked him once, blasting the air from his lungs.

"It seems you've been messing with very dangerous people," Thren told the priest before turning back to Haern. "This man sent the Suns into Veldaren, and specifically after my guild. I'd appreciate knowing why as well."

Laerek rolled off his back and pressed against the nearby wall.

"Karak be my strength," he prayed. "Not pain, nor death, nor threats of this world..."

Thren kicked him in the teeth to stop the prayer.

"Karak will not help you," Thren said, kneeling before him. "And you will feel pain, so much pain, before your death. If you want to do something useful with your words, then talk. The more you talk, the less you suffer."

Haern watched as Thren grabbed Laerek's hand, took his short sword, and slowly sliced into the tendons of his wrist. Laerek let out a cry, yet as Haern watched, he felt no pity, no remorse. Instead he felt himself back as a child, watching his father cut off the hand of a man who had cheated them. Despite the passing of time, Thren was still in charge, still holding the lives of others in his hands. Haern knew he should object. He'd spent his whole childhood rebelling against everything Thren had taught him. Yet this priest had played with all their lives. Everyone Haern knew and loved would be dead if he'd had his way. And so he watched the blood drip to the ground and hardened his heart against it. Had he not just thrust his own blade into the belly of another, all for a name?

"Start talking," Thren said as he continued to saw. He kept his fist clenching down against the veins so Laerek would not bleed out. His sword reached bone, and its sharp edge began to pry into the joint. "Why the Suns? Why did you have to send Grayson after me after all these years?"

"I didn't!" Laerek cried. "The Suns were willing, that's all I know!"

"Then why the Widow?"

Haern crossed his arms and frowned. The Widow? Laerek was behind that as well?

"Never part of our plan," Laerek said. "By Karak, please, it hurts..."

"Who is he?" pressed Thren.

"Stephen Connington," said Zusa from the rooftops, drawing their attention her way. She looked furious, and her gaze frightened Haern more than Thren's. "He was the Widow, your little puppet. Let me guess, priest...you told him Thren killed his father, not the Watcher?"

Laerek's skin was already pale, but it somehow turned paler. Thren pulled away his sword, put the bloody tip against his throat.

"You claimed I killed Leon?" he asked. "I'd have gladly done so, but I wasn't given the privilege. The Watcher here took that from me. So why? What has my guild done to you?"

"Alyssa, as well," Zusa said, leaping to the ground with daggers drawn. "You tried to have her killed. I can't forgive you, not for that."

Laerek's eyes bounced among all three of them, and he saw no comfort in any, no signs he might live. Closing them, he began praying again, until Thren shoved his short sword between his lips. The priest's clattering teeth rattled against the steel. Thren leaned close, and Haern saw how easily his father's gaze broke the man, so much easier than it had been for Haern with Percy.

"Why?" Thren asked. "We're all here, now tell us why."

"I only followed orders," Laerek said when Thren withdrew the blade. Tears ran down his face. "I'm a messenger, just a messenger."

"Messenger for whom?" asked Haern.

Laerek looked at them all. For a brief moment he paused, as if afraid to say, but his will was weak.

"He's my teacher," Laerek said. "A powerful priest named Luther. He sends me his orders by letter from the Stronghold, and I carry them out. That's all I know."

"Luther?" Thren asked, and he looked to the other two. Both shook their heads, not recognizing the name.

"I swear it's true!" Laerek insisted, seeing their doubt.

"One more question," Zusa said, moving closer. Thren stepped away, and bowed as if he were a gentleman making way for a lady. Zusa knelt before Laerek, and glanced down at her daggers.

"You blinded my beloved," she said, looking up at him. "I hope you burn for an eternity."

Her dagger thrust into his throat, twisted, and then tore out, taking flesh and blood with it. Laerek flailed at her with shaking hands, but she held him as she watched him die. When at last he went still, Zusa stood and spit on his corpse.

"I thought you had a question?" Haern asked.

Zusa glared at him, then walked away. At a loss for words, he turned to Thren, whose face was locked in a grim smile. Haern tensed, wondering if he might try something, if their shadowed feud might come to a head now they were alone.

"Clearly she lied," said Thren. And then he laughed.

For some reason Haern couldn't believe it. This was the specter of his nightmares, the lone man he'd feared, above all others, might recognize the face beneath his hood. He'd avoided fighting him so many times over the years, dreaded any sort of confrontation, yet here he was... laughing.

Thren sheathed his swords, and he nodded to the blades in Haern's hands. "Put those away," he said. "Or do you plan on using them still?"

"You're still alive," Haern said. "I'd say that leaves a good chance I'll have need of them."

His father shook his head, and he gestured to Laerek's corpse. "The one controlling that fool is who needs your sabers," he said. "Who am I to you, Watcher?"

"I've been your enemy for years."

"Don't flatter yourself. Was it you who dissolved my guild? Was it you who marched into my territory, who turned my men against me with bribes, who butchered my men and left coins in their throats and eyes? No, that was Victor, that was Grayson, that was that sick man, the Widow. You?" Thren laughed again. "The only thing you have done is keep my men on their toes whenever they prowl the streets. You're stories of the Abyss to impressionable children, a way to terrify them into more proper behavior."

Haern paused a moment, and he felt tempted to sheathe his blades as a gesture of trust. It felt so strange, hearing his father talk like that. To talk as if he'd been defeated.

Thren walked over to the corpse, knelt down so he could stare more closely into the young priest's face.

"Someone manipulated us," he said, and his deep voice softened. "Both of us, you and I. Deep down, I know we are similar. I know the pride you feel in your skills, the ruthlessness with which you rule the empire you've created. Perhaps you won't believe it, but I've been...impressed by what you've accomplished." He stood, turned his way. "My guild is in pieces, and your city flails out of control before your eyes. Both of our accomplishments are turning to ash in our hands, and our futures are bleak and empty. We are not enemies, not anymore. Not when a common enemy would consume us both. So either sheathe your swords and listen to what I have to say... or get out of my damn sight. Your choice."

More than anything, more than the dozens of memories that flashed through his mind, more than the fear of his father and an undeniable desire for his approval, Haern thought he saw something inside his father that desired better. Something that might be worth saving.

He sheathed his sabers, crossed his arms.

"So be it," he said. "Now talk."

"There isn't much to it," Thren said. "We now have a name. The puppet master of this farce. The priest, Luther..."

CHAPTER

35

Would you like me to come with you, my lord?" asked Sef as Victor stepped out the door of his tavern and into the street. Victor fought down his initial denial. His pride had put friends and allies at risk already, and despite the crushing of the Sun Guild, the rest of the city was still filled with men who wished him harm.

"If you wouldn't mind the walk," Victor said instead, forcing a smile. Sef nodded, motioned two other men over. They took up positions, following Victor as he led them along.

"Where is it we go?" Sef asked.

"We go where I lead," Victor said, having no desire for conversation. Thankfully Sef took the hint, and together the four marched toward the center of town.

Bitterness dwelt in Victor's heart as tired and cautious eyes watched him walk the worn dirt roads. It burned him deep inside to require Deathmask's help, and the help of his Ash Guild. No matter how hard he tried to justify it, the fire remained. Was it his own weakness that allowed it? His own inadequacies? But of course, Victor wasn't like them. He didn't hold the power of death in his skilled hands. He was a man. They were the monsters.

But he'd deal with the monsters, if it saved his city. Memories had haunted him over the week, of his past, his family, of times both good and bad. He wanted to relive them, to view them again. He had to remind himself that every sacrifice he made, every ounce of effort he gave, went toward something good. Something pure. The safety of the people of Veldaren. What could be purer than that?

Without need to think, with hardly more than glances at the markings for the street names, he found his way. As they approached he heard Sef shuffle nervously alongside him, clearing his throat to signify his desire to speak.

"Is this..." he asked, then fell silent when Victor glared his way.

"Yes," Victor said, swallowing heavily. "It is."

They stopped before the ruins of the mansion. The upper floor had collapsed completely, but chunks remained of the lower floor, the fire that had gutted the old Kane mansion having not fully consumed the place. The ash was long gone, blown away on the winds of many years. Victor's eyes scanned the wreckage of his old home. Here he saw a window, one of many he'd breathed against in winter, using the frost to draw shapes with his fingers. There was the stump of what had once been a tree on which his father had hung for him a swing. His room on the upper floor he saw no remnant of, knew it foolish to search for. Every toy, every possession of his, had been in either the mansion or the carriage they'd taken in their doomed escape. Everything that had been his, taken.

"The land is still yours," Sef said as the day marched along, and Victor stood lost in memories. "You could rebuild."

"I could," Victor said. "But I won't. Not until the city I would build it in is worthy enough to be called home."

A tired laugh escaped his lips.

"Besides, they would just burn it all down the moment I placed the last brick."

"They?"

Victor waved about him, to the many homes beyond. "The people, the rioters, the thieves, the Trifect…pick one."

He put his back to his old home, hurried on. His next destination was the market, always a place of excitement in his youth. Whenever allowed, he went with his mother and her servants, eager for the smells, the sights, the promise of things he'd not yet seen or heard. On the busiest of days there might even be jugglers, singers, men with fiddles and horns who would play for whatever charity might be thrown into a pot or hat placed at their feet. Victor had always insisted he be allowed to throw the coins in with the others.

There were no singers, no jugglers, just tired men and women. Victor walked among them, and at first the feel was the same. He closed his eyes, let it sink into him. Fresh bread, meat pies, and treats made of crushed apples and cherries. He felt the fire burning in the pit of his stomach start to fade, just a little. Walking among them Victor smiled, tried to let the people see that despite the chaos of the night before, he was still in charge, still to be trusted. They knew who he was now, recognized the symbol on his chest. He'd hoped for smiles. Instead he got sideways glances, if he was not ignored completely.

"Care for something to eat?" Victor asked Sef.

"It depends on what I'm to eat," Sef said. "And if I'm paying."

Victor grinned at his friend. "I'm buying, and you eat what you'd like."

"In that case," Sef said, "I think me and my men here would be very much interested."

As the soldiers bought themselves honey-soaked bread, Victor leaned against a wall erected to help prevent the market from spilling out to the homes beyond. Casually he let his sight roam, let himself take in the people. These people, these desperate merchants, these tired wives, these worried fathers... they were whom he protected.

And then he saw the cloaks among them.

A gray armband here, a green cloak there. Children running through the crowds, with but the thinnest of thread about their wrists to show their allegiances. Even as he watched, one of them attempted, and failed, to steal coin from the pocket of a fat merchant busy haggling over the price of his furs. Victor's hand fell for his sword, but then Sef returned, licking his lips, and Victor pulled it away.

"Come on," he told them, earning confused looks for his gruff tone but not caring to explain.

Next was a park he'd played in often, one of the few places he'd been allowed to go with only a single escort. Who was it who'd gone with him... Burson? Barson? Some old man, graying hair, he'd always looked at Victor as if he were a troublesome pest, and would always be a pest. But that was hardly fair now, Victor thought as he traveled deeper into the rich north of Veldaren. Whatever the man's name, he'd been responsible for the safety of his master's son. Of course he'd been dour. Of course he'd taken things seriously. That was the price of responsibility.

The park, a large area full of bushes, trees, and pathways to hide in, he instead found to be nothing but some grass and a few lone oaks scattered about. There'd always been kids there, he remembered, but he only saw two out despite its being midday. They were dirty, their clothes tattered, and upon seeing Victor arrive with his men they quickly bolted. Victor slowly let out a sigh.

"I know how you feel," Sef said, glancing about the park. "It's always sad to see things change."

"Change," Victor mumbled. "Perhaps. But what if the past was never what you thought it to be?"

Sef shrugged. "That's why it's dangerous to live in the past, my lord."

"Indeed. Take me home, Sef."

Before his inn, with several of the king's guards standing around him in a diamond formation, was the adviser, Gerand. The man looked bored, though at Victor's arrival his eyes flickered with a bit of life.

"Greetings, Victor," said the adviser. "Your soldiers would not tell me when you might return, nor where you went. I'm glad you were not long."

"They could tell you neither for they knew neither," Victor said, nodding curtly. "Might I ask what you're here for?"

From one of the inner pockets of his shirt Gerand pulled a thin scrap of paper rolled tightly and bound with wax. "For you," he said. "I would risk it with no other."

Victor accepted the paper, making sure none of his confusion showed on his face.

"I pray it is good news," he said.

Gerand motioned to his guards to leave. "Then you might need to be praying for a long time," he said as they marched toward the castle. Frowning, Victor broke the wax, unrolled the paper, and read.

Victor,

Given the destruction over the past few weeks, the infighting between the guilds, and Stephen Connington's death, the city's safety does not feel improved by your presence. But even if those do not lay at your feet, I now hear one of the guilds fights alongside you. You are compromised, Victor, and the crown will not pay you to play your games anymore.

Gerand.

Victor crumpled the paper in his hands, tore it, crumpled it again, and dropped it to his feet.

"Burn it," he told one of his soldiers as he stormed inside. He went to his room, hoping for a moment of privacy, but was given none. Before he could even settle into the chair beside his fireplace there came a knock on his door.

"Come in," he said, rubbing his eyes.

The door opened, and in stepped Henris Weeks. The old man was clearly excited, his scrunched face looking even more pinched. In his hand he held several withered documents.

"My lord," he said, "the payment did not arrive this morning as it was supposed to. Do you know..."

"Gerand's thrown us to the wolves," Victor said. "There will be no payment."

Henris looked taken aback. "My lord...then what are we to do? I can only pay a third of our men with what we have left."

Victor leaned back in his chair, put a hand on his chin. "How many men of mine are loyal?" he asked. "Men who would die for me, who believe in what I do?"

Henris shrugged. "I cannot judge the hearts of men, my lord. But there are three hundred who have served you since you were but a child, and whose fathers served your father. Beyond that…"

"Then pay them," Victor said. "Tell the rest to be patient. I will find a way to pay them in time."

"They will not be pleased."

Despite his mood, Victor let out a laugh. "Do you think I care? If they cause problems, then I will deal with them in my own way. You need not worry away the last gray hairs you have, Henris."

"Of course, of course," Henris said, bowing. Victor rubbed his eyes, then realized the old man was not leaving.

"Is there something else?" he asked.

"Indeed," Henris said. "I have here documents given to me by Terrance Gemling, adviser to Lady Alyssa Gemcroft. They're shipping manifests, recording their transactions with John Gandrem in regards to their mines farther north. If you'd look at the logs, particularly the third row…"

"Spare me," Victor said. "What are you trying to tell me, Henris? In plain words, preferably."

The old man licked his lips. "Plain words? Alyssa has been cheating the king out of taxes for the past four years, perhaps even longer."

Victor stood, feeling his jaw tighten. "You are certain?" he asked.

"As I could ever be," Henris said, offering him the documents. "It is all here, hidden of course, and cleverly so."

Victor paced before his fireplace, flicking through the sheets. They were just numbers to him, pages of names, places, costs.

"Is this everything?" he asked. "If I'm to go to the king, I'll need every bit of proof I can get to convict a lady of the Trifect. Is there anything else?"

"You hold in your hands the only proof I could obtain," Henris said. "The rest they themselves will surely have destroyed."

"Good," Victor said. "Good."

He turned and threw the papers onto the fireplace. Henris let out a cry, took a step forward, and then stopped when he looked into Victor's glare.

"Get out," he ordered, and the old man quickly obeyed.

As the door slammed shut, Victor plopped back into his chair and stared at the paper curling and blackening in the fire.

The king was a puppet, and his puppet master had turned on Victor. His men were fiends addicted to gold and nothing more. The guilds stabbed and bickered with one another, finding peace only when they could turn on a mutual enemy such as the Trifect. He was tiring of the games, and even worse, he was failing at them. But all was not lost. Both Deathmask and the Watcher had taught him something, a lesson he would use in the coming days. His stroll about the city that morning had only confirmed it.

The city itself was infected, rotting away to the core. In all of its dark corners were monsters. And to defeat the monsters, he needed monsters.

He thought of Alyssa's beauty, her storied reputation, and, most important of all, her vast wealth.

Monsters... and allies.

Victor poured himself a drink, toasted the burning evidence.

"To a whirlwind courtship," he said, laughed, and drank.

EPILOGUE

No one had slept the rest of the night in the Connington mansion. Guards rushed about, suddenly without anyone in charge, and each one nervous about what the death of Stephen meant to him. Lord Gandrem assumed control with ease, settling into a role he'd known his entire life. He knew how to give men orders, how to instruct them, in ways others wouldn't understand. His place in charge of them would only last a few days, at least until proceedings could begin, and a temporary steward could be placed in charge of the Connington fortune. Zusa respected him, yet feared him as well, for every time she looked she saw Melody there at his side, his hand in hers.

Zusa walked down the hallway, glaring at any guard who looked twice at her. Morning had come, yet the tension remained. It'd been a long couple of years establishing Leon's heir. With no remaining sons, illegitimate or otherwise, it'd be a terrible squabble among the scattered remnants of the Connington family. She felt anger directed at her in the guards, guards who had been treated and paid well, all of that potentially ended by her single thrust of a dagger through their master's eye.

Alyssa lay on her bed, Nathaniel at her side, when Zusa stepped into the bedroom.

"Is all well?" she asked. Nathaniel glanced up at her, and she saw the exhaustion in his eyes, which were bloodshot and wet with tears. Zusa smiled at him, wishing she could lend him strength... not that she had much left to lend.

"I've known better days," Alyssa said. A cloth was over her face, hiding the empty sockets. "The priests say they can do nothing. I've sent Terrance to find the finest glass-smith in the land. I may not be able to see, but I'll have eyes, damn it, beautiful green eyes..."

She was crying, and no squeezing of her hands by her son seemed able to stop it. Zusa felt a burden growing in her chest. She wished she could say something, do something, to make it all better. But she could perform no miracles with her daggers and cloak.

"Nathan, I need a moment with your mother," she said. Nathaniel instinctively held his mother tighter, and Zusa smiled to show nothing was wrong. "It is no worrisome matter," she insisted. "I just wish a few words in private."

"You can wait outside the door," Alyssa told him.

Nathaniel nodded, then blushed upon realizing she couldn't see it.

"Yes, Mother," he said.

Zusa shut the door behind him, then turned back to Alyssa.

"He's so frightened," Alyssa said, putting a hand on her forehead. "I can't blame him. Even with Stephen dead, he thinks the guards will turn on us at any second."

"A wise boy to fear it," Zusa said, sliding up beside the bed. "We should return to our own mansion whenever you are well. I would entrust your life to them no longer."

Alyssa nodded. "I'll tell Terrance to make the preparations."

Zusa sat down, and she struggled to find the proper words. "I killed him," she said. "Not just Stephen, but the man who gave him orders. I tried to make it painful, but I didn't have time. I had to get back to you."

Alyssa reached out her hand, and Zusa took it, pressed it against her cheek. "I'm sorry," Zusa whispered. "I should have been here. I should have been faster, shouldn't have gotten caught..."

"It's not your fault," Alyssa said. "I shouldn't have been so... blind."

She laughed, laughed even though she could hardly breathe, even though she sniffled from her tears, which soaked into the cloth. Zusa squeezed her hand tighter, then kissed her fingertips. "Not again," she said. "I won't let you ever be in danger again. I failed you before, but I swear to fix this. I swear I'll find a way."

"Forget me," Alyssa said. "Nathaniel is all that matters now. His role in our dealings needs to be increased tremendously. Every vulture will be circling. If Nathaniel is to be my heir, he needs to take it now, and show Dezrel his strength."

"But he's so young..."

"And he's endured more than most have in their lifetimes. Gods help me, I'm blind, and he's lost an arm. The vultures won't just be circling, they'll be pecking at our corpses."

Another bitter laugh. Zusa hated to see her so, but she also couldn't deny her argument. Everyone would be searching for weakness now. Potential replacements for Nathaniel would come out of the woodwork.

"I'll kill them all," Zusa whispered. "Any challenger, any threat. I won't lose you, Alyssa. I don't think I could endure it."

Alyssa reached out, and Zusa leaned close so she could wrap

her arms about her. As they embraced, Alyssa kissed her neck, then pressed her forehead against Zusa's breast. "You can't kill the world," Alyssa told her. "And they must come to fear Nathaniel, not you. Just promise that if something should happen to me, you'll raise him as your own."

"Shouldn't your mother be the one..."

More grim laughter interrupted her. "Melody?" Alyssa said. "I lost my eyes because of Stephen's love of her. My torture was punishment for her own. I cannot prove it, but deep down I find it hard to believe Stephen acted on his own. The timing is too perfect. Stephen said it took him a year to discover who my mother really was...but what if it wasn't a year, Zusa? What if her return and Stephen's madness as the Widow were connected, and now she clings to John Gandrem, his wealth, his power..."

"If what you say is true, then we house a dangerous threat to you and your family."

Alyssa's smile was so bitter, so sad, it made Zusa's heart ache. "It wouldn't be the first time," she said, reaching out and clutching Zusa's wrist with a grip like iron. "Promise me. Promise me he'll be your son before anyone else's."

Zusa swallowed, and it felt like nails were caught in her throat. "I promise," she said.

Alyssa leaned back in the bed, and it looked like she relaxed for the first time since her encounter with Stephen. "I need some rest," she said. "Send Nathaniel in if he's still upset."

"Yes, milady."

Zusa left, and felt a pall settle over her. The walls of the mansion confined her, and she headed for the exit, wanting fresh air, wanting to be alone. At the doors to the mansion, Zusa stopped, for a great commotion had started. Soldiers, at least a hundred, were streaming into the mansion, shouting and joking with one another as if they'd arrived for a feast. Every single one bore the Gandrem family crest. Servants ushered them down various hallways, trying to find spare rooms.

In the center of it all stood John Gandrem, greeting his men. And with her arms wrapped around his waist was Melody.

"Our family will be kept safe," Melody said, noticing Zusa standing there amid the sea of confusion. "Do not worry for my daughter, nor her son. You've done much to protect us, but it's time we do this the right way."

Zusa said nothing, just continued to count the men. When the number reached two hundred, she returned to Alyssa's room and hid above the door, her body awash in shadows, her daggers at the ready.

Never again, she thought.

Tarlak could hardly believe what he was hearing, and even if he believed it, he certainly didn't like it.

"Are you sure he wasn't lying?" he asked, plopping down in his chair. Haern stood at the door to his room, hands on the hilts of his swords. "Priests of Karak aren't exactly known for their truthfulness."

"Trust me on this," Haern said, shaking his head. "He didn't lie. Whoever this Luther is, he's set his sights on nearly every major player in Veldaren. The Gemcrofts, the Conningtons, myself, the thief guilds…"

"Why Thren in particular, you think?"

Haern shrugged. "The Suns and Thren have a connection, though I know little more than that."

Tarlak frowned while rocking back and forth. "Every major player," he said. "Every single one but the king…"

Haern chuckled. "Perhaps he thought the king too inept to pose a problem?"

Tarlak shot him a look. "This is no laughing matter. What you're talking about is beyond dangerous."

"I know."

"I don't think you do," Tarlak insisted. "You want to travel all the way to Ker so you can infiltrate the Stronghold, to interrogate a priest whose name you can't be sure is real, and who might not even be there. And this isn't some ordinary building, either. This is the dark paladins' home, their training ground, their own little private fortress. Damn it, Haern, I've heard horror stories about their dungeons that make Thren seem like a pretty butterfly."

He stood, waved a finger. "And most importantly about this nonsensical plan . . . there's no money in it!"

The wizard plopped back down in his chair and rubbed his forehead with his fingers.

"I won't help you," he said. "None of us will."

"I thought not."

Tarlak sighed. "You're still going, aren't you?"

Haern nodded. "They wanted us dead, Tar. You know I can't leave us in danger like that. What happens if he tries again? We still don't know what Luther wanted to accomplish. The Sun Guild was attached to it, and I doubt we've seen the last of them either. But why? What does Karak have to do with any of this? I have to know, no matter the danger."

"So you'll go alone? They'll kill you, you have to know that."

Something about the way Haern stood there felt off. His determined words belied nervousness. There was something he was missing, Tarlak knew, but what . . .

"I know it's suicide to go alone," his friend said after a pause. "That's why I'm *not* going alone."

Haern stepped away from the door, revealing Thren Felhorn

leaning against the doorframe behind him, arms crossed, an amused expression on his face.

"I must say," he said, glancing about Tarlak's room. "I think I expected something more. And forgive me if I may be so bold, wizard, but I don't think anyone has ever referred to me as a pretty butterfly in my entire life."

He smirked as Tarlak's jaw dropped open.

"So please...don't do it again."

A NOTE FROM THE AUTHOR

I hated this book.

That isn't me exaggerating, or saying some sort of cutesy writer/editing thing. I really did hate this book mere months after I self-published it a year or so ago. *Blood of the Underworld* (as it was named at the time) was the first and only book I've written and released solely hoping it made money. Mercenary work does not suit me well, and I really do care about these characters and the trials I put them through. But *BotU* was, at the time, a pretty blatant attempt to cash in on Haern's popularity with my readers. It helped none that I was starting to be bored with Haern as a whole (something I've been blessedly cured of by rereading and working on all the older Shadowdance novels, which has reminded me why I once loved this character so much).

Now, this doesn't mean I thought the book was terrible. Far from it. I knew there were problems, but I honestly thought a lot of the fights and moments I put into the book would make people excited, and make up for any...authorial slacking. But, well...that just meant I was pandering. The original ending, with a smug Haern standing next to an equally smug Thren, pretty much epitomized it all. But the nitty-gritty details? The plot line, the characters' motivations, the behind-the-scenes scaffolding so important to a story? I just winged it. I'd figure it out later. That's what books two and three are for! Just let Haern fight some over-the-top bad guys, pull in references to all my other series for some fanboy love, and all would be fine. Right?

See, there's a problem when I write like that...it leaves me cold for the sequels, and in a bind when I try to come up with what else to do with the characters.

So now comes a chance to rework the book for Orbit, and honestly, this was the one I dreaded the most, far and away. Because I knew when I sat down, took another look at it, that this would be the book that had to grow up the most. All that stuff I slacked off on, tried to leave vague, I couldn't get away with anymore. In trying to recapture the whirlwind nature of *A Dance of Cloaks*, I substituted laziness for recklessness. It's not the same thing, and it's an insult to my readers. (Not to insult those of you who read that version and liked it...I really do still think there's plenty of fun scenes in it, especially involving Grayson and the Bloodcrafts...I just have a hard time seeing past all the flaws that poor book suffered because of yours truly.)

So I examined the plot line, the motivations, and worked to fill in the gaps. My editor, Devi, was incredibly helpful in this, and it was her work with me on the previous three books that helped evolve this one into something that should be far more solid, far more able to stand on its own.

So did I do better this time around? God, I hope so. You all will have to be the judge. But deep down I feel this is now a worthy continuation of the story of the Watcher of Veldaren. And more important, I've laid down the scenes for the final two books, the pawns, the heroes, the motivations, and now I get to play. Now I get to have fun. The Darkhand is coming, Luther's about to make his own reveal from the Paladins, and in the Vile Wedge, a prophet is awakening…

David Dalglish
July 30, 2013

extras

orbit

meet the author

Mike Scott Photography

DAVID DALGLISH currently lives in rural Missouri with his wife, Samantha, and daughters Morgan and Katherine. He graduated from Missouri Southern State University in 2006 with a degree in mathematics and currently spends his free time teaching his children the timeless wisdom of Mario jumping on a turtle shell.

introducing

If you enjoyed
A DANCE OF SHADOWS
look out for

A DANCE OF GHOSTS

Shadowdance: Book 5

by David Dalglish

PROLOGUE

Kadish Fel wore a rut into the dirt floor as he paced in the center of the large warehouse. The smell of dust overwhelmed his nose, and he sneezed often. All around were large squares of hay stacked to the ceiling, hay Kadish would sell to the outlying farms come winter. He kept his hands clasped behind his back, for it was the only way to keep himself from drawing his swords and twirling them as a nervous tic. But drawn weapons wouldn't do, not when he needed his ambush to succeed.

"Not sure I've ever seen you so nervous," said Carlisle, a squat man who helped Kadish with the more brutal affairs of his Hawk Guild. "You really think this Darkhand will be that frightening in person?"

Kadish stopped his pacing, just for a moment.

"You know his reputation," he said, running a hand through his auburn hair.

"Aye, I do," laughed Carlisle. "But I also know people love to tell tales, and that the tales get larger with the telling. This guy lives three kingdoms away, and every story making its way here probably went through many tellings before ever reaching us."

Carlisle dug into his pocket, took out a pinch of snuff and snorted it.

"Besides," he continued, rubbing his eyes as they watered. "I don't care if this guy's the biggest shit in all of Mordeina; he's still coming into our city. Our *home*. That arrogant prick dies tonight."

Kadish looked to the rafters, the tops of the mountains of hay. Hidden above were nearly twenty members of his Hawk Guild, every last one armed with crossbow bolts tipped with poison. On the ground were ten more, their daggers ready. In but a moment, Kadish could bring the wrath of his entire guild upon the man he was soon to meet for the first time. Yet still he felt he was the one in danger.

Muzien the Darkhand, no matter how bloated his reputation, no matter how far he was from his home, was still a man to fear.

"Perhaps he won't show," Kadish said as the minutes crawled, midnight passing and the truly late hours arriving. "He might have anticipated our ambush."

Carlisle sat down on a single bundle of hay, grunting and shifting at its lack of comfort. He took another hit of snuff, then shook his head.

"Or maybe he's abandoned coming into Veldaren altogether. That Victor fellow, how long ago was it, three weeks..."

"Five," said Kadish.

"Five, right. Whatever. Victor's men thrashed the Sun Guild, drove 'em out of the city like they were rats on a ship. Fuck, even the fabled Grayson Lightborn got his ass killed. Perhaps

Muzien took one look at our city and decided he didn't want to share his right-hand man's fate?"

"Then why set up this meeting if he was just going to turn tail and slither back to Mordeina?"

Carlisle spit.

"He's an elf. Who says he has to make sense?"

Kadish shrugged. Well, Carlisle did have a point there. Still, the reputation the Darkhand carried...

"No," Kadish said. "The Sun Guild isn't finished with our city just yet. He's here, in Veldaren. And he'll be here for our meeting, even if he makes us wait a few hours."

"What makes you so certain?"

Kadish crossed his arms and leaned against one of the nine support beams throughout the middle of the building. The wood was rough and splintered, but his long brown cloak kept him safe from its discomfort. His brow furrowed, and he let his voice drop in hopes that only Carlisle, and not the rest of his hidden men, would hear.

"Because a man with such a reputation as Muzien's doesn't get a reputation like that through accident," he said. "He gets it by working his ass off for it, and making sure nothing tarnishes it. He's like Thren in that regard, except even better if we're to believe the stories. By Karak, I think every child alive has heard the tale of Muzien's Red Wine."

Carlisle snickered.

"Well," he said. "Make sure you don't drink anything that elf offers you, then, eh?"

"Indeed. But my point is, calling us here for a meeting and then flaking... all it takes is a few whispers by me and everyone hears of his cowardice, his unreliability. He won't allow it, no matter how petty. He wants us afraid, every single one of us. I have a feeling we're not the first he'll talk to tonight."

449

"Perhaps," said Carlisle. "But we'll sure as shit be the *last* he talks to."

"I pray we are."

With a sudden bang the worn door blocking the only entrance to the building smacked open. Despite the many hours of waiting, despite his fear of the unknown guildmaster of the Suns, Kadish felt relief that the time had finally come. In through the door walked two hard-looking men dressed in dark grays and tightly fitted clothing. Daggers gleamed from their belts. They wore no cloaks, instead bearing the four-pointed star sewn just above their hearts. From what Kadish had learned, the rings in their ears signified solo kills, and each had at least a dozen hoops and studs. They strode in without pause, their eyes scanning every corner of the room. Kadish swallowed, trusting his men to be adequately hidden.

And then in stepped the Darkhand. He was tall, and despite the long coat he wore, it was striking how slender an elf Muzien was. That slenderness belied a smooth strength, for each step he took was carefully weighted, every twitch of his muscles like that of a feline predator. His hair was a dark umber, the front of which was hooked into two braids and tied behind his head. From his hips swayed two swords, mimicking him in length and slenderness. Upon entering the building Muzien glanced about the place, seeing the tall stacks of hay, and smirked. That done, he brought his attention to Kadish as he moved to join his two acquaintances. The moment those cool blue eyes settled on Kadish he felt his scrotum tighten, felt the air around him thicken. Kadish had met hard men, had spent decades among those who viewed life as something to trade and fuck and cut short without a second thought.

He'd not seen eyes quite like Muzien's. Beneath that gaze Kadish felt like an insect seeking an audience with the boot about to crush him beneath its heel.

"Wel…welcome to Veldaren," Kadish said, gathering his senses. He expected better of himself, and he used his wounded pride to find the strength to stand a little taller, and let a bit of mockery enter his voice. "I pray you won't be staying long?"

Muzien stood several feet opposite Kadish, with his body-guards on either side. His long pale fingers slowly twirled a gold band on the index finger of his left hand—which, true to his name, appeared to have been crafted out of coals instead of flesh.

"I'll stay until my task here is done," he said, openly staring at Kadish. Disliking the cryptic answer, Kadish felt himself snap.

"Not sure that's wise," he said. "Your kind ain't wanted here, Muzien. You think your little trick with your ears fools anybody?"

Muzien tilted his head slightly to one side, as if amused. The tops of his ears, where there should have been the distinctive upturned curve of his race, were instead two mutilated scars.

"What was done to my ears was not done for you, nor the wretches who fill this city," the elf said. His voice was deep and aged. "Nor do I care if I am unwanted. That did not stop my Sun Guild in Mordeina, and it shall not stop us here. Now please, I've come to hear your answer, not your pathetic attempts at insult."

"To get an answer you need to ask questions," Carlisle said, earning himself a glare from Muzien. "So far I don't think me and my guildmaster here have heard one yet."

"Is this toad yours?" Muzien asked. "I guess I should take comfort in knowing that mankind shows no greater patience here than it has anywhere else in our world."

"He only speaks my mind, if a bit hastily," Kadish said. He wasn't happy with Carlisle's outburst either, but he would still defend one of his own over the accusations of some foreign elf guildmaster. "You asked to meet me, so here I am. You said you

451

have questions, and I'm here to answer. Ask away, and I'll do my best to play the good host."

Kadish put his hands behind his back and tried to look relaxed. In truth he was preparing to dive aside the second any of the three drew their blades. The moment he shouted out, his guild would reveal its ambush, but until then he wanted to learn what he could about the Sun Guild's intentions, just in case someone else took up Muzien's mantle after his death.

"I have but two questions," said Muzien. "First...where is Thren Felhorn?"

Kadish was honestly surprised. "Thren?" he asked. "Why do you care?"

At Muzien's glare, Kadish shrugged.

"Fine then, don't tell me," he said. "But Thren's gone missing, ever since he disbanded his Spider Guild. Rumors on the street claim your right hand Grayson killed him, but others said he got away only to be killed by Lord Victor Kane."

"So he is dead?" Muzien asked. "Has anyone seen his body?"

Again Kadish shrugged.

"Not that I know of."

"Then he isn't dead."

It was spoken so simply, with such finality, Kadish didn't bother to argue. What did it matter if the legendary Thren Felhorn was dead? His guild had been disbanded, his territory swallowed up by the remaining guilds. He was a nonentity now, a relic of the past in an underworld willing to move on and forget within the blink of an eye.

"Well, there's question one," Kadish said. "What's your second, so we can get this over with and I can go find myself a bed and a pair of tits?"

Still Muzien twisted the ring on his finger, as if it was nothing more than a nervous tic of his own. But it seemed strange to think that...seemed strange to even consider a man with those cold blue eyes ever being nervous about anything. The gold of the band appeared almost ludicrous contrasted against the dark flesh beneath it.

"I offer you and your guild the same chance I will offer the Wolves, the Serpents, the Ash, and all the rest," said the elf. "Despite whatever setbacks you think I have suffered, be assured our takeover of Veldaren is inevitable. The Sun Guild rises, and all who would stand against us shall fall."

"Big words," Kadish mumbled. "You think we've not heard the same a hundred times before? There's always a new challenger on the streets."

Muzien smiled.

"You've not had a challenger like me. Listen well, Kadish Fel, for it is your only chance to survive this night unharmed. Toss aside your cloaks and accepted the pointed star. There will be a place for everyone in my guild, for I will need strong hands and sharp minds to shape the future of Veldaren. You will have a position of honor, one worthy of the position you once held. All others will be given roles suited to their talents. No blood will be spilled. No wars fought between guilds. My victory is inevitable, so let us not waste the time, nor end lives unnecessarily."

Kadish could hardly believe what he was hearing, and despite the deep pit of fear in his belly, he laughed.

"Is that so?" he asked. "Inevitable? You are truly something special, Muzien, but I fear you've let your pride overwhelm your common sense. *Hawks, now!*"

Out from the hay sprang his men, slipping out from behind bales, falling down from the rafters onto piles, dark sheets meant to hide them during their long wait discarded. Before the two bodyguards could draw their blades a half-dozen arrows plunged into each of their bodies, dropping them.

Blood pooled at Muzien's feet as he stood there, still twirling his ring. He'd not even blinked at the sudden ambush.

Kadish drew his own sword, took a step closer to Muzien.

"Not everyone here is as cowardly as you'd believe," he said. "Now tell me why you've come to Veldaren, and why now?"

"Or what?" asked Muzien. "You'll kill me?"

"Look around you," Kadish said. "My guild is here, and ready. However many you brought with you, it doesn't matter. My arrows have you sighted. My swords are ready to plunge into your heart and lungs. You walked right into my home, you egotistical elf, so do you really think I wouldn't be ready for an intruder like you?"

Slowly Muzien shook his head.

"Ready with an ambush, perhaps," he said. "I expected that. But for you to be stupid enough to spring it? No. No, I did not."

The door to the warehouse slammed shut with a heavy thud.

"You and your guild fail to realize how far out of your depth you really are," Muzien said as the rest of the Hawk Guild turned to the door, unsure of what was about to transpire. "You cannot see Veldaren's fate even though it is as clear and undeniable as the rising sun. Your whores, your drug trades of leafs and powders, your *territory* as you would call it, will be swept into my arms. You could have continued on under my care. You could have had your place."

A few of Kadish's men pushed against the doors, lightly at first, then with their entire bodies flung against it. The wood rattled but would not move.

"You could have lived," said Muzien.

Kadish turned to the archers still in place.

"Kill him!" he shouted.

The arrows flew, but Muzien never moved. His body became

a blur, the sight of it somehow hurting Kadish's head. And then the arrows thudded into the dirt, leaving Muzien standing there, not a drop bleeding from his untouched form. The pit of fear in Kadish's stomach turned to full-blown terror. As if lost in a dream he stepped closer to the elf and raised his sword. Muzien only stared at him with an expression that was equal parts pity and condescension. Still his swords remained buckled at his sides. Taking in a deep breath, Kadish plunged his sword forward.

It disappeared into Muzien's stomach without a hint of resistance, all the way up to Kadish's hand. He felt nothing, only air. When he pulled the blade back, he knew his life was over.

"Do not resist," said Muzien. "Let the smoke take you. Your death will be more peaceful that way."

Kadish dropped his sword as the elf ceased the turning of his ring. Muzien's image flickered, then faded away until it was as if he'd never been there at all.

All around him he heard screams, banging at the doors, people begging to be let out. Others were swearing they would turn, they would join the Sun Guild. Kadish glanced to the door, saw even Carlisle was one of the ones willing to turn. It should have disappointed him, but it didn't. Kadish was willing to toss aside his own cloak now, but he knew it was beyond that. He had seen that look in Muzien's eye. He knew his place now, what he meant to the Darkhand. They were but vermin to be destroyed.

From the very walls came the first hints of smoke, followed by the flickering tongues of fire.

Muzien watched as the building burned, twelve members of his Sun Guild forming a perfect circle surrounding it and holding torches aloft as if in silent ritual. The screams from within took several minutes to stop, and it wasn't until they finally did that he spoke.

"He said he doesn't know where Thren is hiding."

Beside him stood his new right hand, a stocky man named Ridley with a pockmarked face.

"Did he at least offer an idea to explain the absence?"

Muzien nodded.

"He did. He said he believed Thren to be dead, though no proof of it has surfaced."

Ridley took a step forward and tossed his own torch onto the burning wreckage. A large crack followed, one of the support beams having weakened so much it broke under the strain of the roof, which crumbled inward along with it.

"Of your students, who was the better, Grayson or Thren?" asked Ridley.

"Grayson."

"Easy enough. Thren is still alive."

Muzien cocked his head at that.

"How so?" he asked. "If the stronger and the more skilled has perished, why then should Thren also have survived?"

Ridley gave him a crooked smile.

"Because that's the way this world works, Muzien. It's the best of us who die before their time, the ones who the world gives cruel jokes and ignoble deaths."

"If that is true, then why do I still live?"

Ridley winked. "Because you're *not* the best of us. You're the worst of us, Muzien, the very worst."

At that the Darkhand had to smile. He looked to the sleeping city, which, despite the fire he'd set, would not dare come to put it out, not while so many of his guild walked the streets in all directions, ordering men and women to return to their beds should they poke their heads out of their doors. The city was alive, Muzien knew, a living, breathing conglomerate of beings, and like any being it could be made to fear, and fear him it would.

But there was still one man out there who wouldn't fear him, who could be a great asset to his plan, or its most terrible threat.

"Where have you gone, my student?" Muzien asked with a breathless whisper that was carried away by the night wind along with the smoke, ash, and all else that remained of the Hawk Guild.

introducing

If you enjoyed
A DANCE OF SHADOWS
look out for

PROMISE OF BLOOD

The Powder Mage Trilogy: Book 1

by Brian McClellan

It's a bloody business overthrowing a king...
Field Marshal Tamas's coup against his king sent corrupt
aristocrats to the guillotine and brought bread to the starving. But
it also provoked war with the Nine Nations, internal attacks by
royalist fanatics, and the greedy scramble for money and power
of Tamas's supposed allies: the Church, workers' unions, and
mercenary forces.

It's up to a few...
Stretched to his limit, Tamas is relying heavily on his few
remaining powder mages, including the embittered Taniel,
a brilliant marksman who also happens to be his estranged son,
and Adamat, a retired police inspector whose loyalty
is being tested by blackmail.

But when gods are involved...
Now, as attacks batter them from within and without, the
credulous are whispering about omens of death and destruction.
Just old peasant legends about the gods waking to walk the earth.
No modern educated man believes that sort of thing.
But they should...

CHAPTER 1

Adamat wore his coat tight, top buttons fastened against a wet night air that seemed to want to drown him. He tugged at his sleeves, trying to coax more length, and picked at the front of the jacket where it was too close by far around the waist. It'd been half a decade since he'd even seen this jacket, but when summons came from the king at this hour, there was no time to get his good one from the tailor. Yet this summer coat provided no defense against the chill snaking through the carriage window.

The morning was not far off but dawn would have a hard time scattering the fog. Adamat could feel it. It was humid even for early spring in Adopest, and chillier than Novi's frozen toes. The soothsayers in Noman's Alley said it was a bad omen. Yet who listened to soothsayers these days? Adamat reasoned it would give him a cold and wondered why he had been summoned out on a pit-made night like this.

The carriage approached the front gate of Skyline and moved on without a stop. Adamat clutched at his pantlegs and peered out the window. The guards were not at their posts. Odder still, as they continued along the wide path amid the fountains, there were no lights. Skyline had so many lanterns, it could be seen all the way from the city even on the cloudiest night. Tonight the gardens were dark.

Adamat was fine with this. Manhouch used enough of their taxes for his personal amusement. Adamat stared out into the gardens at the black maws where the hedge mazes began and imagined shapes flitting back and forth in the lawn. What was…ah, just a sculpture. Adamat sat back, took a deep breath. He could hear his heart beating, thumping, frightened, his stomach tightening. Perhaps they *should* light the garden lanterns…

A little part of him, the part that had once been a police inspector, prowling nights such as these for the thieves and pickpockets in dark alleys, laughed out from inside. *Still your heart, old man,* he said to himself. *You were once the eyes staring back from the darkness.*

The carriage jerked to a stop. Adamat waited for the coachman to open the door. He might have waited all night. The driver rapped on the roof. "You're here," a gruff voice said.

Rude.

Adamat stepped from the coach, just having time to snatch his hat and cane before the driver flicked the reins and was off, clattering into the night. Adamat uttered a quiet curse after the man and turned around, looking up at Skyline.

The nobility called Skyline Palace "the Jewel of Adro." It rested on a high hill east of Adopest so that the sun rose above it every morning. One particularly bold newspaper had compared it to a starving pauper wearing a diamond ring. It was an apt comparison in these lean times. A king's pride doesn't fill the people's bellies.

He was at the main entrance. By day, it was a grand avenue of marbled walks and fountains, all leading to a pair of giant, silver-plated doors, themselves dwarfed by the sheer façade of the biggest single building in Adro. Adamat listened for the soft footfalls of patrolling Hielmen. It was said the king's personal

461

guard were everywhere in these gardens, watching every secluded corner, muskets always loaded, bayonets fixed, their gray-and-white sashes somber among the green-and-gold splendor. But there were no footfalls, nor were the fountains running. He'd heard once that the fountains only stopped for the death of the king. Surely he'd not have been summoned here if Manhouch were dead. He smoothed the front of his jacket. Here, next to the building, a few of the lanterns were lit.

A figure emerged from the darkness. Adamat tightened his grip on his cane, ready to draw the hidden sword inside at a moment's notice.

It was a man in uniform, but little could be discerned in such ill light. He held a rifle or a musket, trained loosely on Adamat, and wore a flat-topped forage cap with a stiff visor. Only one thing could be certain…he was not a Hielman. Their tall, plumed hats were easy to recognize, and they never went without them.

"You're alone?" a voice asked.

"Yes," Adamat said. He held up both hands and turned around.

"All right. Come on."

The soldier edged forward and yanked on one of the mighty silver doors. It rolled outward slowly, ponderously, despite the man putting his weight into it. Adamat moved closer and examined the soldier's jacket. It was dark blue with silver braiding. Adran military. In theory, the military reported to the king. In practice, one man held their leash: Field Marshal Tamas.

"Step back, friend," the soldier said. There was a note of impatience in his voice, some unseen stress—but that could have been the weight of the door. Adamat did as he was told, only coming forward again to slip through the entrance when the soldier gestured.

"Go ahead," the soldier directed. "Take a right at the diadem and head through the Diamond Hall. Keep walking until you find yourself in the Answering Room." The door inched shut behind him and closed with a muffled thump.

Adamat was alone in the palace vestibule. Adran military, he mused. Why would a soldier be here, on the grounds, without any sign of the Hielmen? The most frightening answer sprang to mind first. A power struggle. Had the military been called in to deal with a rebellion? There were a number of powerful factions within Adro: the Wings of Adom mercenaries, the royal cabal, the Mountainwatch, and the great noble families. Any one of them could have been giving Manhouch trouble. None of it made sense, though. If there had been a power struggle, the palace grounds would be a battlefield, or destroyed outright by the royal cabal.

Adamat passed the diadem—a giant facsimile of the Adran crown—and noted it was in as bad taste as rumor had it. He entered the Diamond Hall, where the walls and floor were of scarlet, accented in gold leaf, and thousands of tiny gems, which gave the room its name, glittered from the ceiling in the light of a single lit candelabra. The tiny flames of the candelabra flickered as if in the wind, and the room was cold.

Adamat's sense of unease deepened as he neared the far end of the gallery. Not a sign of life, and the only sound came from his own echoing footfalls on the marble floor. A window had been shattered, explaining the chill. The result of one of the king's famous temper tantrums? Or something else? He could hear his heart beating in his ears. There. Behind a curtain, a pair of boots? Adamat passed his hand before his eyes. A trick of the light. He stepped over to reassure himself and pulled back the curtain.

A body lay in the shadows. Adamat bent over it, touched the

skin. It was warm, but the man was most certainly dead. He wore gray pants with a white stripe down the side and a matching jacket. A tall hat with a white plume lay on the floor some ways away. A Hielman. The shadows played on a young, clean-shaven face, peaceful except for a single hole in the side of his skull and the dark, wet stain on the floor.

He'd been right. A struggle of some kind. Had the Hielmen rebelled, and the military been brought in to deal with them? Again, it didn't make any sense. The Hielmen were fanatically loyal to the king, and any matters within Skyline Palace would have been dealt with by the royal cabal.

Adamat cursed silently. Every question compounded itself. He suspected he'd find some answers soon enough.

Adamat left the body behind the curtain. He lifted his cane and twisted, bared a few inches of steel, and approached a tall doorway flanked by two hooded, scepter-wielding sculptures. He paused between the ancient statues and took a deep breath, letting his eyes wander over a set of arcane script scrawled into the portal. He entered.

The Answering Room made the Hall of Diamonds look small. A pair of staircases, one to either side of him and each as wide across as three coaches, led to a high gallery that ran the length of the room on both sides. Few outside the king and his cabal of Privileged sorcerers ever entered this room.

In the center of the room was a single chair, on a dais a handbreadth off the floor, facing a collection of knee pillows, where the cabal acknowledged their liege. The room was well lit, though from no discernible source of light.

A man sat on the stairs to Adamat's right. He was older than Adamat, just into his sixtieth year with silver hair and a neatly trimmed mustache that still retained a hint of black. He had a strong but not overly large jaw and his cheekbones were well defined. His skin was darkened by the sun, and there were deep lines at the corners of his mouth and eyes. He wore a dark-blue soldier's uniform with a silver representation of a powder keg pinned above the heart and nine gold service stripes sewn on the right breast, one for every five years in the Adran military. His uniform lacked an officer's epaulettes, but the weary experience in the man's brown eyes left no question that he'd led armies on the battlefield. There was a single pistol, hammer cocked, on the stair next to him. He leaned on a sheathed small sword and watched as a stream of blood slowly trickled down each step, a dark line on the yellow-and-white marble.

"Field Marshal Tamas," Adamat said. He sheathed his cane sword and twisted until it clicked shut.

The man looked up. "I don't believe we've ever met."

"We have," Adamat said. "Fourteen years ago. A charity ball thrown by Lord Aumen."

"I have a terrible time with faces," the field marshal said. "I apologize."

Adamat couldn't take his eyes off the rivulet of blood. "Sir. I was summoned here. I wasn't told by whom, or for what reason."

"Yes," Tamas said. "I summoned you. On the recommendation of one of my Marked. Cenka. He said you served together on the police force in the twelfth district."

Adamat pictured Cenka in his mind. He was a short man with an unruly beard and a penchant for wines and fine food. He'd seen him last seven years ago. "I didn't know he was a powder mage."

"We try to find anyone with an affinity for it as soon as possible," Tamas said, "but Cenka was a late bloomer. In any case"—he waved a hand—"we've come upon a problem."

Adamat blinked. "You . . . want my help?"

The field marshal raised an eyebrow. "Is that such an unusual request? You were once a fine police investigator, a good servant of Adro, and Cenka tells me that you have a perfect memory."

"Still, sir."

"Eh?"

"I'm still an investigator. Not with the police, sir, but I still take jobs."

"Excellent. Then it's not so odd for me to seek your services?"

"Well, no," Adamat said, "but sir, this is Skyline Palace. There's a dead Hielman in the Diamond Hall and..." He pointed at the stream of blood on the stairs. "Where's the king?"

Tamas tilted his head to the side. "He's locked himself in the chapel."

"You've staged a coup," Adamat said. He caught a glimpse of movement with the corner of his eye, saw a soldier appear at the top of the stairs. The man was a Deliv, a dark-skinned northerner. He wore the same uniform as Tamas, with eight golden stripes on the right breast. The left breast of his uniform displayed a silver powder keg, the sign of a Marked. Another powder mage.

"We have a lot of bodies to move," the Deliv said.

Tamas gave his subordinate a glance. "I know, Sabon."

"Who's this?" Sabon asked.

"The inspector that Cenka requested."

"I don't like him being here," Sabon said. "It could compromise everything."

"Cenka trusted him."

"You've staged a coup," Adamat said again with certainty.

"I'll help with the bodies in a moment," Tamas said. "I'm old, I need some rest now and then." The Deliv gave a sharp nod and disappeared.

"Sir!" Adamat said. "What have you done?" He tightened his grip on his cane sword.

Tamas pursed his lips. "Some say the Adran royal cabal had the most powerful Privileged sorcerers in all the Nine Nations, second only to Kez," he said quietly. "Yet I've just slaughtered every one of them. Do you think I'd have trouble with an old inspector and his cane sword?"

Adamat loosened his grip. He felt ill. "I suppose not."

"Cenka led me to believe that you were pragmatic. If that is the case, I would like to employ your services. If not, I'll kill you now and look for a solution elsewhere."

"You've staged a coup," Adamat said again.

Tamas sighed. "Must we keep coming back to that? Is it so shocking? Tell me, can you think of any fewer than a dozen factions within Adro with reason to dethrone the king?"

"I didn't think any of them had the skill," Adamat said. "Or the daring." His eyes returned to the blood on the stairs, before his mind traveled to his wife and children, asleep in their beds. He looked at the field marshal. His hair was tousled; there were drops of blood on his jacket—a lot, now that he thought to look. Tamas might as well have been sprayed with it. There were dark circles under his eyes and a weariness that spoke of more than just age.

"I will not agree to a job blindly," Adamat said. "Tell me what you want."

"We killed them in their sleep," Tamas said without preamble. "There's no easy way to kill a Privileged, but that's the best. A mistake was made and we had a fight on our hands." Tamas looked pained for a moment, and Adamat suspected that the fight had not gone as well as Tamas would have liked. "We prevailed. Yet upon the lips of the dying was one phrase."

Adamat waited.

"'You can't break Kresimir's Promise,'" Tamas said. "That's what the dying sorcerers said to me. Does it mean anything to you?"

Adamat smoothed the front of his coat and sought to recall old memories. "No. 'Kresimir's Promise'...'Break'...'Broken'...Wait—'Kresimir's Broken Promise.'" He looked up. "It was the name of a street gang. Twenty...twenty-two years ago. Cenka couldn't remember that?"

Tamas continued. "Cenka thought it sounded familiar. He was certain you'd remember it."

"I don't forget things," Adamat said. "Kresimir's Broken Promise was a street gang with forty-three members. They were all young, some of them no more than children, the oldest not yet twenty. We were trying to round up some of the leaders to put a stop to a string of thefts. They were an odd lot—they broke into churches and robbed priests."

"What happened to them?"

Adamat couldn't help but look at the blood on the stairs. "One day they disappeared, every one of them—including our informants. We found the whole lot a few days later, forty-three bodies jammed into a drain culvert like pickled pigs' feet. They'd been massacred by powerful sorceries, with excessive brutality. The marks of the king's royal cabal. The investigation ended there." Adamat suppressed a shiver. He'd not once seen a thing like that, not before or since. He'd witnessed executions and riots and murder scenes that filled him with less dread.

The Deliv soldier appeared again at the top of the stairs. "We need you," he said to Tamas.

"Find out why these mages would utter those words with their final breath," Tamas said. "It may be connected to your street gang. Maybe not. Either way, find me an answer. I don't like the riddles of the dead." He got to his feet quickly, moving like a man twenty years younger, and jogged up the stairs after the Deliv. His boot splashed in the blood, leaving behind red prints. "Also," he called over his shoulder, "keep silent about what you have seen here until the execution. It will begin at noon."

"But…" Adamat said. "Where do I start? Can I speak with Cenka?"

Tamas paused near the top of the stairs and turned. "If you can speak with the dead, you're welcome to."

Adamat ground his teeth. "How did they say the words?" he said. "Was it a command, or a statement, or…?"

Tamas frowned. "An entreaty. As if the blood draining from their bodies was not their primary concern. I must go now."

"One more thing," Adamat said.

Tamas looked to be near the end of his patience.

"If I'm to help you, tell me why all of this?" He gestured to the blood on the stairs.

"I have things that require my attention," Tamas warned.

Adamat felt his jaw tighten. "Did you do this for power?"

"I did this for me," Tamas said. "And I did this for Adro. So that Manhouch wouldn't sign us all into slavery to the Kez with the Accords. I did it because those grumbling students of philosophy at the university only play at rebellion. The age of kings is dead, Adamat, and I have killed it."

Adamat examined Tamas's face. The Accords was a treaty to be signed with the king of Kez that would absolve all Adran debt but impose strict tax and regulation on Adro, making it little more than a Kez vassal. The field marshal had been outspoken about the Accords. But then, that was expected. The Kez had executed Tamas's late wife.

"It is," Adamat said.

"Then get me some bloody answers." The field marshal whirled and disappeared into the hallway above.

Adamat remembered the bodies of that street gang as they were being pulled from the drain in the wet and mud, remembered the horror etched upon their dead faces. *The answers may very well be bloody.*